Pride and Prejudice for Teens

a simplified retelling of Jane Austen's classic romance

by Jane Austen and Gerry Baird

Cover Design: SelfPubBookCovers.com/Roman

ISBN: 1530143292
ISBN-13: 978-1530143290

PREFACE

I have loved Pride and Prejudice ever since I first read it in my high school English class, but I remember struggling with the long sentences, sophisticated vocabulary and archaic terms found in the book. Here is an example of a 104-word sentence from the novel:

"It was generally evident whenever they met, that he did admire her; and to her it was equally evident that Jane was yielding to the preference which she had begun to entertain for him from the first, and was in a way to be very much in love; but she considered with pleasure that it was not likely to be discovered by the world in general, since Jane united, with great strength of feeling, a composure of temper and a uniform cheerfulness of manner which would guard her from the suspicions of the impertinent."

I have endeavoured in this edition to make a classic work more accessible by breaking long sentences into smaller ones. I have also gently modernized the text and punctuation while honouring, to the degree possible, the beauty and intent of the original. Here is the rewritten version of the sentence above:

"It was generally evident whenever they met that he *did* admire her, and it was equally evident that Jane was on her way to being very much in love. But Elizabeth considered with pleasure that it was not likely to be discovered by the world in general, since Jane's natural reserve and kindness to everyone would protect her from suspicion."

I am deeply indebted to the volume "The Annotated Pride and Prejudice, Revised and Expanded Edition" published by David M. Shapard (New York: Anchor, 2012), which provided invaluable insight into the words and world of Jane Austen.

CHAPTER 1

It is a truth universally acknowledged that a single man in possession of a good fortune must be in search of a wife.

This truth is so well fixed in the minds of the surrounding families that he is considered as the rightful property of some one or other of their daughters, even if the feelings or views of such a man on his first entering a neighbourhood are little known.

"My dear Mr. Bennet," said his wife to him one day, "have you heard that Netherfield Park is rented at last?"

Mr. Bennet replied that he had not.

"But it is," returned she, "for Mrs. Long has just been here, and she told me all about it."

Mr. Bennet made no answer.

"Do not you want to know who has taken it?" cried his wife impatiently.

"*You* want to tell me, and I have no objection to hearing it."

This was invitation enough.

"Why, my dear, you must know, Mrs. Long says that Netherfield is taken by a young man of large fortune from the north of England. He came down on Monday in a coach with four horses to see the place, and was so much delighted with it that he made an agreement with Mr. Morris immediately. He is to move in before the end of September, and some of his servants are to be in the house by the end of next week."

"What is his name?"

"Bingley."

"Is he married or single?"

"Oh! Single, my dear, to be sure! A single man of large fortune; four or five thousand a year. What a fine thing for our girls!"

"How so? How can it affect them?"

"My dear Mr. Bennet," replied his wife, "how can you be so tiresome? You must know that I am thinking of his marrying one of them."

"Is that his purpose in settling here?"

"Purpose! Nonsense, how can you talk so! But it is very likely that he *may* fall in love with one of them, and therefore you must visit him as soon as he comes."

"I see no occasion for that. You and the girls may go, or you may send them by themselves, which perhaps will be still better. Since you are as beautiful as any of them, Mr. Bingley might like you the best of the party."

"My dear, you flatter me. I certainly *have* had my share of beauty, but I do not pretend to be anything extraordinary now. When a woman has five grown-up daughters she ought to stop thinking of her own beauty."

"In such cases a woman has not often much beauty to think of."

"But, my dear, you must indeed go and see Mr. Bingley when he comes into the neighbourhood."

"It is not necessary, I assure you."

"But consider your daughters. Only think what a benefit it would be for one of them. Sir William and Lady Lucas are determined to go, solely for that reason, for in general, you know, they visit no newcomers. Indeed you must go, for it will be impossible for us to visit him if you do not."

"You are overly concerned with formality, surely. I dare say Mr. Bingley will be very glad to see you, and I will send a few lines by you to assure him of my hearty consent to his marrying whichever he chooses of the girls. Although I must throw in a good word for my little Lizzy."

"I desire you will do no such thing. Lizzy is not a bit better than the others, and I am sure she is not half so beautiful as Jane, nor half so good-natured as Lydia. But you are always giving *her* the preference."

"They have none of them much to recommend them," he replied. "They are all silly and ignorant, like other girls, but Lizzy has something more of intelligence and wit than her sisters."

"Mr. Bennet, how can you abuse your own children in such a way! You take delight in upsetting me. You have no compassion on my poor nerves."

"You mistake me, my dear. I have a high respect for your nerves. They are my old friends. I have heard you mention them often these twenty years at least."

"Ah! You do not know what I suffer."

"But I hope you will get over it, and live to see many young men of four thousand a year come into the neighbourhood."

"It will be no use to us if twenty such should come, since you will not visit them."

"Depend upon it, my dear, that when there are twenty, I will visit them all."

Mr. Bennet was so odd a mixture of wit, sarcastic humour, reserve, and peculiarity that the experience of twenty-three years had been insufficient to make his wife understand his character. Her mind was less difficult to grasp. She was a woman of limited understanding, little information, and unpredictable temper. Whenever she was unhappy she thought she was developing a nervous condition. The business of her life was to get her daughters married; its solace was visiting and gossip.

CHAPTER 2

Mr. Bennet was among the earliest of those who visited Mr. Bingley. He had always intended to do so, though to the last he assured his wife that he would not go. Until the evening after the visit was paid she had no knowledge of it. It was then disclosed in the following manner: — Observing his second daughter employed in trimming a hat, he suddenly addressed her with —

"I hope Mr. Bingley will like it, Lizzy."

"We have no way of knowing *what* Mr. Bingley likes," said her mother resentfully, "since we are not to visit."

"But you forget, mama," said Elizabeth, "that we shall meet him at the assemblies, and that Mrs. Long has promised to introduce him."

"I do not believe Mrs. Long will do any such thing. She has two nieces of her own. She is a selfish, hypocritical woman, and I have nothing good to say about her."

"Nor have I," said Mr. Bennet, "and I am glad to find that you do not depend on her serving you."

Mrs. Bennet made no reply, but, unable to contain herself, began scolding one of her daughters.

"Don't keep coughing so Kitty, for Heaven's sake! Have a little compassion on my nerves. You tear them to pieces."

"Kitty has no discretion in her coughs," said her father. "She times them poorly."

"I do not cough for my own amusement," replied Kitty fretfully. "When is your next ball, Lizzy?"

"Two weeks from tomorrow."

"Yes, so it is," cried her mother, "and Mrs. Long does not come back until the day before, so it will be impossible for her to introduce him, for she will not know him herself."

"Then, my dear, you may have the advantage over your friend, and introduce Mr. Bingley to *her.*"

"Impossible, Mr. Bennet, impossible, when I am not acquainted with him myself. How can you be so teasing?"

"I honour your discretion. Two weeks' acquaintance is certainly very little. One cannot know what a man really is by the end of it. But if *we* do not introduce him then somebody else will. After all, Mrs. Long and her nieces must be introduced. Therefore, as she will think it an act of kindness, if you decline to do it, then I will do it myself."

The girls stared at their father. Mrs. Bennet said only, "Nonsense, nonsense!"

"What can be the meaning of that exclamation?" cried he. "Do you consider the forms of introduction, and the importance that is placed on them, as nonsense? I cannot quite agree with you *there.* What do you say, Mary? For you are a young lady of deep reflection, I know, and read great books."

Mary wished to say something very wise, but knew not how.

"While Mary is sorting out her ideas," he continued, "let us return to Mr. Bingley."

"I am sick of Mr. Bingley," cried his wife.

"I am sorry to hear *that.* Why did not you tell me before? If I had known it this morning I certainly would not have visited him. It is very unfortunate, but as I have actually paid the visit, we cannot escape the acquaintance now."

The astonishment of the ladies was just what he wished; that of Mrs. Bennet perhaps surpassing the rest. After her initial excitement, though, she began to declare that it was what she had expected all along.

"How good it was of you, my dear Mr. Bennet! But I knew I would persuade you eventually. I was sure you loved your girls too well to neglect such an acquaintance. Well, how pleased I am! And it is such a good joke, too, that you should have gone this morning, and never said a word about it till now."

"Now, Kitty, you may cough as much as you choose," said Mr. Bennet. Then he left the room, tired of his wife's jubilant exclamations.

"What an excellent father you have, girls!" said she, when the door was shut. "I do not know how you will ever pay him back for his kindness; or me either, for that matter. At our time of life it is not so easy, I can tell you, to be making new acquaintance every day; but for your sakes, we would do anything. Lydia, my love, though you *are* the youngest, I dare say Mr. Bingley will dance with you at the next ball."

"Oh!" said Lydia stoutly, "I am not worried on that account; for though I *am* the youngest, I'm also the tallest."

The rest of the evening was spent wondering how soon he would return Mr. Bennet's visit, and determining when they should ask him to dinner.

CHAPTER 3

Mrs. Bennet, even with the assistance of her five daughters, was unable to draw from her husband any satisfactory description of Mr. Bingley. They attacked him in various ways — with direct questions and clever guesses; but he eluded the skill of them all. Thus they were at last forced to accept the secondhand knowledge of their neighbour, Lady Lucas. Her report was highly favourable. Sir William had been delighted with him. He was quite young, wonderfully handsome, extremely agreeable, and, to top it off, he meant to be at the next ball with a large party. Nothing could be more delightful! To be fond of dancing was a certain step towards falling in love, and very cheerful hopes about winning Mr. Bingley's heart were entertained.

"If I can but see one of my daughters happily settled at Netherfield," said Mrs. Bennet to her husband, "and all the others equally well married, I shall have nothing to wish for."

In a few days Mr. Bingley returned Mr. Bennet's visit, and sat about ten minutes with him in his library. He had hoped to see the young ladies, of whose beauty he had heard much; but he saw only the father. The ladies were somewhat more fortunate, for they had the advantage of determining from an upper window that he wore a blue coat, and rode a black horse.

An invitation to dinner was sent soon afterwards. Mrs. Bennet had already planned the courses that were to do credit to her oversight, when an answer arrived which postponed it all. Mr. Bingley was needed in London the following day, and, consequently, unable to accept the honour of their invitation, etc. Mrs. Bennet was quite troubled. She could not imagine what business he could have in town so soon after his arrival in Hertfordshire. She began to fear that he might be always running about from one place to another, and never settled at Netherfield as he ought to be. Lady Lucas calmed her fears a little by suggesting the idea of his being gone to London only to get a large party for the ball. A report soon followed that Mr.

Bingley was to bring twelve ladies and seven gentlemen with him to the assembly. The girls grieved over such a number of ladies, but were comforted the day before the ball by hearing that instead of twelve he had brought only six with him from London — his five sisters and a cousin. And when the party entered the assembly room it consisted of only five altogether — Mr. Bingley, his two sisters, the husband of the eldest, and another young man.

Mr. Bingley was good-looking and gentlemanlike; he had a pleasant countenance, and relaxed, sincere manners. His sisters were elegant women of high social standing. His brother-in-law, Mr. Hurst, possessed the appearance of a gentleman. But his friend Mr. Darcy soon drew the attention of the room by his fine, tall person, handsome features, and noble disposition. It was reported, and the report was known by all within five minutes after his entrance, that he had an income of ten thousand a year. The gentlemen pronounced him to be a fine figure of a man. The ladies declared he was much handsomer than Mr. Bingley, and he was looked at with great admiration for about half the evening. Then his manners produced a distaste which turned the tide of his popularity; for he was discovered to be proud, to be above his company, and impossible to please. Even his large estate in Derbyshire could not then save him from having a most forbidding, disagreeable character, and being unworthy to be compared with his friend.

Mr. Bingley had soon made himself acquainted with all the distinguished people in the room. He was lively and unreserved, danced every dance, was displeased that the ball closed so early, and talked of giving one himself at Netherfield. Such friendly qualities must speak for themselves. What a contrast between him and his friend! Mr. Darcy danced only once with Mrs. Hurst and once with Miss Bingley. He declined being introduced to any other lady, and spent the rest of the evening walking around the room, speaking occasionally to one of the members of his own party. His character was decided. He was the proudest, most disagreeable man in the world, and everybody hoped that he would never come there again. Among the most outspoken against him was Mrs. Bennet, whose dislike of his general behaviour was sharpened into resentment by his having snubbed one of her daughters.

Elizabeth Bennet had been required, because there were more ladies in attendance than gentlemen, to sit down for two dances. During part of that time Mr. Darcy had been standing near enough for her to overhear a conversation between him and Mr. Bingley, who came from the dance for a few minutes, to encourage his friend to join it.

"Come, Darcy," said he, "I must have you dance. I hate to see you standing by yourself in this tiresome manner. It would be much better if you danced."

"I certainly shall not. You know how I detest it, unless I am particularly acquainted with my partner. At such an assembly as this it would be impossible. Your sisters are dancing with other gentlemen, and there is not another woman in the room whom it would not be a punishment to me to stand up with."

"I would not be as critical as you are," cried Bingley, "for a kingdom! Upon my honour, I never met with so many pleasant girls in my life as I have this evening; and there are several of them who are uncommonly pretty."

"*You* are dancing with the only beautiful girl in the room," said Mr. Darcy, looking at the eldest Miss Bennet.

"Oh! She is the most beautiful creature I ever beheld! But there is one of her sisters sitting down just behind you, who is very pretty, and I dare say very agreeable. Do let me ask my partner to introduce you."

"Which do you mean?" and turning round, he looked for a moment at Elizabeth, till catching her eye, he withdrew his own and coldly said, "She is tolerable; but not beautiful enough to tempt *me*; and I am in no mood at present to spend time with young ladies who are snubbed by other men. You had better return to your partner and enjoy her smiles, for you are wasting your time with me."

Mr. Bingley followed his advice. Mr. Darcy walked off, and Elizabeth remained with no very kind feelings towards him. She told the story, however, with great spirit among her friends and family; for she had a lively, playful personality, which delighted in anything ridiculous.

The evening overall went pleasantly for the whole family. Mrs. Bennet had seen her eldest daughter much admired by the Netherfield party. Mr. Bingley had danced with her twice, and she had been highly regarded by his sisters. Jane was as much gratified by this as her mother could be, though in a quieter way. Elizabeth felt Jane's pleasure. Mary had heard herself mentioned to Miss Bingley as the most accomplished girl in the neighbourhood, and Catherine and Lydia had been fortunate enough to be never without partners, which was all that they had yet learned to care for at a ball. They returned, therefore, in good spirits to Longbourn, the village where they lived, and of which they were the principal inhabitants. They found Mr. Bennet still up. While reading a book he never noticed the passage of time; and on the present occasion he had a good deal of curiosity about an evening which had produced such high expectations. He had rather hoped that all his wife's views on the stranger would be disappointed; but he soon found that he had a very different story to hear.

"Oh! My dear Mr. Bennet," as she entered the room, "we have had a most delightful evening, a most excellent ball. I wish you had been there. Jane was so admired, nothing could be like it. Everybody said how good she looked. Mr. Bingley thought her quite beautiful, and danced with her twice.

Only think of *that* my dear; he actually danced with her twice! And she was the only girl in the room that he asked a second time. First he asked Miss Lucas. I was so displeased to see him stand up with her! But, however, he did not admire her at all: indeed, nobody can, you know; and he seemed quite struck with Jane as she was dancing. So he inquired who she was, and got introduced, and asked her for the next dance. Then he danced with Miss King, then Maria Lucas, then with Jane again, and then with Lizzy."

"If he had had any compassion for *me*," cried her husband impatiently, "he would not have danced half so much! For God's sake, say no more of his partners. O that he had sprained his ankle in the first dance!"

"Oh! my dear," continued Mrs. Bennet, "I am quite delighted with him. He is so excessively handsome! And his sisters are charming women. I never in my life saw anything more elegant than their dresses. I dare say the lace upon Mrs. Hurst's gown — "

Here she was interrupted again. Mr. Bennet protested against any description of apparel. She therefore changed the subject and related, with much bitterness and some exaggeration, the shocking rudeness of Mr. Darcy.

"But I can assure you," she added, "that Lizzy does not lose much by not catching his eye; for he is a most disagreeable, horrid man, not at all worth pleasing. So high and so conceited that there was no enduring him! He walked here, and walked there, believing himself so very great! Not beautiful enough to dance with! I wish you had been there, my dear, to have given him one of your reprimands. I quite detest the man."

CHAPTER 4

When Jane and Elizabeth were alone, Jane, who had been reserved in her praise of Mr. Bingley before, expressed to her sister how very much she admired him.

"He is just what a young man ought to be," said she, "sensible, good-humoured, lively; and I never saw such wonderful manners! — so friendly, such a perfect gentleman!"

"He is also handsome," said Elizabeth, "which a young man ought to be, if he possibly can. His character is thereby complete."

"I was very much flattered by his asking me to dance a second time. I did not expect such a compliment."

"You didn't? *I* did for you. But that is one great difference between us. Compliments always take *you* by surprise, and *me* never. What could be more natural than his asking you again? He could not help seeing that you were about five times as pretty as every other woman in the room and didn't ask you a second time simply out of courtesy. But he certainly is very agreeable, and you have my permission to like him. You have liked many a more tiresome person."

"Dear Lizzy!"

"Oh! You are a great deal too inclined, you know, to like people in general. You never see a fault in anybody. Everyone in the world is good and agreeable in your eyes. I never heard you speak unkindly about a human being in my life."

"I do not wish to speak unkind things about anyone, but I always say what I think."

"I know you do; and it is *that* which makes it so incredible. With *your* good sense to be so honestly blind to the follies and nonsense of others! Pretended good will is common enough — one sees it everywhere. But to be completely accepting without some selfish purpose or design —

to take the good of everybody's character and make it still better, and say nothing of the bad — belongs to you alone. And so you like this man's sisters too, do you? Their manners are not as good as his."

"Certainly not — at first. But they are very pleasing women when you converse with them. Miss Bingley is to live with her brother, and manage his household; and I am much mistaken if we shall not find a very charming neighbour in her."

Elizabeth listened in silence, but was not convinced. Their behaviour at the assembly had not been calculated to please in general. With more quickness of observation and less ease of temper than her sister, and with the advantage of being an outside observer, she was not so quick to approve of them. They were in fact very refined ladies; not deficient in good-humour when it suited them, nor unable to be agreeable when they chose it, but proud and conceited. They were rather beautiful, had been educated in one of the best private boarding schools in town, had a fortune of twenty thousand pounds, and were in the habit of spending more than they should. They particularly enjoyed associating with people of rank, and were therefore in every respect entitled to think well of themselves and poorly of others. They came from a respectable family in the north of England; a circumstance they emphasized over the fact that their brother's fortune and their own had been acquired through trade.

Mr. Bingley inherited property to the amount of nearly a hundred thousand pounds from his father, who had intended to purchase an estate, but did not live to do it. Mr. Bingley intended to purchase his own estate, and sometimes decided which county he would like it to be in; but as he now had a good house with plenty of game for shooting, many of those who best knew him doubted whether he might not spend the remainder of his days at Netherfield and leave the next generation to purchase.

His sisters were very anxious for him to have an estate of his own; but, though he was now established only as a tenant, Miss Bingley was by no means unwilling to manage his household. Mrs. Hurst, who had married a man of more status than fortune, was no less disposed to consider his house as her home when it suited her. Mr. Bingley had not been of age two years when he was tempted by a fortunate recommendation to look at Netherfield House. He did look at it, and into it, for half an hour — was pleased with the situation and the main rooms, satisfied with what the owner said in its praise, and took it immediately.

Between him and Darcy there was a very steady friendship, in spite of a great difference of character. Bingley was endeared to Darcy by the easiness, openness, and flexibility of his temper, though no disposition could offer a greater contrast to his own. Darcy in turn held Bingley in the highest regard. Darcy was more intelligent than Bingley, who was by no means deficient. But Darcy was clever. He was at the same time haughty, reserved, and difficult to please. His disposition, though gentlemanlike, was not inviting. In that respect his friend had the advantage. Bingley was sure of being liked wherever he appeared; Darcy was continually giving offence.

The manner in which they spoke of the Meryton assembly was typical of them. Bingley had never met with pleasanter people or prettier girls in his life, and everybody had been most kind and attentive to him. There had been no formality, no stiffness. He had soon felt acquainted with everyone in the room, and as to Miss Bennet, he could not conceive an angel more beautiful. Darcy, on the other hand, had seen a collection of people in whom there was little beauty and no fashion. He had no interest in getting to know any of them better, and he therefore received neither attention nor pleasure from the company. Miss Bennet he acknowledged to be pretty, but she smiled too much.

Mrs. Hurst and her sister agreed that Miss Bennet smiled too much; but still they admired her and liked her, and pronounced her to be a sweet girl – one they would like to know better. Miss Bennet was therefore established as a sweet girl, and their brother felt authorised by their good opinion to think of her as he chose.

CHAPTER 5

Within a short walk of Longbourn lived a family with whom the Bennets were particularly close. Sir William Lucas had been formerly in business in Meryton, where he had made a tolerable fortune, and risen to the honour of knighthood after giving a speech to the King during his mayoralty. The distinction had perhaps been felt too strongly. It had given him a dislike for his business, and to his residence in a small market town; and, leaving them both, he had removed with his family to a house about a mile from Meryton. He named the house Lucas Lodge, and it was a place where he could think with pleasure of his own importance, and, unshackled by business, occupy himself solely in being civil to all the world. For, though elated by his rank, it did not render him self-centered; on the contrary, he was all attention to everybody. By nature inoffensive, friendly and obliging, the honor he received from the King had made him courteous.

Lady Lucas was a very good kind of woman, not too clever to be a valuable neighbour to Mrs. Bennet. They had several children. The eldest of them, a sensible, intelligent young woman of twenty-seven, was Elizabeth's intimate friend.

That the Miss Lucases and the Miss Bennets should meet to talk over a ball was absolutely necessary; and the morning after the assembly brought the Lucases to Longbourn to hear and to communicate.

"*You* began the evening well, Charlotte," said Mrs. Bennet, with civil self-command, to Miss Lucas. You were Mr. Bingley's first choice."

"Yes, but he seemed to like his second better."

"Oh! You mean Jane, I suppose, because he danced with her twice. To be sure that *did* seem as if he admired her — indeed I rather believe he *did* — I heard something about it — but I hardly know what — something about Mr. Robinson."

"Perhaps you mean what I overheard between him and Mr. Robinson: did not I mention it to you? Mr. Robinson's asking him how he liked our Meryton balls, and whether he did not think there were a great many pretty women in the room, and *which* he thought the prettiest? And his answering immediately to the last question — 'Oh! the eldest Miss Bennet, beyond a doubt; there cannot be two opinions on that point.'"

"Upon my word! Well, that was very decided indeed — that does seem as if — but, however, it may all come to nothing, you know."

"*My* overhearings were more to the purpose than *yours*, Eliza," said Charlotte. "Mr. Darcy is not so well worth listening to as his friend, is he? Poor Eliza! To be only just *tolerable*."

"I beg you would not put it into Lizzy's head to be troubled by his poor treatment, for he is such a disagreeable man that it would be quite a misfortune to be liked by him. Mrs. Long told me last night that he sat close to her for half an hour without once opening his lips."

"Are you quite sure, ma'am? Is not there a little mistake?" said Jane. "I certainly saw Mr. Darcy speaking to her."

"Ay — because she asked him at last how he liked Netherfield, and he could not avoid answering her — but she said he seemed very angry at being spoken to."

"Miss Bingley told me," said Jane, "that he never speaks much, except among people he knows well. With *them* he is remarkably agreeable."

"I do not believe a word of it, my dear. If he had been so very agreeable, he would have talked to Mrs. Long. But I can guess how it was: everybody says that he is filled with pride. I dare say he had heard somehow that Mrs. Long does not keep a carriage, and had come to the ball in a hired one."

"I do not mind his not talking to Mrs. Long," said Miss Lucas, "but I wish he had danced with Eliza."

"Another time, Lizzy," said her mother. "I would not dance with *him*, if I were you."

"I believe, ma'am, I may safely promise you *never* to dance with him."

"His pride," said Miss Lucas, "does not offend *me* as much as pride usually does, because there is an excuse for it. One cannot wonder that so very fine a young man, with family, fortune, everything in his favour, should think highly of himself. If I may so express it, he has a *right* to be proud."

"That is very true," replied Elizabeth, "and I could easily forgive *his* pride, if he had not mortified *mine*."

"Pride," observed Mary, who prided herself on the wisdom of her reflections, "is a very common failing, I believe. By all that I have ever read, I am convinced that it is very common indeed. Human nature is particularly prone to it, and there are very few of us who do not experience a feeling of self-importance because of some quality or other, real or imaginary. Vanity and pride are different things, though the words are often used interchangeably. A person may be proud without being vain. Pride relates more to our opinion of ourselves, vanity to what we would have others think of us."

"If I were as rich as Mr. Darcy," cried a young Lucas, who came with his sisters, "I should not care how proud I was. I would keep a pack of foxhounds, and drink a bottle of wine every day."

"Then you would drink a great deal more than you should," said Mrs. Bennet, "and if I were to see you doing it, I would take away your bottle immediately."

The boy protested that she would not. She continued to declare that she would, and the argument ended only with the visit.

CHAPTER 6

The ladies of Longbourn soon visited those of Netherfield. The visit was returned in kind. Miss Bennet's pleasing manners grew on the good will of Mrs. Hurst and Miss Bingley. Though the mother was found to be intolerable, and the younger sisters not worth speaking to, a wish of being better acquainted with *them* was expressed towards the two eldest. By Jane, this attention was received with the greatest pleasure, but Elizabeth still saw haughtiness in their treatment of everybody, hardly excepting even her sister, and could not like them. Their kindness to Jane, such as it was, arose in all probability from the influence of their brother's admiration. It was generally evident whenever they met that he *did* admire her, and it was equally evident that Jane was on her way to being very much in love. But Elizabeth considered with pleasure that it was not likely to be discovered by the world in general, since Jane's natural reserve and kindness to everyone would protect her from suspicion. She mentioned this to her friend Miss Lucas.

"It may perhaps be agreeable," replied Charlotte, "to keep such things from public view, but it is sometimes a disadvantage to be so very guarded. If a woman conceals her affection with the same skill from her would-be lover, she may lose the opportunity of securing his admiration. It will then be but poor consolation to believe the world equally unaware of her attachment. There is so much gratitude or vanity in almost every relationship that it is not safe to leave any to itself. We can all *begin* freely — a slight preference is natural enough; but there are very few of us who have heart enough to be really in love without encouragement. In nine cases out of ten it is better for a woman to show *more* affection than she feels. Bingley likes your sister undoubtedly, but he may never do more than like her if she does not encourage him."

"But she does encourage him, as much as her nature will allow. If *I* can perceive her regard for him, he must be stupid, indeed, not to discover it too."

"Remember, Eliza, that he does not know Jane as well as you do."

"But if a woman is attracted to a man, and does not try to hide it, he will eventually discover it."

"Perhaps he will, if he sees enough of her. But, though Bingley and Jane meet often, it is never for many hours together. As they always see each other in large mixed parties, it is impossible that every moment should be spent in conversing together. Jane should therefore make the most of every half-hour in which she can command his attention. When they are married, there will be leisure for falling in love as much as she chooses."

"Your plan is a good one," replied Elizabeth, "where nothing is in question but the desire of marrying well. If I were determined to get a rich husband, or any husband, I dare say I should adopt it. But these are not Jane's feelings; she is not acting by design. As yet, she cannot even be certain of the degree of her own regard, nor of its reasonableness. She has known him for only two weeks. She danced four dances with him at Meryton; she saw him one morning at his own house, and has since dined in company with him four times. This is not quite enough to make her understand his character."

"Not as you represent it. Had she merely *dined* with him, she might only have discovered whether he had a good appetite. But you must remember that four evenings have been also spent together — and four evenings may do a great deal."

"Yes, these four evenings have enabled them to determine that they both like Blackjack better than Commerce. But with respect to any other essential characteristic, I do not imagine that much has been revealed."

"Well," said Charlotte, "I wish Jane success with all my heart. If she were married to him tomorrow, I think she would have as good a chance of happiness as she would if she studied his character for a year. Happiness in marriage is entirely a matter of chance. If the dispositions of the parties are ever so well known to each other, or ever so similar beforehand, it does not increase their happiness in the least. They always continue to grow sufficiently unlike afterwards to have their share of frustration. It is better to know as little as possible of the defects of the person with whom you are to spend your life."

"You make me laugh, Charlotte, but it is not prudent. You know it is not, and you would never act in this way yourself."

Occupied in observing Mr. Bingley's attentions to her sister, Elizabeth was far from suspecting that she was herself becoming an object of some interest in the eyes of his friend. Mr. Darcy had at first scarcely believed her to be pretty. He had looked at her without admiration at the ball, and when they next met he looked at her only to criticise. But no sooner had he made it clear to himself and his friends that she had hardly a good feature in her face, than he began to find it was made uncommonly intelligent by the beautiful expression of her dark eyes. To this discovery others equally mortifying were added. Though he had detected with a critical eye more than one failure of perfect symmetry in her form, he was forced to acknowledge her figure to be light and pleasing. In spite of his determining that her manners were not those of the highest society, he was taken in by their easy playfulness. Of this she was perfectly unaware — to her he was only the man who made himself agreeable nowhere, and who had not thought her beautiful enough to dance with.

He began to wish to know more of her, and as a step towards conversing with her himself, he listened to her conversation with others. His doing so drew her notice. It was at Sir William Lucas's, where a large group was assembled.

"What does Mr. Darcy mean," said she to Charlotte, "by listening to my conversation with Colonel Forster?"

"That is a question which Mr. Darcy only can answer."

"But if he does it anymore I shall certainly let him know that I see what he is doing. He has a very critical eye, and if I do not start matching wits with him I shall soon grow afraid of him."

On his approaching them soon afterwards, though without seeming to have any intention of speaking, Miss Lucas dared her friend to mention such a subject to him. Elizabeth, accepting the challenge, immediately turned to him and said —

"Did not you think, Mr. Darcy, that I expressed myself uncommonly well just now, when I was teasing Colonel Forster about giving us a ball at Meryton?"

"With great energy, but it is a subject which always makes a lady energetic."

"Such cutting words!"

"It will be *her* turn soon to be teased," said Miss Lucas. "I am going to open the piano, Eliza, and you know what follows."

"You are a very strange creature by way of a friend! Always wanting me to play and sing before anybody and everybody! If my vanity had taken a musical turn, you would have been invaluable. But as it is, I would really rather not play for those who must be in the habit of hearing the very best performers." On Miss Lucas's persevering, however, she added, "Very well; if it must be so, it must." And gravely glancing at Mr. Darcy, "There is a fine old saying, which everybody here is of course familiar with — 'Keep your breath to cool your porridge' — and I shall keep mine to swell my song."

Her performance was pleasing, though by no means exceptional. After a song or two, and before she could reply to the requests of several who asked her to sing again, she was eagerly followed at the instrument by her sister Mary. Having worked hard for knowledge and accomplishments, in consequence of being the only plain one in the family, Mary was always impatient to show off her skill.

Mary had neither natural ability nor taste; and though vanity had motivated her to work hard, it had given her likewise a conceited manner ill-suited to the degree of skill she had reached. Elizabeth, casual and unassuming, had been listened to with much more pleasure, though not playing half so well. Mary, at the end of a long concerto, was glad to receive praise and gratitude by switching to Scotch and Irish dances at the request of her younger sisters. They, with some of the Lucases and two or three officers, joined eagerly in dancing at one end of the room.

Mr. Darcy stood near them in silent indignation at such a mode of spending the evening, to the exclusion of all conversation. He was too much consumed by his own thoughts to perceive that Sir William Lucas was sitting next to him, till Sir William thus began —

"What a charming amusement for young people this is, Mr. Darcy! There is nothing like dancing. I consider it as one of the first refinements of polished societies."

"Certainly, sir; and it has the advantage also of being popular among the less polished societies of the world. Every savage can dance."

Sir William only smiled. "Your friend performs delightfully," he continued after a pause, on seeing Bingley join the group, "and I am certain you are an fine dancer yourself, Mr. Darcy."

"You saw me dance at Meryton, I believe, sir."

"Yes, indeed, and received no inconsiderable pleasure from the sight. Do you often dance at court?"

"Never, sir."

"Do you not think it would be a proper compliment to the place?"

"It is a compliment which I never pay to any place if I can avoid it."

"You have a house in town, I assume?"

Mr. Darcy nodded.

"I had once some thoughts of settling in town myself — for I am fond of superior society; but I did not feel quite certain that the air of London would agree with Lady Lucas."

He paused in hopes of an answer, but his companion was not disposed to make any. As Elizabeth at that instant moved towards them, he was struck with the notion of doing a very gallant thing, and called out to her —

"My dear Miss Eliza, why are you not dancing? — Mr. Darcy, you must allow me to present this young lady to you as a very desirable partner. You cannot refuse to dance, I am sure, when so much beauty is before you."

And, taking her hand, he would have given it to Mr. Darcy, who, though extremely surprised, was not unwilling to receive it. But she instantly drew back, and said with some distress to Sir William —

"Indeed, sir, I have not the least intention of dancing. I beg you not to suppose that I moved this way in order to find a partner."

Mr. Darcy, with grave propriety, requested to be allowed the honour of her hand, but in vain. Elizabeth was determined; nor could Sir William at all shake her purpose by his attempt at persuasion.

"You excel so much in the dance, Miss Eliza, that it is cruel to deny me the happiness of seeing you. And though this gentleman dislikes the amusement in general, he can have no objection, I am sure, to oblige us for one half-hour."

"Mr. Darcy is all politeness," said Elizabeth, smiling.

"He is indeed, but considering the circumstances, my dear Miss Eliza, we cannot wonder at his willingness — for who would object to such a partner?"

Elizabeth looked amused and turned away. Her resistance had not lowered the gentleman's opinion of her; and he was thinking of her with some pleasure when thus approached by Miss Bingley —

"I can guess the subject of your reverie."

"I should imagine not."

"You are considering how miserable it would be to pass many evenings in this manner — in such society; and indeed I am quite of your opinion. I was never more annoyed! The lifelessness, and yet the noise — the nothingness, and yet the self-importance of all these people! What I would give to hear your criticisms of them!"

"Your assumption is completely wrong, I assure you. My mind was more agreeably engaged. I have been meditating on the very great pleasure which a pair of fine eyes in the face of a pretty woman can bestow."

Miss Bingley immediately fixed her eyes on his face, and asked him to tell her what lady had inspired such reflections. Mr. Darcy replied with great boldness —

"Miss Elizabeth Bennet."

"Miss Elizabeth Bennet!" repeated Miss Bingley. "I am all astonishment. How long has she been such a favourite? — and when am I to wish you joy on your upcoming wedding?"

"That is exactly the question which I expected you to ask. A lady's imagination is very rapid; it jumps from admiration to love, and from love to matrimony, in a moment. I knew you would be wishing me joy."

"Well, if you are so serious about it, I shall consider the matter as absolutely settled. You will have a charming mother-in-law, indeed; and, of course, she will be always at Pemberley with you."

He listened to her with perfect indifference while she chose to entertain herself in this manner. As his composure convinced her that all was safe, her wit flowed long.

CHAPTER 7

Mr. Bennet's property consisted almost entirely in an estate of two thousand a year, which, unfortunately for his daughters, was to be inherited by a distant relative. Their mother's fortune, though ample for her situation in life, could but poorly make up for the deficiency of his. Her father had been an attorney in Meryton, and had left her four thousand pounds.

She had a sister married to a Mr. Phillips, who had been a clerk to their father and succeeded him in the business, and a brother settled in London in a respectable line of trade.

The village of Longbourn was only one mile from Meryton; a most convenient distance for the young ladies, who usually went there three or four times a week to visit their aunt and to a hat shop just over the way. The two youngest of the family, Catherine and Lydia, were particularly frequent in these attentions. Their minds were more vacant than their sisters', and when there was nothing better to do, a walk to Meryton was necessary to amuse their morning hours and furnish conversation for the evening. However empty of gossip the country in general might be, they always contrived to learn some from their aunt. At present, indeed, they were well supplied both with news and happiness by the recent arrival of a militia regiment in the neighbourhood. It was to remain the whole winter, and Meryton was the headquarters.

Their visits to Mrs. Philips now produced the most interesting information. Every day added something to their knowledge of the officers' names and backgrounds. Their lodgings were not long a secret, and at length they began to know the officers themselves. Mr. Philips visited them all, and this opened to his nieces a source of happiness previously unknown. They could talk of nothing but officers; and Mr. Bingley's large fortune, the mere mention of which thrilled their mother, was worthless in their eyes when compared to the uniform of an ensign.

After listening one morning to their gushing on this subject, Mr. Bennet coolly observed —

"From all that I can collect by your manner of talking, you must be two of the silliest girls in the country. I have suspected it some time, but I am now convinced."

Catherine was troubled, and made no answer; but Lydia, with perfect indifference, continued to express her admiration of Captain Carter, and her hope of seeing him in the course of the day, as he was going the next morning to London.

"I am astonished, my dear," said Mrs. Bennet, "that you should be so ready to think your own children silly. If I wished to think disdainfully of anybody's children, it should not be of my own."

"If my children are silly, I must hope to be always aware of it."

"Yes — but as it happens, they are all of them very clever."

"This is the only point, I flatter myself, on which we do not agree. I had hoped that our views coincided in every particular, but I must differ from you so far as to think our two youngest daughters uncommonly foolish."

"My dear Mr. Bennet, you must not expect such girls to have the sense of their father and mother. When they get to our age I dare say they will not think about officers any more than we do. I remember the time when I liked a red coat myself very well — and, indeed, so I do still at my heart. If a smart young colonel with five or six thousand a year should want one of my girls, I shall not say no to him. I thought Colonel Forster looked very becoming the other night at Sir William's in his uniform."

"Mama," cried Lydia, "my aunt says that Colonel Forster and Captain Carter do not go so often to Miss Watson's as they did when they first came. She sees them now very often standing in Clarke's library."

Mrs. Bennet was prevented replying by the entrance of a servant with a note for Miss Bennet. It came from Netherfield, and the servant waited for an answer. Mrs. Bennet's eyes sparkled with pleasure, and she was eagerly calling out, while her daughter read —

"Well, Jane, who is it from? What is it about? What does he say? Well, Jane, hurry and tell us; hurry, my love."

"It is from Miss Bingley," said Jane, and then read it aloud.

"My dear Friend, — If you are not so compassionate as to dine today with Louisa and me, we shall be in danger of hating each other for the rest of our lives. When two women spend the entire day together it can never end without a quarrel. Come as soon as you can on the receipt of this. My brother and the gentlemen are to dine with the officers. — Yours ever,
CAROLINE BINGLEY."

"With the officers!" cried Lydia. "I wonder why my aunt did not tell us of *that*."

"Dining out," said Mrs. Bennet, " is very unlucky."

"Can I have the carriage?" said Jane.

"No, my dear, you had better go on horseback, because it seems likely to rain, and then you must stay all night."

"That would be a good scheme," said Elizabeth, "if you were sure that they would not offer to send her home."

"Oh! But the gentlemen will have Mr. Bingley's carriage to go to Meryton, and the Hursts have no horses for theirs."

"I had much rather go in the coach."

"But, my dear, your father cannot spare the horses, I am sure. They are needed on the farm, Mr. Bennett, are they not?"

"They are needed on the farm much more often than I can get them."

"But if you need them today," said Elizabeth, "my mother's scheme may be set in motion."

She did at last extort from her father an acknowledgment that the horses were needed: Jane was therefore obliged to go on horseback, and her mother walked her to the door with many cheerful predictions of bad weather. Her hopes were soon realized: Jane had not been gone long before it rained hard. Her sisters were worried about her, but her mother was delighted. The rain continued the whole evening without pause: Jane certainly could not come back.

"This was a lucky idea of mine, indeed!" said Mrs. Bennet more than once, as if the credit of making it rain were all her own. Until the next morning, however, she was not aware of all the benefits of her scheme. Breakfast was scarcely over when a servant from Netherfield brought the following note for Elizabeth –

"My dearest Lizzy, — I find myself very unwell this morning, which, I suppose, is to be attributed to my getting wet through yesterday. My kind friends will not hear of my returning home till I am better. They insist also on my seeing Mr. Jones — therefore do not be alarmed if you should hear of his having been to me — and, excepting a sore throat and headache, there is not much the matter with me. — Yours, etc."

"Well, my dear," said Mr. Bennet, when Elizabeth had read the note aloud, "if your daughter has contracted a serious illness — if she should die, it would be a comfort to know that it was all in pursuit of Mr. Bingley, and under your orders."

"Oh! I am not at all afraid of her dying. People do not die of little trifling colds. She will be taken good care of. As long as she stays there, she'll be fine. I would go and see her if I could have the carriage."

Elizabeth, feeling really worried, was determined to go to her, though the carriage was not to be had. As she was no horsewoman, walking was her only alternative. She declared her intention.

"How can you be so silly," cried her mother, "as to think of such a thing in all this mud? You will not be fit to be seen when you get there!"

"I shall be very fit to see Jane — which is all I want."

"Is this a hint to me, Lizzy," said her father, "to send for the horses?"

"No, indeed. I do not wish to avoid the walk. The distance is nothing when one has a clear purpose; only three miles. I shall be back by dinner."

"I admire your kind intentions," observed Mary, "but every impulse of feeling should be guided by reason. In my opinion, exertion should always be in proportion to what is required."

"We will go as far as Meryton with you," said Catherine and Lydia. Elizabeth accepted their company, and the three young ladies set off together.

"If we hurry," said Lydia, as they walked along, "perhaps we may see Captain Carter before he goes."

In Meryton they parted, the two youngest going to the lodgings of one of the officers' wives, and Elizabeth continued her walk alone. She crossed field after field at a quick pace, springing over puddles, anxious to arrive. She soon found herself at last within view of the house, with weary ankles, dirty stockings, and a face glowing with the warmth of exercise.

She was shown into the breakfast parlour, where all but Jane were assembled, and where her appearance created a great deal of surprise. That she should have walked three miles so early in the day, in such dirty weather, and by herself, was almost unimaginable to Mrs. Hurst and Miss Bingley. Elizabeth was convinced that they disdained her for it. She was received, however, very politely by them, and in their brother's manners there was something better than politeness; there was good-humour and kindness. Mr. Darcy said very little, and Mr. Hurst nothing at all. Mr. Darcy was divided between admiring the luster which exercise had given to her complexion, and doubt as to the occasion's justifying her coming so far alone. Mr. Hurst was thinking only of his breakfast.

Her enquiries after her sister were not very favourably answered. Miss Bennet had slept poorly, and though awake, was very feverish and not well enough to leave her room. Elizabeth was glad to be taken to her immediately. Jane, who in her letter had stopped short of expressing a wish for such a visit out of fear of giving alarm or inconvenience, was delighted at her entrance. She was not, however, feeling well enough for much conversation. When Miss Bingley left them alone together, she could attempt little besides expressions of gratitude for the extraordinary kindness she was treated with. Elizabeth silently sat by her.

When breakfast was over they were joined by the sisters, and Elizabeth began to like them herself when she saw how much affection and kindness they showed to Jane. The doctor came, and having examined his patient, said, as might be supposed, that she had caught a violent cold, and that they must endeavour to get the better of it. He advised her to return to bed, and promised her some medicine. The advice was followed readily, for the feverish symptoms increased, and her headache intensified. Elizabeth did not leave her room for a moment, nor were the other ladies often absent: the gentlemen being out, they had, in fact, nothing else to do.

When the clock struck three Elizabeth felt that she must go, and very unwillingly said so. Miss Bingley offered her the carriage, and she only needed a little encouragement to accept it. But when Jane expressed concern in parting with her, Miss Bingley was obliged to convert the offer of the carriage into an invitation to remain at Netherfield for the present. Elizabeth most thankfully agreed, and a servant was dispatched to Longbourn to tell the family she was staying and to bring back a supply of clothes.

CHAPTER 8

At five o'clock the two ladies went to dress, and at half-past six Elizabeth was summoned to dinner. To the polite enquiries which then poured in, and among which she had the pleasure of discerning the much superior compassion of Mr. Bingley's, she could not make a very favourable answer. Jane was by no means better. The sisters, on hearing this, repeated three or four times how much they were grieved, how shocking it was to have a bad cold, and how much they disliked being ill themselves. They then thought no more of the matter, and their indifference towards Jane when she was not present restored Elizabeth to the enjoyment of all her original dislike.

Their brother, indeed, was the only one of the party whom she could regard with any approval. His anxiety for Jane was evident, and his attentions to herself most pleasing, and they prevented her from feeling like an intruder as she believed she was considered by the others. She had very little attention paid to her by any but him. Miss Bingley was captivated by Mr. Darcy, her sister scarcely less so. Mr. Hurst, by whom Elizabeth sat, was a dispassionate man who lived only to eat, drink, and play at cards. When he found she preferred a plain dish to a spiced stew, he had nothing to say to her.

When dinner was over she returned directly to Jane, and Miss Bingley began speaking rudely of her as soon as she was out of the room. Her manners were pronounced to be very bad indeed, a mixture of pride and impropriety; she had no wit, no style, no taste, no beauty. Mrs. Hurst thought the same, and added —

"She has nothing, in short, to recommend her, but being an excellent walker. I shall never forget her appearance this morning. She really looked almost wild."

"She did indeed, Louisa. I could hardly keep my composure. Very foolish to come at all! Why must *she* be scampering about the country, because her sister had a cold? Her hair was so untidy!"

"Yes, and her petticoat. I hope you saw her petticoat. Six inches deep in mud, I am absolutely certain. And the gown which had been let down to hide it not doing its job."

"Your picture may be very exact, Louisa," said Bingley, "but this was all lost upon me. I thought Miss Elizabeth Bennet looked remarkably good when she came into the room this morning. Her dirty petticoat quite escaped my notice."

"*You* observed it, Mr. Darcy, I am sure," said Miss Bingley, "and I am inclined to think that you would not wish to see *your sister* make such an exhibition."

"Certainly not."

"To walk three miles, or four miles, or five miles, or whatever it is, above her ankles in dirt, and alone, quite alone! What could she mean by it? It seems to me to show an awful sort of prideful independence, a most country-town indifference to propriety."

"It shows an affection for her sister that is very pleasing," said Bingley.

"I am afraid, Mr. Darcy," observed Miss Bingley, in a half-whisper, "that this adventure has rather affected your admiration of her fine eyes."

"Not at all," he replied. "They were brightened by the exercise." A short pause followed this speech, and Mrs. Hurst began again —

"I have an excessive regard for Jane Bennet. She is really a very sweet girl, and I wish with all my heart she were well settled. But with such a father and mother, and such low connections, I am afraid there is no chance of it."

"I think I have heard you say that their uncle is an attorney in Meryton."

"Yes, and they have another, who lives somewhere near Cheapside."

"That is *precisely* what one would expect," added her sister, and they both laughed heartily.

"If they had uncles enough to fill *all* Cheapside," cried Bingley, "it would not make them one bit less agreeable."

"But it must significantly lessen their chances of marrying men of any consequence in the world," replied Darcy.

To this speech Bingley made no answer. But his sisters heartily agreed, and indulged their pleasure for some time at the expense of their dear friend's inferior relations.

With a renewal of tenderness, however, they went to her room on leaving the dining-parlour, and sat with her till summoned to coffee. She was still very ill, and Elizabeth would not leave her at all, till late in the evening, when she had the comfort of seeing her asleep. She then felt obligated to go downstairs herself. On entering the drawing room she found the whole party playing cards, and was immediately invited to join them. But, suspecting them to be playing for high stakes, she declined it. Making her sister the excuse, she said she would amuse herself with a book for the short time she could stay downstairs. Mr. Hurst looked at her with astonishment.

"Do you prefer reading to cards?" said he. "That is rather unusual."

"Miss Eliza Bennet," said Miss Bingley, "despises cards. She is a great reader, and has no pleasure in anything else."

"I deserve neither such praise nor such condemnation," cried Elizabeth. "I am *not* a great reader, and I have pleasure in many things."

"In caring for your sister I am sure you have pleasure," said Bingley, "and I hope it will soon be increased by seeing her quite well."

Elizabeth thanked him from her heart, and then walked towards a table where a few books were lying. He immediately offered to fetch her others — all that his library afforded.

"And I wish my collection were larger for your benefit and my own credit. But I am an idle fellow, and though I have not many, I have more than I ever look into."

Elizabeth assured him that she could suit herself perfectly with those in the room.

"I am astonished," said Miss Bingley, "that my father should have left so small a collection of books. What a delightful library you have at Pemberley, Mr. Darcy!"

"It ought to be good," he replied. "It has been the work of many generations."

"And then you have added so much to it yourself. You are always buying books."

"I cannot comprehend the neglect of a family library in such days as these."

"Neglect! I am sure you neglect nothing that can add to the beauties of that noble place. Charles, when you build *your* house, I wish it may be half as delightful as Pemberley."

"I wish it may."

"But I would really advise you to make your purchase in that neighbourhood, and take Pemberley for a kind of model. There is not a finer county in England than Derbyshire."

"With all my heart, I will buy Pemberley itself if Darcy will sell it."

"I am talking of possibilities, Charles."

"Upon my word, Caroline, I should think it more possible to get Pemberley by purchase than by imitation."

Elizabeth was so much caught by what passed as to leave her very little attention for her book. Setting it aside, she drew near the card-table and stationed herself between Mr. Bingley and his eldest sister to observe the game.

"Is Miss Darcy much grown since the spring?" said Miss Bingley. "Will she be as tall as I am?"

"I think she will. She is now about Miss Elizabeth Bennet's height, or rather taller."

"How I long to see her again! I never met with anybody who delighted me so much. Such beauty, such manners! And so extremely accomplished for her age! Her performance on the piano is exquisite."

"It is amazing to me," said Bingley, "how young ladies can have patience to be so very accomplished as they all are."

"All young ladies accomplished! My dear Charles, what do you mean?"

"Yes, all of them, I think. They all paint tables, cover screens, and net purses. I scarcely know any who cannot do all this, and I am sure I never heard a young lady spoken of for the first time without being informed that she was very accomplished."

"Your list of the common extent of accomplishments," said Darcy, "has too much truth. The word is applied to many a woman who deserves it for no other reason than that she can net a purse or cover a screen. But I am very far from agreeing with you in your estimation of ladies in general. I cannot boast of knowing more than half a dozen, in the whole range of my acquaintance, that are really accomplished."

"Nor I, I am sure," said Miss Bingley. "Then," observed Elizabeth, "you must include a great deal in your idea of an accomplished woman."

"Yes, I do include a great deal in it."

"Oh! Certainly," cried his faithful assistant, "no one can be really esteemed accomplished who does not greatly surpass what is usually seen. A woman must have a thorough knowledge of music, singing, drawing, dancing, and the modern languages, to deserve the word. Besides all this, she must possess a certain something in her air and manner of walking, the tone of her voice, her address and expressions, or the word will be but half deserved."

"All this she must possess," added Darcy, "and to all this she must yet add something more: the improvement of her mind by extensive reading."

"I am no longer surprised at your knowing *only* six accomplished women. I rather wonder now at your knowing *any*."

"Are you so critical of your own sex as to doubt the possibility of all this?"

"*I* never saw such a woman. *I* never saw such capacity, and taste, and application, and elegance, as you describe united."

Mrs. Hurst and Miss Bingley both cried out against the injustice of her doubt, and were both protesting that they knew many women who answered this description, when Mr. Hurst interrupted them with bitter complaints of their inattention to the card game. As all conversation was then at an end, Elizabeth soon afterwards left the room.

"Eliza Bennet," said Miss Bingley, when the door was closed on her, "is one of those young ladies who seek to recommend themselves to the other sex by undervaluing their own. With many men, I dare say, it succeeds. But, in my opinion, it is a cheap device, a very devious art."

"Undoubtedly," replied Darcy, to whom this remark was chiefly addressed, "there is deviousness in *all* the arts which ladies sometimes condescend to employ for securing a husband. Anything that comes across as cunning is despicable."

Miss Bingley was not so entirely satisfied with this reply as to continue the subject.

Elizabeth joined them again only to say that her sister was worse, and that she could not leave her. Bingley urged Mr. Jones's being sent for immediately. His sisters, convinced that no country advice could be of any service, recommended sending for one of London's most esteemed physicians. This she would not hear of, but she was not so unwilling to comply with their brother's proposal, and it was settled that Mr. Jones should be sent for early in the morning if Miss Bennet were not decidedly better. Bingley was quite uncomfortable; his sisters declared that they were miserable. They found comfort, however, in singing duets after supper, while he could find no better relief to his feelings than by giving his housekeeper directions that every possible attention might be paid to the sick lady and her sister.

CHAPTER 9

Elizabeth spent most of the night in her sister's room. In the morning she had the pleasure of being able to send a tolerable answer to the enquiries which she very early received from Mr. Bingley by a housemaid. Ssome time afterwards she received and responded to similar enquiries from the two elegant ladies who assisted his sisters. She then requested to have a note sent to Longbourn, desiring her mother to visit Jane and appraise the situation. The note was immediately sent, and its contents as quickly complied with. Mrs. Bennet, accompanied by her two youngest girls, reached Netherfield soon after the family breakfast.

Had she found Jane in any apparent danger, Mrs. Bennet would have been very miserable. But being satisfied on seeing her that her illness was not alarming, she had no wish of her recovering immediately, as her restoration to health would promptly take her away from Netherfield. She would not listen, therefore, to her daughter's proposal of being carried home; neither did the doctor, who arrived about the same time, think it at all advisable. After sitting a little while with Jane, on Miss Bingley's appearance and invitation, the mother and three daughters all joined her in the breakfast parlour. Bingley met them with hopes that Mrs. Bennet had not found Miss Bennet worse than she expected.

"Indeed I have, sir," was her answer. "She is a great deal too ill to be moved. Mr. Jones says we must not think of moving her. We must impose a little longer on your kindness."

"Moved!" cried Bingley. "It must not be thought of. My sister, I am sure, will not hear of her leaving."

"You may depend upon it, madam," said Miss Bingley with cold civility, "that Miss Bennet shall receive every possible attention while she remains with us."

Mrs. Bennet thanked them profusely.

"I am sure," she added, "if it was not for such good friends, I do not know what would become of her. For she is very ill indeed, and suffers a great deal, though with the greatest patience in the world, which is always the way with her. She has, without exception, the sweetest temper I ever saw. I often tell my other girls they are nothing compared to *her*. You have a sweet room here, Mr. Bingley, and a charming view from that gravel walk. I do not know a place in the country that is equal to Netherfield. You will not think of leaving it in a hurry, I hope, though you have but a short lease."

"Whatever I do is done in a hurry," replied he; "and therefore if I should resolve to leave Netherfield, I should probably be off in five minutes. At present, however, I consider myself as quite settled here."

"That is exactly what I would expect of you," said Elizabeth.

"You begin to understand me, do you?" cried he, turning towards her.

"Oh! yes — perfectly."

"I wish I might take this for a compliment; but to be so easily seen through, I am afraid, is pitiful."

" Not necessarily. A deep, intricate character is not inherently better than one such as yours."

"Lizzy," cried her mother, "remember where you are, and do not go on in the wild manner that you are allowed to at home."

"I did not know before," continued Bingley immediately, "that you were a studier of character. It must be an amusing study."

"Yes, but intricate characters are the *most* interesting. They have at least that advantage."

"The country," said Darcy, "can in general supply but few subjects for such a study. In a country neighbourhood you move in a very limited and unchanging society."

"But people themselves change so much that there is something new to be observed in them forever."

"Yes, indeed," cried Mrs. Bennet, offended by his manner of mentioning a country neighbourhood. "I assure you there is quite as much of *that* going on in the country as in town."

Everybody was surprised, and Darcy, after looking at her for a moment, turned silently away. Mrs. Bennet, who believed she had gained a complete victory over him, continued her triumph.

"I cannot see that London has any great advantage over the country, for my part, except the shops and public places. The country is a vast deal pleasanter, is not it, Mr. Bingley?"

"When I am in the country," he replied, "I never wish to leave it. And when I am in town, it is pretty much the same. They have each their advantages, and I can be equally happy in either."

"Ay — that is because you have the right disposition. But that gentleman," looking at Darcy, "seemed to think the country was nothing at all."

"Indeed, Mama, you are mistaken," said Elizabeth, blushing for her mother. "You quite misunderstood Mr. Darcy. He only meant that there were not such a variety of people in the country as in town, which you must acknowledge to be true."

"Certainly, my dear, nobody said there were. But as to not meeting with many people in this neighbourhood, I believe there are few neighbourhoods larger. I know we dine with four and twenty families."

Nothing but concern for Elizabeth could enable Bingley to keep his composure. His sister was less delicate, and directed her eye towards Mr. Darcy with a very expressive smile. Elizabeth, for the sake of saying something that might change the topic of conversation, now asked her if Charlotte Lucas had been at Longbourn since *her* coming away.

"Yes, she visited yesterday with her father. What an agreeable man Sir William is, Mr. Bingley — is he not? Such a gentlemen, and so accepting! He has always something to say to everybody. *That* is my idea of good breeding, and those persons who believe they are important, and never open their mouths, quite mistake the matter."

"Did Charlotte dine with you?"

"No, she went home. I believe she was needed to help with the mince-pies. For my part, Mr. Bingley, *I* always keep servants that can do their own work. *My* daughters are brought up differently. But everybody must decide for themselves, and the Lucases are very good sort of girls, I assure you. It is a pity they are not beautiful! Not that *I* think Charlotte so *very* plain — but then she is our particular friend."

"She seems a very pleasant young woman," said Bingley.

"Oh! Dear, yes — but you must admit she is very plain. Lady Lucas herself has often said so, and envied me Jane's beauty. I do not like to boast of my own child, but to be sure, Jane — one does not often see anybody better looking. It is what everybody says. I do not trust my own partiality. When she was only fifteen, there was a gentleman at my brother Gardiner's in town so much in love with her that my sister-in-law was sure he would make her an offer of marriage before we came away. But, however, he did not. Perhaps he thought her too young. However, he wrote some poetry about her, and very pretty it was."

"And so ended his affection," said Elizabeth impatiently. "There has been many a one, I believe, that ended the same way. I wonder who first discovered the effectiveness of poetry in driving away love!"

"I consider poetry to be the *food* of love," said Darcy.

"Of a fine, stout, healthy love it may. Everything nourishes what is strong already. But if it be only a slight, thin sort of preference, I am convinced that one good sonnet will starve it entirely away."

Darcy only smiled, and the general pause which followed made Elizabeth tremble lest her mother should again expose her limited understanding and ill manners. She longed to speak, but could think of nothing to say. After a short silence Mrs. Bennet began repeating her thanks to Mr. Bingley for his kindness to Jane, with an apology for troubling him also with Lizzy. Mr. Bingley was genuinely civil in his answer, and forced his younger sister to be civil also, and say what the occasion required. She performed her part indeed without much graciousness, but Mrs. Bennet was satisfied, and soon afterwards asked for her carriage. Upon this signal, the youngest of her daughters put herself forward. The two girls had been whispering to each other during the whole visit. The result of it was that the youngest should remind Mr. Bingley that he had promised on his first coming into the country to give a ball at Netherfield.

Lydia was a healthy, well-grown girl of fifteen, with a fine complexion and good disposition. She was a favourite with her mother, whose affection had brought her into public at an early age. She had high spirits, and a sort of natural self-importance, which had recently been increased by the attentions of the officers. She was very willing, therefore, to address Mr. Bingley on the subject of the ball, and abruptly reminded him of his promise. She added that it would be the most shameful thing in the world if he did not keep it. His answer to this sudden attack was delightful to their mother's ear —

"I am perfectly ready, I assure you, to keep my commitment. When your sister is recovered, you shall, if you please, name the very day of the ball. But you would not want to be dancing while she is ill."

Lydia declared herself satisfied. "Oh! Yes — it would be much better to wait till Jane is well, and by that time most likely Captain Carter will be at Meryton again. And when you have given *your* ball," she added, "I shall insist on their giving one also. I shall tell Colonel Forster it will be quite a shame if he does not."

Mrs. Bennet and her daughters then departed, and Elizabeth returned instantly to Jane, leaving her own and her relations' behaviour to the remarks of the two ladies and Mr. Darcy. *That* gentleman, however, could not be prevailed on to join in their condemnation of *her*, in spite of all Miss Bingley's witticisms on *fine eyes*.

CHAPTER 10

The day passed much as the day before had done. Mrs. Hurst and Miss Bingley had spent some hours of the morning with Jane, who continued, though slowly, to improve. In the evening Elizabeth joined their party in the drawing room. Mr. Darcy was writing, and Miss Bingley, seated near him, was watching the progress of his letter and repeatedly interrupting and asking him to add messages from her to his sister. Mr. Hurst and Mr. Bingley were playing cards, and Mrs. Hurst was observing their game.

Elizabeth took up some needlework, and was sufficiently amused in listening to the conversation between Darcy and his companion. The lady perpetually complimented him on his handwriting, on the straightness of his lines, or on the length of his letter. Her praises were received with perfect indifference. This resulted in an entertaining dialogue which was exactly in accordance with her opinion of each.

"How delighted Miss Darcy will be to receive such a letter!"

He made no answer.

"You write uncommonly fast."

"You are mistaken. I write rather slowly."

"How many letters you must have occasion to write in the course of the year! Letters of business, too! How tedious *they* must be!"

"It is fortunate, then, that they are my responsibility instead of to yours."

"Please tell your sister that I long to see her."

"I have already told her so once, as you requested."

"I am afraid you do not like your pen. Let me fix it for you. I mend pens remarkably well."

"Thank you — but I always mend my own."

"How is it that you write so evenly?"

He was silent.

"Tell your sister I am delighted to hear of her improvement on the harp. Also let her know that I am quite adore her beautiful little design for a table, and I think it infinitely superior to Miss Grantley's."

"Will you allow me to wait to include your praises till I write again? At present I have not room to do them justice."

"Oh! It does not matter. I shall see her in January. But do you always write such charming long letters to her, Mr. Darcy?"

"They are generally long. But whether always charming, it is not for me to determine."

"It seems to me that a person who can easily write a long letter must possess some skill."

"That will not do for a compliment to Darcy, Caroline," cried her brother, "because he does *not* write with ease. He includes too many four syllable words. Do you not, Darcy?"

"My style of writing is very different from yours."

"Oh!" cried Miss Bingley, "Charles writes in the most careless way imaginable. He leaves out half his words, and scribbles out the rest."

"My ideas flow so rapidly that I have not time to express them — thus my letters sometimes convey no ideas at all to my correspondents."

"Your humility, Mr. Bingley," said Elizabeth, "renders you above criticism."

"Nothing is more deceitful," said Darcy, "than the appearance of humility. It is often only apathy, and sometimes an indirect boast."

"And of which of the two do I stand accused?"

"The indirect boast, for you are really proud of your poor writing skills. You consider them as proceeding from a speed of thought and sloppy execution, which if not admirable, you think at least highly interesting. The power of doing anything quickly is always much prized by the possessor, and often without any attention to the inadequacy of the performance. When you told Mrs. Bennet this morning that if you ever resolved on leaving Netherfield you should be gone in five minutes, you meant it to be a sort of compliment to yourself. Yet what is so praiseworthy about a situation which must leave very necessary business undone, and can be of no real advantage to yourself or anyone else?"

"No," cried Bingley, "this is too much, to remember at night all the foolish things that were said in the morning. And yet, upon my honour, I believed what I said to myself to be true, and I believe it at this moment. At least, therefore, I did not assume the character of needless impulsivity merely to show off before the ladies."

"I dare say you believed it; but I am by no means convinced that you would be gone with such swiftness. Your conduct would be quite as dependent on chance as that of any man I know. If, as you were mounting your horse, a friend were to say, 'Bingley, you had better stay till next week,' you would probably do it, you would probably not go — and at another word, might stay a month."

"You have only proved by this," cried Elizabeth, "that Mr. Bingley did not do justice to his own disposition. You have shown him off now much more than he did himself."

"I am exceedingly gratified," said Bingley, "by your converting what my friend says into a compliment on the goodness of my temper. But I am afraid you are interpreting it in a way which Darcy did not intend. For he would certainly think the better of me if, under such a circumstance, I were to give a flat denial, and ride off as fast as I could."

"Would Mr. Darcy then consider the impulsiveness of your original intention as compensated for by your determination to adhere to it?"

"Upon my word I cannot exactly explain the matter — Darcy must speak for himself."

"You expect me to defend opinions which you choose to call mine, but which I have never stated. However, in this case you must remember, Miss Bennet, that the friend who is supposed to desire his return to the house, and the delay of his plan, has merely desired it without offering one good reason for it."

"To yield readily to the *persuasion* of a friend is no estimable quality to you."

"To yield without a good reason is no compliment to the intelligence of either."

"You appear to me, Mr. Darcy, to allow nothing for the influence of friendship and affection. A regard for the requester would often make one readily yield to a request without regard for the merits of the argument. I am speaking only of such a case as you have supposed about Mr. Bingley. We may as well wait, perhaps, till the circumstance occurs before we discuss the wisdom of his behaviour. But in general and ordinary cases between friend and friend, where one of them is persuaded by the other to make a decision of little consequence, should you think poorly of that person for complying with the desire, without waiting to be argued into it?"

"Should we not, before we proceed on this subject, determine the degree of importance pertaining to this request, as well as the degree of acquaintance between the friends?"

"By all means," cried Bingley, "let us hear all the particulars, not forgetting their comparative height and size. That will have more weight in the argument, Miss Bennet, than you may be aware of. I assure you that, if Darcy were not such a great tall fellow, in comparison with myself, I should not give him half so much respect. I declare I do not know a more intimidating man than Darcy, on particular occasions, and in particular places; at his own house especially, and on a Sunday evening, when he has nothing to do."

Mr. Darcy smiled, but Elizabeth thought she could perceive that he was rather offended, and therefore checked her laugh. Miss Bingley resented the indignity he had received, and spoke harshly to her brother for talking such nonsense.

"I see your design, Bingley," said his friend. "You dislike an argument, and want to silence this."

"Perhaps I do. If you and Miss Bennet will defer yours till I am out of the room I shall be very thankful; and then you may say whatever you like of me."

"What you ask," said Elizabeth, "is no sacrifice on my side. And Mr. Darcy had better finish his letter."

Mr. Darcy took her advice, and did finish his letter.

When that business was over, he asked Miss Bingley and Elizabeth for the favor of some music. Miss Bingley moved quickly to the piano. After a polite request that Elizabeth would lead the way, which the other earnestly declined, she seated herself.

Mrs. Hurst sang with her sister; and while they were thus employed, Elizabeth could not help observing, as she turned over some music books that lay on the instrument, how frequently Mr. Darcy's eyes were fixed on her. She hardly knew how to suppose that she could be an object of admiration to such a man, and yet that he should look at her because he disliked her was still more strange. She could only imagine, however, at last, that she drew his notice because there was a something wrong with her, at least in his view. This conclusion did not pain her. She liked him too little to care for his approval.

After playing some Italian songs, Miss Bingley varied her performance with a lively Scottish air; and soon afterwards Mr. Darcy, drawing near Elizabeth, said to her —

"Do not you feel a great inclination, Miss Bennet, to seize such an opportunity of dancing a reel?"

She smiled, but made no answer. He repeated the question, with some surprise at her silence.

"Oh!" said she, "I heard you before, but I could not immediately determine what to say in reply. You wanted me, I know, to say 'Yes,' that you might have the pleasure of mocking me. But I always delight in preventing those kind of schemes, and cheating a person of their premeditated contempt. I have, therefore, made up my mind to tell you, that I do not want to dance a reel at all — and now despise me if you dare."

"Indeed I do not dare."

Elizabeth, having rather expected to offend him, was amazed at his composure But there was a mixture of sweetness and cheerfulness in her manner which made it difficult for her to offend anybody, and Darcy had never been so captivated by any woman as he was by her. He really believed that, were it not for the inferiority of her connection, he would be in danger of wanting to make her an offer of marriage.

Miss Bingley saw, or suspected enough to be jealous, and her great anxiety for the recovery of her dear friend Jane was increased by a desire to get rid of Elizabeth.

She often tried to provoke Darcy into disliking her guest, by talking of their supposed marriage and planning his happiness in such an alliance.

"I hope," said she, as they were walking together on the Netherfield grounds the next day, "you will give your mother-in-law a few hints, when this desirable event takes place, as to the advantage of keeping quiet. And if you can accomplish it, do cure the younger girls of running after the officers. Also, if I may bring up a sensitive subject, endeavour to check that little something bordering on conceit and disrespect which your lady possesses."

"Have you anything else to propose for my domestic happiness?"

"Oh! yes. Do let the portraits of your uncle and aunt Philips be placed in the gallery at Pemberley. Put them next to your great uncle the judge. They are in the same profession, you know, only in different lines. As for your Elizabeth's picture, you must not attempt to have it painted. For what artist could do justice to those beautiful eyes?"

"It would not be easy, indeed, to catch their expression. But their colour and shape, and the eye-lashes, so remarkably fine, might be copied."

At that moment they were met from another path by Mrs. Hurst and Elizabeth herself.

"I did not know that you intended to walk," said Miss Bingley, in some confusion, fearing they had been overheard.

"The very idea," answered Mrs. Hurst; "running away without telling us that you were coming out."

Then, taking the free arm of Mr. Darcy, she left Elizabeth to walk by herself. The path just admitted three. Mr. Darcy felt their rudeness and immediately said, —

"This path is not wide enough for our party. We had better go into the avenue."

But Elizabeth, who had not the least intention of remaining with them, laughingly answered, —

"No, no, stay where you are. You are charmingly grouped, and perfect just as you are. The picture would be spoiled by admitting a fourth. Goodbye."

She then ran happily off, rejoicing, as she rambled about, in the hope of being at home again in a day or two. Jane was already so much recovered as to intend leaving her room for a couple of hours that evening.

CHAPTER 11

"Not at all," was her answer, "but depend upon it, he means to be critical of us, and our surest way of disappointing him will be to not ask about it."

Miss Bingley, however, was incapable of disappointing Mr. Darcy in anything, and insisted, therefore, on receiving an explanation of his two motives.

"I have not the smallest objection to explaining them," said he, as soon as she allowed him to speak.

You either choose this method of passing the evening because you are in each other's confidence, and have secret affairs to discuss, or because you are conscious that your figures appear to the greatest advantage in walking. If the first, I should be completely in your way, and if the second, I can admire you much better as I sit by the fire."

"Oh! Shocking!" cried Miss Bingley. "I never heard anything so abominable. How shall we punish him for such a speech?"

"It can be easily done, if you so desire," said Elizabeth. "We can all plague and punish one another. Tease him — laugh at him. Close as you are, you must know how it is to be done."

"But upon my honour I do *not*. I do assure you that my knowledge of him has not yet taught me *that*. Tease calmness of temper and presence of mind! No, no — I feel he may get the better of us there. And as to laughter, we will not expose ourselves, if you please, by attempting to laugh for no reason.."

"Mr. Darcy is not to be laughed at!" cried Elizabeth. "That is an uncommon advantage, and uncommon I hope it will continue, for it would be a great loss to *me* to have many such acquaintances. I dearly love a laugh."

"Miss Bingley," said he, "has given me credit for more than I deserve. The wisest and the best of men — no, the wisest and best of their actions — may be made to look ridiculous by a person always looking for a good joke."

"Certainly," replied Elizabeth, "there are such people, but I hope I am not one of *them*. I hope I never ridicule what is wise or good. Follies and nonsense, whims and inconsistencies *do* interest me, I admit, and I laugh at them whenever I can. But these, I suppose, are precisely what you lack."

"Perhaps that is not possible for anyone. But it has been a goal of mine to avoid those weaknesses which often expose an otherwise good character to ridicule."

"Such as vanity and pride."

"Yes, vanity is a weakness indeed. But pride — where there is a real superiority of character, pride will be always kept within its proper bounds."

Elizabeth turned away to hide a smile.

"Your inquisition of Mr. Darcy is over, I presume," said Miss Bingley; "and pray what is the result?"

"I am perfectly convinced by it that Mr. Darcy has no defect. He admits it himself."

"No," said Darcy, "I have made no such claim. I have faults enough, but they are not, I hope, of judgment. My temperament I dare not vouch for. It is, I believe, too strict — certainly too strict for the convenience of the world. I cannot forget the follies and vices of others as soon as I ought, nor their offences against myself. My temper would perhaps be called resentful. My good opinion once lost is lost forever."

"*That* is a failing indeed!" cried Elizabeth. "Uncompromising resentment *is* a character flaw . But you have chosen your fault well. I really cannot *laugh* at it. You are safe from me."

"There is, I believe, in every disposition a tendency to some particular evil — a natural defect which not even the best education can overcome."

"And *your* defect is a tendency to hate everybody."

"And yours," he replied with a smile, "is to wilfully misunderstand them."

"Do let us have a little music," cried Miss Bingley, tired of a conversation in which she had no part. "Louisa, you will not mind my waking Mr. Hurst?""

Her sister made not the smallest objection, and the piano was opened. Darcy, after a few moments' thought, was not sorry about it. He began to feel the danger of paying Elizabeth too much attention.

CHAPTER 12

Elizabeth wrote the next morning to her mother asking that the carriage be sent for them in the course of the day. But Mrs. Bennet had planned on her daughters remaining at Netherfield till the following Tuesday, which would exactly finish Jane's week. Her answer, therefore, was not well received, at least not by Elizabeth, for she was impatient to get home. Mrs. Bennet sent them word that they could not possibly have the carriage before Tuesday, and she added that if Mr. Bingley and his sister encouraged them to stay longer, she could get along fine without them. Elizabeth was positively resolved, however, against staying longer — nor did she expect it would be asked. Fearful of being considered as intruding, she urged Jane to borrow Mr. Bingley's carriage immediately, and it was decided that their original plan to leave Netherfield that morning should be mentioned.

The communication excited many exclamations of concern, and enough was said of wishing them to stay at least till the following day to work on Jane. Miss Bingley was then sorry that she had proposed the delay, for her jealousy and dislike of one sister much exceeded her affection for the other.

The master of the house heard with real sorrow that they were to go so soon, and repeatedly tried to persuade Miss Bennet that it would not be safe for her — that she was not enough recovered. But Jane was firm where she felt herself to be right.

To Mr. Darcy it was welcome intelligence: Elizabeth had been at Netherfield long enough. She attracted him more than he liked — and Miss Bingley was uncivil to *her*, and more irritating than usual to himself. He wisely resolved to be particularly careful that no sign of admiration should *now* escape him. Steady to his purpose, he scarcely spoke ten words to her through the whole of Saturday, and though they were at one time left by themselves for half an hour, he devoted himself entirely to his book, and would not even look at her.

On Sunday, after morning church service, the separation so agreeable to almost all took place. Miss Bingley's civility to Elizabeth renewed itself, as well as her affection for Jane. When they parted, after assuring Jane of the pleasure it would always give her to see her either at Longbourn or Netherfield, and embracing her most tenderly, she even shook hands with Elizabeth, who took leave of the whole party in the liveliest spirits.

They were not welcomed home very kindly by their mother. Mrs. Bennet was surprised at their coming, and thought them very wrong to give so much trouble. She was worried Jane had caught cold again; but their father, though very brief in his expressions of pleasure, was really glad to see them. He had felt their importance in the family circle. The evening conversation, when they were all assembled, had lost much of its excitement, and almost all its sense, by the absence of Jane and Elizabeth.

They found Mary, as usual, deep in the study of music theory and human nature, and had some new observations on morality to listen to. Catherine and Lydia had information for them of a different sort. Much had been done and much had been said in the regiment since the previous Wednesday. Several of the officers had dined lately with their uncle, a private had been flogged, and it had actually been hinted that Colonel Forster was going to be married.

CHAPTER 13

"I hope, my dear," said Mr. Bennet to his wife, as they were at breakfast the next morning, "that you have planned a good dinner today, because I have reason to expect an addition to our family party."

"Who do you mean, my dear? I know of nobody that is coming, I am sure, unless Charlotte Lucas should happen to call in — and I hope *my* dinners are good enough for her. I do not believe she often sees such at home."

"The person of whom I speak is a gentleman, and a stranger."

Mrs. Bennet's eyes sparkled. "A gentleman and a stranger! It is Mr. Bingley, I am sure. Why, Jane — you never dropped a hint of this, you sly thing! Well, I am sure I shall be extremely glad to see Mr. Bingley. — But — good lord! How unlucky! There is not a bit of fish to be got today. Lydia, my love, ring the bell. I must speak to Hill this moment."

"It is *not* Mr. Bingley," said her husband. "It is a person whom I never saw in the whole course of my life."

This produced a general astonishment, and he had the pleasure of being eagerly questioned by his wife and five daughters at once. — After entertaining himself some time with their curiosity, he thus explained —

"About a month ago I received this letter, and about two weeks ago I answered it, for I thought it a case of some delicacy requiring immediate attention. It is from my cousin, Mr. Collins, who, when I am dead, may turn you all out of this house as soon as he pleases."

"Oh! My dear," cried his wife, "I cannot bear to hear that mentioned. Please do not talk of that horrid man. I do think it is the most repugnant thing in the world that your estate should be entailed away from your own children. I am sure, if I had been you, I should have tried long ago to do something about it."

Jane and Elizabeth attempted to explain to her the nature of an entail. They had often attempted it before, but it was a subject on which Mrs. Bennet was beyond the reach of reason. She continued to rant bitterly against the cruelty of settling an estate away from a family of five daughters to a man whom nobody cared anything about.

"It certainly is a most loathsome affair," said Mr. Bennet, "and nothing can clear Mr. Collins from the guilt of inheriting Longbourn. But if you will listen to his letter, you may perhaps be a little softened by his manner of expressing himself."

"No, I am sure I shall not; and I think it was very inappropriate of him to write to you at all, and very hypocritical. I hate such false friends. Why could not he keep on quarrelling with you, as his father did before him?"

"Why, indeed? He does seem to have had some concerns about that, as you will hear."

"Hunsford, near Westerham, Kent,
15th October.
DEAR SIR, — The disagreement subsisting between yourself and my late honoured father always gave me much discomfort. Since I have had the misfortune to lose him, I have frequently wished to heal the breach. But for some time I was kept back by my own doubts, fearing lest it might seem disrespectful to his memory for me to be on good terms with anyone with whom it had always pleased him to be at variance. — "There, Mrs. Bennet." — My mind, however is now made up on the subject, for having recently been ordained as a clergyman I have been so fortunate as to be distinguished by the patronage of the Right Honourable Lady Catherine de Bourgh, widow of Sir Lewis de Bourgh, who in her kindness has offered me the valuable rectory of this parish, where it shall be my earnest endeavour to offer grateful respect towards her Ladyship, and be ever ready to perform those rites and ceremonies which are instituted by the Church of England. As a clergyman, moreover, I feel it my duty to promote and establish the blessing of peace in all families within the reach of my influence. On these grounds I flatter myself that my present offer of goodwill is highly praiseworthy, and that the circumstance of my being next to inherit Longbourn estate will be kindly overlooked on your side, and not lead you to reject the peace offering. I do not wish to be the means of injuring your good daughters, and hope you will allow me to apologise for it, as well as to assure you of my readiness to make it up to them — but of this hereafter. If you should have no objection to receive me into your house, I propose myself the satisfaction of waiting on you and your family Monday, November 18th, by four o'clock, and shall probably trespass on your hospitality till the Saturday following, which I can do without any inconvenience, as Lady Catherine does not object to my occasional absence on a Sunday, provided that some other clergyman is engaged to do the duty of the day. — I remain, dear sir, with respectful compliments to your lady and daughters, your well-wisher and friend,
    "William Collins."

"At four o'clock, therefore, we may expect this peace-making gentleman," said Mr. Bennet, as he folded up the letter. "He seems to be a most thoughtful and polite young man, upon my word, and I believe he will be a valuable acquaintance, especially if Lady Catherine should be so indulgent as to let him come to us again."

"There is some sense in what he says about the girls, however, and if he wants to make them any amends, I shall not be the person to discourage him."

"Though it is difficult," said Jane, "to guess in what way he can mean to make it up to us, the desire is certainly to his credit."

Elizabeth was struck with his extraordinary respect for Lady Catherine, and his kind intention of christening, marrying, and burying his parishioners whenever it was required.

"He must be an oddity, I think," said she. "I cannot figure him out. There is something of self-importance in his style. — And what can he mean by apologizing for being next in the entail? — We cannot suppose he would help it if he could. — Can he be a prudent man, sir?"

"No, my dear, I think not. I have great hopes of finding him quite the opposite. There is a mixture of humility and self-importance in his letter which is very promising. I am impatient to see him."

"In point of composition," said Mary, "his letter does not seem defective. The idea of the peace offering perhaps is not wholly new, yet I think it is well expressed."

To Catherine and Lydia, neither the letter nor its writer were in any degree interesting. It was next to impossible that their cousin should come in a scarlet coat, and it was now some weeks since they had received pleasure from spending time with a man in any other colour. As for their mother, Mr. Collins's letter had done away much of her ill-will, and she was preparing to see him with a degree of composure which astonished her husband and daughters.

Mr. Collins arrived on time and was received with great politeness by the whole family. Mr. Bennet indeed said little, but the ladies were ready enough to talk. Mr. Collins seemed neither in need of encouragement nor inclined to be silent himself. He was a tall, heavy-looking young man of twenty-five. His air was grave and stately, and his manners were very formal. He had not been long seated before he complimented Mrs. Bennet on having so fine a family of daughters. He said he had heard much of their beauty, but that in this instance fame had fallen short of the truth. He then added that he was sure she would see them all in due time well married. This manner of speaking was not much to the taste of some of his hearers. But Mrs. Bennet, who never argued with a compliment, answered most readily –

"You are very kind, sir, I am sure; and I wish with all my heart it may prove so, for otherwise they will be quite destitute."

"You allude, perhaps, to the entail of this estate."

"Ah! Sir, I do indeed. It is a grievous affair to my poor girls, you must admit. Not that I mean to find fault with _you_, for such things I know are all chance in this world. There is no knowing how estates will go when once they become entailed."

"I am very aware, madam, of the hardship to my fair cousins, and could say much on the subject. But I am cautious of appearing too forward. I can assure the young ladies, however, that I come prepared to admire them. At present I will not say more, but perhaps when we are better acquainted — "

He was interrupted by a summons to dinner, and the girls smiled at each other. They were not the only objects of Mr. Collins's admiration. The hall, the dining-room, and all its furniture were examined and praised. His approval of everything would have touched Mrs. Bennet's heart, but for the mortifying belief of his viewing it all as his own future property. The dinner too in its turn was highly admired, and he begged to know to which of his fair cousins had cooked the meal. But here he was set right by Mrs. Bennet, who assured him with some sharpness that they were very well able to keep a good cook, and that her daughters never worked in the kitchen. He apologised for having displeased her. In a softened tone she declared herself not at all offended, but he continued to apologise for about a quarter of an hour.

CHAPTER 14

During dinner Mr. Bennet scarcely spoke at all, but when the servants were withdrawn he thought it time to have some conversation with his guest. He therefore started a subject in which he expected him to shine by observing that he seemed very fortunate in his patroness. Lady Catherine de Bourgh's attention to his wishes, and consideration for his comfort, appeared very remarkable. Mr. Bennet could not have chosen better. Mr. Collins was eloquent in her praise. The subject elevated him to more than his usual seriousness, and with a self-important demeanor he claimed that "he had never in his life witnessed such behaviour in a person of rank — such courtesy and attention to her inferiors, as he had himself experienced from Lady Catherine. She had been graciously pleased to approve of both the sermons which he had already had the honour of preaching before her. She had also asked him twice to dine at Rosings, and had sent for him only the Saturday before, to join her at cards in the evening. Lady Catherine was reckoned proud by many people he knew, but *he* had never seen anything but kindness in her. She had always spoken to him as she would to any other gentleman; she made not the smallest objection to his socializing with others in the neighbourhood, nor to his leaving his parish occasionally for a week or two, to visit his relations. She had even condescended to advise him to marry as soon as he could, provided he chose carefully. And she had once paid him a visit in his humble home, where she had perfectly approved all the changes he had been making, and had even suggested some herself, — some shelves in the closets upstairs."

"That is all very proper and civil, I am sure," said Mrs. Bennet, "and I dare say she is a very agreeable woman. It is a pity that noble ladies in general are not more like her. Does she live near you, sir?"

"The garden in which stands my humble home is separated only by a lane from Rosings Park, her ladyship's residence."

"I think you said she was a widow, sir? Has she any family?"

"She has one only daughter, the heiress of Rosings, and of very extensive property."

"Ah!" cried Mrs. Bennet, shaking her head, "then she is better off than many girls. And what sort of young lady is she? Is she beautiful?"

"She is a most charming young lady indeed. Lady Catherine herself says that Miss De Bourgh is far superior to others of her sex because there is that in her features which marks the young woman of distinguished birth. She is unfortunately of a sickly nature, which has prevented her acquiring many accomplishments. But she is perfectly friendly, and often condescends to drive by my humble home in her little carriage and ponies."

"Has she been presented at court? I do not remember her name among the ladies."

"Her unfortunate state of health prevents her being in town, and by that means, as I told Lady Catherine myself one day, the British court has been deprived of its brightest ornament. Her ladyship seemed pleased with the idea, and you may imagine that I am happy on every occasion to offer those little delicate compliments which are always acceptable to ladies. I have more than once observed to Lady Catherine that her charming daughter seemed born to be a duchess, and that the most elevated rank, instead of giving her importance, would be enhanced by her. These are the kind of little things which please her ladyship, and it is a sort of attention which I conceive myself particularly bound to pay."

"You judge very properly," said Mr. Bennet, "and it is happy for you that you possess the talent of flattering with delicacy. May I ask whether these pleasing attentions are conceived in the moment or planned in advance?"

"They arise chiefly from what is passing at the time, and though I sometimes amuse myself with suggesting and arranging such little elegant compliments as may be adapted to ordinary occasions, I always wish to make them sound as natural as possible."

Mr. Bennet's expectations were fully answered. His cousin was as absurd as he had hoped, and he listened to him with the fondest enjoyment. He maintained at the same time complete composure, and except in an occasional glance at Elizabeth, he required no partner in his pleasure.

By teatime, however, he had had enough, and Mr. Bennet was glad to take his guest into the drawing room again, and, when tea was over, glad to invite him to read aloud to the ladies. Mr. Collins readily assented, and a book was produced; but on beholding it he started back, and begging pardon, protested that he never read novels. Kitty stared at him, and Lydia exclaimed. Other books were produced, and after some deliberation he chose Fordyce's Sermons. Lydia gaped as he opened the volume, and before he had, with very monotonous solemnity, read three pages, she interrupted him with —

"Do you know, Mama, that my uncle Philips talks of firing his servant Richard; and if he does, Colonel Forster will hire him. My aunt told me so herself on Saturday. I shall walk to Meryton tomorrow to hear more about it, and to ask when Mr. Denny comes back from town."

Lydia was bid by her two eldest sisters to hold her tongue; but Mr. Collins, much offended, laid aside his book, and said —

"I have often observed how little young ladies are interested by serious books, though written solely for their benefit. It amazes me, I admit; for, certainly, there can be nothing so advantageous to them as education. But I will no longer bore my young cousin."

Then, turning to Mr. Bennet, he invited him to join him in a game of backgammon. Mr. Bennet accepted the challenge, observing that he acted very wisely in leaving the girls to their own trifling amusements. Mrs. Bennet and her daughters apologised most civilly for Lydia's interruption, and promised that it should not occur again, if he would resume his book. But Mr. Collins, after assuring them that he bore his young cousin no ill will, and should never resent her behaviour as any affront, seated himself at another table with Mr. Bennet, and prepared for backgammon.

CHAPTER 15

Mr. Collins was not a sensible man, and this natural deficiency had been but little assisted by education or society, since he spent the greatest part of his life under the guidance of an illiterate and miserly father. Though he studied at one of the universities, he had merely done the minimum required, without gaining any useful understanding. The strict manner in which his father had brought him up had given him originally great humility of manner; but it was now a good deal contradicted by the self-conceit of a weak head, living in seclusion, and the consequential feelings of early and unexpected prosperity. A fortunate chance had recommended him to Lady Catherine de Bourgh when the living of Hunsford was vacant. The respect which he felt for her high rank, and his admiration for her as his patroness, mingled with a very good opinion of himself and his authority as a clergyman, made him altogether a mixture of pride and flattery, self-importance and humility.

Having now a good house and very sufficient income, he intended to marry. In seeking a reconciliation with the Longbourn family he meant to choose one of the daughters, if he found them as beautiful and kind as they were represented by common report. This was his plan of amends — of atonement — for inheriting their father's estate, and he thought it an excellent one.

His plan did not vary on seeing them. Miss Bennet's lovely face confirmed his views, and as she was the oldest he felt it right to address her particularly. For the first evening *she* was his settled choice. The next morning, however, made an alteration; for a quarter-of-an-hour's conversation with Mrs. Bennet before breakfast produced from her, amid smiles and general encouragement, a caution against the very Jane he had fixed on.

"As to her *younger* daughters she could not take upon her to say — she could not positively answer — but she did not *know* of any developing romance. Her *eldest* daughter, she must just mention, was likely to be very soon engaged."

Mr. Collins had only to change from Jane to Elizabeth — and it was soon done — done while Mrs. Bennet was stirring the fire. Elizabeth, equally next to Jane in birth and beauty, was the next obvious choice.

Mrs. Bennet smiled at the thought, and trusted that she might soon have two daughters married. The man whom she could not bear to speak of the day before was now high in her good graces.

Lydia's intention of walking to Meryton was not forgotten. Every sister except Mary agreed to go with her, and Mr. Collins was to join them, at the request of Mr. Bennet, who was most anxious to get rid of him and have his library to himself. Mr. Collins had followed him there after breakfast, and there he would otherwise have remained, talking to Mr. Bennet, with little cessation, of his house and garden at Hunsford. Such doings made Mr. Bennet quite uncomfortable. In his library he had been always sure of leisure and tranquillity. Though prepared, as he told Elizabeth, to meet with folly and conceit in every other room in the house, he was used to be free from them there. He was therefore most prompt in inviting Mr. Collins to join his daughters in their walk. Mr. Collins, being in fact much better fitted for a walker than a reader, was extremely well pleased to close his large book and go.

In pompous nothings on his side, and civil responses on that of his cousins, their time passed till they entered Meryton. The attention of the younger ones was then no longer to be gained by *him*. Their eyes were immediately wandering up the street in quest of the officers, and nothing less than a very smart bonnet indeed, or a really new muslin in a shop window, could recall them.

But the attention of every lady was soon caught by a young man, whom they had never seen before, of most gentlemanlike appearance, walking with an officer on the other side of the street. The officer was Mr. Denny, concerning whose return from London Lydia came to inquire, and he bowed as they passed. All were struck with the stranger's air, all wondered who he could be. Kitty and Lydia, determined if possible to find out, led the way across the street, under the guise of wanting something in an opposite shop. Fortunately they had just reached the sidewalk when the two gentlemen, turning back, had arrived at the same spot. Mr. Denny addressed them directly, and requested permission to introduce his friend, Mr. Wickham, who had returned with him the day before from town, and he was happy to say had accepted a commission in their corps. This was exactly as it should be, for the young man needed only a uniform to make him completely charming. His appearance was greatly in his favour. He had all the best part of handsomeness, a fine countenance, a good figure, and very pleasing manners. The introduction was followed up on his side by a happy readiness of conversation — a readiness at the same time perfectly correct and unassuming. The whole party were still standing and talking together very agreeably when the sound of horses drew their notice, and Darcy and Bingley were seen riding down the street. On recognizing the ladies of the group the two gentlemen came directly towards them and began the usual civilities. Bingley was the principal spokesman, and Miss Bennet the principal object. He was then, he said, on his way to Longbourn to inquire after her. Mr. Darcy bowed, and was beginning to determine not to fix his eyes on Elizabeth, when they were suddenly arrested by the sight of the stranger. Elizabeth, happening to see the countenance of both as they looked at each other, was astonished at the effect of the meeting. Both changed colour; one looked white, the other red. Mr. Wickham, after a few moments, touched his hat — a salutation which Mr. Darcy coldly returned. What could be the meaning of it? — It was impossible to imagine; it was impossible not to long to know.

In another minute Mr. Bingley, without seeming to have noticed what passed, took leave and rode on with his friend.

Mr. Denny and Mr. Wickham walked with the young ladies to the door of Mr. Philips's house and then said their farewells, in spite of Miss Lydia's pressing entreaties that they would come in, and even in spite of Mrs. Philips' throwing up the parlour window and loudly seconding the invitation.

Mrs. Philips was always glad to see her nieces, and the two eldest, from their recent absence, were particularly welcome. She eagerly expressed her surprise at their sudden return home, which, as their own carriage had not fetched them, she should have known nothing about, if she had not happened to see Mr. Jones's shop-boy in the street, who had told her that they were not to send anymore medicines to Netherfield because the Miss Bennets had left. Her civility was then directed towards Mr. Collins after Jane introduced him. She received him with her very best politeness, which he returned with as much more, apologising for his intrusion, without any previous acquaintance with her. Mrs. Philips was quite awed by such an excess of good manners, but her contemplation of one stranger was soon put an end to by exclamations and inquiries about the other. She could only tell her nieces what they already knew: that Mr. Denny had brought him from London, and that he was to have a lieutenant's commission. She had been watching him the last hour, she said, as he walked up and down the street. Had Mr. Wickham appeared, Kitty and Lydia would certainly have done same, but unluckily no one passed the window now except a few of the officers, who, in comparison with the stranger, were become "stupid, disagreeable fellows." Some of them were to dine with the Philips' the next day, and their aunt promised to make her husband visit Mr. Wickham, and give him an invitation also, if the family from Longbourn would come in the evening. This was agreed to, and Mrs. Philips protested that they would have a nice comfortable noisy game of cards, and a little bit of hot supper afterwards. The prospect of such delights was very cheering, and they parted in mutual good spirits. Mr. Collins repeated his apologies while leaving the room, and was assured with unwearying civility that they were perfectly needless.

As they walked home, Elizabeth related to Jane what she had seen pass between the two gentlemen. Though Jane would have defended either or both, had they appeared to be wrong, she could no more explain such behaviour than her sister.

Mr. Collins on his return highly gratified Mrs. Bennet by admiring Mrs. Philips' manners and politeness. He claimed that, except Lady Catherine and her daughter, he had never seen a more elegant woman. She had not only received him with the utmost civility, but had even pointedly included him in her invitation for the next evening, although utterly unknown to her before. Something, he supposed, might be attributed to his connection with them, but yet he had never met with so much attention in the whole course of his life.

CHAPTER 16

As no objection was made to the young people's engagement with their aunt, and all Mr. Collins' anxieties about leaving Mr. and Mrs. Bennet for a single evening during his visit were most steadily resisted, the coach conveyed him and his five cousins at a suitable hour to Meryton. The girls had the pleasure of hearing, as they entered the drawing room, that Mr. Wickham had accepted their uncle's invitation and was then in the house.

When this information was given and they had all taken their seats, Mr. Collins was at leisure to look around him and admire. He was so much struck with the size and furnishings of the room that he declared he might almost have supposed himself in the small summer breakfast parlour at Rosings. His comparison did not at first convey much gratification, but when Mrs. Philips understood from him what Rosings was, and who was its proprietor — when she had listened to the description of only one of Lady Catherine's drawing rooms and found that the chimney-piece alone had cost eight hundred pounds, she felt all the force of the compliment, and would hardly have resented a comparison with the housekeeper's room.

In describing to her all the grandeur of Lady Catherine and her mansion, with occasional comments in praise of his own humble abode and the improvements it was receiving, he was happily employed until the gentlemen joined them. He found in Mrs. Philips a very attentive listener, whose opinion of his importance increased with what she heard, and who was resolving to retell it all to her neighbours as soon as she could. To the girls, who could not listen to their cousin, and who had nothing to do but to wish for an instrument, it was a long wait. At last, however, the gentlemen did approach, and when Mr. Wickham walked into the room, Elizabeth felt that she had not been thinking of him with the smallest degree of unreasonable admiration. The officers of of his regiment were in general a very creditable, gentlemanlike set, and the best of them were of the present party. But Mr. Wickham was as far beyond them all in person, countenance, air, and walk, as *they* were superior to the broad-faced, stuffy uncle Philips, breathing port wine, who followed them into the room.

Mr. Wickham was the happy man towards whom almost every female eye was turned, and Elizabeth was the happy woman by whom he finally seated himself. The agreeable manner in which he immediately fell into conversation, though it was only about the weather, and on the probability of a rainy season, made her feel that the commonest, dullest, most threadbare topic might be rendered interesting by the skill of the speaker.

With such rivals for the notice of the women as Mr. Wickham and the officers, Mr. Collins seemed likely to sink into insignificance. To the young ladies he certainly was nothing, but he had still at intervals a kind listener in Mrs. Philips, and was, by her attentiveness, most abundantly supplied with coffee and muffins.

When the card tables were placed, he had an opportunity of obliging her in return, by sitting down to whist.

"I know little of the game at present," said he, "but I shall be glad to improve my skills, for in my situation of life — " Mrs. Philips was very thankful for his compliance, but could not wait for his reason.

Mr. Wickham did not play whist, and with ready delight he was received at the other table between Elizabeth and Lydia. At first there seemed danger of Lydia's absorbing his attention entirely, for she was a most determined talker. But being likewise extremely fond of the game, she soon grew too eager in making bets and exclaiming about prizes to pay attention to anyone in particular. In between turns, Mr. Wickham was therefore at leisure to talk to Elizabeth, and she was very willing to hear him, though what she chiefly wished to hear she could not hope to be told — the history of his acquaintance with Mr. Darcy. She dared not even mention that gentleman. Her curiosity, however, was unexpectedly satisfied. Mr. Wickham began the subject himself. He inquired how far Netherfield was from Meryton, and after receiving her answer, asked in an hesitating manner how long Mr. Darcy had been staying there.

"About a month," said Elizabeth, and then, unwilling to let the subject drop, added, "He is a man of very large property in Derbyshire, I understand."

"Yes," replied Wickham, "his estate there is a noble one. Ten thousand per year. You could not have met with a person more capable of giving you certain information about that than myself, for I have been connected with his family in a particular manner from my infancy."

Elizabeth could not but look surprised.

"You may well be surprised, Miss Bennet, at such a claim, after seeing, as you probably did, the very cold manner of our meeting yesterday. Are you much acquainted with Mr. Darcy?"

"As much as I ever wish to be," cried Elizabeth. "I have spent four days in the same house with him, and I think him very disagreeable."

"I have no right to give *my* opinion," said Wickham, "as to his being agreeable or otherwise. I am not qualified to form one. I have known him too long and too well to be a fair judge. It is impossible for *me* to be impartial. But I believe your opinion of him would in general astonish — and perhaps you should not express it quite so strongly anywhere else. "

"Upon my word, he is not at all liked in Hertfordshire. Everybody is disgusted with his pride. You will not find him more favourably spoken of by anyone."

"I cannot pretend to be sorry," said Wickham, after a short interruption, "that he or that any man should not be esteemed beyond what is deserved, but with *him* I believe it does not often happen. The world is blinded by his fortune and importance, or frightened by his high and imposing manners, and sees him only as he chooses to be seen."

"I should take him, even on *my* slight acquaintance, to be an ill-tempered man." Wickham only shook his head.

"I wonder," said he, at the next opportunity of speaking, "whether he is likely to be in this country much longer."

"I do not at all know; but I *heard* nothing of his going away when I was at Netherfield. I hope your plans will not be affected by his being in the neighbourhood."

"Oh! no — it is not for *me* to be driven away by Mr. Darcy. If *he* wishes to avoid seeing *me*, he must go. We are not on friendly terms, and it always gives me pain to meet him, but I have no reason for avoiding *him* but what I might proclaim to all the world — a sense of very great mistreatment, and most painful regrets at his being what he is. His father, Miss Bennet, the late Mr. Darcy, was one of the best men that ever breathed, and the truest friend I ever had. I can never be in company with this Mr. Darcy without being grieved to the soul by a thousand tender recollections. His behaviour to myself has been scandalous, but I believe I could forgive him anything and everything to avoid disappointing the hopes and disgracing the memory of his father."

Elizabeth found her interest of the subject increasing, and listened with all her heart; but the delicacy of it prevented farther inquiry.

Mr. Wickham began to speak on more general topics: Meryton, the neighbourhood, the people, appearing highly pleased with all that he had yet seen, and speaking of the latter especially with gentle gallantry.

"It was the prospect of constant society, and good society," he added, "which was my chief inducement to enter the regiment. I knew it to be a most respectable, agreeable corps, and my friend Denny convinced me farther by his account of their present location, and the very great attentions and excellent acquaintance Meryton offered them. Society, I believe, is necessary to me. I have been a disappointed man, and my spirits will not bear solitude. I *must* have employment and society. A military life is not what I was intended for, but circumstances have now made it necessary. The church *ought* to have been my profession — I was brought up for the church, and I should at this time have been in possession of a most valuable living, had it pleased the gentleman we were speaking of just now."

"Indeed!"

"Yes — the late Mr. Darcy bequeathed me the next presentation of the best living in his will. He was my godfather, and excessively attached to me. I cannot do justice to his kindness. He meant to provide for me amply, and thought he had done it; but when the living became available it was given elsewhere."

"Good heavens!" cried Elizabeth. "But how could *that* be? — How could his will be disregarded? — Why did not you seek legal redress?"

"There was enough uncertainty in the terms of the bequest as to give me no hope from law. A man of honour could not have doubted the intention, but Mr. Darcy chose to doubt it — or to treat it as a merely conditional recommendation, and to assert that I had forfeited all claim to it by extravagance and imprudence. Certain it is, that the living became vacant two years ago, exactly as I was of an age to hold it, and that it was given to another man. I cannot accuse myself of having really done anything to deserve to lose it. I have an unguarded temper, and I may perhaps have sometimes spoken my opinion *of* him, and *to* him, too freely. I can recall nothing worse. But the fact is, that we are very different sort of men, and that he hates me."

"This is quite shocking! He deserves to be publicly disgraced."

"Some time or other he *will* be — but it shall not be by *me*. Till I can forget his father, I can never defy or expose *him*."

Elizabeth commended him for such feelings, and thought him handsomer than ever as he expressed them.

"But what," said she, after a pause, "can have been his motive? What can have caused him to behave so cruelly?"

"A thorough, determined dislike of me — a dislike which I cannot but attribute in some measure to jealousy. Had the late Mr. Darcy liked me less, his son might have accepted me better; but his father's uncommon attachment to me irritated him, I believe, very early in life. He had not a temper to bear the sort of competition in which we stood — the sort of preference which was often given me."

"I had not thought Mr. Darcy so bad as this. Though I have never liked him, I had not thought so very ill of him. — I had supposed him to be despising his fellow-creatures in general, but did not suspect him of descending to such malicious revenge, such injustice, such inhumanity as this!"

After a few minutes reflection, however, she continued, "I *do* remember his boasting one day, at Netherfield, of the inflexibility of his resentments, of his having an unforgiving temper. His disposition must be dreadful."

"I will not trust myself on the subject," replied Wickham, "*I* can hardly be just to him."

Elizabeth was again deep in thought, and after a time exclaimed, "To treat in such a manner the godson, the friend, the favourite of his father!" — She could have added, "A young man too, like *you*, whose very countenance may vouch for your being friendly" — but she contented herself with, "And one, too, who had probably been his own companion from childhood, connected together, as I think you said, in the closest manner!"

"We were born in the same parish, and the greatest part of our youth was passed together. Occupants of the same house, sharing the same amusements, objects of the same parental care. *My* father began life in the profession which your uncle, Mr. Philips, appears to do so much credit to — but he gave up everything to be of use to the late Mr. Darcy, and devoted all his time to the care of the Pemberley property. He was most highly esteemed by Mr. Darcy, a most intimate, confidential friend. Mr. Darcy often acknowledged himself to be under the greatest obligations to my father's management. When, immediately before my father's death, Mr. Darcy gave him a voluntary promise of providing for me, I am convinced that he felt it to be as much a debt of gratitude to *him* as of affection to myself."

"How strange!" cried Elizabeth. "How abominable! I wonder that the very pride of this Mr. Darcy has not made him just to you! If from no better motive, that he should not have been too proud to be dishonest, for dishonesty I must call it."

"It *is* abominable," replied Wickham. "Almost all his actions may be traced to pride; and pride has often been his best friend. It has brought him closer to virtue than any other feeling. But we are none of us consistent, and in his behaviour to me there were stronger impulses even than pride."

"Can such abominable pride as his have ever done him good?"

"Yes. It has often led him to be generous — to give his money freely, to display hospitality, to assist his tenants, and relieve the poor. The pride of a son — for he is very proud of what his father was — has done this. Not to appear to disgrace his family, to degenerate from the popular qualities, or lose the influence of the Pemberley House, is a powerful motive. He has also *brotherly* pride, which, with *some* brotherly affection, makes him a very kind and careful guardian of his sister, and you will hear him generally described as the most attentive and best of brothers."

"What sort of a girl is Miss Darcy?"

He shook his head. "I wish I could call her friendly. It gives me pain to speak ill of a Darcy. But she is too much like her brother — very, very proud. As a child, she was affectionate and pleasing, and extremely fond of me; and I have devoted hours and hours to her amusement. But she is nothing to me now. She is a beautiful girl, about fifteen or sixteen, and highly accomplished. Since her father's death her home has been London, where a lady lives with her and supervises her education."

After many pauses and many attempts at other subjects, Elizabeth could not help reverting once more to the first, and saying —

"I am astonished at his friendship with Mr. Bingley! How can Mr. Bingley, who seems good-humour itself, and is, I really believe, truly amiable, be in friendship with such a man? How can they suit each other? Do you know Mr. Bingley?"

"Not at all."

"He is a sweet-tempered, friendly, charming man. He cannot know what Mr. Darcy is."

"Probably not; — but Mr. Darcy can please where he chooses. He does not lack *those* abilities. He can be a warm companion if he thinks it worth his while. Among those who are at all his equals in importance, he is a very different man from what he is to the less prosperous. His pride never deserts him; but with the rich he is open-minded, just, sincere, rational, honourable, and perhaps even agreeable.."

The whist party soon afterwards breaking up, the players gathered round the other table, and Mr. Collins took his station between his cousin Elizabeth and Mrs. Philips. The usual inquiries as to his success were made by the latter. It had not been very great: he had lost every point; but when Mrs. Philips began to express her concern thereupon, he assured her with much earnestness that it was not of the least importance, that he considered the money as a mere trifle, and begged she would not make herself uneasy.

"I know very well, madam," said he, "that when persons sit down to a card table they must take their chance of these things — and happily I am not in such circumstances as to make five shillings any concern. There are undoubtedly many who could not say the same, but thanks to Lady Catherine de Bourgh, I am removed far beyond the necessity of regarding little matters."

After observing Mr. Collins for a few moments, Mr. Wickham asked Elizabeth in a low voice whether her relation were very well acquainted with the family of de Bourgh.

"Lady Catherine de Bourgh," she replied, "has very lately given him a living. I hardly know how Mr. Collins was first introduced to her, but he certainly has not known her long."

"You know of course that Lady Catherine de Bourgh and Lady Anne Darcy were sisters. Consequently she is aunt to the present Mr. Darcy."

"No, indeed, I did not. I knew nothing at all of Lady Catherine's connections. I never heard of her existence till the day before yesterday."

"Her daughter, Miss de Bourgh, will have a very large fortune, and it is believed that she and her cousin will unite the two estates."

This information made Elizabeth smile, as she thought of poor Miss Bingley. Vain indeed must be all her attentions, vain and useless her affection for his sister and her praise of himself, if he were already destined for another.

"Mr. Collins," said she, "speaks highly both of Lady Catherine and her daughter. But from some particulars that he has related of her ladyship, I suspect his gratitude misleads him, and that in spite of her being his patroness, she is an arrogant, conceited woman."

"I believe her to be both in a great degree," replied Wickham; "I have not seen her for many years, but I very well remember that I never liked her, and that her manners were dictatorial and insulting. She has the reputation of being remarkably sensible and clever, but I rather believe she derives part of her abilities from her rank and fortune, part from her authoritative manner, and the rest from the pride of her nephew, who insists that everyone connected with him should have an understanding of the first class."

Elizabeth and Mr. Wickham continued talking together with mutual satisfaction till supper put an end to cards and gave the rest of the ladies their share of Mr. Wickham's attentions. There could be no conversation in the noise of Mrs. Philips's supper party, but his manners recommended him to everybody. Whatever he said was said well, and whatever he did was done gracefully. Elizabeth went away with her head full of him. She could think of nothing but Mr. Wickham, and of what he had told her, all the way home. There was not time for her even to mention his name as they went, however, for neither Lydia nor Mr. Collins were once silent. Lydia talked incessantly of cards, of the prizes she had lost and the prizes she had won. Mr. Collins, in describing the civility of Mr. and Mrs. Philips, claimed that he did not in the least regard his losses at whist, enumerated all the dishes at supper, and repeatedly feared that he crowded his cousins. He therefore had more to say than he could manage before the carriage stopped at Longbourn House.

CHAPTER 17

Elizabeth related to Jane the next day what had passed between Mr. Wickham and herself. Jane listened with astonishment and concern. She did not know how to believe that Mr. Darcy could be so unworthy of Mr. Bingley's regard, yet it was not in her nature to question the honesty of a young man of such amiable appearance as Wickham. The possibility of his having really endured such unkindness was enough to evoke all her tender feelings, and nothing therefore remained to be done but to think well of them both: to defend the conduct of each, and to attribute to accident or mistake whatever could not be otherwise explained.

"They have both," said she, "been deceived, I dare say, in some way or other, of which we can form no idea. Interested people have perhaps misrepresented each to the other. It is, in short, impossible for us to know the causes or circumstances which may have alienated them, without actual blame on either side."

"Very true, indeed. And now, my dear Jane, what have you got to say in behalf of the interested people who have probably been concerned in the business? Do exonerate *them* too, or we shall be obliged to think ill of somebody."

"Laugh as much as you choose, but you will not laugh me out of my opinion. My dearest Lizzy, do but consider in what a disgraceful light it places Mr. Darcy, to be treating his father's favourite in such a manner — one whom his father had promised to provide for. It is impossible. No man of common humanity, no man who had any value for his character, could be capable of it. Can his closest friends be so completely deceived in him? Impossible!"

"I can much more easily believe Mr. Bingley's being aware of Mr. Darcy's indiscretions than that Mr. Wickham should invent such a history of himself as he gave me last night: names, facts, everything mentioned without ceremony. If it is not so, let Mr. Darcy contradict it. Besides, there was truth in his looks."

"It is difficult indeed — it is distressing. One does not know what to think."

"I beg your pardon; one knows exactly what to think."

But Jane could think with certainty on only one point — that Mr. Bingley, if he was aware of Mr. Darcy's infamous behavior, would have much to suffer when the details of it became public knowledge.

The two young ladies were summoned from the garden where this conversation passed by the arrival of some of the very persons of whom they had been speaking. Mr. Bingley and his sisters came to give their personal invitation for the long expected ball at Netherfield, which was to be held the following Tuesday. The two ladies were delighted to see their dear friend again — saying it had been ages since they last met — and repeatedly asked what she had been doing with herself since their separation. To the rest of the family they paid little attention: avoiding Mrs. Bennet as much as possible, saying very little to Elizabeth, and nothing at all to the others. They were soon gone again, rising from their seats with an urgency which took their brother by surprise, and hurrying off as if eager to escape from Mrs. Bennet's civilities.

The prospect of the Netherfield ball was extremely agreeable to every female of the family. Mrs. Bennet chose to consider it as given in honor of her eldest daughter. She was also particularly flattered by receiving the invitation from Mr. Bingley himself instead of a ceremonious invitation. Jane pictured to herself a happy evening in the company of her two friends, and the attentions of their brother. Elizabeth thought with pleasure of dancing a great deal with Mr. Wickham, and of seeing a confirmation of everything in Mr. Darcy's looks and behaviour. The happiness anticipated by Catherine and Lydia depended less on any single event, or any particular person. Though they each, like Elizabeth, meant to dance half the evening with Mr. Wickham, he was by no means the only partner who could satisfy them, and a ball was, at any rate, a ball. Even Mary could assure her family that she had no prejudice against it.

"As long as I can have my mornings to myself," said she, "it is enough. I think it no sacrifice to join occasionally in evening engagements. Society has claims on us all; and I profess myself one of those who consider intervals of recreation and amusement as desirable for everybody."

Elizabeth's spirits were so high on the occasion that, though she did not often speak unnecessarily to Mr. Collins, she could not help asking him whether he intended to accept Mr. Bingley's invitation. She was rather surprised to find that he had no reservations whatsoever, and was very far from dreading a rebuke either from the Archbishop or Lady Catherine de Bourgh by venturing to dance.

"I am by no means of the opinion, I assure you," said he, "that a ball of this kind, given by a young man of character, to respectable people, can have any evil tendency. And I am so far from objecting to dancing myself that I shall hope to be honoured with the hands of all my fair cousins in the course of the evening. I take this opportunity of requesting yours, Miss Elizabeth, for the two first dances especially — a preference which I trust my cousin Jane will attribute to the right cause, and not to any disrespect for her."

Elizabeth felt herself completely betrayed. She had planned to be partnered with Wickham for those very dances; and to have Mr. Collins instead! Her playfulness had never been worse timed. There was no help for it, however. Mr. Wickham's happiness and her own was delayed a little longer, and Mr. Collins's proposal accepted with as much grace as she could manage. It did not lift her spirits when she realized his request suggested the possibility of something more. It now first struck her that *she* was selected from among her sisters as worthy of being the mistress of Hunsford Parsonage, and of assisting to form a card table at Rosings in the absence of more suitable visitors. The idea soon became conviction as she observed his increasing civilities toward herself, and heard his frequent attempts at complimenting her wit and vivacity. Though more astonished than gratified by this effect of her charms, it was not long before her mother gave her to understand that the probability of their marriage was exceedingly agreeable to *her*. Elizabeth, however, did not choose to take the hint, being well aware that a serious dispute must be the result of any reply. Mr. Collins might never make the offer, and till he did, it was useless to quarrel about him.

If there had not been a Netherfield ball to prepare for and talk of, the younger Miss Bennets would have been in a pitiable state at this time, for from the day of the invitation to the day of the ball there was enough rain to prevent their walking to Meryton once. No aunt, no officers, no news could be sought after. Even Elizabeth felt some trial of her patience in weather which totally prevented the furthering of her acquaintance with Mr. Wickham. Nothing less than a dance on Tuesday could have made such a Friday, Saturday, Sunday, and Monday endurable to Kitty and Lydia.

CHAPTER 18

Until Elizabeth entered the drawing room at Netherfield and looked in vain for Mr. Wickham among the cluster of red coats there assembled, a doubt of his being present had never occurred to her. She had dressed with more than usual care, and prepared in the highest spirits for the conquest of his heart, trusting that it might be won in the course of the evening. But in an instant arose the dreadful suspicion of his being purposely snubbed. Though this was not exactly the case, the absolute fact of his absence was pronounced by his friend Mr. Denny, to whom Lydia eagerly applied, and who told them that Wickham had been obliged to go to town on business the day before, and was not yet returned. He added, with a significant smile

———

"I do not imagine his business would have called him away just now, if he had not wished to avoid a certain gentleman here."

This part of his intelligence, though unheard by Lydia, was caught by Elizabeth, and it assured her that Darcy was not less to blame for Wickham's absence than if her first assumption had been correct. Every feeling of displeasure against Mr. Darcy was so sharpened by immediate disappointment that she could hardly reply with tolerable civility to the polite inquiries which he directly afterwards approached to make. Attention, forbearance and patience with Darcy were injurious to Wickham. She was resolved against any sort of conversation with him, and turned away with a degree of disappointment which she could not wholly overcome even in speaking to Mr. Bingley, whose blind acceptance of Mr. Darcy upset her.

But Elizabeth was not formed for ill-humour, and though every prospect of her own was destroyed for the evening, it could not dwell long on her spirits. Having told all her griefs to Charlotte Lucas, whom she had not seen for a week, she was soon able to make a voluntary transition to the oddities of her cousin, and to point him out to her. The two first dances, however, brought a return of distress; they were dances of mortification. Mr. Collins, awkward and solemn, apologising instead of paying attention, and often moving wrong without being aware of it, gave her all the shame and misery which a disagreeable partner for a couple of dances can give. The moment of her release from him was ecstasy.

She danced next with an officer and had the refreshment of talking of Wickham and hearing that he was universally liked. When those dances were over she returned to Charlotte Lucas and was in conversation with her when she found herself suddenly addressed by Mr. Darcy. He took her so much by surprise in his application for her hand, that, without knowing what she did, she accepted him. He walked away again immediately, and she was left to fret over her own lack of presence of mind; Charlotte tried to console her.

"I dare say you will find him very agreeable."

"Heaven forbid! *That* would be the greatest misfortune of all! To find a man agreeable whom one is determined to hate! Do not wish me such ill-will."

When the dancing recommenced, however, and Darcy approached to claim her hand, Charlotte could not help cautioning her in a whisper not to be a fool and allow her preference for Wickham to make her appear unpleasant in the eyes of a man ten times more influential. Elizabeth made no answer and took her place in the set, amazed at the dignity she was able to command while standing opposite Mr. Darcy, and reading in her neighbours' looks their equal amazement in beholding it. They stood for some time without speaking a word, and she began to imagine that their silence was to last through the two dances, and at first was resolved not to break it; till suddenly, fancying that it would be the greater punishment to her partner to oblige him to talk, she made some slight observation on the dance. He replied, and was again silent. After a pause of some minutes she addressed him a second time with — "It is *your* turn to say something now, Mr. Darcy — *I* talked about the dance, and *you* ought to make some kind of remark on the size of the room, or the number of couples."

He smiled, and assured her that whatever she wished him to say should be said.

"Very well. That reply will do for the present. Perhaps by and by I may observe that private balls are much pleasanter than public ones. But *now* we may be silent."

"Do you generally follow such conversational forms, then, while you are dancing?"

"Sometimes. One must speak a little, you know. It would look odd to be entirely silent for half an hour together. And yet for the advantage of *some*, conversation ought to be arranged so that they may have the trouble of saying as little as possible."

"Are you consulting your own feelings in the present case, or do you imagine that you are gratifying mine?"

"Both," replied Elizabeth, "for I have always seen a great similarity in our preferences. We are each of an unsocial, quiet disposition, unwilling to speak unless we expect to say something that will amaze the whole room."

"This is no very striking resemblance of your own character, I am sure," said he. "How near it may be to *mine*, I cannot pretend to say. *You* think it a faithful portrait undoubtedly."

"It is not for *me* to decide such things."

He made no answer, and they were again silent till they had gone down the dance, when he asked her if she and her sisters walked to Meryton often. She answered that they did, and, unable to resist the temptation, added, "When you met us there the other day, we had just been forming a new acquaintance."

The effect was immediate. A deeper shade of pompousness overspread his features, but he said not a word, and Elizabeth, though blaming herself for her own weakness, could not go on. At length Darcy spoke, and in a constrained manner said, "Mr. Wickham is blessed with such good manners as may ensure his *making* friends. Whether he may be equally capable of *retaining* them, is less certain."

"He has been so unlucky as to lose *your* friendship," replied Elizabeth with emphasis, "and in a manner which he is likely to suffer from all his life."

Darcy made no answer, and seemed desirous to change the subject. At that moment Sir William Lucas appeared close to them, meaning to pass through the set to the other side of the room. But on perceiving Mr. Darcy he stopped with a bow of superior courtesy to compliment him on his dancing and his partner.

"I have been most highly gratified indeed, my dear sir. Such very skilled dancing is not often seen. It is evident that you belong to the best circles. Allow me to say, however, that your fair partner does not disgrace you. I must hope to have this pleasure often repeated, especially when a certain desirable event, my dear Miss Eliza (glancing at her sister and Bingley), shall take place. What congratulations will then flow in! I appeal to Mr. Darcy — but let me not interrupt you, sir. You will not thank me for detaining you from the bewitching conversation of that young lady, whose bright eyes are telling me it is time to move on."

The latter part of this address was scarcely heard by Darcy, but Sir William's mention of his friend seemed to strike him forcibly. His eyes were then directed with a very serious expression towards Bingley and Jane, who were dancing together. Recovering himself, however, he turned to his partner and said, "Sir William's interruption has made me forget what we were talking of."

"I do not think we were speaking at all. Sir William could not have interrupted any two people in the room who had less to say to each other. We have tried two or three subjects already without success, and what we are to talk of next I cannot imagine."

"What think you of books?" said he, smiling.

"Books! I am sure we never read the same, or not with the same feelings."

"I am sorry you think so; but if that be the case, there can at least be no lack of material for conversation. We may compare our different opinions."

"No — I cannot talk of books in a ballroom; my head is always full of something else."

"The *present* always occupies you in such scenes, does it?" said he, with a look of doubt.

"Yes, always," she replied, without knowing what she said, for her thoughts had wandered far from the subject, as soon afterwards appeared by her suddenly exclaiming, "I remember hearing you once say, Mr. Darcy, that you hardly ever forgave, that your resentment once created could not be undone. You are very cautious, I suppose, as to its *being created*."

"I am," said he, with a firm voice.

"And never allow yourself to be blinded by prejudice?"

"I hope not."

"It is particularly important for those who never change their opinion to be certain of judging properly at first."

"May I ask the purpose of these questions?"

"Merely to the illustration of *your* character," said she, endeavouring to shake off her serious tone. "I am trying to make it out."

"And what have you learned?"

She shook her head. "Nothing at all. I hear such different accounts of you as puzzle me exceedingly."

"I can readily believe," he answered gravely, "that opinions may vary greatly with respect to me. I would like to request, Miss Bennet, that you not attempt to determine my character at the present moment, as there is reason to fear that the results would be less than flattering."

"But if I do not examine it now, I may never have another opportunity."

"I would by no means interrupt any pleasure of yours," he coldly replied. She said no more, and they went down the other dance and parted in silence; on each side dissatisfied, though not to an equal degree. In Darcy's breast there was a powerful feeling towards her which allowed him to quickly forgive her and direct all his anger against another.

They had not long separated when Miss Bingley came towards her, and with a scornfully civil expression thus began: — "So, Miss Eliza, I hear you are quite delighted with George Wickham! Your sister has been talking to me about him and asking me a thousand questions. I find that the young man forgot to tell you, among his other communications, that he was the son of old Wickham, the late Mr. Darcy's steward. Let me recommend you, however, as a friend, not to give implicit confidence to all his claims. As to Mr. Darcy's treating him poorly, it is perfectly false. On the contrary, Darcy has always always remarkably kind to him, though George Wickham has treated Mr. Darcy in a most infamous manner. I do not know the particulars, but I know very well that Mr. Darcy is not in the least to blame, and that he cannot bear to hear George Wickham mentioned. Though my brother could not avoid including him in his invitation to the officers, he was excessively glad to find that he had chosen not to come. His being in this area at all is a most insufferable thing, indeed, and I wonder how he could presume to do it. I pity you, Miss Eliza, for this discovery of your favourite's guilt; but really, considering his low birth, one could not expect much better."

"His guilt and his low birth appear by your account to be the same," said Elizabeth angrily, "for I have heard you accuse him of nothing worse than of being the son of Mr. Darcy's steward. Of *that*, I can assure you, he informed me himself."

"I beg your pardon," replied Miss Bingley, turning away with a sneer. "Excuse my interference; it was kindly meant."

"Arrogant girl!" said Elizabeth to herself. "You are much mistaken if you expect to influence me by such an attack as this. I see nothing in it but your own wilful ignorance and the malice of Mr. Darcy." She then sought her eldest sister, who had talked with Bingley about the same subject. Jane met her with a smile of such sweet complacency, a glow of such happy expression, as sufficiently indicated how well she was satisfied with the events of the evening. Elizabeth instantly read her feelings, and at that moment concern for Wickham, resentment against his enemies, and everything else, gave way before the hope of Jane's happiness.

"I want to know," said she, with a countenance no less smiling than her sister's, "what you have learned about Mr. Wickham. But perhaps you have been too pleasantly engaged to think of any third person, in which case you may be sure of my pardon."

"No," replied Jane, "I have not forgotten him, but I have nothing satisfactory to tell you. Mr. Bingley does not know the whole of his history, and is quite ignorant of the circumstances which have offended Mr. Darcy. But he will vouch for the good conduct, the integrity and honour of his friend, and is perfectly convinced that Mr. Wickham has deserved much less attention from Mr. Darcy than he has received. I am sorry to say that by his account as well as his sister's, Mr. Wickham is by no means a respectable young man. I am afraid he has been very dishonourable, and has deserved to lose Mr. Darcy's regard."

"Mr. Bingley does not know Mr. Wickham himself?"

"No. He never saw him till the other morning at Meryton."

"This account, then, is what he has received from Mr. Darcy, I am sure. But what does he say of the living?"

"He does not exactly recollect the circumstances, though he has heard them from Mr. Darcy more than once. But he believes that it was left to him *conditionally*."

"I have not a doubt of Mr. Bingley's sincerity," said Elizabeth warmly, "but you must excuse my not being convinced by assurances only. Mr. Bingley's defence of his friend was a very good one, I dare say. But since he is unacquainted with several parts of the story and has learned the rest from that friend himself, I shall venture still to think of both gentlemen as I did before."

She then changed the discussion to one more gratifying to each, and on which there could be no difference of sentiment. Elizabeth listened with delight to the happy, though modest hopes which Jane entertained of Bingley's regard, and said all in her power to encourage her confidence in it. On their being joined by Mr. Bingley himself, Elizabeth withdrew to Miss Lucas, to whose inquiry after the pleasantness of her last partner she had scarcely replied before Mr. Collins came up to them and told her with great excitement that he had just been so fortunate as to make a most important discovery.

"I have found out," said he, "by a singular accident that there is now in the room a near relation of my patroness. I happened to overhear the gentleman himself mentioning to Miss Bingley the names of his cousin Miss de Bourgh and of her mother Lady Catherine. Who would have thought of my meeting with, perhaps, a nephew of Lady Catherine de Bourgh in this assembly! I am most thankful that the discovery is made in time for me to pay my respects to him, which I am now going to do, and trust he will excuse my not having done it before. My total ignorance of the connection must be my excuse."

"You are not going to introduce yourself to Mr. Darcy!"

"Indeed I am. I shall entreat his pardon for not having done it earlier. I believe him to be Lady Catherine's *nephew*. It will be in my power to assure him that her ladyship was quite well when I saw her last week."

Elizabeth tried hard to dissuade him from such a plan, assuring him that Mr. Darcy would consider his addressing him without introduction as an offence rather than a compliment to his aunt. It was not in the least necessary that there should be any notice on either side, she continued, and that if it were it was Mr. Darcy, the superior gentleman, who should begin the acquaintance. Mr. Collins listened to her with the determination to do as he pleased, and, when she ceased speaking, replied thus: — "My dear Miss Elizabeth, I have the highest opinion in the world of your excellent judgment in all matters within the scope of your understanding. But permit me to say that there must be a wide difference between the established forms of ceremony among the general populace and those which regulate the clergy. Give me leave to observe that I consider the clerical office as equal in point of dignity with the highest rank in the kingdom — provided that a proper humility of behaviour is at the same time maintained. You must, therefore, allow me to follow the dictates of my conscience on this occasion, which leads me to perform what I look on as a point of duty. Pardon me for neglecting to profit by your advice, which on every other subject shall be my constant guide, though in the case before us I consider myself more able by education and study to decide what is right than a young lady like yourself." And with a low bow he left her to attack Mr. Darcy, whose reception of his advances she eagerly watched, and whose astonishment at being so addressed was very evident. Her cousin prefaced his speech with a solemn bow: and though she could not hear a word of it, she felt as if hearing it all, and saw in the motion of his lips the words "apology," "Hunsford," and "Lady Catherine de Bourgh." It upset her to see him make a mockery of himself in front of such a man. Mr. Darcy was eyeing him with unrestrained surprise, and when at last Mr. Collins allowed him time to speak, replied with an air of distant civility. Mr. Collins, however, was not discouraged from speaking again, and Mr. Darcy's contempt seemed abundantly increasing with the length of his second speech. At the end of it he only made him a slight bow and moved another way. Mr. Collins then returned to Elizabeth.

"I have no reason, I assure you," said he, "to be dissatisfied with my reception. Mr. Darcy seemed much pleased with the attention. He answered me with the utmost civility, and even paid me the compliment of saying that he was so well convinced of Lady Catherine's judgment as to be certain she could never bestow a favour unworthily. It was really a very kind thought. Upon the whole, I am much pleased with him."

As Elizabeth had no longer any interest of her own to pursue, she turned her attention almost entirely to her sister and Mr. Bingley. The series of agreeable reflections which her observations generated made her perhaps almost as happy as Jane. She pictured her settled in that very house, in all the happiness which a marriage of true affection could bestow; and she felt capable, under such circumstances, of endeavouring even to like Bingley's two sisters. Her mother's thoughts she plainly saw were along the same lines, and she determined not to venture near her lest she might hear too much. When they sat down to supper, therefore, she considered it most unlucky to find herself near her. And she was further upset to discover that her mother was talking to Lady Lucas freely, openly, and of nothing else but of her expectation that Jane would be soon married to Mr. Bingley. — It was an exciting subject, and Mrs. Bennet seemed incapable of fatigue while listing the advantages of the match. His being such a charming young man, and so rich, and living but three miles from them, were the first points of self-congratulation; and then it was such a comfort to think how fond the two sisters were of Jane, and to be certain that they must desire the connection as much as she did. It was, moreover, such a promising thing for her younger daughters, as Jane's marrying so well must throw them in the way of other rich men. She concluded with many good wishes that Lady Lucas might soon be equally fortunate, though evidently and triumphantly believing there was no chance of it.

In vain did Elizabeth endeavour to slow the rapidity of her mother's words, or persuade her to describe her happiness in a less audible whisper. For, to her inexpressible horror, she could perceive that most of it was overheard by Mr. Darcy, who sat opposite to them. Her mother only scolded her for being nonsensical.

"What is Mr. Darcy to me that I should be afraid of him? I am sure we owe him no such particular civility as to be obliged to say nothing *he* may not like to hear."

"For heaven's sake, madam, speak lower. What advantage can it be to you to offend Mr. Darcy? You will never commend yourself to his friend by so doing."

Nothing that she could say, however, had any influence. Her mother continued to talk of her views in the same loud tone. Elizabeth blushed and blushed again with shame and anger. She could not help frequently glancing at Mr. Darcy, though every glance convinced her of what she dreaded; for though he was not always looking at her mother, she was convinced that he was listening to every word she spoke. The expression of his face changed gradually from indignant contempt to a composed and steady seriousness.

At length, however, Mrs. Bennet had no more to say, and Lady Lucas, who had been long yawning at the repetition of delights which she saw no likelihood of sharing, was left to the comforts of cold ham and chicken. Elizabeth now began to revive. But not long was the interval of tranquillity; for when supper was over, singing was talked of, and she had the mortification of seeing Mary preparing to oblige the company. By many significant looks and silent entreaties did she endeavour to prevent her — but in vain: Mary would not understand them; such an opportunity of performing was delightful to her, and she began her song. Elizabeth's eyes were fixed on her with most painful sensations, and she watched her progress through the several stanzas with impatience. Mary, on receiving amongst the thanks of the table the hint of a hope that she might be prevailed on to favour them again, paused for half a minute and began another. Her powers were by no means fitted for such a display: her voice was weak, and her manner unnatural. Elizabeth was in agonies. She looked at Jane to see how she bore it, but Jane was very composedly talking to

Bingley. She looked at his two sisters and saw them making signs of derision at each other, and at Darcy, who continued impenetrably grave. She looked at her father to entreat his interference, lest Mary should be singing all night. He took the hint, and when Mary had finished her second song, said aloud, "That will do extremely well, child. You have delighted us long enough. Let the other young ladies have time to perform."

Mary, though pretending not to hear, was somewhat flustered, and Elizabeth, sorry for her, and sorry for her father's speech, was afraid her attempts to remedy the situation had done no good.

"If I," said Mr. Collins, "were so fortunate as to be able to sing, I should have great pleasure, I am sure, in obliging the company with an air; for I consider music as a very innocent diversion, and perfectly compatible with the profession of a clergyman. I do not mean, however, to say that we can be justified in devoting too much of our time to music, for there are certainly other things to be accomplished. The rector of a parish has much to do. In the first place, he must make such an agreement for tithes as may be beneficial to himself and not offensive to his patron. He must write his own sermons; and the time that remains will not be too much for his parish duties, and the care and improvement of his dwelling, which he cannot be excused from making as comfortable as possible. And I do not think it of light importance that he should have attentive and conciliatory manners towards everybody, especially towards those to whom he owes his preferment. He cannot neglect that duty; nor could I think well of the man who should omit an occasion of proclaiming his respect towards anybody connected with the family." And with a bow to Mr. Darcy he concluded his speech, which had been spoken so loud as to be heard by half the room. Many stared — many smiled; but no one looked more amused than Mr. Bennet himself, while his wife seriously praised Mr. Collins for having spoken so well, and observed in a half-whisper to Lady Lucas that he was a remarkably clever, good kind of young man.

To Elizabeth it appeared that had her family made an agreement to look as ridiculous as possible during the evening, it would have been impossible for them to play their parts with more spirit or finer success. She consoled herself by thinking that for Bingley and her sister some of the exhibition had escaped his notice, and that his feelings were not of a sort to be much distressed by the folly which he must have witnessed. That his two sisters and Mr. Darcy, however, should have such an opportunity of mocking her relations was bad enough, and she could not determine whether the silent contempt of the gentleman, or the insolent smiles of the ladies, were more intolerable.

The rest of the evening brought her little amusement. She was vexed by Mr. Collins, who continued most perseveringly by her side, and though he could not prevail with her to dance with him again made it impossible for her to dance with others. In vain did she ask him to dance with somebody else, offering to introduce him to any young lady in the room. He assured her that, as to dancing, he was perfectly indifferent to it. His chief object was, by delicate attentions, to recommend himself to her, and he therefore made a point of remaining close to her the whole evening. There was no arguing with him upon the subject. She owed her greatest relief to her friend Miss Lucas, who often joined them, and good-naturedly engaged Mr. Collins in conversation.

She was at least free from the offence of Mr. Darcy's farther notice. Though often standing within a very short distance of her, doing nothing in particular, he never came near enough to speak. She felt it to be the probable consequence of her mention of Mr. Wickham, and rejoiced in it.

The Longbourn party were the last of all the company to depart, and by a scheme of Mrs. Bennet had to wait for their carriages a quarter of an hour after everybody else was gone, which gave them time to see how heartily they were wished away by some of the family. Mrs. Hurst and her sister scarcely opened their mouths, except to complain of fatigue, and were evidently impatient to have the house to themselves. They rebuffed every attempt of Mrs. Bennet at conversation, and by so doing threw a dullness over the whole party, which was very little relieved by the long speeches of Mr. Collins. He was complimenting Mr. Bingley and his sisters on the elegance of their entertainment, and the hospitality and politeness which had marked their behaviour to their guests. Darcy said nothing at all. Mr. Bennet, in equal silence, was enjoying the scene. Mr. Bingley and Jane were standing together, a little detached from the rest, and talked only to each other. Elizabeth preserved as steady a silence as either Mrs. Hurst or Miss Bingley. Even Lydia was too fatigued to utter more than the occasional exclamation of "Lord, how tired I am!" accompanied by a violent yawn.

When at length they arose to take leave, Mrs. Bennet was most pressingly civil in her hope of seeing the whole family soon at Longbourn, and addressed herself particularly to Mr. Bingley, to assure him how happy he would make them by eating a family dinner with them at any time, without the ceremony of a formal invitation. Bingley was all grateful pleasure, and he readily promised to take the earliest opportunity of visiting her after his return from London, where he was obliged to go the next day for a short time.

Mrs. Bennet was perfectly satisfied, and left the house with the delightful belief that, allowing for the necessary preparations, she should undoubtedly see her daughter settled at Netherfield in the course of three or four months. Of having another daughter soon married to Mr. Collins, she thought upon with equal certainty, and with considerable, though not equal, pleasure. Elizabeth was the least dear to her of all her children; and though the man and the match were quite good enough for *her*, the worth of each was eclipsed by Mr. Bingley and Netherfield.

CHAPTER 19

The next day opened a new scene at Longbourn. Mr. Collins made his formal proposal. Having resolved to do it without delay, as his leave of absence extended only to the following Saturday, he set about it in a very orderly manner, with all the observances which he supposed a regular part of the business. On finding Mrs. Bennet, Elizabeth, and one of the younger girls together soon after breakfast, he addressed the mother in these words: "May I hope, madam, for your assistance with your fair daughter Elizabeth, by requesting the honour of a private conversation with her this morning?"

Before Elizabeth had time for anything but a blush of surprise, Mrs. Bennet instantly answered, "Oh dear! Yes — certainly. I am sure Lizzy will be very happy — I am sure she can have no objection. Come, Kitty, I want you upstairs." And gathering her work together, she was hurrying away when Elizabeth called out —

"Dear ma'am, do not go. I beg you will not go. Mr. Collins must forgive me. He can have nothing to say to me that anybody need not hear. I am going away myself."

"No, no, nonsense, Lizzy. I desire you to stay where you are." And upon Elizabeth's seeming really, with fretful and embarrassed looks, about to escape, she added, "Lizzy, I *insist* upon your staying and hearing Mr. Collins."

Elizabeth would not oppose such a request — and a moment's consideration making her also realize that it would be wisest to get it over with as soon and as quietly as possible, she sat down again, trying to conceal her distress. Mrs. Bennet and Kitty walked off, and as soon as they were gone Mr. Collins began.

"Believe me, my dear Miss Elizabeth, that your modesty, so far from doing you any disservice, rather adds to your other perfections. You would have been less amiable in my eyes had there *not* been this little unwillingness, but allow me to assure you, that I have your respected mother's permission for this address. You can hardly doubt the purpose of my discourse, however your natural delicacy may lead you to react; my attentions have been too obvious to be mistaken. Almost as soon as I entered the house, I singled you out as the companion of my future life. But before I am run away with by my feelings on this subject, perhaps it will be advisable for me to state my reasons for marrying — and, moreover, for coming into Hertfordshire with the design of selecting a wife, as I certainly did."

The idea of Mr. Collins, with all his solemn composure, being run away with by his feelings, made Elizabeth so near laughing that she could not use the short pause he allowed in any attempt to stop him farther, and he continued —

"My reasons for marrying are, first, that I think it a right thing for every clergyman in prosperous circumstances (like myself) to set the example of matrimony in his parish; secondly, that I am convinced it will add very greatly to my happiness; and thirdly — which perhaps I ought to have mentioned earlier, that it is the particular advice and recommendation of the very noble lady whom I have the honour of calling patroness. Twice has she condescended to give me her opinion (unasked too!) on this subject; and it was but the very Saturday night before I left Hunsford — while we were playing cards, and Mrs. Jenkinson was arranging Miss de Bourgh's footstool — that she said, 'Mr. Collins, you must marry. A clergyman like you must marry. Choose properly, choose a gentlewoman for *my* sake; and for your *own*. Let her be an active, useful sort of person, not brought up wealthy, but able to make a small income go a long way. This is my advice. Find such a woman as soon as you can, bring her to Hunsford, and I will visit her.' Allow me, by the way, to observe, my fair cousin, that I do not believe the notice and kindness of Lady Catherine de Bourgh is among the least of the advantages in my power to offer. You will find her manners beyond anything I can describe; and your wit and vivacity, I think, must be acceptable to her, especially when tempered with the silence and respect which her rank will inevitably invite. Now that you know my general intention in favour of matrimony; it remains to be told why my views were directed to Longbourn instead of my own neighbourhood, where, I assure you, there are many amiable young women. But the fact is, that being, as I am, to inherit this estate after the death of your honoured father (who, however, may live many years longer), I could not but resolve to choose a wife from among his daughters, that the loss to them might be as little as possible, when the melancholy event takes place — which, however, as I have already said, may not be for several years. This has been my motive, my fair cousin, and I flatter myself it will not sink me in your esteem. And now nothing remains for me but to assure you in the most passionate language of the violence of my affection. To wealth I am perfectly indifferent, and shall make no demand of that nature on your father, since I am well aware that it could not be complied with. On that head, therefore, I shall be uniformly silent; and you may assure yourself that no condemnation shall ever pass my lips when we are married."

It was absolutely necessary to interrupt him now.

"You are too hasty, sir," she cried. "You forget that I have made no answer. Let me do it without farther loss of time. Accept my thanks for the compliment you are paying me. I am very aware of the honour of your proposals, but it is impossible for me to do otherwise than decline them."

"I am not now to learn," replied Mr. Collins, with a formal wave of the hand, "that it is usual with young ladies to reject the addresses of the man whom they secretly mean to accept, when he first applies for their favour. Sometimes the refusal is repeated a second or even a third time. I am therefore by no means discouraged by what you have just said, and shall hope to lead you to the altar before long."

"Upon my word, sir," cried Elizabeth, "your hope is rather an extraordinary one after my declaration. I do assure you that I am not one of those young ladies (if such young ladies there are) who are so daring as to risk their happiness on the chance of being asked a second time. I am perfectly serious in my refusal. You could not make *me* happy, and I am convinced that I am the last woman in the world who would make *you* so. Were your friend Lady Catherine to know me, I am persuaded she would find me in every respect poorly qualified for such a situation."

"Were it certain that Lady Catherine would think so," said Mr. Collins very gravely — "but I cannot imagine that her ladyship would at all disapprove of you. And you may be certain that when I have the honour of seeing her again, I shall speak in the highest terms of your modesty, economy, and other qualifications."

"Indeed, Mr. Collins, all praise of me will be unnecessary. You must allow me to decide for myself, and pay me the compliment of believing what I say. I wish you very happy and very rich, and by refusing your hand I am doing everything in my power to prevent your being otherwise. In making me the offer, you must have satisfied your conscience with regard to my family, and may take possession of Longbourn estate whenever it falls to you without any guilt. This matter may be considered, therefore, as finally settled." And standing as she thus spoke, she would have left the room if Mr. Collins had not addressed her —

"When I do myself the honour of speaking to you next on this subject, I shall hope to receive a more favourable answer than you have now given me. Though I am far from accusing you of cruelty at present, because I know it to be the established custom of your sex to reject a man on the first application. Perhaps you have even now said as much to encourage me as would be consistent with the true delicacy of the female character."

"Really, Mr. Collins," cried Elizabeth with frustration, "you puzzle me exceedingly. If what I have said can appear to you in the form of encouragement, I know not how to express my refusal in such a way as may convince you of its being one."

"You must allow me to flatter myself, my dear cousin, that your refusal of my proposal is merely words of course. My reasons for believing it are briefly these: it does not appear to me that my hand is unworthy of your acceptance, or that what I can offer would be anything other than highly desirable. My situation in life, my connections with the family of De Bourgh, and my relationship to your own, are circumstances highly in my favour; and you should take it into farther consideration that, in spite of your many attractions, it is by no means certain that another offer of marriage may ever be made you. Your wealth is unhappily so insignificant that it will in all likelihood undo the effects of your loveliness and amiable qualifications. As I must therefore conclude that you are not serious in your rejection of me, I shall choose to attribute it to your wish of increasing my love by suspense, according to the usual practice of elegant females."

"I do assure you, sir, that I have no part whatever in that kind of elegance which consists in tormenting a respectable man. I would rather be paid the compliment of being believed sincere. I thank you again and again for the honour you have done me in your proposals, but to accept them is absolutely impossible. My feelings in every respect forbid it. Can I speak plainer? Do not consider me now as an elegant female, intending to plague you, but as a rational creature, speaking the truth from her heart."

"You are uniformly charming!" cried he, with an air of awkward gallantry, "and I am persuaded that, when sanctioned by the express authority of both your excellent parents, my proposals will not fail of being acceptable."

To such perseverance in wilful self-deception Elizabeth would make no reply, and immediately and in silence withdrew. She determined, if he persisted in considering her repeated refusals as flattering encouragement, to apply to her father, whose refusal might be uttered in such a manner as must be decisive, and whose behaviour at least could not be mistaken for the flirtatious torment of an elegant female.

CHAPTER 20

Mr. Collins was not left long to the silent contemplation of his successful love. Mrs. Bennet, having waited in the hallway to watch for the end of the conversation, no sooner saw Elizabeth open the door and with quick step pass her towards the staircase than she entered the breakfast room and congratulated both him and herself in warm terms on the happy prospect of their nearer connection. Mr. Collins received and returned these with equal pleasure, and then proceeded to relate the particulars of their interview. He said he had every reason to be satisfied, since the refusal which his cousin had steadfastly given him would naturally flow from her bashful modesty and the genuine delicacy of her character.

This information, however, startled Mrs. Bennet. She would have been glad to be equally satisfied that her daughter had meant to encourage him by protesting against his proposals, but she dared not to believe it, and could not help saying so.

"But depend upon it, Mr. Collins," she added, "that Lizzy shall be brought to reason. I will speak to her about it myself directly. She is a very headstrong, foolish girl, and does not know what is best for her, but I will *make* her know it."

"Pardon me for interrupting you, madam," cried Mr. Collins, "but if she is really headstrong and foolish, I know not whether she would altogether be a very desirable wife to a man in my situation, who naturally looks for happiness in the marriage state. If, therefore, she actually persists in rejecting my proposal, perhaps it would be better not to force her into accepting me, because if she indeed has such defects of temper she could not contribute much to my happiness."

"Sir, you quite misunderstand me," said Mrs. Bennet, alarmed. "Lizzy is only headstrong in such matters as these. In everything else she is as good-natured a girl as ever lived. I will go directly to Mr. Bennet and we shall very soon settle it with her, I am sure."

She would not give him time to reply, but hurrying instantly to her husband, called out as she entered the library, "Oh! Mr. Bennet, you are needed immediately; we are all in an uproar. You must come and make Lizzy marry Mr. Collins, for she vows she will not have him, and if you do not hurry he will change his mind and not have *her*."

Mr. Bennet raised his eyes from his book as she entered and fixed them on her face with a calm unconcern which was not in the least altered by her communication.

"I do not have the pleasure of understanding you," said he, when she had finished her speech. "Of what are you talking?"

"Of Mr. Collins and Lizzy. Lizzy declares she will not have Mr. Collins, and Mr. Collins begins to say that he will not have Lizzy."

"And what am I to do on the occasion? It seems like hopeless business."

"Speak to Lizzy about it yourself. Tell her that you insist upon her marrying him."

"Let her be called down. She shall hear my opinion."

Mrs. Bennet rang the bell, and Miss Elizabeth was summoned to the library.

"Come here, child," cried her father as she appeared. " I understand that Mr. Collins has made you an offer of marriage. Is it true?" Elizabeth replied that it was.

Very well. And this offer of marriage you have refused?"

"I have, sir."

"Very well. We now come to the point. Your mother insists upon your accepting it. Is it not so, Mrs. Bennet?"

"Yes, or I will never see her again."

"An unhappy alternative is before you, Elizabeth. From this day you must be a stranger to one of your parents. Your mother will never see you again if you do *not* marry Mr. Collins, and I will never see you again if you *do*."

Elizabeth could not help smiling at such a conclusion of such a beginning, but Mrs. Bennet, who had persuaded herself that her husband was on her side, was excessively disappointed.

"What do you mean, Mr. Bennet, by talking in this way? You promised me to *insist* upon her marrying him."

"My dear," replied her husband, "I have two small favours to request. First, that you will allow me the free use of my intellect on the present occasion; and secondly, of my room. I shall be glad to have the library to myself as soon as may be."

Not yet, however, in spite of her disappointment in her husband, did Mrs. Bennet abandon her purpose. She talked to Elizabeth again and again, alternately coaxing and threatening her. She endeavoured to get Jane on her side, but Jane, with all possible mildness, declined interfering. Elizabeth, sometimes with real earnestness and sometimes with playfulness, replied to her attacks. Though her approach varied, her determination never did.

Mr. Collins, meanwhile, was meditating in solitude on what had happened. He thought too well of himself to understand what motive his cousin could have for refusing him, and though his pride was hurt, he suffered in no other way. His regard for her was quite imaginary, and the possibility of her deserving her mother's reproach prevented his feeling any regret.

While the family was in this confusion, Charlotte Lucas came to spend the day with them. She was met in the hallway by Lydia, who, running to her, cried in a half-whisper, "I am glad you have come, for there is such fun here! What do you think has happened this morning? Mr. Collins has made an offer to Lizzy, and she will not have him."

Charlotte had hardly time to answer before they were joined by Kitty, who came to tell the same news. No sooner had they entered the breakfast room, where Mrs. Bennet was alone, than she likewise began the subject, calling on Miss Lucas for her compassion and entreating her to persuade her friend Lizzy to comply with the wishes of all her family. "Please, my dear Miss Lucas," she added in a melancholy tone, "for nobody is on my side; I am cruelly used, and nobody feels for my poor nerves."

Charlotte's was spared the necessity of replying by the entrance of Jane and Elizabeth.

"Ah, there she comes," continued Mrs. Bennet, "looking as unconcerned as may be, and caring no more for us than if we did not exist, provided she can have her own way. But I tell you what, Miss Lizzy — if you take it into your head to go on refusing every offer of marriage in this way, you will never get a husband at all — and I am sure I do not know who is to support you when your father is dead. *I* shall not be able to — and so I warn you. I am done with you from this very day. I told you in the library, you know, that I should never speak to you again, and you will find me as good as my word. I have no pleasure in talking to disobedient children. Not that I have much pleasure, indeed, in talking to anybody. People who suffer as I do from nervous complaints can have no great interest in talking. Nobody can tell what I suffer! But it is always so. Those who do not complain are never pitied."

Her daughters listened in silence to this speech, aware that any attempt to reason with or sooth her would only increase the irritation. She talked on, therefore, without interruption from any of them, till they were joined by Mr. Collins. He entered with an air more stately than usual, and on perceiving him she said to the girls, "Now, I do insist that you, all of you, hold your tongues, and let Mr. Collins and me have a little conversation together."

Elizabeth quietly left the room. Jane and Kitty followed, but Lydia stood her ground, determined to hear all she could. Charlotte, after being detained by the civility of Mr. Collins, whose inquiries after herself and all her family were very brief, satisfied herself with walking to the window and pretending not to hear. In a distressed voice Mrs. Bennet thus began the projected conversation: — "Oh! Mr. Collins!"

"My dear madam," replied he, "let us be forever silent on this subject. Far be it from me," he continued, in a voice that expressed his displeasure, "to resent the behaviour of your daughter. Accepting inevitable evils is the duty of us all; the particular duty of a young man who has been as fortunate as I have been. Perhaps it is for the best, as I have begun to feel a doubt of my positive happiness had my fair cousin honoured me with her hand. I have often observed that resignation is never so perfect as when the blessing denied begins to lose somewhat of its value in our estimation. You will not, I hope, consider me as showing any disrespect to your family, my dear madam, by thus withdrawing my design without having paid yourself and Mr. Bennet the compliment of requesting you to interpose your authority in my behalf. My conduct may, I fear, be objectionable in having accepted my refusal from your daughter's lips instead of your own. But we all make mistakes. I have certainly meant well through the whole affair. My object has been to secure an amiable companion for myself, with due consideration for the advantage of all your family, and if my *civility* has been at all reprehensible, I here beg leave to apologise."

CHAPTER 21

The discussion of Mr. Collins's offer was now nearly at an end, and Elizabeth had only to suffer from the uncomfortable feelings surrounding it and occasionally from some derogatory comment by her mother. As for the gentleman himself, *his* feelings were chiefly expressed not by embarrassment or dejection or by trying to avoid her, but by stiffness of manner and resentful silence. He hardly spoke to her, and the attentions which he had been paying her were transferred for the rest of the day to Miss Lucas, whose civility in listening to him was a timely relief to them all, and especially to her friend.

The next day produced no change in Mrs. Bennet's ill-humour or ill-health. Mr. Collins was also in the same state of angry pride. Elizabeth had hoped that his resentment might shorten his visit, but his plan did not appear in the least affected by it. He intended to leave on Saturday, and until Saturday he still meant to stay.

After breakfast the girls walked to Meryton to inquire if Mr. Wickham were returned, and to lament over his absence from the Netherfield ball. He joined them on their entering the town and walked them to their aunt's, where his regret and frustration, and the concern of everybody, was well talked over. To Elizabeth, however, he voluntarily acknowledged that the necessity of his absence *had* been self-imposed.

"I found," said he, "as the time drew near, that I had better not meet Mr. Darcy; that to be in the same room, the same party with him for so many hours together, might be more than I could bear, and that scenes might arise unpleasant to more than myself."

She highly approved his forbearance, and they had time for a full discussion of it as Wickham and another officer walked back with them to Longbourn. During the walk he paid particularly attention to her. His accompanying them was a double advantage; she felt the compliment it offered to herself, and it was most acceptable as an occasion of introducing him to her father and mother.

Soon after their return a letter was delivered to Miss Bennet; it came from Netherfield, and was opened immediately. The envelope contained a sheet of elegant paper, well covered with a lady's fair, flowing hand. Elizabeth saw her sister's countenance change as she read it, and saw her dwelling intently on some particular passages. Jane recollected herself soon, and, putting the letter away, tried to join with her usual cheerfulness in the general conversation. But Elizabeth felt an anxiety on the subject which drew her attention even from Wickham. No sooner had he and his companion departed than a glance from Jane invited her to follow her upstairs. When they had reached their room, Jane, taking out the letter, said, "This is from Caroline Bingley; what it contains has surprised me a great deal. The whole party have left Netherfield by this time, and are on their way to town — and without any intention of coming back again. You shall hear what she says."

She then read the first sentence aloud, which comprised the information of their having just resolved to follow their brother to town directly, and of their meaning to dine that day in Grosvenor street, where Mr. Hurst had a house. The next was in these words: "I do not pretend to regret anything I shall leave in Hertfordshire except your company, my dearest friend; but we will hope, at some future period, to enjoy again the delightful friendship we have known, and in the meantime may lessen the pain of separation by a very frequent and most unreserved correspondence. I am counting on you for that." To these expressions Elizabeth listened with total distrust; and though the suddenness of their removal surprised her, she saw nothing in it really to lament. It was not to be supposed that their absence from Netherfield would prevent Mr. Bingley's being there, and as to the loss of their company, she was persuaded that Jane must soon cease to care about it, in the enjoyment of his.

"It is unfortunate," said she, after a short pause, "that you are unable to see your friends before they leave the area. But may we not hope that the period of future happiness to which Miss Bingley looks forward may arrive sooner than she is aware, and that the delightful friendship between you will be renewed with yet greater satisfaction once you are married? Mr. Bingley will not be detained in London by them."

"Caroline decidedly says that none of the party will return to Hertfordshire this winter. I will read it to you.

"'When my brother left us yesterday, he imagined that the business which took him to London might be concluded in three or four days. But as we are certain it cannot be so, and at the same time convinced that when Charles gets to town he will be in no hurry to leave it again, we have determined on following him there, that he may not be obliged to stay in a comfortless hotel. Many of my acquaintance are already there for the winter. I wish I could hear that you, my dearest friend, had an intention of making one in the crowd — but of that I despair. I sincerely hope your Christmas in Hertfordshire may abound in the happiness which that season generally brings, and that the gentlemen you associate with will be so numerous as to prevent your feeling the loss of the three of whom we shall deprive you."

"It is evident by this," added Jane, "that he will come back no more this winter."

"It is only evident that Miss Bingley does not want him to."

"Why do you think that? It must be his own doing. He is his own master. But you do not know *all*. I *will* read you the passage which particularly hurts me. I will keep no secrets from *you*."

"'Mr. Darcy is impatient to see his sister; and, to confess the truth, *we* are scarcely less eager to meet her again. I really do not think Georgiana Darcy has her equal for beauty, elegance, and accomplishments. The affection she inspires in Louisa and myself is heightened into something still more interesting from the hope we dare to entertain of her being hereafter married to my brother. I do not know whether I ever before mentioned to you my feelings on this subject, but I will not leave without confiding them, and I trust you will not think them unreasonable. My brother admires her greatly already; he will have frequent opportunity now of seeing her. Her relations all wish for the connection as much as his own, and a sister's bias is not misleading me, I think, when I call Charles most capable of engaging any woman's heart. With all these circumstances to favour an attachment, and nothing to prevent it, am I wrong, my dearest Jane, in indulging the hope of an event which will secure the happiness of so many?"

"What do you think of *this* sentence, my dear Lizzy?" said Jane as she finished it. "Is it not clear enough? Does it not expressly declare that Caroline neither expects nor wishes me to be her sister-in-law, that she is perfectly convinced of her brother's indifference, and that if she suspects the nature of my feelings for him she intends (most kindly!) to put me on my guard? Can there be any other opinion on the subject?"

"Yes, there can; for mine is totally different. Will you hear it?"

"Most willingly."

"You shall have it in few words. Miss Bingley sees that her brother is in love with you, and wants him to marry Miss Darcy. She follows him to town in the hope of keeping him there, and tries to persuade you that he does not care about you."

Jane shook her head.

"Indeed, Jane, you ought to believe me. No one who has ever seen you together can doubt his affection. Miss Bingley, I am sure, cannot. She is not such a simpleton. Could she have seen half as much love in Mr. Darcy for herself, she would have ordered her wedding dress. But the case is this: we are not rich enough or grand enough for them, and she is anxious to get Miss Darcy for her brother from the notion that when there has been *one* family alliance, she may have less trouble in achieving a second. There is certainly some ingenuity in her plan, and I dare say it would succeed if Miss de Bourgh were out of the way. But, my dearest Jane, you cannot seriously imagine that because Miss Bingley tells you her brother greatly admires Miss Darcy, he is in the smallest degree less aware of *your* merit than when he saw you on Tuesday. Do not believe it is in her power to persuade him that instead of being in love with you he is very much in love with her friend."

"If we thought alike of Miss Bingley," replied Jane, "your representation of all this might make me feel much better. But I know the foundation is unjust. Caroline is incapable of wilfully deceiving anyone, and all that I can hope in this case is that she is deceived herself."

"That is right. You could not have come up with a better explanation, since you will not take comfort in mine. Believe her to be deceived, by all means. You have now absolved her of guilt, and must fret no longer."

"But, my dear sister, can I be happy, even supposing the best, in accepting a man whose sisters and friends are all want him to marry someone else?"

"You must decide for yourself," said Elizabeth; "and if you find that the misery of offending his two sisters is enough to overcome the happiness of being his wife, I advise you by all means to refuse him."

"How can you speak so?" said Jane, faintly smiling. "You must know that though I should be exceedingly grieved at their disapproval, I could not hesitate."

"I did not think you would: and that being the case, I cannot consider your situation with much compassion."

"But if he returns no more this winter, my choice will never be required. A thousand things may arise in six months!"

The idea of his returning no more Elizabeth treated with the utmost contempt. It appeared to her merely the suggestion of Caroline's wishes, and she could not for a moment suppose that those wishes, however openly or artfully spoken, could influence a young man so totally independent of everyone.

She expressed to her sister as forcibly as possible what she felt on the subject, and had soon the pleasure of seeing its happy effect. Jane was gradually led to hope that Bingley would return to Netherfield and answer every wish of her heart.

Mrs. Bennet, when she heard of the departure of the family, bemoaned it as exceedingly unlucky that the ladies should happen to go away just as they were all getting to know each other. At some length, she had the consolation of thinking that Mr. Bingley would be soon down again and soon dining at Longbourn. The conclusion of all was the comfortable declaration that, though he had been invited only to a small family dinner, she would make sure there were two full courses.

CHAPTER 22

The Bennets were planning to dine with the Lucases, and again during the greater part of the day Miss Lucas was so kind as to listen to Mr. Collins. Elizabeth took an opportunity of thanking her. "It keeps him in good humour," said she, "and I am more obliged to you than I can express." Charlotte assured her friend of her satisfaction in being useful, and that it amply repaid her for the little sacrifice of her time. This was true, but Charlotte's kindness extended farther than Elizabeth knew; its object was nothing else than to save her from any return of Mr. Collins's proposals by engaging them towards herself. Such was Miss Lucas's scheme, and it was going so well that when they parted at night she would have felt almost sure of success if he had not been to leave Hertfordshire so very soon. But here she did injustice to his character, for it led him to escape out of Longbourn House the next morning with admirable slyness, and hasten to Lucas Lodge to throw himself at her feet. He was anxious to avoid the notice of his cousins, from a conviction that if they saw him depart they could not fail to guess his plan. He was not willing to have the attempt known till its success could be known likewise. Though feeling almost secure, and with reason, for Charlotte had been tolerably encouraging, he was comparatively cautious since the adventure of Wednesday. His reception, however, was of the most flattering kind. Miss Lucas saw him from an upper window as he walked towards the house and instantly set out to meet him accidentally in the lane. But little had she dared to hope that so much love and eloquence awaited her there.

In as short a time as Mr. Collins's long speeches would allow, everything was settled between them to the satisfaction of both. As they entered the house he earnestly entreated her to name the wedding day, and though such a request must be delayed for the present, the lady felt no inclination to toy with his happiness. The dullness with which he was favoured by nature must prevent his courtship from having the sort of charm that could make a woman wish for its continuance. Miss Lucas, who accepted him solely from the pure and disinterested desire of financial security, cared not how soon that security was gained.

Sir William and Lady Lucas were speedily applied to for their consent, and it was bestowed with joy. Mr. Collins's present circumstances made it a most suitable match for their daughter, to whom they could give little fortune, and his prospects of future wealth were exceedingly promising. Lady Lucas began directly to calculate, with more interest than the matter had ever excited before, how many years longer Mr. Bennet was likely to live. Sir William gave it as his decided opinion that, whenever Mr. Collins should be in possession of the Longbourn estate, it would be a good idea for both he and his wife to make their appearance at St. James's. The whole family, in short, were properly overjoyed on the occasion. The younger girls formed hopes of *coming out* a year or two sooner than they might otherwise have done; and the boys were relieved from their worries of Charlotte's dying an old maid and always requiring their financial support. Charlotte herself was tolerably composed. She had gained her point, and had time to consider it. Her thoughts were in general satisfactory. Mr. Collins, to be sure, was neither intelligent nor amiable; his company was tedious, and his love for her must be imaginary. But still he would be her husband. Without thinking highly either of men or of matrimony, marriage had always been her object; it was the only honourable provision for well-educated young women of small fortune, and however uncertain of giving happiness must be their best escape from poverty. This escape she had now obtained; and at the age of twenty-seven, without having ever been beautiful, she felt all the good luck of it. The least agreeable circumstance in the business was the surprise it must give to Elizabeth Bennet, whose friendship she valued beyond that of any other person. Elizabeth would wonder, and probably would disapprove of her decision; and though her resolve could not to be shaken, her feelings must be hurt by such condemnation. She resolved to give her the information herself, and therefore told Mr. Collins, when he returned to Longbourn to dinner, to drop no hint of what had passed before any of the family. A promise of secrecy was of course readily given, but it could not be kept without difficulty. The curiosity excited by his long absence burst forth in such very direct questions on his return as required some skill to evade. He was at the same time exercising great self-denial, for he was longing to tell the world of his successful love.

As he was to begin his journey too early the next morning to see any of the family, the goodbyes were said the evening before. Mrs. Bennet, with great politeness and cordiality, said how happy they should be to see him at Longbourn again whenever his other responsibilities might allow him to visit them.

"My dear madam," he replied, "this invitation is particularly gratifying, because it is what I have been hoping to receive. You may be very certain that I shall accept it it as soon as possible."

They were all astonished; and Mr. Bennet, who could by no means wish for so speedy a return, immediately said —

"But is there no danger of Lady Catherine's disapproval here, my good sir? It would be better to neglect your relations than run the risk of offending your patroness."

"My dear sir," replied Mr. Collins, "I am particularly obliged to you for this friendly caution, and you may depend upon my not taking such a step without her ladyship's consent."

"You cannot be too careful. Risk anything rather than her displeasure. If you find it likely to be raised by your coming to us again, which I should think exceedingly probable, stay quietly at home, and be satisfied that *we* shall take no offence."

"Believe me, my dear sir, my gratitude is warmly excited by such affectionate attention. Depend upon it, you will speedily receive from me a letter of thanks for this, as well as f every other hospitality during my stay in Hertfordshire. As for my fair cousins, though my absence may not be long enough to render it necessary, I shall now take the liberty of wishing them health and happiness, not excepting my cousin Elizabeth."

With proper civilities the ladies then withdrew, all of them equally surprised to find that he was planning a quick return. Mrs. Bennet wished to understand by it that he thought of proposing to one of her younger girls, and Mary might have been prevailed on to accept him. She rated his abilities much higher than any of the others. There was something in his reflections which struck her. Though by no means so clever as herself, she thought that if encouraged to read and improve himself by such an example as hers, he might become a very agreeable companion. But on the following morning, every hope of this kind was done away. Miss Lucas visited soon after breakfast, and in a private conference with Elizabeth related the events of the day before.

The possibility of Mr. Collins's fancying himself in love with her friend had occurred to Elizabeth within the last day or two. But that Charlotte could encourage him seemed almost as far from possibility as that she could encourage him herself, and her astonishment was consequently so great as to overcome at first the bounds of civility. She could not help crying out —

"Engaged to Mr. Collins! My dear Charlotte, impossible!"

The steadiness with which Miss Lucas had told her story gave way to a momentary confusion here on receiving such direct criticism. Although, as it was no more than she expected, she soon regained her composure, and calmly replied —

"Why should you be surprised, my dear Eliza? Do you think it impossible that Mr. Collins should be able to procure any woman's good opinion because he was not so happy as to succeed with you?"

But Elizabeth had now composed herself, and was able to assure her with tolerable firmness that the prospect of their relationship was highly gratifying to her, and that she wished her all imaginable happiness.

"I see what you are feeling," replied Charlotte. "You must be surprised, very much surprised — since Mr. Collins was so recently wishing to marry you. But when you have had time to think it all over, I hope you will be satisfied with what I have done. I am not romantic, you know; I never was. I ask only a comfortable home; and considering Mr. Collins's character, connections, and situation in life, I am convinced that my chance of happiness with him is as fair as most people can boast on entering the marriage state."

Elizabeth quietly answered "Undoubtedly," and after an awkward pause they returned to the rest of the family. Charlotte did not stay much longer, and Elizabeth was then left to reflect on what she had heard. It was a long time before she became at all reconciled to the idea of so unsuitable a match. The strangeness of Mr. Collins's making two offers of marriage within three days was nothing in comparison of his being now accepted. She had always felt that Charlotte's opinion of matrimony was not exactly like her own, but she could not have supposed it possible that she would have sacrificed every better feeling to financial advantage. Charlotte as the wife of Mr. Collins was a most humiliating picture! And to the pain of a friend disgracing herself was added the distressing conviction that it was impossible for that friend to be tolerably happy in the life she had chosen.

CHAPTER 23

Elizabeth was sitting with her mother and sisters, reflecting on what she had heard and doubting whether she was authorised to mention it, when Sir William Lucas himself appeared. He had been sent by his daughter to announce her engagement to the family. With many compliments to them, and much self-congratulation on the prospect of a connection between the two families, he unfolded the matter. His audience was not merely wondering, but disbelieving. Mrs. Bennet, with more perseverance than politeness, protested he must be entirely mistaken; and Lydia, always unguarded and often uncivil, boisterously exclaimed —

"Good Lord! Sir William, how can you tell such a story? Do you not know that Mr. Collins wants to marry Lizzy?"

Nothing less than the good manners of a gentleman could have borne without anger such treatment, but Sir William's good-breeding carried him through it all. Though he was certain about the truth of his information, he listened to all their protestations with the most patient courtesy.

Elizabeth, feeling it her duty to relieve him from so unpleasant a situation, now confirmed his account, by mentioning her prior knowledge of it from Charlotte herself. She endeavoured to put a stop to the exclamations of her mother and sisters by the earnestness of her congratulations to Sir William, in which she was readily joined by Jane. She also added a variety of remarks on the happiness that might be expected from the match, the excellent character of Mr. Collins, and the convenient distance of Hunsford from London.

Mrs. Bennet was, in fact, too much overpowered to say a great deal while Sir William remained; but no sooner had he left them than her feelings found a rapid vent. In the first place, she persisted in disbelieving the whole of the matter; secondly, she was very sure that Mr. Collins had been tricked; thirdly, she trusted that they would never be happy together;

and fourthly, that the match might be broken off. Two things were certain however: first, that Elizabeth was the real cause of all the mischief; and second, that she herself had been barbarously used by them all. On these two points she dwelt throughout the rest of the day. Nothing could console and nothing appease her. Nor did that day exhaust her resentment. A week passed before she could see Elizabeth without scolding her, a month before she could speak to Sir William or Lady Lucas without being rude, and many months before she could at all forgive their daughter.

Mr. Bennet's emotions were much more tranquil on the occasion. It gratified him, he said, to discover that Charlotte Lucas, whom he had been used to think tolerably intelligent, was as foolish as his wife, and more foolish than his daughter!

Jane confessed herself a little surprised at the match, but she said less of her astonishment than of her earnest desire for their happiness; nor could Elizabeth persuade her to consider it unlikely. Kitty and Lydia were far from envying Miss Lucas, for Mr. Collins was only a clergyman. It affected them in no other way than as a piece of news to spread at Meryton.

Lady Lucas could not but feel a sense of triumph on being able to boast to Mrs. Bennet about the comfort of having a daughter well married. She called at Longbourn rather oftener than usual to say how happy she was, though Mrs. Bennet's sour looks and ill-natured remarks should have been enough to drive happiness away.

Between Elizabeth and Charlotte there was a restraint which kept them mutually silent on the subject. Elizabeth felt persuaded that no real closeness could ever exist between them again. Her disappointment in Charlotte made her turn with fonder regard to her sister, of whose good character she was sure her opinion could never be shaken. She grew daily more anxious for her sister's happiness, however, as Bingley had now been gone a week, and nothing was heard of his return.

Jane had sent Caroline an early answer to her letter, and was counting the days till she might reasonably hope to hear again. The promised letter of thanks from Mr. Collins arrived on Tuesday, addressed to their father, and written with all the gratitude which a year's stay with the family might have justified. He then proceeded to inform them, with many joyful expressions, of his happiness in having obtained the affection of their neighbour, Miss Lucas, and then explained that it was merely with the view of spending time with her that he had been so ready to accept their kind invitation to see him again at Longbourn. He hoped to be able to return two weeks from Monday, for Lady Catherine, he added, so heartily approved his marriage that she wished it to take place as soon as possible. He trusted this would be an unanswerable argument with his amiable Charlotte to name an early day for making him the happiest of men.

Mr. Collins' return to Hertfordshire was no longer a matter of pleasure to Mrs. Bennet. On the contrary, she complained of it as much as her husband. It was very strange that he should come to Longbourn instead of to Lucas Lodge; it was also very inconvenient and exceedingly troublesome. She hated having visitors in the house while her health was so poor, and lovers were of all people the most disagreeable. Such were the gentle murmurs of Mrs. Bennet, and they gave way only to the greater distress of Mr. Bingley's continued absence.

Neither Jane nor Elizabeth were comfortable on this subject. Day after day passed away without bringing any other tidings of him than the news which had begun to circulate in Meryton of his coming no more to Netherfield the whole winter. This report angered Mrs. Bennet, and she never failed to contradict it as a most scandalous falsehood.

Even Elizabeth began to fear — not that Bingley was indifferent — but that his sisters would be successful in keeping him away. Unwilling as she was to believe an idea so destructive of Jane's happiness, and so dishonourable to the devotion of her lover, she could not prevent its frequently recurring. The united efforts of his two unfeeling sisters and of his overpowering friend, assisted by the attractions of Miss Darcy and the amusements of London, might be too much, she feared, for the strength of his attachment.

As for Jane, *her* anxiety was, of course, more painful than Elizabeth's; but whatever she felt she was desirous of concealing, and between herself and Elizabeth, therefore, the subject was never brought up. But as no such concerns restrained her mother, an hour seldom passed in which she did not talk of Bingley, express her impatience for his arrival, or even require Jane to confess that if he did not come back, she should think herself very ill used. It required all Jane's steady mildness to bear these attacks.

Mr. Collins returned most punctually, but his reception at Longbourn was not quite as gracious as it had been on his first introduction. He was too happy, however, to need much attention; and, luckily for the others, the time he spent with Charlotte relieved them from a great deal of his company. The better part of every day was spent by him at Lucas Lodge, and he sometimes returned to Longbourn only in time to make an apology for his absence before the family went to bed.

Mrs. Bennet was really in a most pitiable state. The very mention of anything concerning the match threw her into agony, and wherever she went she was sure of hearing it talked of. The sight of Miss Lucas was abhorrent to her. As in the future mistress of her house, she regarded Charlotte with jealous abhorrence. Whenever she came to see them, Mrs. Bennet was convinced she was simply anticipating the hour of possession. Whenever she spoke in a low voice to Mr. Collins, she was convinced that they were talking of the Longbourn estate and resolving to turn herself and her daughters out of the house as soon as Mr. Bennet was dead. She complained bitterly of all this to her husband.

"Indeed, Mr. Bennet," said she, "it is very painful to think that Charlotte Lucas will ever be mistress of this house, that *I* should be forced to make way for *her*, and live to see her take my place in it!"

"My dear, do not give in to such gloomy thoughts. Let us hope for better things. Let us flatter ourselves that *I* will outlive you."

This was not very consoling to Mrs. Bennet, and therefore, instead of making any answer, she went on as before—

"I cannot bear to think that they should have all this estate. If it was not for the entail, I should not mind it."

"What should not you mind?"

"I should not mind anything at all."

"Let us be thankful that you are preserved from a state."

"I never can be thankful, Mr. Bennet, for anything about the entail. How anyone could have the conscience to entail away an estate from one's own daughters, I cannot understand; and all for the sake of Mr. Collins too! Why should *he* have it more than anybody else?"

"I leave it to yourself to determine," said Mr. Bennet.

CHAPTER 24

Miss Bingley's letter arrived, and put an end to doubt. The very first sentence conveyed the assurance of their being all settled in London for the winter, and concluded with her brother's regret at not having had time to pay his respects to his friends in Hertfordshire before he left the country.

Hope was over, entirely over. When Jane found the strength to read the rest of the letter, she found little, except the professed affection of the writer, that could give her any comfort. Miss Darcy's praise occupied the greater part of it. Her many attractions were again dwelt on, and Caroline boasted joyfully of their increasing closeness, venturing to predict the surety of the match between Miss Darcy and her brother. She wrote also with great pleasure of her brother's being a guest in Mr. Darcy's house, and mentioned with raptures some plans in regard to new furniture.

Elizabeth, to whom Jane very soon communicated all this, heard it in silent indignation. Her heart was divided between concern for her sister and resentment against all the others. To Caroline's claim of her brother's interest in Miss Darcy she gave no heed. That he was really fond of Jane, she doubted no more than she had ever done. Much as she had always liked him, she could not think without anger on that easiness of temper which now made him the slave of his manipulative friends and family. Had his own happiness been the only sacrifice, he might have been allowed to do as he pleased; but her sister's was involved in it, as she thought he must be aware himself. It was a subject, in short, on which reflection would be long indulged, but nothing could ever come of it. She thought of little else; and yet, whether Bingley's regard had really died away, or was suppressed by the interference of others, her sister's situation remained the same.

A day or two passed before Jane had courage to speak of her feelings to Elizabeth. On Mrs. Bennet's leaving them together, after a longer tirade than usual about Netherfield and its master, she could not help saying —

"Oh that my dear mother had more command over herself! She can have no idea of the pain she gives me by her continual complaints about him. But I will not succumb to grief. It cannot last long. He will be forgotten, and we shall all be as we were before."

Elizabeth looked at her sister with disbelief, but said nothing.

"You doubt me," cried Jane, slightly colouring. "Indeed you have no reason. He may live in my memory as the most amiable man of my acquaintance, but that is all. I have nothing either to hope or fear, and nothing to criticize him for. A little time therefore — I shall certainly try to get over it."

With a stronger voice she soon added, "I have this comfort at present, that it has not been more than a misunderstanding on my side, and that it has done no harm to anyone but myself."

"My dear Jane!" exclaimed Elizabeth, "you are too good. Your sweetness and disinterestedness are really angelic; I do not know what to say to you. I feel as if I had never done you justice, or loved you as you deserve."

Miss Bennet eagerly rejected her compliments, and threw back the praise on her sister.

"No," said Elizabeth, "this is not fair. You wish to think all the world respectable, and are hurt if I speak ill of anybody. I only want to think you perfect, and you reject my every attempt. It is certain that I shall never be as good as you. There are few people whom I really love, and still fewer of whom I think well. The more I see of the world, the more am I dissatisfied with it. Every day confirms my belief of the inconsistency of everyone, and of the little confidence that can be placed on the appearance of either merit or sense. I have met with two instances lately: one I will not mention, the other is Charlotte's marriage. It is nonsensical! In every view it is nonsensical!"

"My dear Lizzy, do not give in to such feelings as these. They will ruin your happiness. You are not taking into account differences of situation and temper. Consider Mr. Collins's respectability, and Charlotte's prudent, steady character. Remember that she comes from a large family; that as to fortune it is a most suitable match; and be ready to believe, for everybody's sake, that she may feel something like regard and esteem for our cousin."

"To oblige you, I would try to believe almost anything, but no one else could be benefited by such a belief as this. Were I persuaded that Charlotte had any regard for him, I should only think worse of her intelligence than I now do of her heart. My dear Jane, Mr. Collins is a conceited, pompous, narrow-minded, silly man. You know he is; and you must feel, as well as I do, that the woman who marries him cannot be thinking straight. You shall not defend her, though it is Charlotte Lucas. You shall not, for the sake of one individual, change the meaning of principle and integrity, nor endeavour to persuade yourself or me that selfishness is prudence."

"I must think your language too strong in speaking of both," replied Jane, "and I hope you will be convinced of it by seeing them happy together. But enough of this. You hinted at something else. You mentioned *two* instances. I cannot misunderstand you, but I beg you, dear Lizzy, not to pain me by thinking *that person* to blame, and saying your opinion of him is sunk. We must not be so ready to believe ourselves intentionally injured. We must not expect a lively young man to always be guarded and careful. It is very often nothing but our own vanity that deceives us. Women believe admiration means more than it does."

"And men give them every reason to!"

"If it is purposely done, their guilt cannot be absolved; but I had no idea there was as much cunning in the world as some persons imagine."

"I am far from attributing any part of Mr. Bingley's conduct to cunning," said Elizabeth, "but without scheming to do wrong, or to make others unhappy, there may be error, and there may be misery. Thoughtlessness, lack of attention to other people's feelings, and lack of resolution, will do the business."

"And do you attribute it to either of those?'

"Yes; to the last. But if I go on, I shall displease you by saying what I think of persons you esteem. Stop me while you can."

"You persist, then, in supposing his sisters influence him."

"Yes, in conjunction with his friend."

"I cannot believe it. Why should they try to influence him? They can only wish his happiness; and if he is attached to me, no other woman can secure it."

"Your first position is false. They may wish many things besides his happiness; they may wish his increase of wealth and consequence; they may wish him to marry a girl who has money, great connections, and pride."

"Beyond a doubt they *do* wish him to choose Miss Darcy," replied Jane, "but this may be from better feelings than you are supposing. They have known her much longer than they have known me: no wonder if they love her better. But, whatever may be their own wishes, it is very unlikely they should have opposed their brother's. What sister would think herself at liberty to do it, unless there were something very objectionable? If they believed him attached to me, they would not try to part us; if he were so, they could not succeed. By supposing such an affection, you make everybody acting unnaturally and wrong, and me most unhappy. Do not distress me by the idea. I am not ashamed of having been mistaken — or, at least, it is slight, it is nothing in comparison to what I should feel in thinking ill of him or his sisters. Let me see it in the best light, in the light in which it may be understood."

Elizabeth could not oppose such a wish, and from this time Mr. Bingley's name was scarcely ever mentioned between them.

Mrs. Bennet still continued to wonder and complain about his returning no more, and though a day seldom passed in which Elizabeth did not explain the matter clearly, there seemed little chance of her ever considering it with less perplexity. Her daughter endeavoured to convince her of what she did not believe herself, that his attentions to Jane had been merely the effect of a common and transient liking, which ceased when he saw her no more. Though the probability of the statement was acknowledged at the time, she had the same story to repeat every day. Mrs. Bennet's best comfort was that Mr. Bingley would return in the summer.

Mr. Bennet treated the matter differently. "So, Lizzy," said he one day, "your sister has been rejected, it seems. I congratulate her. Next to being married, a girl likes to be a little heartbroken now and then. It is something to think of, and gives her a sort of distinction among her companions. When is your turn to come? You certainly don't want to be outdone by Jane. Now is your time. There are officers enough at Meryton to disappoint all the young ladies in the country. Let Wickham be your man. He is a pleasant fellow, and would jilt you thoroughly."

"Thank you, sir, but a less agreeable man would satisfy me. We must not all expect Jane's good fortune."

"True," said Mr. Bennet, "but it is a comfort to think that if something of that kind may happen, you have an affectionate mother who will always make the most of it."

Mr. Wickham's company helped to dispel the gloom which recent events had bestowed on many of the Longbourn family. They saw him often, and to his other recommendations was now added that of general unreserve. The whole of what Elizabeth had already heard, his claims on Mr. Darcy, and all that he had suffered from him, was now openly acknowledged and publicly known. Everybody was pleased to think how much they had always disliked Mr. Darcy before they had known anything of the matter.

Miss Bennet was the only creature who could suppose there might be any extenuating circumstances in the case, unknown to the society of Hertfordshire. Her mild and steady nature always pleaded for allowances, and urged the possibility of mistakes — but by everybody else Mr. Darcy was condemned as the worst of men.

CHAPTER 25

After a week spent in declarations of love and schemes of happiness, Mr. Collins was removed from his amiable Charlotte by the arrival of Saturday. The pain of separation, however, was reduced on his side by preparations for the reception of his bride. He had reason to hope that, shortly after his next return into Hertfordshire, the day would be decided upon that was to make him the happiest of men. He left his relations at Longbourn with as much ceremony as before, wishing his fair cousins health and happiness and promising their father another letter of thanks.

On the following Monday Mrs. Bennet had the pleasure of receiving her brother and his wife, who came as usual to spend Christmas at Longbourn. Mr. Gardiner was an intelligent, gentlemanlike man, greatly superior to his sister in both disposition and education. The Netherfield ladies would have had difficulty in believing that a man who lived by commerce, and within view of his own stores, could have been so agreeable. Mrs. Gardiner, who was several years younger than Mrs. Bennet and Mrs. Philips, was an amiable, elegant woman, and a great favourite with all her Longbourn nieces. Between the two eldest and herself especially there existed a very warm relationship. They had frequently stayed with her in town.

The first part of Mrs. Gardiner's business on her arrival was to distribute her presents and describe the newest fashions. When this was done she had a less active part to play, and it became her turn to listen. Mrs. Bennet had many grievances to relate, and much to complain of. They had all been very ill-used since she last saw her sister. Two of her girls had been on the point of marriage, but it came to nothing.

"I do not blame Jane," she continued, "for Jane would have married Mr. Bingley if he had asked. But Lizzy! Oh, sister! It is mortifying to think that she might have been Mr. Collins's wife by this time, had not it been for her own obstinacy. He made her an offer in this very room, and she refused him. The consequence of it is that Lady Lucas will have a daughter married before I have, and that Longbourn estate is just as much entailed as ever. The Lucases are very cunning people indeed, sister. They think only of what they can get. I am sorry to say it of them, but so it is. It agitates my nerves and affects my health to be thwarted so in my own family, and to have neighbours who think of themselves before anybody else. However, your coming just at this time is the greatest of comforts, and I am very glad to hear what you tell us of the latest fashions."

Mrs. Gardiner, to whom the greater part of this news had been given before, in the course of Jane and Elizabeth's correspondence with her, made her sister a slight answer, and, in compassion to her nieces, changed the topic.

When alone with Elizabeth afterwards she spoke more on the subject. "It seems likely to have been a desirable match for Jane," said she. "I am sorry it did not work out. But these things happen so often! A young man, such as you describe Mr. Bingley, so easily falls in love with a pretty girl for a few weeks, and when chance separates them, he easily forgets her."

"An excellent consolation in its way," said Elizabeth, "but it will not do for *us*. We do not suffer due to *chance*. It does not often happen that the interference of friends will persuade a young man of independent fortune to think no more of a girl whom he was violently in love with only a few days before."

"But that expression of 'violently in love' is so overused and cliché that it tells me very little. It is as often applied to feelings which arise from an hour's acquaintance as to a real, strong attachment. Tell me, how *violent was* Mr. Bingley's love?"

"I never saw a more promising inclination. He was growing quite inattentive to other people, and wholly taken in by her. Every time they met it was more decided and remarkable. At his own ball he offended two or three young ladies by not asking them to dance; and I spoke to him twice myself without receiving an answer. Could there be clearer symptoms? Is not general rudeness the very essence of love?"

"Oh, yes! Of that kind of love which I suppose him to have felt. Poor Jane! I am sorry for her, because, with her disposition, she may not get over it immediately. It would have been better if it had happened to *you*, Lizzy; you would have laughed yourself out of it sooner. But do you think she would be prevailed on to go back with us? A change of scene might help — and perhaps a little relief from home may be as useful as anything."

Elizabeth was exceedingly pleased with this proposal, and felt persuaded of her sister's ready acceptance.

"I hope," added Mrs. Gardiner, "that no consideration with regard to this young man will influence her. We live in so different a part of town, all our connections are so different, and, as you well know, we go out so little, that it is very improbable they should meet at all, unless he comes to see her."

"And *that* is quite impossible; for he is now in the custody of his friend, and Mr. Darcy would not allow him to call on Jane in such a part of London! My dear aunt, how could you think of it? Mr. Darcy may, perhaps, have *heard* of such a place as Gracechurch Street, but he would hardly think a month of bathing enough to cleanse him from its impurities, were he once to enter it. And, depend upon it, Mr. Bingley never goes anywhere without him."

"Even better. I hope they will not meet at all. But Jane corresponds with the sister, does she not? *She* will not be able to help visiting."

"She will drop the acquaintance entirely."

But in spite of the certainty in which Elizabeth affected to place this point, as well as the still more interesting one of Bingley's being withheld from seeing Jane, she felt a peace on the subject which convinced her, on examination, that she did not consider it entirely hopeless. It was possible, and sometimes she thought it probable, that his affection might be reawakened, and the influence of his friends successfully combated by the more natural influence of Jane's attractions.

Miss Bennet accepted her aunt's invitation with pleasure, and the Bingleys were no more in her thoughts at the time than as she hoped that, by Caroline's not living in the same house with her brother, she might occasionally spend a morning with her without any danger of seeing him.

The Gardiners stayed a week at Longbourn. Mrs. Bennet had so carefully provided for the entertainment of her brother and sister that they did not once sit down to a family dinner. When they dined at home, some of the officers always joined them — of which Mr. Wickham was sure to be one. On these occasions Mrs. Gardiner, suspicious of Elizabeth's warm recommendation of him, narrowly observed them both. Without believing them, from what she saw, to be very seriously in love, their preference of each other was plain enough to make her a little uneasy. She resolved to speak to Elizabeth on the subject before she left Hertfordshire, and represent to her the foolishness of encouraging such an attachment.

There was one benefit to Wickham's company, however. Mrs. Gardiner had seen Pemberley, and known the late Mr. Darcy by character perfectly well. She had spent a considerable time in that part of Derbyshire, and she and Wickham had, therefore, many acquaintances in common. Here consequently was an inexhaustible subject of conversation. In comparing her recollection of Pemberley with the detailed description which Wickham could give, and in bestowing her tribute of praise on the character of Darcy's father, she was delighting both him and herself. On being made acquainted with the present Mr. Darcy's treatment of him, she recollected having heard Mr. Fitzwilliam Darcy formerly spoken of as a very proud, ill-natured boy.

CHAPTER 26

Mrs. Gardiner's caution to Elizabeth was punctually and kindly given on the first opportunity she had of speaking to her alone. After honestly telling her what she thought, she thus went on —

"You are too sensible a girl, Lizzy, to fall in love merely because you are warned against it; and therefore I am not afraid of speaking openly. Seriously, be careful. Do not involve yourself or endeavour to involve him in a relationship which the lack of fortune would make so very unwise. I have nothing to say against *him*; he is a most charming young man; and if he had the fortune he ought to have, I would think you could not do better. But as it is, you must not let your emotions run away with you. You have sense, and we all expect you to use it. Your father would depend on *your* resolution and good conduct, I am sure. You must not disappoint your father."

"My dear aunt, this is being serious indeed."

"Yes, and I hope to encourage you to be serious likewise."

"Well, then, you need not be concerned. I will take care of myself, and of Mr. Wickham too. He shall not be in love with me, if I can prevent it."

"Elizabeth, you are not serious now."

"I beg your pardon, I will try again. At present I am not in love with Mr. Wickham; no, I certainly am not. But he is, beyond all comparison, the most agreeable man I ever saw — and if he becomes really attached to me — I believe it would be better if he did not. I see the imprudence of it. Oh! *That* abominable Mr. Darcy! My father's opinion of me does me the greatest honor, and I should be miserable if I were to lose it. My father, however, is partial to Mr. Wickham. In short, my dear aunt, I should be very sorry to be the means of making any of you unhappy. But since we see every day that where there is affection, young people are seldom withheld by immediate lack of fortune from entering into engagements with each other, how can I promise to be wiser than them? All that I can promise you, therefore, is not to be in a hurry. I will not be in a hurry to believe myself the primary subject of his affections. "

"Perhaps it would be a good idea to discourage him from coming here so very often. At least, you should not *encourage* your mother to invite him."

"As I did the other day," said Elizabeth, with a conscious smile. "Very true, it will be wise to refrain from *that*. But do not imagine that he is always here so often. It is because of your visit that he has been so frequently invited this week. You know my mother's ideas about the necessity of constant company for her friends. But really, and upon my honour, I will try to do what I think to be wisest; and now I hope you are satisfied."

Her aunt assured her that she was, and Elizabeth, having thanked her for the kindness of her advice, departed; — a wonderful instance of wisdom being offered on such a point without being resented.

Mr. Collins returned to Hertfordshire soon after the Gardiners and Jane had departed But as he stayed with the Lucases, his arrival was no great inconvenience to Mrs. Bennet. His marriage was now fast approaching, and she repeatedly said, in an ill-natured tone, that she "*wished* they might be happy." Thursday was to be the wedding day, and on Wednesday Miss Lucas paid her farewell visit. When she stood to leave, Elizabeth, ashamed of her mother's ungracious and reluctant good wishes, accompanied her out of the room. As they went downstairs together, Charlotte said —

"I shall count on hearing from you very often, Eliza."

"*That* you certainly shall."

"And I have another favour to ask. Will you come and see me?"

"We shall often meet, I hope, in Hertfordshire."

"I am not likely to leave Kent for some time. Promise me, therefore, to come to Hunsford."

Elizabeth could not refuse, though she imagined little pleasure in the visit.

"My father and Maria are to come to me in March," added Charlotte, "and I hope you will consent to join them. Indeed, Eliza, you will be as welcome to me as either of them."

The wedding took place: the bride and bridegroom set off for Kent from the church door, and everybody had as much to say, or to hear, on the subject as usual. Elizabeth soon heard from her friend, and their correspondence was as regular and frequent as it had ever been, although not quite as open as before. Elizabeth could never address her without feeling that all the comfort of their close friendship was over. She determined to do her part as a correspondent, but it was for the sake of what had been rather than what was. Charlotte's first letters were received with a good deal of eagerness. Elizabeth was curious to know how she would speak of her new home, how she would like Lady Catherine, and how happy she would claim to be. Charlotte wrote cheerfully, seemed surrounded with comforts, and mentioned only those things she found praiseworthy. The house, furniture, neighbourhood, and roads, were all to her taste .Lady Catherine's behaviour was most friendly and obliging. Elizabeth perceived that she must wait for her own visit there to discover the truth.

Jane had already written a few lines to her sister to announce their safe arrival in London, and when she wrote again, Elizabeth hoped it would be in her power to say something of the Bingleys.

Her impatience for this second letter was as well rewarded as impatience generally is. Jane had been a week in town without either seeing or hearing from Caroline. She excused it, however, by supposing that her last letter to her friend from Longbourn had, by some accident, been lost.

"My aunt," she continued, "is going tomorrow into that part of the town, and I shall take the opportunity of visiting Grosvenor Street."

She wrote again when the visit was paid, and she had seen Miss Bingley. "I did not think Caroline in good spirits," were her words, "but she was very glad to see me, and reproached me for giving her no notice of my coming to London. I was right, therefore; my last letter had never reached her. I inquired after their brother, of course. He was well, but so busy with Mr. Darcy that they scarcely ever saw him. I found that Miss Darcy was expected to dinner. I wish I could have seen her. My visit was not long, as Caroline and Mrs. Hurst were going out. I dare say I shall soon see them here."

Elizabeth shook her head over this letter. It convinced her that chance alone could inform Mr. Bingley of her sister's being in town.

Four weeks passed away, and Jane saw nothing of him. She endeavoured to persuade herself that she did not regret it, but she could no longer ignore Miss Bingley's inattention. After waiting at home every morning for two weeks, and inventing every evening a fresh excuse for her, the visitor did at last appear. But the shortness of her stay, and yet more, the alteration of her manner, would allow Jane to deceive herself no longer. The letter which she wrote on this occasion to her sister will prove what she felt.

"My dearest Lizzy will, I am sure, be incapable of boasting about her better judgment, at my expense, when I confess that I have been entirely deceived in Miss Bingley's regard for me. But, my dear sister, though events have proved you right, do not think me obstinate if I still claim that, considering what her behaviour was, my confidence was as natural as your suspicion. I do not at all comprehend her reason for wishing to be so friendly with me, but if the same circumstances were to recur, I am sure I should be deceived again. Caroline did not return my visit till yesterday, and not a note, not a line, did I receive in the meantime. When she did come, it was very evident that she had no pleasure in it. She made a slight, formal apology for not visiting before, said not a word of wishing to see me again, and was in every respect so different a creature that when she went away I was perfectly resolved to continue the acquaintance no longer. She was very wrong in singling me out as she did I can safely say that every advance began on her side. But I pity her, because she must feel that she has been acting wrong, and because I am very sure that concern for her brother is the cause of it. I am sure she no longer harbors any fears of her brother's marrying me now, because, if he had at all cared about me, we must have met long, long ago. He knows of my being in town, I am certain, from something she said herself; and yet it would seem, by her manner of talking, as if she wanted to persuade herself that he is really partial to Miss Darcy. I cannot understand it. If I were not afraid of judging harshly, I should be almost tempted to say that there is a strong appearance of deceit in all this. But I will endeavour to banish every painful thought, and think only of what will make me happy — your affection, and the unvarying kindness of my dear uncle and aunt. Let me hear from you very soon. Miss Bingley said something of his never returning to Netherfield again, of giving up the house. We had better not mention it. I am extremely glad that you have such pleasant accounts from our friends at Hunsford. Please go see them, with Sir William and Maria. I am sure you will be very comfortable there. — Your's, etc."

This letter gave Elizabeth some pain, but her spirits returned as she considered that Jane would no longer be duped by the sister at least. All expectation from the brother was now absolutely over. She would not even wish for any renewal of his attentions. His character sunk on every review of it, and as a punishment for him, as well as a possible advantage to Jane, she seriously hoped he might really soon marry Mr. Darcy's sister, as by Wickham's account she would make him abundantly regret what he had thrown away.

Mrs. Gardiner about this time reminded Elizabeth of her promise concerning that gentleman, and required information. Elizabeth had such to send as might rather give contentment to her aunt than to herself. His apparent partiality had subsided; his attentions over. He was the admirer of someone else. Elizabeth could see it and write of it without any great pain. Her heart had been but slightly touched, and her vanity was satisfied with believing that *she* would have been his only choice, had his financial situation permitted it. The sudden acquisition of ten thousand pounds was the most remarkable charm of the young lady to whom he was now becoming better acquainted. But Elizabeth, less clear-sighted perhaps in his case than in Charlotte's, did not condemn him for his wish of financial independence. Nothing, on the contrary, could be more natural; and while able to suppose that it cost him a few struggles to let her go, she was ready to call it a wise and desirable measure for both, and could very sincerely wish him happiness.

All this was acknowledged to Mrs. Gardiner, and after relating the circumstances, she thus went on: "I am now convinced, my dear aunt, that I have never been much in love. For had I really experienced that pure and elevating passion, I should at present detest his very name, and wish him all manner of evil. But my feelings are not only cordial towards *him*; they are even impartial towards Miss King. I cannot make myself hate her at all, and I am not in the least unwilling to think her a very good sort of girl. There can be no love in all this. My guardedness has been effective. Though I should certainly be a more interesting object to all my acquaintance were I madly in love with him, I cannot say that I regret my comparative insignificance. Kitty and Lydia take his defection much more to heart than I do. They are young in the ways of the world, and not yet open to the mortifying conviction that handsome young men—just as plain ones— must have something to live on."

CHAPTER 27

January and February passed by with no greater events than these in the Longbourn family, interrupted by little beyond the walks to Meryton, sometimes muddy and sometimes cold. March was to take Elizabeth to Hunsford. She had not at first thought very seriously of going there, but Charlotte, she soon found, was depending on the plan. Elizabeth gradually came to consider it herself with greater pleasure as well as greater certainty. Absence had increased her desire of seeing Charlotte again, and weakened her disgust of Mr. Collins. It would be a change of pace for her, and as her mother and uncompanionable sisters ensured that home could not be faultless, a little change was not unwelcome for its own sake. The journey would, moreover, give her a chance to visit Jane, and as the time for departure drew near, she would have been very sorry for any delay. Everything, however, went smoothly, and was finally settled as Charlotte had planned. Elizabeth was to accompany Sir William and his second daughter. The decision to spend a night in London was made, and the plan became as perfect as a plan could be.

The only pain was in leaving her father, who would certainly miss her, and who was so distressed at her leaving that he told her to write to him, and almost promised to answer her letter.

The farewell between her and Mr. Wickham was perfectly friendly. His present interest could not make him forget that Elizabeth had been the first to excite and to deserve his attention. She was the first to listen and pity, the first to be admired. In his manner of bidding her farewell, wishing her every enjoyment, reminding her of what she was to expect in Lady Catherine de Bourgh, there was an attentiveness which she felt must ever attach her to him with a most sincere regard. She parted from him convinced that, whether married or single, he must always be her model of the amiable and pleasing.

Her fellow travellers the next day were not of a kind to make her think him less agreeable. Sir William Lucas and his daughter Maria, a good-humoured girl who was as empty-headed as himself, had nothing to say that could be worth hearing. Elizabeth listened to them with about as much delight as the rattle of the carriage. She loved absurdities, but she had been subjected to Sir William's for too long. He could tell her nothing new of the wonders of his presentation and knighthood, and his civilities were worn out, like his information.

It was a journey of only twenty-four miles, and they began it so early as to be in Gracechurch Street by noon. As they drove to Mr. Gardiner's door, Jane was at a drawing room window watching for their arrival. When they entered she was there to welcome them, and Elizabeth, looking earnestly in her face, was pleased to see it as healthy and lovely as ever. On the stairs were several little boys and girls, whose eagerness for their cousin's appearance would not allow them to wait in the drawing room, and whose shyness, as they had not seen her for a year, prevented their coming lower. All was joy and kindness. The day passed most pleasantly away: the morning in shopping, and the evening at one of the theatres.

Elizabeth then contrived to sit by her aunt. Their first subject was her sister; and she was more grieved than astonished to hear, in reply to her minute enquiries, that though Jane was always in tolerably good spirits, there were periods of dejection. It was reasonable, however, to hope that they would not continue long. Mrs. Gardiner gave her the particulars also of Miss Bingley's visit in Gracechurch Street, and repeated conversations occurring at different times between Jane and herself, which proved that Jane had, from her heart, given up the acquaintance.

Mrs. Gardiner then consoled her niece regarding Wickham's desertion, and complimented her on bearing it so well.

"But, my dear Elizabeth," she added, "what sort of girl is Miss King? I should be sorry to think our friend only interested in her because of her money."

"My dear aunt, when it comes to marriage, what is the difference between the fortune seekers and the merely practical? Where does prudence end, and greed begin? Last Christmas you were afraid of his marrying me, because it would be financially unwise; and now, because he is trying to get a girl with only ten thousand pounds, you want to find out if he is greedy."

"If you will only tell me what sort of girl Miss King is, I shall know what to think."

"She is a very good kind of girl, I believe. I know nothing bad about her."

"But he paid her not the smallest attention till her grandfather's death made her inherit this fortune."

"No — why should he? If it were not allowable for him to gain *my* affections because I had no money, what occasion could there be for paying his regards a girl whom he did not care about, and who was equally poor?"

"But it seems indelicate to direct his attentions towards her so soon after this event."

"A man in difficult financial circumstances does not have time for all those elegant behaviours which other people may observe. If *she* does not object to it, why should *we*?"

"*Her* not objecting, does not justify *him*. It only proves that she is deficient in sense herself."

"Well," cried Elizabeth, "have it as you choose. *He* shall be mercenary, and *she* shall be foolish."

"No, Lizzy, that is what I do *not* choose. I should be sorry, you know, to think ill of a young man who has lived so long in Derbyshire."

"Oh! If that is all, I have a very poor opinion of young men who live in Derbyshire. Their intimate friends who live in Hertfordshire are not much better. I am sick of them all. Thank Heaven! I am going tomorrow where I shall find a man who has not one agreeable quality, who has neither manner nor sense to recommend him. Dull men are the only ones worth knowing, after all."

Before they were separated by the conclusion of the play, she had the unexpected happiness of an invitation to accompany her uncle and aunt on a trip which they planned to take in the summer.

"We have not quite determined how far we shall go," said Mrs. Gardiner, "but, perhaps, to the Lakes."

No scheme could have been more agreeable to Elizabeth, and her acceptance of the invitation was most ready and grateful. "My dear, dear aunt," she rapturously cried, "what delight! What happiness! You give me fresh life. Goodbye to disappointment. What are men to rocks and mountains? What hours of raptures we shall experience! And when we *do* return, it shall not be like other travellers, without being able to give one accurate idea of anything. We *will* know where we have gone — we *will* recollect what we have seen. Lakes, mountains, and rivers shall not be jumbled together in our imaginations. Let *our* descriptions be less intolerable than those of most travellers."

CHAPTER 28

Every object in the next day's journey was new and interesting to Elizabeth, and her spirits were in a state of enjoyment. She had seen her sister looking so well as to banish all fear for her health, and the prospect of her trip to the north was a constant source of delight.

When they left the highway for the lane to Hunsford, every eye was in search of the Parsonage, and every turn expected to bring it in view. The fence of Rosings Park was their boundary on one side. Elizabeth smiled at the recollection of all that she had heard of its inhabitants.

At length the Parsonage was discernible. The garden sloping to the road, the house standing in it, the green fence posts, and the laurel hedge; everything declared they were arriving. Mr. Collins and Charlotte appeared at the door, and the carriage stopped at the small gate which led by a short gravel walk to the house amidst the nods and smiles of the whole party. In a moment they were all out, rejoicing at the sight of each other. Mrs. Collins welcomed her friend with the liveliest pleasure, and Elizabeth was more and more satisfied with coming when she found herself so affectionately received. She saw instantly that her cousin's manners were not altered by his marriage: his formal civility was just what it had been, and he detained her some minutes at the gate to enquire after all her family. They were then, with no other delay than his pointing out the elegance of the entrance, taken into the house. As soon as they were in the parlour he welcomed them a second time, with great formality, to his humble abode, and repeated all his wife's offers of refreshment.

Elizabeth was prepared to see him in his glory; and she could not help seeing that in displaying the good proportion of the room, its aspect and its furniture, he addressed himself particularly to her, as if wishing to make her feel what she had lost in refusing him. But though everything seemed neat and comfortable, she was not able to gratify him by any sigh of remorse, and rather looked with wonder at her friend that she could have so cheerful an air with such a companion. When Mr. Collins said anything of which his wife might reasonably be ashamed, which certainly was not infrequent, she involuntarily turned her eye on Charlotte. Once or twice she could discern a faint blush, but in general Charlotte wisely did not hear. After sitting long enough to admire every article of furniture in the room, to give an account of their journey, and of all that had happened in London, Mr. Collins invited them to take a stroll in the garden. It was large and well laid out, and he was responsible for its care. To work in his garden was one of his greatest pleasures, and Elizabeth admired the command of countenance with which Charlotte talked of the benefits of his being outdoors, and admitted she encouraged it as much as possible. Here, leading the way through every section, and scarcely allowing them time to utter the praises he asked for, every detail was pointed out with a degree of precision which left beauty entirely behind. He could number the fields in every direction, and could tell how many trees there were in the most distant clump. But of all the views which his garden, or which the country or the kingdom could boast, none were to be compared with the sight of Rosings, afforded by an opening in the trees that bordered the grounds nearly opposite the front of his house. It was a stately modern building, well positioned on high ground.

From his garden Mr. Collins would have led them round his two meadows; but the ladies, not having proper footwear, turned back. While Sir William accompanied him, Charlotte took her sister and friend over to the house, extremely well pleased, probably, to have the opportunity of showing it without her husband's help. It was rather small, but well-built and convenient. Everything was decorated and arranged with a neatness and consistency of which Elizabeth gave Charlotte all the credit. When Mr. Collins could be forgotten, there was really a great air of comfort throughout, and by Charlotte's evident enjoyment of it, Elizabeth supposed he must often be forgotten.

She had already learned that Lady Catherine was still in the country. It was spoken of again while they were at dinner, when Mr. Collins joined in, observed —

"Yes, Miss Elizabeth, you will have the honour of seeing Lady Catherine de Bourgh next Sunday at church, and I need not say you will be delighted with her. She is all kindness, and I am sure you will be honoured by her notice when the service is over. I have scarcely any hesitation in saying that she will include you and my sister Maria in every invitation with which she honours us during your stay here. Her behaviour to my dear Charlotte is charming. We dine at Rosings twice every week, and are never allowed to walk home. Her ladyship's carriage is regularly ordered for us. I *should* say one of her ladyship's carriages, for she has several."

"Lady Catherine is a very respectable, sensible woman indeed," added Charlotte, "and a most attentive neighbour."

"Very true, my dear, that is exactly what I say. She is the sort of woman whom one cannot regard too highly."

The evening was spent mostly in talking over Hertfordshire news, and telling again what had been already written. When it closed, Elizabeth, in the solitude of her chamber, had to meditate upon Charlotte's degree of contentment and composure in bearing with her husband, and to acknowledge that it was all done very well. She had also to anticipate how her visit would go: the quiet moments at home, the vexatious interruptions of Mr. Collins, and the visits to Rosings.

About the middle of the next day, as she was in her room getting ready for a walk, a sudden noise below seemed to send the whole house in confusion. After listening a moment, she heard somebody running upstairs in a violent hurry, calling loudly for her. She opened the door and met Maria on the landing, who, breathless with agitation, cried out —

"Oh, my dear Eliza! Hurry and come to the dining room, for there is such a sight to be seen! I will not tell you what it is. Make haste, and come down this moment."

Elizabeth asked questions in vain; Maria would tell her nothing more, and down they ran into the dining room, in quest of this wonder! It was two ladies stopping in a low carriage at the garden gate.

"And is this all?" cried Elizabeth. "I expected at least that the pigs had gotten into the garden, and here is nothing but Lady Catherine and her daughter!"

"No, my dear," said Maria, quite shocked at the mistake, "it is not Lady Catherine. The old lady is Mrs. Jenkinson, who lives with them; the other is Miss De Bourgh. Only look at her. She is quite a little creature. Who would have thought she could be so thin and small!"

"She is quite rude to keep Charlotte out of doors in all this wind. Why does she not come in?"

"Oh, Charlotte says she hardly ever does. It is the greatest of favours when Miss De Bourgh comes in."

"I like her appearance," said Elizabeth, struck with other ideas. "She looks sickly and out of humour. Yes, she will do for him very well. She will make him a very proper wife."

Mr. Collins and Charlotte were both standing at the gate in conversation with the ladies, and Sir William, to Elizabeth's amusement, was stationed in the doorway, in earnest contemplation of the greatness before him, and constantly bowing whenever Miss De Bourgh looked that way.

At length there was nothing more to be said; the ladies drove on, and the others returned inside. Mr. Collins no sooner saw the two girls than he began to congratulate them on their good fortune, which Charlotte explained by letting them know that the whole party was invited to dine at Rosings the next day.

CHAPTER 29

Mr. Collins's triumph, in consequence of this invitation, was complete. The power of displaying the grandeur of his patroness to his wondering visitors, and of letting them see her civility towards himself and his wife, was exactly what he had wished for. That an opportunity of doing it should be given so soon was such an instance of Lady Catherine's favor that he knew not how to admire it enough.

"I confess," said he, "that I should not have been at all surprised by her Ladyship's asking us on Sunday to drink tea and spend the evening at Rosings. I rather expected, from my knowledge of her kindness, that it would happen. But who could have foreseen such an attention as this? Who could have imagined that we should receive an invitation to dine there (an invitation, moreover, including the whole party) so immediately after your arrival!"

"I am less surprised at what has happened," replied Sir William, "from the knowledge of what the manners of the great really are, which my position in life has allowed me to acquire. At court such instances of elegant breeding are not uncommon."

Scarcely anything was talked of the whole day or the next morning except their visit to Rosings. Mr. Collins was carefully instructing them in what they were to expect so the sight of such rooms, so many servants, and so splendid a dinner might not wholly overpower them.

When the ladies were separating to make their final preparations, he said to Elizabeth —

"Do not make yourself uneasy, my dear cousin, about your clothing. Lady Catherine is far from requiring that elegance of dress in us which becomes herself and daughter. I would advise you merely to put on whatever of your clothes is superior to the rest — there is no occasion for anything more. Lady Catherine will not think the worse of you for being simply dressed. She likes to have the distinction of rank preserved."

While they were dressing, he came two or three times to their different doors, to recommend their being quick, as Lady Catherine very much objected to being kept waiting for her dinner. Such formidable accounts of her ladyship, and her manner of living, quite frightened Maria Lucas, and she looked forward to her introduction at Rosings with as much uneasiness as her father had felt about his presentation at St. James's.

As the weather was fine they had a pleasant walk of about half a mile across the park. Every park has its beauty and its prospects. Elizabeth saw much to be pleased with, though she could not be in such raptures as Mr. Collins expected the scene to inspire. But she was mildly impressed by his enumeration of the windows in front of the house, and his relation of what the glass altogether had originally cost Sir Lewis De Bourgh.

When they ascended the steps to the hall, Maria's alarm was every moment increasing, and even Sir William did not look perfectly calm. Elizabeth's courage did not fail her. She had heard nothing of Lady Catherine that inspired awe, and the mere stateliness of money and rank she thought she could witness without intimidation.

From the entrance hall, of which Mr. Collins pointed out, with a rapturous air, the fine proportion and furnishings, they followed the servants to the room where Lady Catherine, her daughter, and Mrs. Jenkinson were sitting. Her ladyship, with great condescension, arose to receive them. As Mrs. Collins had determined with her husband that the introductions should be done by her, it was performed in a proper manner, without any of those apologies and thanks which he would have thought necessary.

In spite of having been at St. James's, Sir William was so completely awed by the grandeur surrounding him that he had but just courage enough to make a very low bow. He then took his seat without saying a word, and his daughter, frightened almost out of her senses, sat on the edge of her chair, not knowing which way to look. Elizabeth found her faculties quite adequate for the scene, and could calmly observe the three ladies before her. Lady Catherine was a tall, large woman with strongly marked features which might once have been beautiful. Her manner of receiving them did not make her visitors forget their inferior rank. Whatever she said was spoken in so authoritative a tone as emphasized her self-importance, and brought Mr. Wickham immediately to Elizabeth's mind. Upon further observance, she believed Lady Catherine to be exactly what he had represented.

When, after examining the mother, in whose appearance she soon found some resemblance of Mr. Darcy, she turned her eyes on the daughter. She could almost have joined in Maria's astonishment at her being so thin and small. There was neither in figure nor face any likeness between the ladies. Miss De Bourgh was pale and sickly; her features, though not plain, were not beautiful either. She spoke very little, except in a low voice to Mrs. Jenkinson, in whose appearance there was nothing remarkable, and who was entirely engaged in listening to what she said and doing as she asked.

After sitting a few minutes they were all sent to one of the windows to admire the view. Mr. Collins joined them to point out its beauties, and Lady Catherine kindly informed them that it was much better to look at in the summer.

The dinner was exceedingly fine, and there were all the servants and all the fancy dinnerware which Mr. Collins had promised. As he had likewise foretold, he took his seat at the foot of the table, by her ladyship's desire, and looked as if he felt that life could furnish nothing greater. He carved and ate and praised with delight, and every dish was commended, first by him and then by Sir William, who was now recovered enough to echo whatever his son in law said. Lady Catherine seemed gratified by their excessive admiration, and gave most gracious smiles, especially when any dish on the table was new to them. The party did not supply much conversation. Elizabeth was ready to speak whenever there was an opening, but she was seated between Charlotte and Miss De Bourgh — the former of whom was engaged in listening to Lady Catherine, and the latter said not a word to her all through the meal. Mrs. Jenkinson was mainly employed in watching how little Miss De Bourgh ate, pressing her to try some other dish, and fearing she felt ill. Maria thought speaking was out of the question, and the gentlemen did nothing but eat and admire.

When the ladies returned to the drawing room, there was little to be done but to hear Lady Catherine talk, which she did without any pause until coffee came in. She delivered her opinion on every subject in so decisive a manner as to prove she was not used to have her judgment contested. She inquired into Charlotte's domestic concerns familiarly and minutely, and gave her a great deal of advice as to the management of them all. She told her how everything ought to be regulated in so small a family as hers, and instructed her as to the care of her cows and her poultry. Elizabeth found that nothing was beneath this great Lady's attention that could furnish her with an occasion of dictating to others. In the intervals of her conversation with Mrs. Collins, she addressed a variety of questions to Maria and Elizabeth, but especially to the latter, of whose connections she knew the least, and who, she observed to Mrs. Collins, was a very genteel, pretty kind of girl. She asked her, at different times, how many sisters she had, whether they were older or younger than herself, whether any of them were likely to be married, whether they were beautiful, where they had been educated, what carriage her father kept, and what had been her mother's maiden name? Elizabeth felt all the incivility of her questions, but answered them very composedly. Lady Catherine then observed —

"Your father's estate is entailed on Mr. Collins, I think. For your sake," turning to Charlotte, "I am glad. But otherwise I see no reason for entailing estates away from the female line. It was not thought necessary in Sir Lewis de Bourgh's family. Do you play and sing, Miss Bennet?"

"A little."

"Oh! Then some time or other we shall be happy to hear you. Our instrument is a quality one, probably superior to yours. You shall try it someday. Do your sisters play and sing?"

"One of them does."

"Why did not you all learn? You ought all to have learned. The Miss Webbs all play, and their father has not so good an income as yours. Do you draw?"

"No, not at all."

"What, none of you?"

"Not one."

"That is very strange. But I suppose you had no opportunity. Your mother should have taken you to town every spring to be taught by masters."

"My mother would have had no objection, but my father hates London."

"Has your governess left you?"

"We never had a governess."

"No governess! How is that possible? Five daughters brought up at home without a governess! I never heard of such a thing. Your mother must have been quite a slave to your education."

Elizabeth could hardly help smiling, as she assured her that had not been the case.

"Then, who taught you? Who took care of you? Without a governess, you must have been neglected."

"Compared with some families, I believe we were; but those who wished to learn never lacked the means. We were always encouraged to read, and had all the masters that were necessary. Those who chose to be idle certainly had the opportunity."

"No doubt, but that is what a governess will prevent. If I had known your mother, I would have advised her most strenuously to engage one. I always say that nothing is to be done in education without steady and regular instruction, and nobody but a governess can give it. It's impressive how many families I have been the means of supplying in that way. I am always glad to get a young person well placed. Four nieces of Mrs. Jenkinson are most delightfully situated through my means, and it was just the other day when I recommended another young person, who was merely accidentally mentioned to me, and the family are quite delighted with her. Mrs. Collins, did I tell you of Lady Metcalfe's calling yesterday to thank me? She finds Miss Pope a treasure. 'Lady Catherine,' said she, 'you have given me a treasure.' Are any of your younger sisters out, Miss Bennet?"

"Yes, ma'am, all."

"All! What, all five out at once? Very odd! And you only the second. The younger ones out before the elder are married! Your younger sisters must be very young?"

"Yes, my youngest is not sixteen. Perhaps *she* is too young to be much in company. But really, ma'am, I think it would be very hard upon younger sisters if they did not have their share of society and amusement, simply because the elder do not have the means or inclination to marry early. The last born has as much right to the pleasures of youth as the first. And to be kept back on *such* a motive! I think it would not be very likely to promote sisterly affection or peace of mind."

"Upon my word," said her ladyship, "you give your opinion very decidedly for so young a person. Pray, what is your age?"

"With three younger sisters grown up," replied Elizabeth smiling, "your ladyship can hardly expect me to say."

Lady Catherine seemed quite astonished at not receiving a direct answer, and Elizabeth suspected that she was the first creature who had ever dared to trifle with so much dignified rudeness.

"You cannot be more than twenty, I am sure; therefore you need not conceal your age."

"I am not yet twenty-one."

When the gentlemen had joined them, and tea was over, the card-tables were brought out. Lady Catherine, Sir William, and Mr. and Mrs. Collins sat down to quadrille. Miss De Bourgh chose to play casino, and the two girls had the honour of assisting Mrs. Jenkinson to make up her party. Their table was excessively dull. Scarcely a syllable was uttered that did not relate to the game, except when Mrs. Jenkinson expressed her fears of Miss De Bourgh's being too hot or too cold, or having too much or too little light. A great deal more conversation occurred at the other table. Lady Catherine was usually the one speaking — stating the mistakes of the three others, or relating some anecdote about herself. Mr. Collins was employed in agreeing to everything her Ladyship said, thanking her for every hand he won, and apologising if he thought he had won too many. Sir William did not say much. He was filling his memory with anecdotes and noble names.

When Lady Catherine and her daughter had played as long as they wanted, the tables were put away, the carriage was offered to Mrs. Collins, gratefully accepted, and immediately ordered. The party then gathered around the fire to hear Lady Catherine determine what weather they were to have on the morrow. From these instructions they were summoned by the arrival of the coach. With many speeches of thankfulness on Mr. Collins's side, and as many bows on Sir William's, they departed. As soon as they had driven from the door, Elizabeth was asked by her cousin to give her opinion of all that she had seen at Rosings, which, for Charlotte's sake, she made more favourable than it really was. But her commendation, though costing her some trouble, could by no means satisfy Mr. Collins, and he was very soon obliged to take her ladyship's praise into his own hands.

CHAPTER 30

Sir William stayed only a week at Hunsford, but his visit was long enough to convince him of his daughter's being most comfortably settled, and of her possessing such a husband and such a neighbour as were not often seen. While Sir William was with them Mr. Collins devoted his mornings to driving him out in his inexpensive open carriage and showing him the country. But when he went away, the whole family returned to their usual employments. Elizabeth was thankful to find that they did not see more of her cousin as a result, for he spent the greater part of the time between breakfast and dinner either at work in the garden, or in reading and writing in his own library, which was near the front of the house. The room in which the ladies sat faced the back of the house. Elizabeth at first had rather wondered that Charlotte should not prefer the dining room for common use. It was a better sized room, and had a pleasanter view. But she soon saw that her friend had an excellent reason for what she did, for Mr. Collins would undoubtedly have been much less in his own place had they been nearer to him, and she gave Charlotte credit for the arrangement.

From the drawing room they could distinguish nothing in the lane, and were indebted to Mr. Collins for the knowledge of what carriages went along, and how often especially Miss De Bourgh drove by. He never failed to inform them of this event, though it happened almost every day. She frequently stopped at the Parsonage and had a few minutes' conversation with Charlotte, but was scarcely ever prevailed on to get out.

Very few days passed in which Mr. Collins did not walk to Rosings, and not many in which his wife did not think it necessary to go likewise. Until Elizabeth thought of the economic value a good relationship with Lady Catherine could have to any children that may be born to Charlotte and Mr. Collins, she could not understand the sacrifice of so many hours. Now and then they were honoured with a call from her ladyship, and nothing escaped her observation that was happening in the room during these visits. She examined how they spent their time, looked at their work, and advised them to do it differently. She found fault with the arrangement of the furniture, or detected the housemaid in negligence. If she accepted any offer to dine with them, she seemed to do it only for the sake of finding out that Mrs. Collins' cuts of meat were too large for her family.

Elizabeth soon perceived that Lady Catherine was actively involved in the affairs of the nearby residents, the minutest concerns of which were carried to her by Mr. Collins. Whenever any in her care were disposed to be quarrelsome, discontented, or too poor, she went to the village to settle their differences, silence their complaints, and scold them into harmony and plenty.

The entertainment of dining at Rosings was repeated about twice a week. Excepting the loss of Sir William, and there being only one card table in the evening, it was just as it had been before. Their other engagements were few, as the style of living of the neighbourhood in general was beyond the Collins' reach. This, however, was no difficulty for Elizabeth, and she spent her time comfortably enough. There were half-hours of pleasant conversation with Charlotte, and the weather was so fine for the time of year that she often had great enjoyment outdoors. Her favourite walk, and where she frequently went while the others were calling on Lady Catherine, was along the open grove which bordered that side of the park. There was a nice sheltered path which no one seemed to value but herself, and there she felt beyond the reach of Lady Catherine's curiosity.

In this quiet way the first two weeks of her visit soon passed away. Easter was approaching, and the week preceding it was to bring an addition to the family at Rosings, which in so small a circle must be important. Elizabeth had heard soon after her arrival that Mr. Darcy was expected there in the course of a few weeks. Though she would have preferred almost anyone to him, his coming would give her someone comparatively new to look at in their Rosings parties. She might also be amused to see how hopeless Miss Bingley's plans to secure him were, by his behaviour to his cousin, for whom he was evidently destined by Lady Catherine. By her his coming was talked of with the greatest satisfaction. She spoke of him in terms of the highest admiration, and seemed almost angry to find that Miss Lucas and herself were already acquainted with him.

His arrival was soon known at the Parsonage, for Mr. Collins was walking the whole morning within view of the lodges opening into Hunsford Lane in order to have the first glimpse of it. After making his bow as the carriage turned into the Park, he hurried home with the news. On the following morning he hurried to Rosings to pay his respects. There were two nephews of Lady Catherine there, for Mr. Darcy had brought with him a Colonel Fitzwilliam, the younger son of his uncle, and to the great surprise of all the party, when Mr. Collins returned, the gentlemen accompanied him. Charlotte had seen them from her husband's room crossing the road, and immediately running into the other she told the girls what an honour they might expect, adding —

"I may thank you, Eliza, for this piece of civility. Mr. Darcy would never have come so soon to visit me."

Elizabeth had scarcely time to deny all right to the compliment before their approach was announced by the doorbell, and shortly afterwards the three gentlemen entered the room. Colonel Fitzwilliam, who led the way, was about thirty. He was not handsome, but in person and manner most truly a gentleman. Mr. Darcy looked just as he had looked in Hertfordshire. He paid his compliments with his usual reserve to Mrs. Collins, and whatever might be his feelings towards her friend, viewed her with every appearance of composure. Elizabeth merely curtseyed to him without saying a word.

Colonel Fitzwilliam entered into conversation immediately with the readiness and ease of a well-bred man, and he talked very pleasantly. But his cousin, after having made a slight observation on the house and garden to Mrs. Collins, sat for some time without speaking to anybody. At length, however, his civility was so far awakened as to inquire of Elizabeth after the health of her family. She answered him in the usual way, and after a moment's pause, added –

"My eldest sister has been in town these three months. Have you never happened to see her there?"

She was perfectly aware that he never had, but she wished to see whether he would betray any consciousness of what had passed between the Bingleys and Jane. She thought he looked a little confused as he answered that he had never been so fortunate as to encounter Miss Bennet in London. The subject was pursued no farther, and the gentlemen soon afterwards went away.

CHAPTER 31

Colonel Fitzwilliam's manners were very much admired at the Parsonage, and the ladies all felt that he must add considerably to the pleasure of their engagements at Rosings. It was some days, however, before they received an invitation, for while there were visitors in the house they could not be necessary. It was not till Easter Sunday, almost a week after the gentlemen's arrival, that they were honoured by such an attention, and then they were merely asked on leaving church to come there in the evening. For the last week they had seen very little of either Lady Catherine or her daughter. Colonel Fitzwilliam had visited the parsonage more than once during that time, but Mr. Darcy they had only seen at church.

The invitation was accepted, of course, and at the appointed time they joined the party in Lady Catherine's drawing room. Her ladyship received them civilly, but it was plain that their company was by no means as meaningful as when she could get nobody else. She was, in fact, almost engrossed by her nephews, speaking to them, especially to Darcy, much more than to any other person in the room.

Colonel Fitzwilliam seemed really glad to see them; anything was a welcome relief to him at Rosings, and Mrs. Collins' pretty friend had moreover caught his notice very much. He now seated himself by her and talked so agreeably of Kent and Hertfordshire, of travelling and staying at home, of new books and music, that Elizabeth had never been half so well entertained in that room before. They conversed with so much spirit and flow as to draw the attention of Lady Catherine herself, as well as that of Mr. Darcy. *His* eyes had been soon and repeatedly turned towards them with a look of curiosity. That her ladyship shared the feeling was more openly acknowledged, for she did not hesitate to call out —

"What is that you are saying, Fitzwilliam? What is it you are talking of? What are you telling Miss Bennet? Let me hear what it is."

"We are speaking of music, madam," said he, when no longer able to avoid a reply.

"Of music! Then pray speak aloud. It is of all subjects my delight. I must have my share in the conversation if you are speaking of music. There are few people in England, I suppose, who have more true enjoyment of music than myself, or a better natural taste. If I had ever learned, I would have been very proficient. And so would Anne, if her health had allowed her to play. I am confident that she would have performed delightfully. How is Georgiana's playing, Darcy?"

Mr. Darcy spoke with affectionate praise of his sister's proficiency.

"I am very glad to hear such a good account of her," said Lady Catherine. "Tell her from me, that she cannot expect to excel if she does not practise a great deal."

"I assure you, madam," he replied, "that she does not need such advice. She practises very constantly."

"So much the better. It cannot be done too much; and when I next write to her, I shall charge her not to neglect it on any account. I often tell young ladies that no excellence in music is to be acquired without constant practice. I have told Miss Bennet several times that she will never play really well unless she practices more. Though Mrs. Collins has no instrument, she is very welcome, as I have often told her, to come to Rosings every day and play the piano in Mrs. Jenkinson's room. She would be in nobody's way, you know, in that part of the house."

Mr. Darcy looked a little ashamed of his aunt's rudeness and made no answer.

When coffee was over Colonel Fitzwilliam reminded Elizabeth of having promised to play for him, and she sat down at the instrument. He drew a chair near her. Lady Catherine listened to half a song, and then talked, as before, to her other nephew, until he walked away from her. He moved with purposefulness towards the piano, stationing himself so as to command a full view of the fair performer. Elizabeth saw what he was doing, and at the first convenient pause, turned to him with a smile and said

———

"Perhaps you mean to frighten me, Mr. Darcy, by coming in all this formality to hear me. But I will not be alarmed, even though your sister *does* play so well. There is a stubbornness about me that never can bear to be frightened at the will of others. My courage always rises with every attempt to intimidate me."

"I shall not say that you are mistaken," he replied, "because you could not really believe me to entertain any design of alarming you. I have had the pleasure of your acquaintance long enough to know that you find great enjoyment in occasionally professing opinions which in fact are not your own."

Elizabeth laughed heartily at this picture of herself, and said to Colonel Fitzwilliam, "Your cousin will convince you not to believe a word I say. I am particularly unlucky in meeting with a person so well able to expose my real character, in a place where I had hoped to pass myself off with some degree of credit. Indeed, Mr. Darcy, it is very ungenerous in you to mention all that you knew to my disadvantage in Hertfordshire. It may provoke me to retaliate, and things could come out that will shock your relations to hear."

"I am not afraid of you," he said smilingly.

"Tell me what you have to accuse him of," cried Colonel Fitzwilliam. "I should like to know how he behaves among strangers."

"You shall hear then — but prepare yourself for something very dreadful. The first time of my ever seeing him in Hertfordshire, you must know, was at a ball — and at this ball, what do you think he did? He danced only four dances! I am sorry to pain you, but so it was. He danced only four dances, though gentlemen were scarce; and, to my certain knowledge, more than one young lady was sitting down without a partner. Mr. Darcy, you cannot deny it."

"I had not at that time the honour of knowing any lady in the assembly beyond my own party."

"True, and nobody can *ever* be introduced in a ball room. Well, Colonel Fitzwilliam, what should I play next? My fingers await your orders."

"Perhaps," said Darcy, "it would have been better if I had I sought an introduction, but I am poorly qualified to recommend myself to strangers."

"Shall we ask your cousin the reason for this?" said Elizabeth, still addressing Colonel Fitzwilliam. "Shall we ask him why a man of sense and education, and who has lived among the best of society, is poorly qualified to recommend himself to strangers?"

"I can answer your question," said Fitzwilliam, "without asking him. It is because he will not make the effort."

"I certainly have not the talent which some people possess," said Darcy, "of conversing easily with those I have never seen before. I cannot catch their tone of conversation, or appear interested in their concerns, as I often see done."

"My fingers," said Elizabeth, "do not move over this instrument in the masterly manner which I see so many women's do. They have not the same force or rapidity, and do not produce the same expression. But then I have always supposed it to be my own fault, because I have not made the effort to practise. It is not that I do not believe *my* fingers as capable as any other woman's of superior playing."

Darcy smiled and said, "You are perfectly right. You have spent your time in much better pursuits. No one hearing you can think anything is lacking. Neither of us does things solely for the benefit of strangers."

Here they were interrupted by Lady Catherine, who called out to know what they were talking of. Elizabeth immediately began playing again. Lady Catherine approached, and, after listening for a few minutes, said to Darcy—

"Miss Bennet would not make any mistakes if she practised more, and could have the advantage of a London master. She has very good fingering, though her taste is not equal to Anne's. Anne would have been a delightful performer, had her health allowed her to learn."

Elizabeth looked at Darcy to see how cordially he assented to his cousin's praise; but neither at that moment nor at any other could she discern any sign of love. From the whole of his behaviour to Miss De Bourgh she derived this comfort for Miss Bingley, that he might have been just as likely to marry *her*, had she been his relation.

Lady Catherine continued her remarks on Elizabeth's performance, mixing with them many instructions on performance and taste. Elizabeth received them with all great tolerance, and, at the request of the gentlemen, remained at the instrument till her ladyship's carriage was ready to take them all home.

CHAPTER 32

Elizabeth was sitting by herself the next morning, writing to Jane while Mrs. Collins and Maria were gone on business into the village, when she was startled by a ring at the door. As she had heard no carriage, she thought it might be Lady Catherine, and was putting away her half-finished letter that she might escape all uncivil questions, when the door opened. To her very great surprise Mr. Darcy, and Mr. Darcy only, entered the room.

He seemed astonished too on finding her alone, and apologised for his intrusion by letting her know that he had understood all the ladies were at home.

They then sat down, and when her enquiries after Rosings were made, seemed in danger of sinking into total silence. It was absolutely necessary, therefore, to think of something. Recollecting *when* she had seen him last in Hertfordshire, and feeling curious to know what he would say on the subject of their hasty departure, she observed —

"How very suddenly you all left Netherfield last November, Mr. Darcy! It must have been a most agreeable surprise to Mr. Bingley to see you all follow him there so soon, for, if I remember correctly, he went but the day before. He and his sisters were well, I hope, when you left London?"

"Perfectly so, thank you."

She found that she was to receive no other answer, and, after a short pause, added —

"I think I have understood that Mr. Bingley has no plans to ever return to Netherfield again?"

"I have never heard him say so, but it is likely he will spend very little of his time there in the future. He has many friends, and he is at a time of life when friends and engagements are continually increasing."

"If he means to be but little at Netherfield, it would be better for the neighbourhood if he gave up the place entirely, for then we might possibly get a settled family there. But, perhaps, Mr. Bingley did not take the house so much for the convenience of the neighbourhood as for his own, and we must expect him to keep or leave it on the same principle."

"I should not be surprised," said Darcy, "if he were to give it up as soon as he finds a suitable estate to purchase."

Elizabeth made no answer. She was afraid of talking longer of his friend, and, having nothing else to say, was now determined to leave the trouble of finding a subject to him.

He took the hint and soon began with, "This seems like a very comfortable house. Lady Catherine, I believe, did a great deal to it when Mr. Collins first came to Hunsford."

"I believe she did — and I am sure she could not have bestowed her kindness on a more grateful person."

"Mr. Collins appears very fortunate in his choice of a wife."

"Yes, indeed. His friends may well rejoice in his having found one of the very few sensible women who would have accepted him. My friend has an excellent understanding — though I am not certain that I consider her marrying Mr. Collins as the wisest thing she ever did. She seems perfectly happy, however, and in a practical light it is certainly a very good match for her."

"It must be very agreeable to her to be settled so close own family and friends."

"Close, you call it? It is nearly fifty miles."

"And what is fifty miles of good road? Little more than half a day's journey. Yes, I call it very close."

"I should never have considered the distance as one of the *advantages* of the match," cried Elizabeth. "I should never have said Mrs. Collins was settled *near* her family."

"It is a proof of your own attachment to Hertfordshire. Anything beyond the very neighbourhood of Longbourn, I suppose, would appear far."

As he spoke there was a sort of smile which Elizabeth believed she understood. He must be supposing her to be thinking of Jane and Netherfield, and she blushed as she answered —

"I do not mean to say that a woman may not be settled too near her family. The far and the near must be relative, and depend on many varying circumstances. Where there is fortune to make the expense of travelling unimportant, distance becomes no obstacle. But that is not the case *here*. Mr. and Mrs. Collins have a comfortable income, but not one that will allow frequent journeys. I am persuaded my friend would not call herself *near* her family under less than *half* the present distance."

Mr. Darcy drew his chair a little towards her and said, "*You* cannot have a right to such very strong local attachment. *You* cannot have been always at Longbourn."

Elizabeth looked surprised. The gentleman experienced some change of feeling; he drew back his chair, took a newspaper from the table, and, glancing over it, said, in a colder voice —

"Are you pleased with Kent?"

A short dialogue on the subject of the country ensued, on either side calm and concise — and soon put to an end by the entrance of Charlotte and her sister, just returned from their walk. They were surprised to see Mr. Darcy alone with Elizabeth. He related the mistake which had occasioned his intruding on Miss Bennet, and after sitting a few minutes longer without saying much to anybody, he went away.

"What can be the meaning of this?" said Charlotte, as soon as he was gone. "My dear Eliza, he must be in love with you, or he would never have visited us in this familiar way."

But when Elizabeth told of his silence, it did not seem very likely, even to Charlotte's wishes, to be the case. After various guesses, they could at last only suppose his visit to proceed from the difficulty of finding anything to do, which was a probable explanation due to the time of year. All hunting sports were over and would not resume until autumn. Indoors there was Lady Catherine, books, and a billiard table, but gentlemen cannot be always inside. In the nearness of the Parsonage, or the pleasantness of the walk to it, or of the people who lived in it, the two cousins found reasons from this period to walk there almost every day. They visited at various times of the morning, sometimes separately, sometimes together, and now and then accompanied by their aunt. It was plain to them all that Colonel Fitzwilliam came because he enjoyed visiting them. Elizabeth was reminded by her own satisfaction in being with him, as well as by his evident admiration for her, of her former favourite George Wickham. Though, in comparing them, she admitted there was less captivating softness in Colonel Fitzwilliam's manners, she believed he might have the best informed mind.

But why Mr. Darcy came so often to the Parsonage was more difficult to understand. It could not be for socializing, as he frequently sat there ten minutes together without opening his lips. When he did speak, it seemed to be out of necessity rather than choice. He seldom appeared very lively. Mrs. Collins knew not what to make of him. Colonel Fitzwilliam's occasionally laughing at his dullness proved that he was behaving differently than he normally did, which her own knowledge of him could not have told her. As she would have liked to believe this change the effect of love, and the object of that love her friend Eliza, she began observing him more closely. She watched him whenever they were at Rosings, and whenever he came to Hunsford, but without much success. He certainly looked at her friend a great deal, but the expression of that look was difficult to interpret. It was an earnest, steadfast gaze, but she often doubted whether there was much admiration in it, and sometimes it seemed nothing but absence of mind.

She had once or twice suggested to Elizabeth the possibility of his being partial to her, but Elizabeth always laughed at the idea. Mrs. Collins did not think it right to press the subject, from the danger of raising expectations which might only end in disappointment, for in her opinion there could be no doubt that all her friend's dislike would vanish if she could suppose him to be in her power.

In her kind schemes for Elizabeth she sometimes pictured her marrying Colonel Fitzwilliam. He was beyond comparison the pleasantest man; he certainly admired her, and his situation in life was most suitable. But, to counterbalance these advantages, Mr. Darcy had considerable influence in the church, and his cousin could have none at all.

CHAPTER 33

More than once did Elizabeth, on her walk within the Park, unexpectedly meet Mr. Darcy. She felt all the frustration of the mischance that should bring him where no one else was brought, and, to prevent its ever happening again, took care to inform him at first that it was a favourite haunt of hers. How it could occur a second time, therefore, was very odd! Yet it did, and even a third. It seemed like he was there to purposely torment her, or attempting to make up for his previous ill-treatment of her, for on these occasions it was not merely a few formal enquiries and an awkward pause and then away, but he actually thought it necessary to turn back and walk with her. He never said a great deal, nor did she give herself the trouble of talking or of listening much. But it struck her in the course of their third *encounter* that he was asking some odd unconnected questions — about her pleasure in being at Hunsford, her love of solitary walks, and her opinion of Mr. and Mrs. Collins' happiness. It distressed her a little, and she was quite glad to find herself at the gate in the fence opposite the Parsonage.

She was kept herself busy one day as she walked by rereading Jane's last letter, and dwelling on some passages which proved that Jane had not been in good spirits, when, instead of being again surprised by Mr. Darcy, she saw, on looking up, that Colonel Fitzwilliam was coming towards her. Putting away the letter immediately and forcing a smile, she said — "I did not know before that you ever walked this way."

"I have been making the tour of the park," he replied, "as I generally do every year, and intend to close it with a call at the Parsonage. Are you going much farther?"

"No, I would have turned back in a moment."

And accordingly she did turn back, and they walked towards the Parsonage together.

"Are you planning to leave Kent on Saturday?" said she.

"Yes — if Darcy does not put it off again. But I am at his mercy. He arranges things just as he pleases."

"And if not able to please himself in the arrangement, he has at least great pleasure in the power of choice. I do not know anybody who seems more to enjoy the power of doing what he likes than Mr. Darcy."

"He likes very much to have his own way," replied Colonel Fitzwilliam. "But so do we all. It is only that he has greater ability to have it than many others, because he is rich, and others are poor. I speak feelingly. A younger son, you know, must never know how it feels to receive such an inheritance and must be accustomed to self-denial and dependence."

"In my opinion, the younger son of an earl can know very little of either. Now, seriously, what have you ever known of self-denial and dependence? When have you been prevented by lack of money from going wherever you chose, or purchasing anything you truly wanted?"

"These are insightful questions — and perhaps I cannot say that I have experienced many hardships of that nature. But in matters of greater weight, I may suffer from the lack of money. Younger sons cannot marry whomever they choose."

"Except when they choose women of fortune, which I think they very often do."

"Our spending habits make us too dependent, and there are not many in my rank of life who can afford to marry without some thoughts about money."

"And just what is the usual price of an earl's younger son? Unless the elder brother is very sickly, I suppose you would not ask above fifty thousand pounds."

He answered her in the same joking style, and the subject was dropped. They walked for a few moments in silence, and then she said —

"I imagine your cousin brought you down with him chiefly for the sake of having somebody to order around. I wonder he does not marry, to secure a lasting convenience of that kind. But perhaps his sister does as well for the present, and, as she is under his sole care, he may do what he likes with her."

"No," said Colonel Fitzwilliam, "that is an advantage which he must share with me. I am joined with him in the guardianship of Miss Darcy."

"Are you, indeed? And what sort of guardians do you make? Does your charge give you much trouble? Young ladies of her age are sometimes a little difficult to manage, and if she has the true Darcy spirit, she probably likes to have her own way."

As she spoke she observed him looking at her earnestly; and the manner in which he immediately asked her why she supposed Miss Darcy likely to give them any uneasiness, convinced her that she had somehow or other got pretty near the truth. She directly replied —

"You need not be frightened. I never heard anything bad about her; and I dare say she is one of the most good-spirited creatures in the world. She is a very great favourite with some ladies of my acquaintance — Mrs. Hurst and Miss Bingley. I think I have heard you say that you know them."

"I know them a little. Their brother is a pleasant, gentlemanlike man — he is a great friend of Darcy's."

"Oh yes," said Elizabeth drily — "Mr. Darcy is uncommonly kind to Mr. Bingley, and takes a good deal of care of him."

"Care of him! — Yes, I really believe Darcy *does* take care of him in those points where he takes little care himself. From something that he told me in our journey here, I have reason to think Bingley very much indebted to him. But I ought to beg his pardon, for I have no right to suppose that Bingley was the person meant. It was all supposition."

"What is it you mean?"

"It is a circumstance which Darcy, of course, would not wish to be generally known, because if it were to get round to the lady's family it would be an unpleasant thing."

"You may depend upon my not mentioning it."

"And remember that I have not much reason for supposing it to be Bingley. What he told me was merely this: that he congratulated himself on having lately saved a friend from the inconveniences of a most impractical marriage, but without mentioning names or any other particulars, and I only suspected it to be Bingley from believing him the kind of young man to get into a scrape of that sort, and from knowing them to have been together the whole of last summer."

"Did Mr. Darcy give you his reasons for this interference?"

"I understood that there were some very strong objections against the lady."

"And what devices did he use to separate them?"

"He did not talk to me of his devices," said Fitzwilliam, smiling. "He only told me what I have now told you."

Elizabeth made no answer, and walked on, her heart swelling with indignation. After watching her a little, Fitzwilliam asked her why she was so thoughtful.

"I am thinking of what you have been telling me," said she. "Your cousin's conduct does not seem entirely commendable. Why was he to be the judge?"

"You are rather disposed to call his interference overly intrusive?"

"I do not see what right Mr. Darcy had to decide on the propriety of his friend's choice, or why, upon his own judgment alone, he was to determine and direct in what manner that friend was to be happy. But," she continued, recollecting herself, "as we know none of the particulars, it is not fair to condemn him. It is not to be supposed that there was much affection in the case."

"That is certainly possible," said Fitzwilliam, "but it is lessening the honour of my cousin's triumph very much."

This was spoken in jest; but it appeared to her so correct a picture of Mr. Darcy that she would not trust herself with an answer, and therefore she abruptly changed the conversation and they talked about lesser matters till they reached the Parsonage. There, shut into her own room as soon as their visitor left them, she could think without interruption of all that she had heard. It was not to be supposed that any other people could be meant than those with whom she was connected. There could not exist in the world *two* men, over whom Mr. Darcy could have such boundless influence. That he had played a role in separating Mr. Bingley and Jane she had never doubted; but she had always attributed to Miss Bingley the principal design and arrangement of them. If his own vanity, however, did not mislead him, *he* was the cause. His pride and caprice were the cause of all that Jane had suffered, and still continued to suffer. He had ruined for a while every hope of happiness for the most affectionate, generous heart in the world; and no one could say how lasting an evil he might have inflicted.

"There were some very strong objections against the lady," were Colonel Fitzwilliam's words; and these strong objections probably were, her having one uncle who was an attorney, and another who was in business in London.

"To Jane herself," she exclaimed, "there could be no possibility of objection; all loveliness and goodness as she is! Her understanding is excellent, and her manners are captivating. Neither could anything be spoken against my father, who, though he has some peculiarities, has abilities which Mr. Darcy himself need not disdain, and respectability which he will probably never reach." When she thought of her mother, indeed, her confidence gave way a little; but she would not allow that any objections *there* had material weight with Mr. Darcy. *His* pride, she was convinced, would receive a deeper wound from the lack of importance in his friend's connections, than from their lack of intelligence; and she was quite decided at last that he had been partly governed by this worst kind of pride, and partly by the wish of retaining Mr. Bingley for his sister.

The agitation and tears which the subject occasioned brought on a headache, and it grew so much worse towards the evening that, added to her unwillingness to see Mr. Darcy, she decided not to join her cousins when they went to Rosings, where they had been invited to tea. Mrs. Collins, seeing that she was really unwell, did not press her to go, and as much as possible prevented her husband from pressing her. But Mr. Collins could not conceal his concerns about Lady Catherine's being rather displeased by her staying at home.

CHAPTER 34

When they were gone, Elizabeth, as if intending to maximize her vexation with Mr. Darcy, chose for her employment the examination of all the letters which Jane had written to her since being in Kent. They contained no actual complaint, nor was there any recitation of past wrongs, or any communication of present suffering. But in all, and in almost every line of each, there was a lack of that cheerfulness which she had previously possessed, and which had been scarcely ever been interrupted. Elizabeth noticed every sentence conveying the idea of unhappiness, with an attention which it had hardly received on the first reading. Mr. Darcy's shameful boast of what misery he had been able to inflict gave her a keener sense of her sister's sufferings. It was some consolation to think that his visit to Rosings was to end on the day after next, and a still greater that in less than a fortnight she would be with Jane again, and enabled to contribute to the recovery of her spirits by all that affection could do.

While thus occupied, she was suddenly roused by the sound of the door-bell, and to her utter amazement she saw Mr. Darcy walk into the room. In a hurried manner he immediately began an enquiry after her health, attributing his visit to a wish of hearing that she were better. She answered him with cold civility. He sat down for a few moments and then got up and walked about the room. Elizabeth was surprised, but said not a word. After a silence of several minutes, he came towards her in an agitated manner, and thus began —

"In vain have I struggled. It will not do. My feelings will not be repressed. You must allow me to tell you how passionately I admire and love you."

Elizabeth's astonishment was beyond expression. She stared, coloured, doubted, and was silent. This he considered sufficient encouragement; and the avowal of all that he felt, and had long felt for her, immediately followed. He spoke eloquently; but there were feelings besides those of the heart to be detailed, and he was not more expressive on the subject of tenderness than of pride. His sense of her inferiority — of its being a degradation — of the family obstacles which reason had always opposed, were dwelt on with a consideration which seemed to be caused by the sense of his own superiority he was wounding. It certainly didn't make Elizabeth any more disposed towards him.

In spite of her deeply rooted dislike she could not be unaware of the compliment of such a man's affection, and though her intentions did not vary for an instant she was at first sorry for the pain he was to receive. As he continued to speak her resentment grew, however, and she lost all compassion in anger. She tried, however, to compose herself to answer him with patience, when he had finished his speech. He concluded with representing to her the strength of that attachment which, in spite of all his endeavours, he had found impossible to conquer, and with expressing his hope that it would now be rewarded by her acceptance of his hand. As he said this, she could easily see that he had no doubt of a favourable answer. Such a circumstance could only exasperate farther, and when he ceased speaking the colour rose into her cheeks, and she said —

"In such cases as this, it is, I believe, the established mode to express a sense of obligation for the sentiment, however unequally it may be returned. It is natural that obligation should be felt, and if I could *feel* gratitude, I would now thank you. But I cannot — I have never desired your good opinion of me, and you have certainly bestowed it most unwillingly. I am sorry to have inflicted pain on anyone. It has been most unconsciously done, however, and I hope will be of short duration. The feelings which, you tell me, have long prevented the acknowledgment of your regard will certainly prevail after this explanation."

Mr. Darcy, who was leaning against the mantelpiece with his eyes fixed on her face, seemed to catch her words with more surprise than resentment. His complexion became pale with anger, and the disturbance of his mind was visible in every feature. He was struggling for the appearance of composure, and would not open his lips till he believed himself to have attained it. The pause was to Elizabeth's feelings dreadful. At length, in a voice of forced calmness, he said –

"And this is all the reply which I am to have the honour of expecting! I might, perhaps, wish to be informed why, with so little *attempt* at civility, I am thus rejected. But it is of little importance."

"I might as well inquire," replied she, "why with so evident a design of offending and insulting me, you chose to tell me that you liked me against your will, against your reason, and even against your better judgment? Was not this some excuse for incivility, if I *was* uncivil? But I have other reasons. You know I have. Had not my own feelings decided against you — had they been indifferent, or had they even been favourable, do you think that any consideration would tempt me to accept the man who has been the means of ruining, perhaps forever, the happiness of a most beloved sister?"

As she pronounced these words Mr. Darcy changed colour; but the emotion was short, and he listened without attempting to interrupt her while she continued –

"I have every reason in the world to think ill of you. No motive can excuse the unjust part you played *there*. You dare not, you cannot deny that you have been the principal, if not the only means of dividing them from each other — of exposing one to the censure of the world for impulsiveness and inconstancy, the other to its derision for disappointed hopes, and involving them both in misery of the strongest kind."

She paused, and saw with indignation that he was listening with an air which proved him wholly unmoved by any feeling of remorse. He even looked at her with a smile of disbelief.

"Can you deny that you have done it?" she repeated.

With assumed serenity he then replied, "I have no wish of denying that I did everything in my power to separate my friend from your sister, or that I rejoice in my success. Towards *him* I have been kinder than towards myself."

"But it is not merely this affair," she continued, "on which my dislike is founded. Long before it had taken place my opinion of you was decided. Your character was unfolded in the account which I received many months ago from Mr. Wickham. On this subject, what can you have to say? In what imaginary act of friendship can you here defend yourself?

"You take an eager interest in that gentleman's concerns," said Darcy, in a less tranquil tone, and with a heightened colour.

"Anyone who knows what his misfortunes have been cannot help feeling an interest in him."

"His misfortunes!" repeated Darcy contemptuously. "Yes, his misfortunes have been great indeed."

"And you are the cause of them," cried Elizabeth with energy. "You have reduced him to his present state of relative poverty. You have withheld the advantages which you must know were intended for him. You have deprived him of the best years of his life, of that independence which would otherwise have been his. You have done all this! And yet you can treat the mention of his misfortunes with contempt and ridicule."

"And this," cried Darcy, as he walked with quick steps across the room, "is your opinion of me! This is how you see me! I thank you for explaining it so fully. My faults, according to this calculation, are heavy indeed! But perhaps," added he, stopping in his walk, and turning towards her, "these offences might have been overlooked, had not your pride been hurt by my honest confession of the reasons which prevented my forming any serious plans to secure you. These bitter accusations might have been suppressed, had I, with greater discretion, concealed my struggles, and flattered you into the belief of my being compelled by reason, by feeling, by everything. But I do not play such games. Nor am I ashamed of the feelings I related. They were natural and just. Could you expect me to rejoice in the inferiority of your connections? To congratulate myself on the hope of relations whose condition in life is so decidedly beneath my own?"

Elizabeth felt herself growing more angry every moment; yet she tried to speak with composure when she said —

"You are mistaken, Mr. Darcy, if you suppose that the mode of your proposal affected me in any other way than to spare me the concern which I might have felt in refusing you, had you behaved in a more gentlemanlike manner."

She saw him visibly react to this, but he said nothing, and she continued —

"You could not have made me the offer of your hand in any possible way that would have tempted me to accept it."

Again his astonishment was obvious; and he looked at her with an expression of mingled disbelief and mortification. She went on —

"From the very beginning — from the first moment, I may almost say — of my acquaintance with you, your manners convinced me of your arrogance, your conceit, and your selfish disdain of the feelings of others. I had not known you a month before I felt that you were the last man in the world whom I could ever be convinced to marry."

"You have said quite enough, madam. I perfectly comprehend your feelings, and have now only to be ashamed of what my own have been. Forgive me for having taken up so much of your time, and accept my best wishes for your health and happiness."

And with these words he hastily left the room, and Elizabeth heard him the next moment open the front door and quit the house.

The tumult of her mind was now painfully great. She knew not how to support herself, and from actual weakness sat down and cried for half an hour. Her astonishment, as she reflected on what had passed, was increased by every thought of it. That she should receive an offer of marriage from Mr. Darcy! That he had been in love with her for so many months! So much in love as to wish to marry her in spite of all the objections which had made him prevent his friend's marrying her sister, and which must be even stronger in his own case–. It was gratifying to have inspired unconsciously so strong an affection. But his pride, his abominable pride — his shameless confession of what he had done with respect to Jane — his unpardonable assurance in acknowledging, though he could not justify it, and the unfeeling manner in which he had mentioned Mr. Wickham, his cruelty towards whom he had not attempted to deny, soon overcame the pity which the consideration of his love for her had for a moment excited. She continued in such agitating reflections till the sound of Lady Catherine's carriage made her realize how unready she was to encounter Charlotte's observation, and she hurried her away to her room.

CHAPTER 35

Elizabeth awoke the next morning to the same thoughts and agitations which had plagued her as she fell asleep. She could not yet recover from the surprise of what had happened: it was impossible to think of anything else. Totally unable to concentrate on anything, she resolved, soon after breakfast, to indulge herself in air and exercise. She was proceeding directly to her favourite walk when the recollection of Mr. Darcy's sometimes coming there stopped her, and instead of entering the park she turned up the lane, which led her farther from the main road. The park fence was still the boundary on one side, and she soon passed one of the gates into the ground.

After walking two or three times along that part of the lane, she was tempted, by the pleasantness of the morning, to stop at the gates and look into the park. The five weeks which she had now spent in Kent had made a great difference in the country, and every day was adding to the foilage of the trees. She was on the point of continuing her walk when she caught a glimpse of a gentleman within a grove that ran along the edge of the park. He was moving that way, and fearful of its being Mr. Darcy she directly retreated. But the person who advanced was now near enough to see her, and stepping forward with eagerness, called her name. She had turned away, but on hearing herself called, though in a voice which proved it to be Mr. Darcy, she moved again towards the gate. He had by that time reached it also, and, holding out a letter, which she instinctively took, said, with a look of haughty composure, "I have been walking in the grove some time in the hope of meeting you. Will you do me the honour of reading that letter?" And then, with a slight bow, turned again into the park and was soon out of sight.

With no expectation of pleasure, but with the strongest curiosity, Elizabeth opened the letter, and, to her still increasing wonder, perceived an envelope containing two sheets of letter-paper. Making her way down the lane, she then began it. It was dated from Rosings, at eight o'clock in the morning, and was as follows –

"Be not alarmed, madam, on receiving this letter, by the apprehension of its containing any repetition of those sentiments or renewal of those offers which were last night so unappealing to you. I write without any intention of paining you, or embarrassing myself, by dwelling on wishes which, for the happiness of both, cannot be too soon forgotten. The effort which the writing, and the reading, of this letter must occasion should have been spared had not my character required it to be done. You must, therefore, pardon the freedom with which I demand your attention. Your feelings, I know, will bestow it unwillingly, but my sense of fairness demands it.

"Two offences of a very different nature, and by no means of equal magnitude, you last night laid at my feet. The first-mentioned was that, heedless of the feelings of either, I had separated Mr. Bingley from your sister; and the other, that I had ruined the prosperity and prospects of Mr. Wickham — wilfully and wantonly to have thrown off the companion of my youth, the acknowledged favourite of my father, a young man who had scarcely any other means than what we could provide him — would be deplorable. But from that blame which was last night so liberally bestowed, respecting each circumstance, I shall hope to be exonerated, when the following account of my actions and their motives has been read.

"I had not been long in Hertfordshire before I saw, as did many others, that Bingley preferred your eldest sister to any other young woman in the country. But it was not till the evening of the dance at Netherfield that I had any notion of this feeling becoming a serious attachment. I had often seen him in love before. At that ball, while I had the honour of dancing with you, I was first made acquainted, by Sir William Lucas's accidental information, that Bingley's attentions to your sister had created a general expectation of their marriage. He spoke of it as a certain event, of which the time alone remained to be decided. From that moment I observed my friend's behaviour attentively; and I could then perceive that his preference for Miss Bennet was beyond what I had ever witnessed in him. Your sister I also watched. Her look and manners were open, cheerful, and engaging as ever, but without any symptom of particular regard, and I remained convinced from the evening's scrutiny that although she received his attentions with pleasure, she did not return the sentiment. If *you* have not been mistaken here, *I* must have been in an error. Your superior knowledge of your sister must make the latter probable. If it be so, if I have been misled by such error to inflict pain on her, your resentment has not been unreasonable. But I shall not hesitate to assert that your sister's behavior was such as might have given the most acute observer a conviction that, however amiable her temper, her heart was not likely to be easily won. That I was desirous of believing she was indifferent is certain — but I will venture to say that my investigations and decisions are not usually influenced by my hopes or fears. I did not believe her to be indifferent because I wished it; I believed it because of what I saw. As I last night acknowledged, there were many reasons for objecting to their marriage. The situation of your mother's family compared to that total lack of propriety so frequently, so almost uniformly betrayed by herself, by your three younger sisters, and occasionally even by your father. Forgive me. It pains me to offend you. But amidst your concern for the defects of your nearest relations, and your displeasure at this representation of them, let it give you consolation to consider that you have conducted yourself so as to avoid any share of the like condemnation, and this praise is no less generally bestowed on you than on your eldest sister. I will only say farther, that from what occurred that evening my opinion of all parties was confirmed, and every concern heightened which could have led me before to save my friend from what I believed would be a most unhappy connection. He left Netherfield for London on the day following, as you know, with the plan of soon returning.

"The part which I acted is now to be explained. His sisters' uneasiness had been equally excited with my own, and we felt that no time was to be lost in detaching their brother. We therefore shortly resolved on joining him in London. We accordingly went — and there I readily engaged in the office of pointing out to my friend the drawbacks of such a choice. I described them earnestly, but while this might have delayed his determination, I do not suppose that it would ultimately have prevented the marriage, had it not been seconded by the assurance which I gave of your sister's indifference. He had before believed her to return his affection with sincere, if not with equal regard. But Bingley has great natural modesty, with a stronger dependence on my judgment than on his own. To convince him, therefore, that he had deceived himself, was no great difficulty. To persuade him against returning to Hertfordshire when that conviction had been given was scarcely the work of a moment. I cannot blame myself for having done this. There is but one part of my conduct in the whole affair on which I do not reflect with satisfaction. It is that I concealed from him your sister's being in town. I knew it myself, as it was known to Miss Bingley, but her brother is even yet ignorant of it. That they might have met without ill consequence is perhaps probable, but his regard did not appear to me enough extinguished for him to see her without some danger. Perhaps this concealment, this disguise was beneath me. It is done, however, and it was done for the best. On this subject I have nothing more to say, no other apology to offer. If I have wounded your sister's feelings, it was unknowingly done, and though the motives which governed me may to you very naturally appear insufficient, I cannot condemn them.

"With respect to that other, more weighty accusation, of having injured Mr. Wickham, I can only refute it by laying before you the whole of his connection with my family. Of what he has *particularly* accused me I am ignorant, but the truth that I am about to relate can be confirmed by more than one witness.

"Mr. Wickham is the son of a very respectable man, who had for many years the management of all the Pemberley lands, and whose good conduct in the discharge of his trust naturally inclined my father to be of service to him. On George Wickham, who was his godson, his kindness was therefore liberally bestowed. My father supported him at school, and afterwards at Cambridge — most important assistance, as his own father, always poor from the extravagance of his wife, would have been unable to give him a gentleman's education. My father was not only fond of this young man's company, as his manners were always engaging, he had also the highest opinion of him. Hoping the church would be his profession, he intended to provide for him in it. As for myself, it is many, many years since I first began to think of him in a very different manner. The character defects — the lack of morals, which he was careful to guard from being generally known, could not escape the observation of a young man nearly the same age as himself, and who had opportunities of seeing him in unguarded moments, which Mr. Darcy could not have. Here again I shall give you pain — to what degree you only can tell.

"My excellent father died about five years ago; and his attachment to Mr. Wickham was to the last so steady, that in his will he particularly recommended it to me to promote his advancement in the best manner that his profession might allow. If he chose to be a clergyman, my father desired that a valuable family living might be his as soon as it became available. There was also a legacy of one thousand pounds. His own father did not live long after mine had died, and within half a year from these events Mr. Wickham wrote to inform me that, having finally resolved against pursuing a church profession, he hoped I would not think it unreasonable for him to expect some more immediate monetary advantage. He had some intention, he added, of studying the law, and I must be aware that the amount of one thousand pounds would be very insufficient support. I rather wished than believed him to be sincere; but, at any rate, was perfectly ready to accept his proposal. I knew that Mr. Wickham was ill fitted to be a clergyman; the business was therefore soon settled. He resigned all claim to assistance in the church, were it possible that he could ever be in a situation to receive it, and accepted in return three thousand pounds. All connection between us seemed now dissolved. I thought too ill of him to invite him to Pemberley, or see him in town. In town I believe he chiefly lived, but his studying the law was a mere pretence, and being now free from all restraint, his life was a life of idleness and imprudence. For about three years I heard little of him; but on the decease of the man who held the living which had previously been designated for him, he asked me in a letter to bestow the living upon him. His circumstances, he assured me, and I had no difficulty in believing it, were exceedingly bad. He had found the law a most unprofitable study, and was now absolutely resolved on being ordained, if I would give him the living in question. You will hardly blame me for refusing to comply with this request, or for resisting every repetition of it. His resentment was in proportion to the distress of his circumstances, and he was doubtless as outspoken in his abuse of me to others as he was me directly. After this period every appearance of acquaintance was dropped. How he lived I know not, but last summer he was again most painfully brought to my notice.

"I must now mention a circumstance which I would wish to forget myself, and which no obligation less than the present one should cause me to unfold to any human being. Having said this much, I have no doubt that you will keep it confidential. My sister, who is more than ten years younger than me, was left to the guardianship of my mother's nephew, Colonel Fitzwilliam, and myself. About a year ago she was taken from school and moved to London. Last summer she went with Mrs. Younge, whose care she was in, to Ramsgate. And there also went Mr. Wickham, undoubtedly by design, for there proved to have been a prior acquaintance between him and Mrs. Younge, in whose character we were most unhappily deceived. By her connivance and aid, he recommended himself to Georgiana, whose affectionate heart retained a strong impression of his kindness to her as a child, and she was persuaded to believe herself in love. She consented to an elopement, although she was then but fifteen, which must be her excuse. I joined them unexpectedly a day or two before it was to occur, and then Georgiana, unable to withstand the idea of grieving and offending a brother whom she almost looked up to as a father, acknowledged the whole plan to me. You may imagine what I felt and how I acted. Regard for my sister's reputation and feelings prevented any public exposure, but I wrote to Mr. Wickham, who left the place immediately, and Mrs. Younge was of course removed from her charge. Mr. Wickham's chief object was unquestionably my sister's fortune, which is thirty thousand pounds; but I cannot help supposing that the hope of getting revenge against me was a strong inducement as well.

"This, madam, is a faithful narrative of every event in which we have been concerned together; and if you do not absolutely reject it as false, you will, I hope, absolve me henceforth of cruelty towards Mr. Wickham. I know not in what manner, under what form of falsehood he has imposed on you. But his success is not perhaps to be wondered at, ignorant as you previously were of everything concerning him. Detection could not be in your power, and suspicion certainly not in your disposition.

"You may possibly wonder why all this was not told you last night; but I was not then master enough of myself to know what could or ought to be revealed. For the truth of everything here related, I can appeal more particularly to the testimony of Colonel Fitzwilliam, who, from our near relationship and constant interaction, and, still more as one of the executors of my father's will, has been unavoidably acquainted with every particular of these transactions. If your abhorrence of *me* should make *my* assertions valueless, you cannot be prevented by the same cause from confiding in my cousin. That there may be the possibility of consulting him, I shall endeavour to find some opportunity of putting this letter in your hands in the course of the morning. I will only add, God bless you. Fitzwilliam Darcy."

CHAPTER 36

If Elizabeth, when Mr. Darcy gave her the letter, did not expect it to contain a renewal of his offers, she had formed no expectation at all of its contents. But such as they were, it may be well supposed how eagerly she went through them, and what a variety of conflicting emotions were produced. Her feelings as she read were scarcely to be defined. With amazement did she first understand that he believed an apology could have any effect. She was persuaded that he could have no explanation to give which would justify his behavior. With a strong prejudice against everything he might say, she began his account of what had happened at Netherfield. She read with eagerness, so impatient to know what the next sentence might bring that she was incapable of paying attention to the one before her eyes. His belief of her sister's indifference she instantly decided must be false. His account of the real, the worst objections to the match, made her too angry to have any desire to give him the benefit of the doubt. He expressed no regret for what he had done which satisfied her; his style was not penitent, but haughty. It was all pride and insolence.

But when this subject was followed by his account of Mr. Wickham, when she read with somewhat clearer attention an account of events which, if true, must change entirely the way she looked at him. Astonishment, apprehension, and even horror, overwhelmed her. She wished to discredit it entirely, repeatedly exclaiming, "This must be false! This cannot be! This must be the worst falsehood!" When she had gone through the whole letter, though scarcely paying any attention to the last page or two, she put it hastily away, claiming that she would not give any weight to its contents and that she would never look in it again.

In this state of mind, with thoughts that could not be pacified, she walked on; but it would not do: in half a minute the letter was unfolded again, and collecting herself as well as she could, she again began the mortifying perusal of all that related to Wickham, and forced her frenzied mind to examine the meaning of every sentence. The account of his connection with the Pemberley family was exactly what he had related himself; and the kindness of the late Mr. Darcy, though she had not before known its extent, agreed equally well with his own words. So far each recital confirmed the other; but when she came to the will, the difference was great. What Wickham had said of the living was fresh in her memory, and as she recalled his very words, it was impossible not to feel that there was gross duplicity on one side or the other. When she read and re-read with the closest attention the particulars immediately following Wickham's resigning all claim to the living, of his receiving instead so large a sum as three thousand pounds, again was she forced to admit there could be some truth in Mr. Darcy's account. She put down the letter, weighed every circumstance with as much impartiality as she could command, deliberated on the probability of each statement's truth; but with little success. On both sides it was only claims without evidence. Again she read on, but every line proved more clearly that Mr. Darcy's conduct was such as must make him entirely blameless.

The extravagance and general wastefulness which Mr. Wickham had engaged in exceedingly shocked her; the more so, as she could bring no proof of its falsehood. She had never heard of him before his entrance into the Militia, and no one in Hertfordshire knew him well enough to do otherwise than believe his account of himself. As to his real character, had it been in her power to discover, she had never felt a wish of enquiring. His manners had recommended him at once as the possessor of every virtue. She tried to recollect some instance of goodness, some distinguished trait of integrity or benevolence, that might rescue him from the attacks of Mr. Darcy, but no such recollection befriended her. She could see him instantly before her, with all his charms; but she could remember no more substantial good than the general approval of the neighbourhood, and the regard which his social powers had gained for him there. After pausing on this point a considerable while, she once more continued to read. But, alas! the story which followed, of his designs on Miss Darcy, received some confirmation from what had passed between Colonel Fitzwilliam and herself only the morning before; and finally she was referred for the truth of every particular to Colonel Fitzwilliam himself — from whom she had previously received the information of his concern in all his cousin's affairs, and whose character she had no reason to question. She had almost resolved to ask him about it, but the idea was checked by the awkwardness of the request. At length she deemed it unnecessary by the conviction that Mr. Darcy would never have made such a proposal if he had not been well assured of his cousin's ability to confirm the claims made.

She perfectly remembered everything that had passed in conversation between Wickham and herself, in their first evening at Mr. Philips's. Many of his expressions were still fresh in her memory. She was *now* struck with the impropriety of such communications to a stranger, and wondered how it had escaped her notice before. She remembered that he had boasted of having no fear of seeing Mr. Darcy — that Mr. Darcy might leave the area, but that *he* should stand his ground: yet he had avoided the Netherfield ball the very next week. She remembered also that, till the Netherfield family had left, he had told his story to no one but herself; but that after their departure it had been everywhere discussed: that he had then no reserves, no hesitation to attack Mr. Darcy's character, though he had assured her that respect for the father would always prevent his exposing the son.

How differently did everything now appear in which he was concerned! His attentions to Miss King were now the result of views solely and hatefully mercenary. The mediocrity of her fortune proved no longer the moderation of his wishes, but his eagerness to grasp at anything. His behaviour to herself could now have had no tolerable motive; he had either been deceived with regard to her fortune, or had been gratifying his vanity by encouraging the preference which she believed she had most incautiously shown. Every lingering struggle in his favour grew fainter and fainter. In farther justification of Mr. Darcy, she could not help but admit that Mr. Bingley, when questioned by Jane, had long ago asserted his blamelessness in the affair. Though his manners were proud she had never, —since she had met him, seen anything that betrayed him to be unprincipled or unjust — anything that spoke him of immoral habits. Among his own connections he was esteemed and valued. Even Wickham had praised him as a brother, and she had often heard him speak so affectionately of his sister as to prove him capable of some amiable feeling. Had his actions been what Wickham represented them, so gross a violation of everything right could hardly have been concealed from the world. The friendship between a person capable of it, and such an amiable man as Mr. Bingley, was incomprehensible.

She grew absolutely ashamed of herself. Of neither Darcy nor Wickham could she think without feeling that she had been blind, partial, and prejudiced.

"How despicably have I acted!" she cried. "I, who have prided myself on my good judgment! I, who have valued myself on my abilities, who have often disdained the generous acceptance of my sister, and gratified my vanity in distrust. How humiliating is this discovery! Yet, how deserved a humiliation! Had I been in love, I could not have been more wretchedly blind. But vanity, not love, has been my folly. Pleased with the preference of one, and offended by the neglect of the other, on the very beginning of our acquaintance, I have courted prejudice and ignorance, and driven reason away. Till this moment I never knew myself."

From herself to Jane — from Jane to Bingley, her thoughts were on a path which soon brought to her recollection that Mr. Darcy's explanation *there* had appeared very insufficient, and she read it again. Widely different was the effect of a second perusal. How could she deny his claims in one instance and allow them in the other? He declared himself to have been totally unaware of her sister's attachment, and she could not help remembering what Charlotte's opinion had always been. Neither could she deny the justice of his description of Jane. She felt that Jane's feelings, though strong, were not publicly displayed, and that there was a constant calmness in her demeanor that one rarely saw in a lover.

When she came to that part of the letter in which her family were mentioned in terms of such mortifying, yet deserved reproach, her sense of shame was severe. The justice of the accusation struck her too forcibly to be denied, and the circumstances to which he particularly alluded as having passed at the Netherfield ball could not have made a stronger impression on his mind than on hers.

The compliment to herself and her sister was not unfelt. It soothed, but it could not console her for the contempt which had been self-imposed by the rest of her family. As she considered that Jane's disappointment had in fact been the work of her nearest relations, she felt depressed beyond anything she had ever known before.

After wandering along the lane for two hours, overcome by every variety of thought — re-considering events, determining probabilities, and reconciling herself, as well as she could, to a change so sudden and so important — fatigue, and a recollection of her long absence, made her at length return home. She entered the house with the wish of appearing cheerful as usual, and the resolution of repressing such reflections that would make her unfit for conversation.

She was immediately told that the two gentlemen from Rosings had each called during her absence; Mr. Darcy, only for a few minutes to take leave — but that Colonel Fitzwilliam had been sitting with them at least an hour, hoping for her return, and almost resolving to walk after her till she could be found. Elizabeth pretended to express concern in missing him, but she really rejoiced at it. She could think only of her letter.

CHAPTER 37

The two gentlemen left Rosings the next morning, and Mr. Collins, having been in waiting near the lodges to say his goodbyes, was able to bring home the pleasing intelligence of their appearing in very good health, and in as tolerable spirits as could be expected. To Rosings he then hastened, to console Lady Catherine and her daughter. On his return he brought back, with great satisfaction, an invitation from her ladyship asking them to dine with her.

Elizabeth could not see Lady Catherine without recollecting that, had she chosen it, she might by this time have been presented to her as her future niece. Nor could she think, without a smile, of what her ladyship's indignation would have been. "What would she have said? How would she have behaved?" were questions with which she amused herself.

Their first subject was the departure of the gentlemen. "I assure you, I feel it exceedingly," said Lady Catherine. "I believe nobody feels the loss of friends so much as I do. But I am particularly attached to those young men, and know them to be so very attached to me! They were excessively sorry to go! But they always are. The dear colonel rallied his spirits tolerably till just at last, but Darcy seemed to feel it most strongly. More, I think, than last year. His attachment to Rosings certainly increases."

Mr. Collins here gave a compliment, which was kindly smiled on by the mother and daughter.

Lady Catherine observed, after dinner, that Miss Bennet seemed out of spirits, and immediately accounted for it herself by supposing that she did not want to go home again so soon. She added —

"But if that is the case, you must write to your mother and beg her to let you stay a little longer. Mrs. Collins will be very glad of your company, I am sure."

"I am much obliged to your ladyship for your kind invitation," replied Elizabeth, "but it is not in my power to accept it. I must be in town next Saturday."

"Why, you have only been here only six weeks. I expected you to stay two months. I told Mrs. Collins so before you came. There can be no reason for your going so soon. Mrs. Bennet could certainly spare you for another two weeks."

"But my father cannot. He wrote last week to hurry my return."

"Oh! Your father of course may spare you, if your mother can. Daughters are never of so much importance to a father. And if you will stay another *month*, it will be in my power to take one of you as far as London, for I am going there early in June for a week. There will be room enough for one of you — and indeed, if the weather should happen to be cool, I should not object to taking you both, as neither of you is large."

"You are all kindness, madam, but I believe we must abide by our original plan."

Lady Catherine seemed resigned. "Mrs. Collins, you must send a servant with them. You know I always speak my mind, and I cannot bear the idea of two young women travelling by themselves. It is highly improper. You must send somebody. I have the greatest dislike in the world for that sort of thing. Young women should always be properly guarded and attended, according to their situation in life. When my niece Georgiana went to Ramsgate last summer, I made a point of her having two manservants to go with her. Miss Darcy, the daughter of Mr. Darcy of Pemberley, and Lady Anne would certainly have approved. I am excessively attentive to all those things. You must send John with the young ladies, Mrs. Collins. I am glad it occurred to me to mention it, for it would really be discreditable to *you* to let them go alone."

"My uncle is to send a servant for us."

"Oh! — Your uncle! — He keeps a manservant, does he? I am very glad you have somebody who thinks of those things. Where will you change horses? — Oh! Bromley of course. If you mention my name at the Bell, you will be attended to."

Lady Catherine had many other questions to ask respecting their journey, and as she did not answer them all herself, attention was necessary. Elizabeth considered this to be fortunate, for with a mind so occupied she might otherwise have forgotten where she was. Reflection must be reserved for solitary hours. Whenever she was alone, she gave in to it as the greatest relief. Not a day went by without a solitary walk, in which she might indulge in all the delight of unpleasant recollections.

Mr. Darcy's letter she now knew almost by heart. She studied every sentence, and her feelings towards its writer were at times widely different. When she remembered the tone of his letter, she was still full of indignation. But when she considered how unjustly she had condemned him, her anger was turned against herself and his disappointed feelings became the object of compassion. His interest in her elicited gratitude, and his general character deserved respect. But she could not for a moment regret her refusal of him, or feel the slightest inclination ever to see him again. In her own past behaviour there was a constant source of embarrassment, and in the unfortunate manners of her family she felt an even deeper sense of shame. There was no way to change that situation. Her father, contented with laughing at them, would never make an effort to restrain the irresponsible behavior of his youngest daughters. And her mother, with such poor manners herself, was entirely unaware of the problem. Elizabeth had frequently united with Jane in an endeavour to check the foolishness of Catherine and Lydia. But while they were supported by their mother's indulgence, what chance could there be of improvement? Catherine, weak-spirited, irritable, and completely under Lydia's guidance, had been always offended by their advice. And Lydia, self-willed and careless, would scarcely even listen to them. They were ignorant, idle, and vain. While there was an officer in Meryton, they would flirt with him. And while Meryton was within walking distance of Longbourn, they would be going there forever.

Anxiety on Jane's behalf was another prevailing concern. Mr. Darcy's explanation, by restoring Bingley to all her former good opinion, heightened the sense of what Jane had lost. His affection was proved to have been sincere, and his conduct blameless, except perhaps in the implicit trust he placed in his friend. How grievous then was the thought that, of a marriage so desirable in every respect, with so much potential for happiness, Jane had been deprived by the folly and bad manners of her own family!

When to these recollections was added the exposing of Wickham's character, it may be easily believed that the happy spirits which had seldom been depressed before were now so much affected as to make it almost impossible for her to appear tolerably cheerful.

Their visits to Rosings were as frequent during the last week of her stay as they had been at first. The very last evening was spent there, and her ladyship again inquired into the minute particulars of their journey, gave them directions as to the best method of packing, and was so urgent on the necessity of placing gowns in a certain way that Maria thought herself obliged, on her return, to undo all the work of the morning and pack her trunk anew.

When they parted, Lady Catherine wished them a good journey, and invited them to come to Hunsford again next year. Miss De Bourgh exerted herself so far as to curtsey and hold out her hand to both.

CHAPTER 38

On Saturday morning Elizabeth and Mr. Collins met for breakfast a few minutes before the others appeared, and he took the opportunity of paying the parting civilities which he felt were indispensable.

"I do not know, Miss Elizabeth," said he, "if Mrs. Collins has yet expressed her feelings about your kindness in coming to us, but I am very certain you will not leave the house without receiving her thanks for it. The favour of your company has been much felt, I assure you. We know how little there is to tempt anyone to our humble home. Our plain manner of living, our small rooms and few servants, and the little we see of the fashionable world must make Hunsford extremely dull to a young lady like yourself. But I hope you will believe us grateful for your company, and know that we have done everything in our power to prevent your spending your time unpleasantly."

Elizabeth was eager with her thanks and assurances of happiness. She had spent six weeks with great enjoyment, and the pleasure of being with Charlotte, and the kind attentions she had received, must make *her* feel obliged. Mr. Collins was gratified, and with a smile replied –

"It gives me the greatest pleasure to hear that you have passed your time agreeably. We have certainly done our best, and we most fortunately have it in our power to introduce you to very superior society. From our connections with Rosings, the frequent means of varying the humble home scene, I think we may flatter ourselves that your Hunsford visit cannot have been entirely troublesome. Our situation with regard to Lady Catherine's family is indeed the sort of extraordinary advantage and blessing which few can boast. You see on what a footing we are. You see how continually we are invited there. In truth, I must acknowledge that, with all the disadvantages of this humble parsonage, I should not think anyone living in it deserving of pity while they enjoy the intimacy of Rosings."

Words were insufficient to express his excitement, and he was obliged to walk about the room while Elizabeth tried to balance civility with truth in a few short sentences.

"You may, in fact, carry a very favourable report of us into Hertfordshire, my dear cousin. I flatter myself at least that you will be able to do so. Lady Catherine's great attentions to Mrs. Collins you have seen daily, and altogether I trust it does not appear that your friend has made a bad decision — but on this point it will be as well to be silent. Only let me assure you, my dear Miss Elizabeth, that I can from my heart most heartily wish you equal happiness in marriage. My dear Charlotte and I have but one mind and one way of thinking. There is in everything a most remarkable resemblance of character and ideas between us. We seem to have been made for each other."

Elizabeth could safely say that it was a great happiness where that was the case, and with equal sincerity could add that she firmly believed and rejoiced in his happiness. She was not sorry, however, to have the recital of them interrupted by the entrance of the lady of the house. Poor Charlotte! It was melancholy to leave her to such society! But she had chosen it with her eyes open, and though evidently regretting that her visitors were to go, she did not seem to ask for compassion. Her home and her housekeeping, her parish and her poultry, had not yet lost their charms.

At length the carriage arrived, the trunks were fastened on, the parcels placed within, and it was pronounced to be ready. After an affectionate parting between the friends, Elizabeth was led to the carriage by Mr. Collins. As they walked down the garden, he was asking her to pay his best respects to all her family, not forgetting his thanks for the kindness he had received at Longbourn in the winter. He then handed her in, Maria followed, and the door was on the point of being closed when he suddenly reminded them, with some consternation, that they had forgotten to leave any message for the ladies at Rosings.

"But," he added, "you will of course wish to have your humble respects delivered to them, with your grateful thanks for their kindness to you while you have been here."

Elizabeth made no objection; the door was then allowed to be shut, and the carriage drove off.

"Good gracious!" cried Maria, after a few minutes silence, "it seems but a day or two since we first came! And yet how many things have happened!"

"A great many indeed," said her companion with a sigh.

"We have dined nine times at Rosings, besides drinking tea there twice! How much I shall have to tell!"

Elizabeth privately added, "And how much I shall have to conceal."

Their journey was performed without much conversation, or any alarm. Within four hours of their leaving Hunsford they reached Mr. Gardiner's house, where they were to remain a few days.

Jane looked well, and Elizabeth had little opportunity of determining her state of mind amidst the various engagements which her aunt had reserved for them. But Jane was to go home with her, and at Longbourn there would be leisure enough for observation.

It was not without an effort, meanwhile, that she could wait even for Longbourn, before she told her sister of Mr. Darcy's proposals. To know that she had the power of revealing what would so exceedingly astonish Jane, and must, at the same time, so highly gratify her vanity, was quite tempting. Yet she had not yet decided how much or how little to communicate, and she feared that if she opened the subject she might say something about Bingley which would only grieve her sister farther.

CHAPTER 39

It was the second week in May, in which the three young ladies set out together from Gracechurch Street to return to Hertfordshire. As they drew near the appointed inn where Mr. Bennet's carriage was to meet them, they quickly perceived both Kitty and Lydia looking out of a dining-room upstairs. The two girls had been there for over an hour, happily employed in visiting a nearby hat shop, watching the sentinel on guard, and preparing a salad with cucumbers.

After welcoming their sisters, they triumphantly displayed a table set out with such cold meat as an inn larder usually affords, exclaiming, "Isn't this nice? Isn't it an agreeable surprise?"

"And we mean to treat you all," added Lydia, "but you must lend us the money, for we have just spent ours at the shop out there." Then, showing her purchases — "Look here, I have bought this bonnet. I do not think it is very pretty, but I thought I might as well buy it as not. I shall pull it to pieces as soon as I get home and see if I can make it better."

When her sisters called it ugly, she added with perfect unconcern, "Oh! But there were two or three much uglier in the shop, and when I have bought some prettier coloured satin to trim it with fresh, I think it will be very tolerable. Besides, it will not matter much what one wears this summer, after the officers have left Meryton. They are going in a fortnight."

"Are they indeed!" cried Elizabeth, with the great satisfaction.

"They are going to be camped near Brighton, and I do so want papa to take us all there for the summer! It would be such a delicious scheme, and I dare say would hardly cost anything at all. Mamma would like to go too, of all things! Only think what a miserable summer we shall have otherwise!"

"Yes," thought Elizabeth, "*that* would be a delightful scheme indeed, and further establish our family's poor reputation. Good Heaven! Brighton, and a whole camp full of soldiers, to us, who have been so disgraced already by one poor regiment of militia and the monthly balls of Meryton."

"Now I have got some news for you," said Lydia, as they sat down at table. "What do you think? It is excellent news — capital news — and about a certain person that we all like."

Jane and Elizabeth looked at each other, and the waiter was told that he need not stay. Lydia laughed, and said — "Yes, that is just like your formality and discretion. You thought the waiter must not hear, as if he cared! I dare say he often hears worse things said than I am going to say. But he is an ugly fellow! I am glad he is gone. I never saw such a long chin in my life. Well, but now for my news. It is about dear Wickham. There is no danger of Wickham's marrying Mary King. She is gone down to her uncle at Liverpool: gone to stay. Wickham is safe."

"And Mary King is safe!" added Elizabeth. "Safe from an unwise connection as to fortune."

"She is a great fool for going away, if she liked him."

"But I hope there is no strong attachment on either side," said Jane.

"I am sure there is not on *his*. I will answer for it: he never cared three straws about her — who *could* about such a nasty little freckled thing?"

As soon as all had eaten, and the elder ones paid, the carriage was ordered. After some effort, the whole party, with all their boxes, bags, and parcels, and the unwelcome addition of Kitty's and Lydia's purchases, were seated in it.

"How nicely we are crammed in!" cried Lydia. "I am glad I bought my bonnet, if it is only for the fun of having another hatbox! Well, now let us be quite comfortable and snug, and talk and laugh all the way home. First, let us hear what has happened to you all, since you went away. Have you seen any pleasant men? Have you had any flirting? I was in great hopes that one of you would have got a husband before you came back. Jane will be quite an old maid soon, I declare. She is almost twenty-three! Lord, how ashamed I should be of not being married before twenty-three! My aunt Philips says Lizzy should have accepted Mr. Collins, but *I* do not think there would have been any fun in it. Lord! How I should like to be married before any of you! And then I would chaperone you about to all the balls. Dear me! We had such a good piece of fun the other day at Colonel Forster's. Kitty and me were to spend the day there, and Mrs. Forster promised to have a little dance in the evening (by the way, Mrs. Forster and me are *such* friends!). So she asked the two Harringtons to come, but Harriet was ill, and so Pen was forced to come by herself. And then, what do you think we did? We dressed up Chamberlayne in woman's clothes on purpose to pass for a lady — only think what fun! Not a soul knew of it, but Colonel and Mrs. Forster, and Kitty and me, except my aunt, for we were forced to borrow one of her gowns; and you cannot imagine how good he looked!

When Denny, and Wickham, and Pratt, and two or three more of the men came in, they did not know him in the least. Lord! How I laughed! And so did Mrs. Forster. I thought I should have died. And *that* made the men suspect something, and then they soon found out what was the matter."

With such stories of their parties and good jokes did Lydia, assisted by Kitty's hints and additions, endeavour to amuse her companions all the way to Longbourn. Elizabeth listened as little as she could, but there was no escaping the frequent mention of Wickham's name.

Their reception at home was most kind. Mrs. Bennet rejoiced to see Jane in undiminished beauty, and more than once during dinner did Mr. Bennet say voluntarily to Elizabeth —

"I am glad you are back, Lizzy."

Their party in the dining room was large, for almost all the Lucases came to meet Maria and hear the news. Various were the subjects which occupied them: Lady Lucas was enquiring of Maria, across the table, after the welfare and poultry of her eldest daughter; Mrs. Bennet was doubly engaged, on one hand collecting an account of the present fashions from Jane, who sat some way below her, and, on the other, retelling them all to the younger Miss Lucases; and Lydia, in a voice rather louder than any other person's, was enumerating the various pleasures of the morning to anybody who would hear her.

"Oh! Mary," said she, "I wish you had gone with us, for we had such fun! As we went along, Kitty and me drew up all the blinds, and pretended there was nobody in the coach. I should have gone so all the way, if Kitty had not been motion sick; and when we got to the George, I do think we behaved very handsomely, for we treated the other three with the nicest cold luncheon in the world, and if you would have gone we would have treated you too. And then, when we came away, it was such fun! I thought we never should have got into the coach. I was ready to die of laughter. And then we were so merry all the way home! We talked and laughed so loud that anybody might have heard us ten miles off!"

To this Mary very gravely replied, "Far be it from me, my dear sister, to depreciate such pleasures. But I confess they would have no charms for *me* — I should infinitely prefer a book."

But of this answer Lydia heard not a word. She seldom listened to anybody for more than half a minute, and never listened to Mary at all.

In the afternoon Lydia encouraged the rest of the girls to walk to Meryton, but Elizabeth opposed the scheme. It should not be said that the Miss Bennets could not be at home half a day before they were in pursuit of the officers. There was another reason, too, for her opposition. She dreaded seeing Wickham again, and was resolved to avoid it as long as possible. The comfort to *her* of the regiment's approaching removal was indeed beyond expression. In two weeks they were to go — and once gone, she hoped there could be nothing more to plague her on his account.

She had not been many hours at home before she found that the Brighton scheme, of which Lydia had given them a hint at the inn, was under frequent discussion between her parents. Elizabeth saw that her father had not the smallest intention of yielding. But his answers were at the same time so vague and equivocal, that her mother, though often disheartened, had never yet despaired of succeeding at last.

CHAPTER 40

Elizabeth's impatience to tell Jane what had happened could no longer be overcome. At length, resolving to suppress every particular in which her sister was concerned, and preparing her to be surprised, she related the next morning the scene between Mr. Darcy and herself.

Miss Bennet's astonishment was soon lessened by the strong sisterly partiality which made any admiration of Elizabeth appear perfectly natural, and all surprise was shortly lost in other feelings. She was sorry that Mr. Darcy should have shared his feelings in such a way, but still more was she grieved for the unhappiness which her sister's refusal must have given him.

"His being so sure of succeeding was wrong," said she, " but consider how much it must increase his disappointment."

"Indeed," replied Elizabeth, "I am heartily sorry for him, but he has other feelings which will probably soon drive away his regard for me. You do not blame me, however, for refusing him?"

"Blame you! Oh, no."

"But you blame me for having praised Wickham."

"No — I do not know that you were wrong in saying what you did."

"But you *will* know it, when I have told you what happened the very next day."

She then spoke of the letter, repeating the whole of its contents as far as they concerned George Wickham. What a shock was this for poor Jane, who would willingly have gone through life without believing that so much wickedness existed in the whole race of mankind as was here collected in one individual. Nor was Darcy's vindication, though she was grateful for it, capable of consoling her for such discovery. Most earnestly did she labour to prove the probability of error, and seek to clear one without involving the other.

"This will not do," said Elizabeth. "You never will be able to make both of them good. Take your choice, but you must be satisfied with only one. There is but such a quantity of merit between them, just enough to make one good sort of man, and recently it has been shifting about. For my part, I am inclined to believe the merit to be all Mr. Darcy's, but you shall do as you choose."

It was some time, however, before a smile could be extorted from Jane.

"I do not know when I have been more shocked," said she. "Wickham so very bad! It is almost past belief. And poor Mr. Darcy! Dear Lizzy, only consider what he must have suffered. Such a disappointment! And with the knowledge of your ill opinion too! And having to relate such a thing about his sister! It is really too distressing. I am sure you must feel it so."

"Oh no, my regret and compassion are all done away by seeing you so full of both. I know you will do him such ample justice that I am growing every moment more unconcerned and indifferent. Your emotions are sufficient for us both, and if you lament over him much longer my heart will be as light as a feather."

"Poor Wickham. There is such an expression of goodness in his countenance! Such an openness and gentleness in his manner!"

"There certainly was some great mismanagement in the education of those two young men. One has got all the goodness, and the other all the appearance of it."

"I never thought Mr. Darcy as deficient in the *appearance* of it as you once did."

"And yet I meant to be uncommonly clever in taking so decided a dislike to him, without any reason. It is such a spur to one's faculties, such an opening for wit, to have a dislike of that kind. One may be continually abusive without saying anything just; but one cannot be always laughing at a man without now and then stumbling on something witty."

"Lizzy, when you first read that letter, I am sure your feelings were very different than they are now."

"Indeed, they were. I was very uncomfortable. I may say unhappy. And with no one to speak to of what I felt, no Jane to comfort me and say that I had not been so very weak and vain and nonsensical as I knew I had been! Oh how I wanted you!"

"How unfortunate that you should have used such very strong expressions in speaking of Wickham to Mr. Darcy, for now they *do* appear wholly undeserved."

"Certainly. But the misfortune of speaking with bitterness is a most natural consequence of the prejudices I had been encouraging. There is one point on which I want your advice. I want to be told whether I ought, or ought not, to make what I know of Wickham's character more generally known."

Miss Bennet paused a little and then replied, "Surely there can be no occasion for exposing him so dreadfully. What is your own opinion?"

"That it ought not to be attempted. Mr. Darcy has not authorised me to make his communication public. On the contrary, every particular relative to his sister was meant to be kept as much as possible to myself, and if I endeavour to undeceive people as to the rest of his conduct, who will believe me? The general prejudice against Mr. Darcy is so violent that it would be the death of half the good people in Meryton to attempt to place him in an amiable light. I am not equal to it. Wickham will soon be gone, and therefore it will not matter to anybody here what he really is. Sometime hence it will be all found out, and then we may laugh at their stupidity in not knowing it before. At present I will say nothing about it."

"You are quite right. To have his errors made public might ruin him forever. He is now, perhaps, sorry for what he has done, and anxious to re-establish his character. We must not make him give up on his efforts to improve himself."

The tumult of Elizabeth's mind was eased by this conversation. She had got rid of two of the secrets which had weighed on her for two weeks, and was certain of a willing listener in Jane, whenever she might wish to talk again on either. But there was still something lurking behind, of which prudence prevented the disclosure. She dared not relate the other half of Mr. Darcy's letter, nor explain to her sister how sincerely she had been valued by his friend. Here was knowledge in which no one could partake, and she was sensible that nothing less than a perfect understanding between the parties could justify her in throwing off this last burden. "And then," said she, "if that very improbable event should ever take place, I shall merely be able to tell what Bingley may tell in a much more agreeable manner himself. The liberty of communication cannot be mine till it has lost all its value!"

She was now, on being settled at home, at leisure to observe the real state of her sister's spirits. Jane was not happy. She still had a very tender affection for Bingley. Having never even believed herself in love before, her regard had all the warmth of first attachment, and, from her age and disposition, greater steadiness than most first attachments. So fervently did she value the memory of him, and prefer him to every other man, that all her good sense, and all her attention to the feelings of her friends, were requisite to check the indulgence of such sadness.

"Well, Lizzy," said Mrs. Bennet one day, "what is your opinion *now* of this business of Jane's? For my part, I am determined never to speak of it again to anybody. I told my sister Philips so the other day. I hear that Jane saw nothing of him in London. Well, he is a very undeserving young man — and I do not suppose there is the least chance in the world of her ever getting him now. There is no talk of his coming to Netherfield again in the summer, and I have inquired of everybody, too, who is likely to know."

"I do not believe that he will ever live at Netherfield again."

"Oh, well! It is just as he chooses. Nobody wants him to come. Though I shall always say that he used my daughter extremely ill; and if I was her, I would not have put up with it. Well, my comfort is, I am sure Jane will die of a broken heart, and then he will be sorry for what he has done."

But as Elizabeth could not receive comfort from any such expectation, she made no answer.

"Well, Lizzy," continued her mother, soon afterwards, "and so the Collinses live very comfortably, do they? Well, well, I only hope it will last. And what sort of table do they keep? Charlotte is an excellent manager, I dare say. If she is half as sharp as her mother, she is saving enough. There is nothing extravagant in *their* housekeeping, I dare say."

"No, nothing at all."

"A great deal of good management, depend upon it. Yes, yes. *They* will take care not to outrun their income. *They* will never be distressed for money. Well, much good may it do them! And so, I suppose, they often talk of having Longbourn when your father is dead. They look upon it quite as their own, I dare say, whenever that happens.

"It was a subject which they could not mention before me."

"No, it would have been strange if they had. But I have no doubt they often talk of it between themselves. Well, if they feel good about having an estate that is not lawfully their own, so much the better. *I* should be ashamed of having one that was only entailed on me."

CHAPTER 41

The first week of their return was soon gone. The second began. It was the last of the regiment's stay in Meryton, and all the young ladies in the neighbourhood were accordingly saddened. The dejection was almost universal. The elder Miss Bennets alone were still able to eat, drink, and sleep, and pursue the usual course of their employments. Very frequently were they reproached for this insensitivity by Kitty and Lydia, whose own misery was extreme, and who could not comprehend such hard-heartedness from someone in their own family.

"Good heavens! What is to become of us? What are we to do?" they would often exclaim in the bitterness of woe. "How can you be smiling so, Lizzy?"

Their affectionate mother shared all their grief; she remembered what she had herself endured on a similar occasion, five-and-twenty years ago.

"I am sure," said she, "I cried for two days together when Colonel Millar's regiment went away. It broke my heart."

"I am sure it shall break *mine*," said Lydia.

"If we could only go to Brighton!" observed Mrs. Bennet.

"Oh, yes! — If we could but go to Brighton! But papa is so disagreeable."

"A little sea-bathing would set me up forever."

"And my aunt Philips is sure it would do *me* a great deal of good," added Kitty.

Such were the kind of lamentations resounding perpetually through Longbourn House. Elizabeth tried to be amused by them, but all sense of pleasure was lost in shame. She felt anew the justice of Mr. Darcy's objections, and never had she before been so much disposed to pardon his interference in the affairs of his friend.

But Lydia's gloom was short-lived, for she received an invitation from Mrs. Forster, the wife of the Colonel of the regiment, to accompany her to Brighton. This invaluable friend was a very young woman, and very recently married. A resemblance in good humour and good spirits had recommended her and Lydia to each other, and out of their *three* months' acquaintance they had been quite close for *two*.

The rapture of Lydia on this occasion, her adoration of Mrs. Forster, the delight of Mrs. Bennet, and the mortification of Kitty, are scarcely to be described. Wholly inattentive to her sister's feelings, Lydia flew about the house in restless ecstasy, calling for everyone's congratulations, and laughing and talking with more passion than ever. The luckless Kitty remained in the parlour bemoaning her misfortune.

"I cannot see why Mrs. Forster should not ask *me* as well as Lydia," said she, "though I am *not* her particular friend. I have just as much right to be asked as she has, and more too, for I am two years older."

In vain did Elizabeth attempt to help her see reason, and Jane to make her accept her fate. As for Elizabeth herself, this invitation was so far from exciting in her the same feelings as in her mother and Lydia that she considered it as the death-warrant of all possibility of common sense for the latter. As detestable as such a step must make her, were it known, she could not keep from secretly advising her father not to let her go. She shared with him all the improprieties of Lydia's general behaviour, the little advantage she could derive from the friendship of such a woman as Mrs. Forster, and the probability of her being yet more imprudent with such a companion at Brighton, where the temptations must be greater than at home. He heard her attentively, and then said —

"Lydia will never be satisfied until she has brought shame upon herself in some public place or other, and we can never expect her to do it with so little expense or inconvenience to her family as under the present circumstances."

"If you were aware," said Elizabeth, "of the very great disadvantage to us all which must arise from the public notice of Lydia's unguarded and imprudent manner — nay, which has already arisen from it, I am sure you would make a different decision."

"Already arisen?" repeated Mr. Bennet. "What, has she frightened away some of your lovers? Poor little Lizzy! But do not be upset. Such squeamish youths as cannot bear to be connected with a little absurdity are not worth considering. Come, let me see the list of the pitiful fellows who have been kept away by Lydia's folly."

"Indeed, you are mistaken. I have no such injuries to resent. It is not of specific, but of general misfortune which I am now complaining. Our importance, our respectability in the world, must be affected by the wildness and lack of restraint which define Lydia's character. Excuse me —

for I must speak plainly. If you, my dear father, will not take the trouble of inhibiting her behavior, and of teaching her that her present pursuits are not to be the business of her life, she will soon be beyond repair. Her character will be set, and she will, at sixteen, be the most determined flirt that ever made herself and her family look ridiculous. A flirt, too, in the worst way: without any attraction beyond youth and tolerable figure. Kitty is no better. She will follow wherever Lydia leads. Vain, ignorant, idle, and absolutely uncontrolled! My dear father, can you suppose it possible that they will not be censured and despised wherever they are known, and that their sisters will not be often involved in the disgrace?"

Mr. Bennet saw that her whole heart was in the subject, and affectionately taking her hand, said in reply —

"Do not make yourself uneasy, my love. Wherever you and Jane are known you must be respected and valued; and you will not appear to less advantage for having a couple of — or I may say, three very silly sisters. We shall have no peace at Longbourn if Lydia does not go to Brighton. Let her go, then. Colonel Forster is a sensible man, and will keep her out of any real mischief; and she is luckily too poor to be an object of marital interest to anybody. At Brighton she will be of less importance even as a common flirt than she has been here. The officers will find women better worth their notice. Let us hope, therefore, that her being there may convince her of her own insignificance. At any rate, she cannot grow much worse without us needing to lock her up for the rest of her life."

With this answer Elizabeth was forced to be content, but her own opinion continued the same, and she left him disappointed and sorry. It was not in her nature, however, to increase her frustration by dwelling on it. She was confident of having performed her duty, and to fret over unavoidable evils, or augment them by anxiety, was not a part of her character.

Had Lydia and her mother known of her conversation with her father, their vexation would hardly have found expression in their united indignation. In Lydia's imagination, a visit to Brighton comprised every possibility of earthly happiness. She saw in her mind's eye the streets of that bathing place covered with officers. She saw herself the object of attention to dozens of them at present unknown. She saw all the glories of the camp — its tents stretched forth in beauteous uniformity of lines, crowded with the young and the vibrant, and dazzling with scarlet; and, to complete the view, she saw herself seated beneath a tent, tenderly flirting with at least six officers at once.

Had she known that her sister sought to tear her from such prospects and such realities as these, what would have been her feelings? They could have been understood only by her mother, who might have felt nearly the same. Lydia's going to Brighton was all that consoled her for the melancholy conviction of her husband's never intending to go there himself.

But they were entirely ignorant of what had passed, and their raptures continued, with little interruption, to the very day of Lydia's leaving home.

Elizabeth was now to see Mr. Wickham for the last time. Having been frequently in company with him since her return, agitation was pretty well over; the agitations of former affection entirely so. She had even learned to detect, in the very gentleness which had first delighted her, an insincerity and sameness that now wearied her. In his present behaviour to herself, moreover, she had a fresh source of displeasure, for his preference towards her could only serve, after what she now knew about him, to provoke her. She lost all compassion for him and was offended by his apparent belief that however long, and for whatever cause, his attentions had been withdrawn, her vanity would be gratified, and her preference secured at any time by their renewal.

On the very last day of the regiment's remaining at Meryton he dined, with others of the officers, at Longbourn; and so little was Elizabeth disposed to part from him in good-humour that, on his making some enquiry as to the manner in which her time had passed at Hunsford, she mentioned Colonel Fitzwilliam's and Mr. Darcy's having both spent three weeks at Rosings, and asked him if he were acquainted with the former.

He looked surprised, displeased, alarmed; but with a moment's recollection and a returning smile, replied that he had formerly seen him often; and, after observing that he was a very gentlemanlike man, asked her how she had liked him. Her answer was warmly in his favour. With an air of indifference he soon afterwards added —

"How long did you say that he was at Rosings?"

"Nearly three weeks."

"And you saw him frequently?"

"Yes, almost every day."

"His manners are very different from his cousin's."

"Yes, very different. But I think Mr. Darcy improves on acquaintance."

"Indeed!" cried Wickham with a look which did not escape her. "Is it in his manners that he improves? Has he deigned to add an ounce of civility to his ordinary style? For I dare not hope," he continued in a lower and more serious tone, "that his basic character has changed."

"Oh no!" said Elizabeth. "His character, I believe, is very much as it ever was."

While she spoke, Wickham looked as if scarcely knowing whether to rejoice over her words, or to distrust their meaning. There was a something in her countenance which made him listen with a concerned and anxious attention while she added —

"When I said that he improved on acquaintance, I did not mean that either his mind or manners were in a state of improvement, but that, from knowing him better, his disposition was better understood."

Wickham's alarm now appeared in a heightened complexion and agitated look; for a few minutes he was silent, till, shaking off his embarrassment, he turned to her again, and said in the gentlest of accents—

"You, who so well know my feelings towards Mr. Darcy, will readily understand how sincerely I must rejoice that he is wise enough to assume even the *appearance* of what is right. His pride may be of some service, if not to himself, then to many others, for it must keep him from such further foul misconduct as I have suffered. I only fear that the sort of cautiousness to which you, I imagine, have been alluding, is merely adopted on his visits to his aunt, of whose good opinion and judgment he stands much in awe. His fear of her was always operative, I know, when they were together; and a good deal is to be attributed to his wish of furthering the match with Miss De Bourgh, which I am certain he has very much at heart."

Elizabeth could not repress a smile at this, but she answered only by a slight inclination of the head. She saw that he wanted to resurrect the old subject of his grievances, and she was in no mood to indulge him. The rest of the evening passed with the *appearance*, on his side, of usual cheerfulness, but with no further attempt to pay particular attention to Elizabeth. They parted at last with mutual civility, and possibly a mutual desire of never meeting again.

When the party broke up, Lydia returned with Mrs. Forster to Meryton, from whence they were to set out early the next morning. The separation between her and her family was more noisy than sad. Kitty was the only one who shed tears, but she wept out of and envy. Mrs. Bennet was profuse in her good wishes for the happiness of her daughter, and persistent in her injunctions that she would not miss the opportunity of enjoying herself as much as possible — advice which there was every reason to believe would be taken. In the clamorous happiness of Lydia herself in bidding farewell, the more gentle adieus of her sisters were uttered without being heard.

CHAPTER 42

Had Elizabeth's opinion been all drawn from her own family, she could not have formed a very pleasing picture of marital happiness or domestic comfort. Her father, captivated by youth and beauty, and that appearance of good-humour which youth and beauty generally give, had married a woman whose weak understanding and uneducated mind had very early in their marriage put an end to all real affection for her. Respect, esteem, and confidence had vanished forever; and all his views of domestic happiness were overthrown. But Mr. Bennet was not of a disposition to seek comfort for the disappointment which his own imprudence had brought on in any pleasurable vice. He was fond of the country and of books, and from these tastes derived his principle enjoyments. To his wife he was very little otherwise indebted, although her ignorance and folly did contribute to his amusement. This is not the sort of happiness which a man would in general wish to owe to his wife; but where other forms of entertainment are lacking, the true philosopher will derive benefit from such as are given.

Elizabeth, however, had never been blind to the impropriety of her father's behaviour as a husband. She had always seen it with pain, but she respected his abilities, and she was grateful for his affectionate treatment of herself. So she endeavoured to forget what she could not overlook, and to banish from her thoughts that continual breach of marital obligation and treatment which, in exposing his wife to the ridicule of her own children, was so highly offensive. But she had never felt as strongly as now the disadvantages which must belong to the children of so unsuitable a marriage, nor ever been so fully aware of the evils arising from such a misuse of talents. Rightly used, such talents might at least have preserved the respectability of his daughters, even if they were incapable of enlarging the mind of his wife.

While Elizabeth had rejoiced over Wickham's departure, she found little other cause for satisfaction in the loss of the regiment. Their visits to Meryton were less interesting than before, and at home she had a mother and sister whose constant complaints about the dullness of everything around them threw a real gloom over their domestic circle. Though Kitty might in time regain some sense, since the disturbers of her mind were removed, her other sister was likely to be further advanced in her folly by her stay in Brighton. Upon the whole, therefore, she found, what has been sometimes found before, that an event to which she had looked forward with impatient desire, did not, in taking place, bring all the anticipated satisfaction. It was therefore necessary to name some other period for the commencement of actual happiness — to have some other point on which her wishes and hopes might be placed. Her tour to the Lakes was now the object of her thoughts; it was her best consolation for all the uncomfortable hours which the discontentedness of her mother and Kitty made inevitable. Could she have included Jane in the scheme, every part of it would have been perfect.

"But it is fortunate," thought she, "that I have something to wish for. Were the whole arrangement complete, my disappointment would be certain. But here, by carrying with me one ceaseless source of regret in my sister's absence, I may reasonably hope to have all my expectations of pleasure realized. A scheme of which every part promises delight can never be successful; and general disappointment is only warded off by the defence of some little peculiar vexation."

When Lydia went away, she promised to write very often and with great detail to her mother and Kitty; but her letters were infrequent, and always very short. Those to her mother contained little else than that they were just returned from the library, where such and such officers had joined them; that she had a new gown, or a new parasol, which she would have described more fully, but was obliged to leave off in a hurry, as Mrs. Forster called her, and they were going to the camp. From her correspondence with her sister, there was still less to be learned — for her letters to Kitty, though rather longer, were much too full of secretive communications to be made public.

After the first two or three weeks of her absence, health, good-humour and cheerfulness began to reappear at Longbourn. Everything wore a happier aspect. The families who had been in town for the winter came back again, and summer apparel and summer engagements arose. Mrs. Bennet was restored to her usual discontented serenity; and by the middle of June Kitty was so much recovered as to be able to enter Meryton without tears. This made Elizabeth hope that by the following Christmas she might be so tolerably reasonable as not to mention an officer more than once a day, unless, by some cruel and malicious arrangement at the War Office, another regiment should be quartered in Meryton.

The time fixed for the beginning of their northern tour was now fast approaching, but a letter arrived from Mrs. Gardiner delayed its commencement and reduced its extent. Mr. Gardiner would be prevented by business from setting out till July, and must be in London again within a month. As that left too short a period for them to go so far, and see so much as they had proposed, or at least to see it with the leisure and comfort they had planned on, they were obliged to give up the Lakes, and, according to the present plan, were to go no farther northward than Derbyshire. In that county there was enough to be seen to occupy the greater part of their three weeks; and to Mrs. Gardiner it had a peculiarly strong attraction. The town where she had formerly passed some years of her life, and where they were now to spend a few days, was probably as great an object of her curiosity as all the popular attractions.

Elizabeth was excessively disappointed; she had set her heart on seeing the Lakes, and still thought there might have been time enough. But it was her duty to be satisfied — and certainly her temper to be happy; and all was soon right again.

With the mention of Derbyshire there were many ideas formed. It was impossible for her to see the word without thinking of Pemberley and its owner. "But surely," said she, "I may enter his county with impunity, and rob it of a few souvenirs without his perceiving me."

The period of expectation was now increased. Four weeks were to pass away before her uncle and aunt's arrival. But they did pass away, and Mr. and Mrs. Gardiner, with their four children, did at length appear at Longbourn. The children, two girls of six and eight years old, and two younger boys, were to be left under the care of their cousin Jane, who was the general favourite, and whose steady sense and sweetness of temper perfectly suited her for taking care of them in every way — teaching them, playing with them, and loving them.

The Gardiners stayed only one night at Longbourn, and set off the next morning with Elizabeth in pursuit of novelty and amusement. One enjoyment was certain — that of suitableness as companions; a suitableness which included health and temper to bear inconveniences — cheerfulness to enhance every pleasure — and affection and intelligence.

It is not the object of this work to give a description of Derbyshire, nor of any of the remarkable places through which their route passed: Oxford, Blenheim, Warwick, Kenelworth, Birmingham, etc., are sufficiently known. A small part of Derbyshire is all the present concern. To the little town of Lambton, the scene of Mrs. Gardiner's former residence, and where she had recently learned that some acquaintance still remained, they went, after having seen all the principal wonders of the country. Elizabeth soon discovered that Pemberley was situated within five miles of Lambton. It was not in their direct road, nor more than a mile or two out of it. In talking over their route the evening before, Mrs. Gardiner expressed a desire to see the place again. Mr. Gardiner declared his willingness, and Elizabeth was applied to for her approval.

"My love, should not you like to see a place of which you have heard so much?" said her aunt. "A place, too, with which so many of your acquaintance are connected. Wickham spent his childhood there, you know."

Elizabeth was distressed. She felt that she had no business at Pemberley, and was obliged to make an excuse for not wanting to see it. She must say that she was tired of great houses; after going over so many, she really had no pleasure in fine carpets or satin curtains.

Mrs. Gardiner protested. "If it were merely a fine house richly furnished," said she, "I should not care about it myself; but the grounds are delightful. They have some of the finest woods in the country."

Elizabeth said no more — but her mind could not be at peace. The possibility of meeting Mr. Darcy while viewing the place immediately occurred to her. It would be dreadful! She blushed at the very idea, and thought it would be better to speak openly to her aunt than to take such a risk. But against this there were objections; and she finally resolved that it could be a last resort if her private enquiries as to the absence of the family were unfavourably answered.

Accordingly, when she went to bed for the night, she asked the chambermaid whether Pemberley were not a very fine place, what was the name of its proprietor, and, with no little alarm, whether the family were down for the summer. A most welcome negative followed the last question. Her worries being now removed, she was at leisure to feel a great deal of curiosity to see the house herself; and when the subject was brought up again the next morning, and she was again applied to, could readily answer that she had not really any dislike to the scheme. To Pemberley, therefore, they were to go.

CHAPTER 43

Elizabeth, as they drove along, watched for the first appearance of Pemberley Woods with some anxiety. When at length they turned in at the lodge, her spirits were in a high flutter.

The park was very large, and contained great variety of attractions. They entered it in one of its lowest points, and drove for some time through a beautiful wood.

Elizabeth's mind was too full for conversation, but she saw and admired every remarkable spot and point of view. They gradually ascended for half a mile, and then found themselves at the top of a large hill, where the wood ceased and the eye was instantly caught by Pemberley House, situated on the opposite side of a valley. It was a large, attractive stone building, standing on rising ground, and backed by a ridge of high woody hills. In the front there was a stream and Elizabeth was thoroughly delighted. She had never seen a place for which nature had done more, or where natural beauty had been so little interfered with by poor taste. They were all of them warm in their admiration; and at that moment she felt that to be mistress of Pemberley might be something!

They descended the hill, crossed the bridge, and drove to the door, and all her apprehensions of meeting its owner returned. She dreaded lest the chambermaid had been mistaken. On asking to see the place, they were admitted into the hall; and Elizabeth, as they waited for the housekeeper, had leisure to wonder at her being where she was.

The housekeeper came; a respectable-looking elderly woman who was quite civil. They followed her into the dining parlour. It was a large, well-proportioned room, nicely furnished. Elizabeth, after looking it over, went to a window to take in the view. The hill, crowned with wood, from which they had descended, was beautiful. Every feature of the grounds was good; and she looked on the whole scene — the river, the trees scattered on its banks, and the winding of the valley, as far as she could trace it — with delight. As they passed into other rooms these objects were taking different positions, but from every window there were beauties to be seen. The rooms were lofty and elegant, and their furniture suitable to the fortune of their proprietor. But Elizabeth saw, with admiration of his taste, that it was neither gaudy nor uselessly luxurious; with less splendor, and more real elegance, than the furniture of Rosings.

"And of this place," thought she, "I might have been mistress! With these rooms I might now have been familiarly acquainted! Instead of viewing them as a stranger, I might have enjoyed them as my own, and welcomed to them as visitors my uncle and aunt. But no," — recollecting herself — "that could never be: my uncle and aunt would have been seen as not genteel enough by the master of the house; I should not have been allowed to invite them."

This was a lucky recollection — it saved her from something like regret.

She longed to inquire of the housekeeper whether her master were really absent, but had not courage for it. At length, however, the question was asked by her uncle, and she turned away with alarm while Mrs. Reynolds replied that he was, adding, "But we expect him tomorrow, with a large party of friends." How happy was Elizabeth that their own journey had not by any circumstance been delayed a day! Her aunt now called her over to look at a picture. She approached and saw the likeness of Mr. Wickham hung, amongst several other miniatures, over the mantlepiece. Her aunt asked her, smilingly, how she liked it. The housekeeper came forward and told them it was the picture of a young gentleman, the son of her late master's steward, who had been brought up by him at his own expense. He is now gone into the army," she added; "but I am afraid he has turned out very wild."

Mrs. Gardiner looked at her niece with a smile, but Elizabeth could not return it.

"And that," said Mrs. Reynolds, pointing to another of the miniatures, "is my master — and a very good likeness of him. It was drawn at the same time as the other — about eight years ago."

"I have heard much of your master's fine person," said Mrs. Gardiner, looking at the picture. "It is a handsome face. But, Lizzy, you can tell us whether it looks like him or not."

Mrs. Reynolds's respect for Elizabeth seemed to increase on this hint of her knowing her master.

"Does that young lady know Mr. Darcy?"

Elizabeth coloured, and said — "A little."

"And do you not think him a very handsome gentleman, ma'am?"

"Yes, very handsome."

"I am sure *I* know none so handsome; but in the gallery upstairs you will see a finer, larger picture of him than this. This room was my late master's favourite room, and these miniatures are just as they used to be then. He was very fond of them."

This accounted for Mr. Wickham's portrait being among them.

Mrs. Reynolds then directed their attention to a picture of Miss Darcy, drawn when she was only eight years old.

"And is Miss Darcy as comely as her brother?" said Mr. Gardiner.

"Oh! yes — the most beautiful young lady that ever was seen; and so accomplished! She plays and sings all day long. In the next room is a new instrument just come down for her — a present from my master; she comes here tomorrow with him."

Mr. Gardiner, whose manners were open and pleasant, encouraged her communicativeness by his questions and remarks. Mrs. Reynolds, either from pride or attachment, had evidently great pleasure in talking of her master and his sister.

"Is your master at Pemberley often?"

"Not so much as I could wish, sir; but I dare say he may spend half his time here; and Miss Darcy is always down for the summer months."

"Except," thought Elizabeth, "when she goes to Ramsgate."

"If your master would marry, you might see more of him."

"Yes, sir; but I do not know when *that* will be. I do not know who is good enough for him."

Mr. and Mrs. Gardiner smiled. Elizabeth could not help saying, "It is very much to his credit, I am sure, that you should think so."

"I say no more than the truth, and what everybody will say that knows him," replied the other. Elizabeth thought this was going pretty far, and she listened with increasing astonishment as the housekeeper added, "I have never heard a cross word from him in my life, and I have known him ever since he was four years old."

This was praise indeed, and it directly contrasted with her view of him. That he was not a good-tempered man had been her firmest opinion. Her keenest attention was awakened. She longed to hear more, and was grateful to her uncle for saying —

"There are very few people of whom so much can be said. You are lucky to have such a master."

"Yes, sir, I know I am. If I was to travel throughout the world, I could not find a better. But I have always observed, that they who are good-natured when children, are good-natured when they grow up; and he was always the sweetest-tempered, most generous-hearted boy in the world."

Elizabeth almost stared at her. "Can this be Mr. Darcy?" she thought.

"His father was an excellent man," said Mrs. Gardiner.

"Yes, ma'am, that he was indeed, and his son will be just like him — just as generous to the poor."

Elizabeth listened, wondered, doubted, and was impatient to hear more. Mrs. Reynolds could interest her on no other point. She related the subject of the pictures, the dimensions of the rooms, and the price of the furnishings, in vain. Mr. Gardiner, highly amused by the kind of family prejudice to which he attributed her excessive praise of her master, soon came back to the subject; and she dwelt with energy on his many merits as they proceeded together up the main staircase.

"He is the best landlord, and the best master," said she, "that ever lived; not like the wild young men nowadays, who think of nothing but themselves. There is not one of his tenants or servants but what will give him a good name. Some people call him proud; but I am sure I never saw anything of it. In my opinion, it is only because he does not ramble on like other young men."

"In what an amiable light does this place him!" thought Elizabeth.

"This fine account of him," whispered her aunt as they walked, "is not quite consistent with his behaviour to our poor friend."

"Perhaps we have been deceived."

"That is not very likely; our authority was too good."

On reaching the spacious lobby above, they were shown into a very pretty sitting-room, recently refurnished with greater elegance than the rooms below. They were informed that it was done to give pleasure to Miss Darcy, who had taken a liking to the room when last at Pemberley.

"He is certainly a good brother," said Elizabeth, as she walked towards one of the windows.

Mrs. Reynolds anticipated Miss Darcy's delight, when she entered the room. "And this is always the way with him," she added. "Whatever can give his sister any pleasure is sure to be done in a moment. There is nothing he would not do for her."

The picture-gallery, and two or three of the principal bedrooms, were all that remained to be shown. In the former were many good paintings, but Elizabeth knew little of art. Miss Darcy's crayon drawings had subjects that were usually more interesting, and also more intelligible.

In the gallery there were many family portraits, but they could offer little that might capture the attention of a stranger. Elizabeth walked on in quest of the only face whose features would be known to her. At last she beheld a striking resemblance of Mr. Darcy, with such a smile over the face as she remembered to have sometimes seen when he looked at her. She stood several minutes before the picture in earnest contemplation, and returned to it again before they left the gallery. Mrs. Reynolds informed them that it had been taken in his father's lifetime.

There was certainly at this moment, in Elizabeth's mind, a more gentle sensation towards the original than she had ever felt during their acquaintance. The commendation bestowed on him by Mrs. Reynolds was of no trifling nature. What praise is more valuable than the praise of an intelligent servant? As a brother, a landlord, a master, she considered how many people's happiness were in his care — how much of pleasure or pain it was in his power to bestow — how much of good or evil must be done by him! Every word that had been brought forward by the housekeeper was favourable to his character, and as she stood before the canvas on which he was represented, and fixed his eyes upon herself, she thought of his regard with a deeper sentiment of gratitude than it had ever raised before. She remembered its warmth, and softened its impropriety of expression.

When all of the house that was open to general inspection had been seen, they returned downstairs, and taking leave of the housekeeper, were delivered to the gardener, who met them at the hall door.

As they walked across the lawn towards the river, Elizabeth turned back to look again; her uncle and aunt stopped also: and while the former was wondering aloud when the building was constructed, the owner of it himself suddenly came forward from the road which led behind it to the stables.

They were within twenty yards of each other, and so abrupt was his appearance that it was impossible to avoid his sight. Their eyes instantly met, and the cheeks of each were overspread with the deepest blush. He was absolutely astonished, and for a moment he seemed paralyzed; but shortly recovering himself, he advanced towards the party and spoke to Elizabeth, if not in terms of perfect composure, at least of perfect civility.

She had instinctively turned away; but, stopping on his approach, received his compliments with an embarrassment impossible to be overcome. Had his first appearance, or his resemblance to the picture they had just been examining, been insufficient to assure the other two that they now saw Mr. Darcy, the gardener's expression of surprise on beholding his master, must immediately have betrayed it. They stood a little aloof while he was talking to their niece, who, astonished and confused, scarcely dared lift her eyes to his face, and knew not what answer she returned to his civil enquiries after her family. Amazed at the alteration in his manner since they last parted, every sentence that he uttered was increasing her embarrassment. Every idea of the impropriety of her being found there came into her mind, and the few minutes in which they continued together were some of the most uncomfortable of her life. Nor did he seem much more at ease: when he spoke, his tone had none of its usual calmness; and he repeated his enquiries as to the time of her having left Longbourn, and of her stay in Derbyshire, so often, and in so hurried a way, as plainly displayed his discomposure.

At length every idea seemed to fail him; and, after standing a few moments without saying a word, he suddenly recollected himself, and took leave.

The others then joined her, and expressed their admiration of him; but Elizabeth heard not a word, and, wholly consumed by her own feelings, followed them in silence. She was overpowered by shame and frustration. Her coming there was the most unfortunate, the most ill-judged thing in the world! How strange must it appear to him! In what a disgraceful light might it not strike so vain a man! It might seem as if she had purposely thrown herself in his way again! Oh! Why did she come? Or, why did he come here a day before he was expected? Had they been only ten minutes sooner, they should have been beyond his reach; for it was plain that he had just arrived — had just dismounted from his horse or exited his carriage. She blushed again and again over the ill timing of the unfortunate meeting. And his behaviour, so strikingly altered — what could it mean? That he should even speak to her was amazing! But to speak with such civility, to inquire after her family! Never in her life had she seen his manners so little dignified, never had he spoken with such gentleness as on this unexpected meeting. What a contrast did it offer to the last time she saw him in Rosings Park, when he put his letter into her hand! She knew not what to think, nor how to account for it.

They had now entered a beautiful walk by the side of the water, but it was some time before Elizabeth noticed any of it; and, though she answered mechanically to the repeated appeals of her uncle and aunt, and seemed to direct her eyes to such objects as they pointed out, she paid no attention to the scene. Her thoughts were all fixed on that one spot of Pemberley House, whichever it might be, where Mr. Darcy then was. She longed to know what at that moment was going through his mind — in what manner he thought of her, and whether, in spite of everything, she still mattered to him. Perhaps he had been civil only because he felt himself at ease; yet there had been *that* in his voice which was not like ease. Whether he had felt more of pain or of pleasure in seeing her she could not tell, but he certainly had not seen her with composure.

At length, however, the remarks of her companions on her absence of mind roused her, and she felt the necessity of appearing more like herself.

They entered the woods, and bidding adieu to the river for a while, ascended some of the higher grounds. In spots where the opening of the trees gave the eye power to wander, there were many charming views of the valley, the opposite hills, and the woods. Mr. Gardiner expressed a wish of going round the whole park, but feared it might be too far to walk. With a triumphant smile, they were told that it was ten miles round. It settled the matter; and they pursued the shorter circuit, which brought them again, after some time, to the edge of the water, in one of its narrowest parts.

They crossed it by a simple bridge, in character with the general air of the scene. It was a spot less adorned than any they had yet visited, and the valley here contracted into a glen, allowed room only for the stream and a narrow walk amidst the woods which bordered it. Elizabeth longed to explore its windings; but when they had crossed the bridge and perceived their distance from the house, Mrs. Gardiner, who was not a great walker, could go no farther, and thought only of returning to the carriage as quickly as possible. Her niece was, therefore, obliged to submit, and they made their way towards the house on the opposite side of the river. Their progress was slow, for Mr. Gardiner, though seldom able to indulge the taste, was very fond of fishing, and was so much engaged in watching the occasional appearance of some trout in the water, and talking to the man about them, that he advanced but little. While wandering on in this slow manner, they were again surprised, and Elizabeth's astonishment was quite as great as it had been at first, by the sight of Mr. Darcy approaching them, and at no great distance. The walk was here less sheltered than on the other side, and this allowed them to see him before they met. Elizabeth, however astonished, was at least more prepared for a conversation than before, and she resolved to appear and to speak with calmness, if he really intended to meet them. For a few moments, indeed, she felt that he would probably strike into some other path. This idea lasted while a turn in the walk concealed him from their view. The turn passed, and he was immediately before them. With a glance she saw that he had lost none of his recent civility; and, to imitate his politeness, she began as they met to admire the beauty of the place. But she had not got beyond the words "delightful," and "charming," when she realized that praise of Pemberley from her might be mischievously construed. Her colour changed, and she said no more.

Mrs. Gardiner was standing a little behind; and on her pausing, he asked her if she would do him the honour of introducing him to her friends. This was a stroke of civility for which she was quite unprepared; and she could hardly suppress a smile at his being now seeking the acquaintance of some of those very people against whom his pride had been set when he proposed to her. "What will be his surprise," thought she, "when he finds out who they are? He takes them now for people of fashion."

The introduction, however, was immediately made; and as she named their relationship to herself, she stole a sly look at him, to see how he bore it, and was not without the expectation of his distancing himself as fast as he could from such disgraceful companions. That he was *surprised* by the connection was evident; he sustained it, however, with fortitude, and, so far from going away, turned back with them, and entered into conversation with Mr. Gardiner. Elizabeth could not but be pleased, could not but triumph. It was consoling that he should know she had some relations of whom there was no need to blush. She listened most attentively to all that passed between them, and gloried in every expression, every sentence of her uncle, which marked his intelligence, his taste, or his good manners.

The conversation soon turned to fishing, and she heard Mr. Darcy invite him, with the greatest civility, to fish there as often as he chose while he remained in the neighbourhood, offering at the same time to supply him with fishing tackle, and pointing out those parts of the stream where there was usually most sport. Mrs. Gardiner, who was walking arm-in-arm with Elizabeth, gave her a look expressing her wonder. Elizabeth said nothing, but it gratified her exceedingly; the compliment must be all for herself. Her astonishment, however, was extreme, and continually was she repeating, "Why is he so changed? From what can it proceed? It cannot be for *me* — it cannot be for *my* sake that his manners are thus softened. My reproofs at Hunsford could not work such a change as this. It is impossible that he should still love me."

After walking some time in this way, the two ladies in front, the two gentlemen behind, on resuming their places, after descending to the brink of the river for the better inspection of some curious water-plant, there chanced to be a little alteration. It originated in Mrs. Gardiner, who, fatigued by the exercise of the morning, found Elizabeth's arm inadequate to her support, and consequently preferred her husband's. Mr. Darcy took her place by her niece, and they walked on together. After a short silence, the lady first spoke. She wished him to know that she had been assured of his absence before she came to the place, and accordingly began by observing that his arrival had been very unexpected. "Your housekeeper," she added, "informed us that you would certainly not be here till tomorrow; and indeed, before we left Bakewell, we understood that you were not immediately expected in the country." He acknowledged the truth of it all, and said that business with his steward had occasioned his coming ahead of the rest of the party with whom he had been travelling. "They will join me early tomorrow," he continued, "and among them are some who will claim an acquaintance with you — Mr. Bingley and his sisters."

Elizabeth answered only by a slight bow. Her thoughts were instantly driven back to the time when Mr. Bingley's name had been last mentioned between them; and, if she might judge from his complexion, *his* mind was similarly engaged.

"There is also one other person in the party," he continued after a pause, "who more particularly wishes to be known to you. Will you allow me, or do I ask too much, to introduce my sister to you during your stay at Lambton?"

The surprise of such a request was great indeed. She immediately felt that whatever desire Miss Darcy might have of being acquainted with her must be the work of her brother, and, without looking farther, it was satisfactory; it was gratifying to know that his resentment had not made him think really ill of her.

They now walked on in silence, each of them deep in thought. Elizabeth was not comfortable: that was impossible; but she was flattered and pleased. His wish of introducing his sister to her was a compliment of the highest kind. They soon outstripped the others, and when they had reached the carriage, Mr. and Mrs. Gardiner were half a quarter of a mile behind.

He then asked her to walk into the house; but she declared herself not tired, and they stood together on the lawn. At such a time much might have been said, and silence was very awkward. She wanted to talk, but could not think of a subject. At last she recollected that she had been travelling, and they talked of Matlock and Dovedale. Yet time and her aunt moved slowly — and her patience and her ideas were nearly worn out before the tête-à-tête was over. On Mr. and Mrs. Gardiner's coming up they were all encouraged to go into the house and take some refreshment; but this was declined, and they parted on each side with the utmost politeness. Mr. Darcy helped the ladies into the carriage; and when it drove off, Elizabeth saw him walking slowly towards the house.

The observations of her uncle and aunt now began, and each of them pronounced him to be infinitely superior to anything they had expected. "He is perfectly well-behaved, polite, and unassuming," said her uncle.

"There *is* something a little stately in him, to be sure," replied her aunt; "but it is not unbecoming. I can now say with the housekeeper, that though some people may call him proud, *I* have seen nothing of it."

"I was never more surprised than by his behaviour to us. It was more than civil; it was really attentive; and there was no necessity for such attention. His acquaintance with Elizabeth was very trifling."

"To be sure, Lizzy," said her aunt, "he is not as handsome as Wickham; or, rather, he has not Wickham's personality, for his features are perfectly good. But why did you tell us that he was so disagreeable?"

Elizabeth excused herself as well as she could; said that she had liked him better when they met in Kent than before, and that she had never seen him so pleasant as this morning.

"But perhaps he may be a little whimsical in his civilities," replied her uncle. "Your great men often are; and therefore I shall not take him at his word about fishing, as he might change his mind another day, and warn me off his grounds."

Elizabeth felt that they had entirely mistaken his character, but said nothing.

"From what we have seen of him," continued Mrs. Gardiner, "I really should not have thought that he could have been as cruel to anyone as he has been to Wickham. He does not seem ill-natured. On the contrary, there is something pleasing about his mouth when he speaks. And there is something of dignity in his countenance that would not give one an unfavourable idea of his heart. But, to be sure, the good lady who showed us the house did give him a most flattering character! I could hardly help laughing aloud sometimes. But he is a generous master, I suppose, and *that*, in the eye of a servant, counts for everything."

Elizabeth here felt herself called on to say something in vindication of his behaviour to Wickham; and therefore gave them to understand, in as guarded a manner as she could, that by what she had heard from his relations in Kent, his character was by no means so faulty, nor Wickham's so amiable, as they had been led to believe in Hertfordshire. In confirmation of this she related the particulars of all the events in which they had been connected, without actually naming her authority, but stating it to be such as might be relied on.

Mrs. Gardiner was surprised and concerned; but as they were now approaching the scene of her former pleasures, every idea gave way to the charm of recollection; and she was too much engaged in pointing out to her husband all the interesting spots in its environs to think of anything else. Fatigued as she had been by the morning's walk, they had no sooner dined than she set off again in quest of her former acquaintances, and the evening was spent in the company of old friends.

The events of the day were too full of interest to leave Elizabeth much attention for anyone, and she could do nothing but think, and think with wonder, of Mr. Darcy's civility, and above all, of his wishing her to be acquainted with his sister.

CHAPTER 44

Elizabeth it was certain that Mr. Darcy would bring his sister to visit her the very day after her reaching Pemberley, and was consequently resolved not to be out of sight of the inn the whole of that morning. But her conclusion was false; for on the very morning after their own arrival at Lambton these visitors came. They had been walking around the place with some of their new friends, and were just returned to the inn when the sound of a carriage drew them to a window, and they saw a gentleman and lady in a carriage driving up the street. Elizabeth, immediately recognising the uniform worn by the driver, guessed what it meant, and gave no small degree of surprise to her relations by informing them of the honour which she expected. Her uncle and aunt were all amazement; and the embarrassment of her manner as she spoke, joined to the circumstance itself, and many of the circumstances of the preceding day, opened to them a new idea on the business. Nothing had ever suggested it before, but they now felt that there was no other way of accounting for such attentions than by supposing Mr. Darcy to have a preference for their niece. While these newly born notions were passing in their heads, the disquiet of Elizabeth's feelings was every moment increasing. She was quite amazed at her own unrest; but among other causes of concern, she feared that she could not meet his expectations, and was unequal to such attentions. She was so anxious to please that she suspected every power of pleasing would fail her.

She retreated from the window, fearful of being seen; and as she walked up and down the room, endeavouring to compose herself, saw such looks of enquiring surprise in her uncle and aunt as made everything worse.

Miss Darcy and her brother appeared, and the introduction took place. With astonishment did Elizabeth see that her new acquaintance was at least as much embarrassed as herself. Since her being at Lambton, she had heard that Miss Darcy was exceedingly proud; but the observation of a very few minutes convinced her that she was only exceedingly shy. She found it difficult to obtain even a word from her that was longer than a single syllable.

Miss Darcy was tall, and, though little more than sixteen, her appearance was womanly and graceful. There was sense and good-humour in her face, and her manners were perfectly unassuming and gentle.

They had not been long together before Darcy told her that Bingley was also coming to visit her. She had barely time to express her satisfaction, and prepare for such a visitor, when Bingley's quick step was heard on the stairs, and in a moment he entered the room. All Elizabeth's anger against him had been long done away, but had she still felt any it could hardly have stood its ground against the sincere kindness he expressed on seeing her again. He inquired in a friendly, though general way, after her family, and looked and spoke with the same good-humoured ease that he always did.

To Mr. and Mrs. Gardiner he was scarcely a less interesting person than to herself. They had long wished to see him. The suspicions which had just arisen of Mr. Darcy and their niece directed their observation towards each, and they soon drew from their facial expressions the full conviction that one of them at least was in love. Of the lady's sensations they remained a little in doubt; but that the gentleman was overflowing with admiration was obvious enough.

Elizabeth, on her side, had much to do. She wanted to determine the feelings of each of her visitors; she wanted to compose her own, and to make herself agreeable to all. That second goal, which she feared she might fail to achieve, was of no real import, for those to whom she endeavoured to give pleasure were predisposed in her favour. Bingley was ready, Georgiana was eager, and Darcy determined, to be pleased.

In seeing Bingley, her thoughts naturally flew to her sister; and oh! How much did she long to know whether any of his were directed in a like manner. Sometimes she could believe that he talked less than on former occasions, and once or twice thought that, as he looked at her, he was trying to trace a resemblance. But, though this might be imaginary, she could not be deceived as to his behaviour to Miss Darcy, who had been set up as a rival to Jane. No look appeared on either side that spoke particular regard. Nothing occurred between them that could justify the hopes of his sister. On this point she was soon satisfied; and two or three little circumstances occurred before they parted, which, in her anxious interpretation, hinted at a tender recollection of Jane, and a wish of saying more that might lead to the mention of her, had he dared. He mentioned to her, in a moment when the others were talking together, and in a tone which had something of real regret, that it "was a very long time since he had had the pleasure of seeing her." Before she could reply, he added, "It has been more than eight months. We have not seen each other since the 26th of November, when we were all dancing together at Netherfield."

Elizabeth was pleased to find his memory so exact; and he afterwards took occasion to ask her whether *all* her sisters were at Longbourn, and there was a look and a manner which gave them meaning.

It was not often that she could turn her eyes on Mr. Darcy himself; but, whenever she did catch a glimpse, she saw an expression of general politeness, and in all that he said she heard a tone so different from disdain of his companions, as convinced her that the improvement of manners which she had yesterday witnessed, however temporary its existence might prove, had at least lasted longer than one day. When she saw him thus seeking the acquaintance and good opinion of people with whom any conversation a few months ago would have been a disgrace — when she saw him thus civil, not only to herself, but to the very relations whom he had openly condemned, and remembered his proposal at Hunsford Parsonage — the difference, the change was so great, and struck so forcibly on her mind, that she could hardly keep her astonishment to herself. Never, even in the company of his dear friends at Netherfield, or his dignified relations at Rosings, had she seen him so desirous to please, so free from self-importance or unbending reserve, as now, when nothing of consequence could result from the success of his endeavours, and when his acquaintance with her relatives would expose him to the ridicule of the ladies both of Netherfield and Rosings.

Their visitors stayed with them for more than half an hour, and when they arose to depart, Mr. Darcy called on his sister to join him in expressing their wish of seeing Mr. and Mrs. Gardiner, and Miss Bennet, to dinner at Pemberley, before they left. Miss Darcy readily obeyed. Mrs. Gardiner looked at her niece, desirous of knowing how *she*, whom the invitation most concerned, felt about its acceptance, but Elizabeth had turned away. Presuming, however, that this betrayed rather a momentary embarrassment than any dislike of the idea, and seeing in her husband, who was fond of social gatherings, a perfect willingness to accept it, she ventured to accept, and the day after the next was settled upon.

Bingley expressed great pleasure in the certainty of seeing Elizabeth again, having still a great deal to say to her, and many enquiries to make after all their Hertfordshire friends. Elizabeth, attributing all this to a wish of hearing her speak of her sister, was pleased; and on this account, as well as some others, found herself, when their visitors left them, capable of considering the last half-hour with some satisfaction, though while it was passing the enjoyment of it had been little. Eager to be alone, and fearful of enquiries or hints from her uncle and aunt, she stayed with them only long enough to hear their favourable opinion of Bingley, and then hurried away.

But she had no reason to fear Mr. and Mrs. Gardiner's curiosity; it was not their wish to force her communication. It was evident that she was much better acquainted with Mr. Darcy than they had before realized; it was also evident that he was very much in love with her. They saw much to make them curious, but nothing to justify inquiry.

Of Mr. Darcy it was now their only desire to think well; and, as far as they could tell, there was no fault to find. They could not be unmoved by his politeness; and had they never before heard of him, and made their assessment solely based upon their own observations, the circle in Hertfordshire to which he was known would not have recognised it for Mr. Darcy. There was now reason, however, to believe the housekeeper; and they soon became aware that the authority of a servant who had known him since he was four years old, and whose own manners indicated respectability, was not to be hastily rejected. Neither had anything been found in the reports of their Lambton friends that could materially lessen its weight. They had nothing to accuse him of but pride; pride he probably had, and if not, it would certainly be attributed to him by the inhabitants of a small market-town where the family did not visit. It was acknowledged, however, that he was a generous man, who did much good among the poor.

With respect to Wickham, the travellers soon found that he was not held there in much esteem; for though the greater part of his concerns with the son of his patron were imperfectly understood, it was yet a well-known fact that, on his leaving Derbyshire, he had left many debts behind him, which Mr. Darcy afterwards paid.

As for Elizabeth, her thoughts were at Pemberley this evening more than the last; and the evening was not long enough for her to determine her feelings towards the owner of that mansion; and she lay awake two whole hours endeavouring to figure them out. She certainly did not hate him. No; hatred had vanished long ago, and she was ashamed of ever feeling a dislike towards him. The respect created by the conviction of his valuable qualities, though at first unwillingly admitted, had for some time ceased to be repugnant. Her regard was now further heightened into a friendlier nature by the reports so highly in his favour, which yesterday had produced. But above all, above respect and esteem, there was a motive within her of goodwill which could not be overlooked. It was gratitude — gratitude, not merely for having once loved her, but for loving her still well enough to forgive her manner of rejecting him, and all the unjust accusations which accompanied her rejection. He whom, she had been persuaded, would avoid her as his greatest enemy, seemed, on this accidental meeting, most eager to preserve the acquaintance, and was soliciting the good opinion of her friends and bent on making her known to his sister. Such a change in a man of so much pride excited not only astonishment but gratitude — for to love it must be attributed; and as such, its impression on her was of a sort to be encouraged, as by no means unpleasing, though it could not be exactly defined. She respected, she esteemed, she was grateful to him, she felt a real interest in his welfare; but she was as yet uncertain how far she wished that welfare to depend upon herself. She wondered how much it would contribute to the happiness of both should she employ the power, which she believed she still possessed, of encouraging a renewal of his proposal.

It had been settled in the evening, between the aunt and niece, that such a striking civility as Miss Darcy's, in coming to them on the very day of her arrival at Pemberley, , ought to be imitated. Consequently, they decided to visit her at Pemberley the following morning. Elizabeth was pleased; though when she asked herself the reason, she had very little to say in reply.

Mr. Gardiner left them soon after breakfast. The fishing scheme had been renewed the day before, and he was meeting some of the gentlemen at Pemberley at noon.

CHAPTER 45

Convinced as Elizabeth now was that Miss Bingley's dislike of her had originated in jealousy, she could not help feeling how very unwelcome her appearance at Pemberley must be to her. She was curious to know with how little civility on that lady's side the acquaintance would now be renewed.

On reaching the house, they were shown through the hall into the salon, whose north-facing windows rendered it delightful for summer. The windows, opening to the ground, admitted a most refreshing view of the high woody hills behind the house, and of the beautiful oaks and Spanish chestnuts which were interspersed throughout the lawn.

In this room they were received by Miss Darcy, who was sitting there with Mrs. Hurst and Miss Bingley, and the lady with whom she lived in London. Georgiana's reception of them was very civil, but accompanied by all that embarrassment which, though proceeding from shyness and the fear of doing wrong, could easily give others the impression that she was proud and reserved. Mrs. Gardiner and her niece, however, did her justice, and sympathized with her.

Mrs. Hurst and Miss Bingley acknowledged them with a brief curtsy; and, on their being seated, there was an awkward pause. It was first broken by Mrs. Annesley, a genteel, agreeable looking woman, whose intention to begin some kind of conversation proved her to be more truly well-bred than either of the others. Between her and Mrs. Gardiner, with occasional help from Elizabeth, the conversation was carried on. Miss Darcy looked as if she wished for courage enough to join in it; and sometimes did venture a short sentence when there was the least danger of its being heard.

Elizabeth soon saw that she was herself closely watched by Miss Bingley, and that she could not speak a word, especially to Miss Darcy, without calling her attention. This observation would not have prevented her from trying to talk to the latter, had they not been seated at an inconvenient distance; but she was not sorry to be spared the necessity of saying much. Her own thoughts kept her busy. She expected every moment that some of the gentlemen would enter the room. She wished, she feared that the master of the house might be among them; and whether she wished or feared it most, she could scarcely determine. After sitting in this manner a quarter of an hour without hearing Miss Bingley's voice, Elizabeth was roused by receiving from her a cold enquiry after the health of her family. She answered with equal indifference and brevity, and the other said no more.

The next variation which their visit afforded was produced by the entrance of servants with cold meat, cake, and a variety of all the finest fruits in season; but this did not take place till after many a significant look and smile from Mrs. Annesley to Miss Darcy had been given, to remind her of her duty as hostess. There was now something for the whole party to do — for though they could not all talk, they could all eat; and the beautiful pyramids of grapes, nectarines, and peaches soon brought them together round the table.

While thus engaged, Elizabeth had a fair opportunity of deciding whether she most feared or wished for the appearance of Mr. Darcy, by the feelings which prevailed on his entering the room. In that moment she began to regret that he came.

He had been some time with Mr. Gardiner, who, with two or three other gentlemen from the house, was engaged by the river, and had left him only on learning that the ladies of the family intended to visit Georgiana that morning. No sooner did he appear than Elizabeth wisely resolved to be perfectly relaxed and unembarrassed — a resolution the more necessary to be made, but perhaps not the more easily kept, because she saw that the suspicions of the whole party were awakened against them, and that there was scarcely an eye which did not watch his behaviour when he first came into the room. In no countenance was attentive curiosity as strongly marked as in Miss Bingley's, in spite of the smiles which overspread her face whenever she spoke to one of its objects; for jealousy had not yet made her desperate, and her attentions to Mr. Darcy were by no means over. Miss Darcy, on her brother's entrance, exerted herself much more to talk; and Elizabeth saw that he was anxious for his sister and herself to get acquainted, and encouraged as much as possible every attempt at conversation on either side. Miss Bingley saw all this likewise; and, in the imprudence of anger, took the first opportunity of saying, with sneering civility —

"Miss Eliza, has the Militia left Meryton? They must be a great loss to *your* family."

In Darcy's presence she dared not mention Wickham's name; but Elizabeth instantly comprehended that he was uppermost in her thoughts. The various recollections connected with him gave her a moment's distress; but exerting herself vigorously to repel the ill-natured attack, she presently answered the question in a tolerably calm tone. While she spoke, an involuntary glance showed her Darcy, with a heightened complexion, earnestly looking at her, and his sister overcome with confusion, and unable to lift up her eyes. Had Miss Bingley known what pain she was then giving her beloved friend, she undoubtedly would have chosen a different subject; but she had merely intended to discompose Elizabeth by indirectly mentioning a man to whom she believed her partial, to make her betray an emotion which might injure her in Darcy's opinion, and perhaps to remind the latter of all the follies and absurdities by which some part of her family were connected with the officers. Not a syllable had ever reached her of Miss Darcy's meditated elopement. To no creature had it been revealed, where secrecy was possible, except to Elizabeth; and from all Bingley's connections her brother was particularly anxious to conceal it, from that very wish which Elizabeth had long ago attributed to him, of his desire for a marriage between Mr. Bingley and Miss Darcy.

Elizabeth's collected behaviour, however, soon quieted his emotion; and as Miss Bingley, disappointed, dared not mention Wickham specifically, Georgiana also recovered in time, though not enough to be able to speak anymore. Her brother, whose eye she feared to meet, scarcely remembered her part in the affair; and the very circumstance which had been designed to turn his thoughts from Elizabeth seemed to have fixed them on her more, and more cheerfully.

Their visit did not continue long after the question and answer above mentioned; and while Mr. Darcy was walking them to their carriage, Miss Bingley was venting her feelings in criticisms about Elizabeth's person, behaviour, and dress. But Georgiana would not join her. Her brother's recommendation was enough to ensure her favour: his judgment could not err, and he had spoken in such terms of Elizabeth as to leave Georgiana without the power of finding her anything but lovely and amiable. When Darcy returned to the saloon, Miss Bingley could not help repeating to him some part of what she had been saying to his sister.

"How very ill Eliza Bennet looks this morning, Mr. Darcy," she cried. "I never in my life saw anyone so changed. Louisa and I were agreeing that we would not have even recognized her."

However little Mr. Darcy might have liked such an address, he contented himself with coolly replying that he perceived no other alteration than her being rather tanned — an unsurprising consequence of travelling in the summer.

"For my own part," she rejoined, "I must confess that I never could see any beauty in her. Her face is too thin; her complexion has no brilliance; and her features are not at all beautiful. Her nose lacks definition — there is nothing remarkable in its lines. Her teeth are tolerable, but not extraordinary; and as for her eyes, which have sometimes been called so fine, I never could perceive anything of merit in them. They have a sharp look, which I do not like at all."

Persuaded as Miss Bingley was that Darcy admired Elizabeth, this was not the best method of recommending herself. But angry people are not always wise, and in seeing him at last look somewhat rattled, she had all the success she expected. He was resolutely silent, however, and, from a determination of making him speak, she continued —

"I remember, when we first met her in Hertfordshire, how amazed we all were to find that she was a reputed beauty; and I particularly recollect your saying one night, after they had been dining at Netherfield, '*She* a beauty! I should as soon call her mother a wit.' But afterwards she seemed to improve in your opinion, and I believe you thought her rather pretty at one time."

"Yes," replied Darcy, who could contain himself no longer, "but *that* was only when I first knew her. For the past several months I have considered her to be one of the most beautiful women of my acquaintance."

He then went away, and Miss Bingley was left to all the satisfaction of having forced him to say what gave no one any pain but herself.

Mrs. Gardiner and Elizabeth talked of all that had occurred during their visit as they returned, except what had particularly interested them both. The looks and behaviour of everybody they had seen were discussed, except of the person who had mostly engaged their attention. They talked of his sister, his friends, his house, his fruit — of everything but the man himself; yet Elizabeth was longing to know what Mrs. Gardiner thought of him, and Mrs. Gardiner would have been highly gratified by her niece's introduction of the subject.

CHAPTER 46

Elizabeth had been disappointed about not finding a letter from Jane on their first arrival at Lambton; and this disappointment had been renewed on each of the mornings that had now been spent there. But on the third day her wait was over, and her sister vindicated by the receipt of two letters from her at once, one of which was marked that it had been misdirected elsewhere. Elizabeth was not surprised, as Jane had written the address quite illegibly. They had just been preparing to walk as the letters came in; and her uncle and aunt, leaving her to enjoy them in quiet, set off by themselves. The one misdirected must be the first one read; it had been written five days ago. The beginning contained an account of all their little parties and engagements, with such news as the neighbourhood afforded; but the latter half, which was dated a day later, and written in evident agitation, gave more important intelligence. It was to this effect.

"Since writing the above, dearest Lizzy, something has occurred of a most unexpected and serious nature; but I am afraid of alarming you — be assured that we are all well. What I have to say relates to poor Lydia. An express came at twelve last night, just as we were all gone to bed, from Colonel Forster, to inform us that she was gone off to Scotland with one of his officers; to own the truth, with Wickham! Imagine our surprise. To Kitty, however, it does not seem so wholly unexpected. I am very, very sorry. So imprudent a match on both sides! But I am willing to hope the best, and that his character has been misunderstood. Thoughtless and indiscreet I can easily believe him, but this step — and let us rejoice over it — marks nothing bad at heart. He is not marrying for money at least, for he must know my father can give her nothing. Our poor mother is sadly grieved. My father bears it better. How thankful am I that we never let them know what has been said against him! We must forget it ourselves. They left Saturday night about twelve, but their absence was not noticed until yesterday morning at eight. The message was sent to us immediately. My dear Lizzy, they must have passed within ten miles of us. Colonel Forster gives us reason to expect him here soon. Lydia left a few lines for his wife, informing her of their intention. I must end, for I cannot be long from my poor mother. I am afraid you will not be able to read my handwriting. I hardly know myself what I have written."

Without allowing herself time for consideration, and scarcely knowing what she felt, Elizabeth on finishing this letter instantly seized the other, and opening it with the utmost impatience, read as follows — it had been written a day later than the conclusion of the first.

"By this time, my dearest sister, you have received my hurried letter; I hope this one will be easier to read, but though not pressed for time, my head is so bewildered that I cannot answer for being coherent. Dearest Lizzy, I hardly know what to write, but I have bad news for you, and it cannot be delayed. Imprudent as a marriage between Mr. Wickham and our poor Lydia would be, we are now anxious to be assured it has taken place, for there is reason to fear they are not gone to Scotland. Colonel Forster came yesterday, having left Brighton the day before, not many hours after the express. Though Lydia's short letter to Mrs. Forster gave them to understand that they were going to Gretna Green, something was dropped by Denny expressing his belief that Wickham never intended to go there, or to marry Lydia at all, which was repeated to Colonel Forster, who instantly set off from Brighton, intending to trace their route. He followed them easily to London, but no farther; for on entering that place, they switched to a hired carriage and dismissed the chaise that brought them from Epsom. I know not what to think. After making every possible enquiry on that side London, Colonel Forster came into Hertfordshire, anxiously asking about them at all the turnpikes, and at the inns in Barnet and Hatfield, but without any success — no such people had been seen to pass through. With the kindest concern he came on to Longbourn, and shared his concerns with us in a manner most creditable to his heart. I am sincerely grieved for him and Mrs. Forster, but no one can blame them. Our distress, my dear Lizzy, is very great. My father and mother believe the worst, but I cannot think so ill of him. Many circumstances might make it more eligible for them to be married privately in town than to pursue their first plan; and even if *he* could form such a design against a young woman of Lydia's connections, which is not likely, can I suppose her so lost to everything? Impossible! I grieve to find, however, that Colonel Forster is not disposed to depend upon their marriage; he shook his head when I expressed my hopes, and said he feared Wickham was not a man to be trusted. My poor mother is really ill, and keeps her room. Could she exert herself, it would be better; but this is not to be expected. And as to my father, I never in my life saw him so affected. Everyone is angry with poor Kitty for having concealed their attachment; but as it was a matter of confidence, it is not surprising. I am truly glad, dearest Lizzy, that you have been spared something of these distressing scenes; but now, as the first shock is over, I will say that I long for your return. I am not so selfish, however, as to require for it, if inconvenient. Adieu! I take up my pen again to do what I have just told you I would not; but circumstances are such that I cannot help earnestly begging you all to come here as soon as possible. I know my dear uncle and aunt so well, that I am not afraid of requesting it, though I have still something more to ask of the former. My father is going to London with Colonel Forster to try to find Lydia. What he means to do I do not know; but his excessive distress will not allow him to pursue any measure in the best and safest way, and Colonel Forster is obliged to be at Brighton again tomorrow evening. In such a circumstance, my uncle's advice and assistance would be everything in the world; he will immediately comprehend what I must feel, and I rely upon his goodness."

"Oh! where, where is my uncle?" cried Elizabeth, darting from her seat as she finished the letter, eager to find him without losing another moment; but as she reached the door it was opened by a servant, and Mr. Darcy appeared. Her pale face and impetuous manner startled him, and before he could recover himself enough to speak, she, in whose mind every idea was superseded by Lydia's situation, hastily exclaimed, "I beg your pardon, but I must leave you. I must find Mr. Gardiner this moment, on business that cannot be delayed; I have not an instant to lose."

"Good God! What is the matter?" cried he, with more feeling than politeness; then recollecting himself, "I will not detain you a minute; but let me, or let the servant, go after Mr. and Mrs. Gardiner. You are not well enough; you cannot go yourself."

Elizabeth hesitated, but her knees trembled under her, and she felt how little would be gained by her attempting to pursue them. Calling back the servant, therefore, she commissioned him, though so breathlessly as made her almost unintelligible, to fetch his master and mistress home instantly.

On his leaving the room she sat down, unable to support herself, and looking so miserably ill that it was impossible for Darcy to part from her, or to refrain from saying, in a tone of gentleness and commiseration, "Let me call your maid. Is there nothing you could take to give you relief? A glass of wine? Shall I get you one? You are very ill."

"No, thank you," she replied, endeavouring to recover herself. "There is nothing the matter with me. I am quite well; I am only distressed by some dreadful news which I have just received from Longbourn."

She burst into tears as she alluded to it, and for a few minutes could not speak another word. Darcy, in wretched suspense, could only say something indistinctly of his concern, and observe her in compassionate silence. At length she spoke again. "I have just had a letter from Jane, with such dreadful news. It cannot be concealed from anyone. My youngest sister has left all her friends — has eloped. She has thrown herself into the power of Mr. Wickham. They are gone off together from Brighton. *You* know him too well to doubt the rest. She has no money, no connections, nothing that can tempt him to — she is lost forever."

Darcy was most astonished. "When I consider," she added, in a yet more agitated voice, "that *I* might have prevented it! *I*, who knew what he was. Had I but explained some part of it only — some part of what I learned, to my own family! Had his character been known, this could not have happened. But it is all — all too late now."

"I am grieved, indeed," cried Darcy. "Grieved — shocked. But is it certain — absolutely certain?"

"Oh yes! They left Brighton together on Sunday night, and were traced almost to London, but not beyond: they have certainly not gone to Scotland."

"And what has been done, what has been attempted, to recover her?"

"My father has gone to London, and Jane has written to beg my uncle's immediate assistance; and we shall be off, I hope, in half an hour. But nothing can be done — I know very well that nothing can be done. How is such a man to be persuaded? How are they even to be found? I have not the smallest hope. It is in every way horrible!"

Darcy shook his head in silent acquiescence.

"When *my* eyes were opened to his real character — Oh! Had I known what I ought, what I dared to do! But I knew not — I was afraid of doing too much. Wretched, wretched, mistake!"

Darcy made no answer. He seemed scarcely to hear her, and was walking up and down the room in earnest meditation, his brow contracted, his air gloomy. Elizabeth soon observed, and instantly understood it. Her power was sinking; everything *must* sink under such a proof of family weakness, such an assurance of the deepest disgrace. She could neither wonder nor condemn, but never had she so honestly felt that she could have loved him, as now, when all love must be in vain.

But thoughts of self paled in comparison to her concerns for her family. Lydia — the humiliation, the misery she was bringing on them all, soon swallowed up every private care; and covering her face with her handkerchief, Elizabeth was soon lost to everything else. After a pause of several minutes, she was only recalled to a sense of her situation by the voice of her companion, who, in a manner which, though it spoke compassion, spoke likewise restraint, said, "I am afraid you have been long desiring my absence, nor have I anything to excuse my stay but real, though unavailing, concern. Would to Heaven that anything could be either said or done on my part that might offer consolation to such distress! But I will not torment you with vain wishes. This unfortunate affair will, I fear, prevent my sister's having the pleasure of seeing you at Pemberley today."

"Oh yes. Be so kind as to apologize for us to Miss Darcy. Say that urgent business calls us home immediately. Conceal the unhappy truth as long as possible. I know it cannot be long."

He readily assured her of his secrecy, again expressed his sorrow for her distress, wished it a happier conclusion than there was at present reason to hope, and leaving his compliments for her relations, went away.

As he left the room, Elizabeth felt how improbable it was that they should ever see each other again on such terms of cordiality as had marked their several meetings in Derbyshire. As she considered the whole of their acquaintance, so full of contradictions and upheaval, sighed with frustration at those feelings which would, now that there was no chance of it, have preferred its continuance.

Never, since reading Jane's second letter, had she entertained a hope of Wickham's meaning to marry Lydia. No one but Jane, she thought, could flatter herself with such an expectation. Surprise was the least of her feelings on this development. While the contents of the first letter remained on her mind, she was all surprise — all astonishment that Wickham should marry a girl whom it was impossible he could marry for money; and how Lydia could ever have enticed him had appeared incomprehensible. But now it was all too natural. For such an attachment as this she might have sufficient charms; and though she did not suppose Lydia to be deliberately engaging in an elopement, without the intention of marriage, she had no difficulty in believing that neither her virtue nor her wisdom would prevent her from falling an easy prey.

She had never perceived, while the regiment was in Hertfordshire, that Lydia had any partiality for him; but she was convinced that Lydia had needed only a little encouragement to attach herself to anybody. Sometimes one officer, sometimes another, had been her favourite, as their attentions raised them in her opinion. Her affections had been continually fluctuating, but never without an object. The mischief of neglect and mistaken indulgence towards such a girl! How acutely did she now feel it!

She was anxious to be at home — to hear, to see, to share with Jane the burdens that must now fall wholly upon her, in the midst of such disarray: a father absent, a mother incapable of exertion and requiring constant care. Though almost persuaded that nothing could be done for Lydia, her uncle's interference seemed of the utmost importance, and till he entered the room the misery of her impatience was severe. Mr. and Mrs. Gardiner had hurried back in alarm, supposing by the servant's account that their niece was taken suddenly ill. Satisfying them instantly in that regard, she eagerly communicated the cause of their summons, reading the two letters aloud. Though Lydia had never been a favourite with them, Mr. and Mrs. Gardiner could not but be deeply affected. Not Lydia only, but all were concerned in it; and after the first exclamations of surprise and horror, Mr. Gardiner readily promised every assistance in his power. Elizabeth, though expecting no less, thanked him with tears of gratitude; and everything relating to their journey home was speedily settled. They were to be off as soon as possible. "But what is to be done about Pemberley?" cried Mrs. Gardiner. "John told us Mr. Darcy was here when you sent for us; was it so?"

"Yes; and I told him we should not be able to keep our engagement. *That* is all settled."

"What is all settled?" repeated the other, as she ran into her room to prepare. "And are they upon such terms as for her to disclose the real truth? Oh, that I knew how it was!"

But wishes were vain, or at best could serve only to amuse her in the hurry and confusion of the following hour. Had Elizabeth been at leisure to be idle, she would have remained certain that all employment was impossible to one so wretched as herself; but she had her share of business as well as her aunt, and among the rest there were notes to be written to all their friends in Lambton, with false excuses for their sudden departure. An hour, however, saw the whole completed; and Mr. Gardiner meanwhile having settled his account at the inn, nothing remained to be done but to go. Elizabeth, after all the misery of the morning, found herself, in a shorter space of time than she could have supposed, seated in the carriage on the road to Longbourn.

CHAPTER 47

"I have been thinking it over again, Elizabeth," said her uncle, as they drove from the town, "and really, upon serious consideration, I am much more inclined than I was to believe as your eldest sister does in the matter. It appears to me so very unlikely that any young man should form such a design against a girl who is by no means unprotected or friendless, and who was actually staying in his colonel's family, that I am strongly inclined to hope for the best. Could he expect that her friends would not step forward? Could he expect to be noticed again by the regiment, after such an affront to Colonel Forster? His temptation does not justify the risk."

"Do you really think so?" cried Elizabeth, brightening up for a moment.

"Upon my word," said Mrs. Gardiner, "I am beginning to be of your uncle's opinion. It is really too great a violation of decency, honour, and interest, for him to be guilty of it. I cannot think so very ill of Wickham. Can you yourself, Lizzy, so wholly give him up, as to believe him capable of it?"

"Not, perhaps, of neglecting his own interest; but of every other neglect I can believe him capable. If, indeed, it should be so! But I dare not hope it. Why should they not go on to Scotland, if that had been the case?"

"In the first place," replied Mr. Gardiner, "there is no absolute proof that they have not gone to Scotland."

"Oh! But their switching from the chaise into a hired carriage is such a presumption! And, besides, no traces of them were to be found on the Barnet road."

"Well, then — supposing them to be in London. They may be there, though for the purpose of concealment, for no more exceptionable purpose. It is not likely that money should be very abundant on either side;

and it might strike them that they could be more economically, though less expeditiously, married in London than in Scotland."

"But why all the secrecy? Why any fear of detection? Why must their marriage be private? Oh! no, no — this is not likely. His most particular friend, you see by Jane's account, was persuaded of his never intending to marry her. Wickham will never marry a woman without some money. He cannot afford it. And what claims has Lydia — what attractions has she beyond youth, health, and good-humour, that could make him, for her sake, forego every chance of benefiting himself by marrying well? As to what restraint the fear of disgrace in the corps might throw on a dishonourable elopement with her, I am not able to judge; for I know nothing of the effects that such a step might produce. But as to your other objection, I am afraid it will not do. Lydia has no brothers to step forward and fight a duel on her behalf; and he might imagine, from my father's behaviour, from the little attention he has ever seemed to give to what was going on in his family, that *he* would do as little, and think as little about it, as any father could do, in such a matter."

"But can you think that Lydia is so lost to everything but love of him as to consent to live with him on any other terms than marriage?"

"It does seem that way, and it is most shocking indeed," replied Elizabeth, with tears in her eyes. "But, really, I know not what to say. Perhaps I am not doing her justice. But she is very young; she has never been taught to think about serious moral subjects; and for the last half year — nay, for the whole of it — she has been given up to nothing but amusement and vanity. She has been allowed to spend her time in the most idle and frivolous manner. Since the militia was first quartered in Meryton, nothing but love, flirtation, and officers have been in her head. She has been doing everything in her power, by thinking and talking on the subject, to give greater strength to feelings which are naturally lively enough. And we all know that Wickham has every charm of person and manner that can captivate a woman."

"But you see that Jane," said her aunt, "does not think so ill of Wickham as to believe him capable of the attempt."

"Of whom does Jane ever think ill? And who is there, whatever might be their former conduct, that she would believe capable of such an attempt, till it were proved against them? But Jane knows, as well as I do, what Wickham really is. We both know that he has been degenerate in every sense of the word; that he has neither integrity nor honour; that he is as false and deceitful as he is appealing."

"And do you really know all this?" cried Mrs. Gardiner, whose curiosity as to the mode of her intelligence was all alive.

"I do, indeed," replied Elizabeth, colouring. "I told you, the other day, of his infamous behaviour to Mr. Darcy; and you yourself, when last at

Longbourn, heard in what manner he spoke of the man who had behaved with such forbearance and liberality towards him. And there are other circumstances which I am not at liberty to relate; but his lies about the whole Pemberley family are endless. From what he said of Miss Darcy, I was thoroughly prepared to see a proud, disagreeable girl. Yet he knew to the contrary himself. He must know that she was as amiable and unpretending as we have found her."

"But does Lydia know nothing of this? Can she be ignorant of what you and Jane seem to understand so well?"

"Oh, yes! That is the worst part of this. Until I was in Kent, and saw so much both of Mr. Darcy and his relation, Colonel Fitzwilliam, I was ignorant of the truth myself. And when I returned home, the militia was to leave Meryton in a week or fortnight's time. As that was the case, neither Jane, to whom I related the whole, nor I, thought it necessary to make our knowledge public; for of what use could it be to anyone that the good opinion which all the neighbourhood had of him should then be cast aside? And even when it was settled that Lydia should go with Mrs. Forster, the necessity of opening her eyes to his character never occurred to me. That *she* could be in any danger from the deception never entered my head. That such a consequence as *this* should ensue, you may easily believe was far enough from my thoughts."

"When they left for Brighton, you had no reason, I suppose, to believe them fond of each other?"

"Not the slightest. I can remember no symptom of affection on either side; and had anything of the kind been perceptible, you must be aware that ours is not a family on which such affection should be directed to no effect. When first he entered the corps, Lydia was ready enough to admire him; but so we all were. Every girl in or near Meryton was out of her senses for the first two months; but he never distinguished *her* by any particular attention; and consequently, after a moderate period of extravagant and wild admiration, her fancy for him gave way, and others of the regiment, who treated her with more distinction, again became her favourites."

It may be easily believed, that however little the novelty could be added to their fears and hopes on this interesting subject by its repeated discussion, no other could distract them from it long, during the whole of the journey. From Elizabeth's thoughts it was never absent. Finding place there by the sharpest of all anguish, self-reproach, she could find no interval of ease or forgetfulness.

They travelled as expeditiously as possible, and, sleeping one night on the road, reached Longbourn by dinner time the next day. It was a comfort to Elizabeth to consider that Jane did not have to wait long for their arrival.

The little Gardiners, attracted by the sight of a carriage, were standing on the steps of the house as they entered the yard. When the carriage drove up to the door, the joyful surprise that lighted up their faces, and displayed itself over their whole bodies, was the first pleasing event of their welcome.

Elizabeth jumped out, and, after giving each of them a hasty kiss, hurried into the hall, where Jane, who came running down stairs from her mother's apartment, immediately met her.

Elizabeth, as she affectionately embraced her, whilst tears filled the eyes of both, lost not a moment in asking whether anything had been heard of the fugitives.

"Not yet," replied Jane. "But now that my dear uncle is come, I hope everything will be well."

"Is Father in town?"

"Yes, he went on Tuesday, as I wrote you word."

"And have you heard from him often?"

"We have heard only once. He wrote me a few lines on Wednesday, to say that he had arrived safely, and to give me his address, which I particularly begged him to do. He merely added that he should not write again till he had something of importance to mention."

"And Mother — how is she? How are you all?"

"Mother is tolerably well, I trust; though her spirits are greatly shaken. She is upstairs, and will have great satisfaction in seeing you all. She does not yet leave her dressing room. Mary and Kitty, thank Heaven, are quite well."

"But you — how are you?" cried Elizabeth. "You look pale. How much you must have gone through!"

Her sister, however, assured her that she was perfectly well; and their conversation, which had been passing while Mr. and Mrs. Gardiner were engaged with their children, was now put to an end by the approach of the whole party. Jane ran to her uncle and aunt, and welcomed and thanked them both, with alternate smiles and tears.

When they were all in the drawing room, the questions which Elizabeth had already asked were of course repeated by the others, and they soon found that Jane had no intelligence to give. The hope of good, however, which the benevolence of her heart suggested, had not yet deserted her. She still expected that it would all end well, and that every morning would bring some letter, either from Lydia or her father, to explain their proceedings, and perhaps announce the marriage.

Mrs. Bennet, to whose room they all went, after a few minutes conversation together, received them exactly as might be expected: with tears and lamentations of regret, exclamations against the villainous conduct of Wickham, and complaints of her own sufferings and ill-usage; blaming everybody but the person to whose ill-judging indulgence the errors of her daughter must be principally owing.

"If I had been able," said she, "to carry my point of going to Brighton, with all my family, *this* would not have happened; but poor dear Lydia had nobody to take care of her. Why did the Forsters ever let her go out of their sight? I am sure there was some great neglect or other on their side, for she is not the kind of girl to do such a thing if she had been well looked after. I always thought they were very unfit to be in charge of her; but I was overruled, as I always am. Poor dear child! And now here's Mr. Bennet gone away, and I know he will have a duel with Wickham, wherever he meets him; and then he will be killed, and what is to become of us all? The Collinses will turn us out before he is cold in his grave, and if you are not kind to us, brother, I do not know what we shall do."

They all exclaimed against such extreme ideas, and Mr. Gardiner, after general assurances of his affection for her and all her family, told her that he meant to be in London the very next day, and would assist Mr. Bennet in every endeavour for recovering Lydia.

"Do not give way to useless alarm," added he. "Though it is right to be prepared for the worst, there is no occasion to look on it as certain. It is not quite a week since they left Brighton. In a few days more we may have some news of them; and till we know that they are not married, and have no design of marrying, let us not give up. As soon as I get to town I shall go to my brother, and make him come home with me to Gracechurch Street; and then we may consult together as to what is to be done."

"Oh! My dear brother," replied Mrs. Bennet, "that is exactly what I could most wish for. And now do, when you get to town, find out where they are; and if they are not married already, *make* them marry. And as for wedding-clothes, do not let them wait for that, but tell Lydia she shall have as much money as she needs to buy them, after they are married. And, above all things, keep Mr. Bennet from fighting a duel. Tell him what a dreadful state I am in: that I am frightened out of my wits — and have such tremblings, such flutterings, all over me — such spasms in my side and pains in my head, and such beatings in my heart, that I can get no rest by night nor by day. And tell my dear Lydia not to give any directions about her clothes till she has seen me, for she does not know which are the best shops. Oh, brother, how kind you are! I know you will arrange it all."

But Mr. Gardiner, though he assured her again of his earnest endeavours in the cause, could not avoid recommending moderation in her hopes as her fears; and after talking with her in this manner till dinner was on table, they left her to the company of the housekeeper.

In the dining room they were soon joined by Mary and Kitty, who had been too busily engaged in their separate rooms to make their appearance before. One came from her books, and the other from her mirror. The faces of both, however, were tolerably calm; and no change was visible in either, except that the loss of her favourite sister, or the anger which she had herself incurred in the business, had given something more of fretfulness than usual to the accents of Kitty. As for Mary, she whispered to Elizabeth, with a countenance of grave reflection, soon after they were seated at table —

"This is a most unfortunate affair; and will probably be much talked of. But we must stem the tide of malice, and pour into the wounded bosoms of each other the balm of sisterly consolation."

Then, perceiving in Elizabeth no inclination to reply, she added, "Unhappy as the event must be for Lydia, we may draw from it this useful lesson: that loss of virtue in a female is irretrievable — that one false step involves her in endless ruin — that her reputation is no less brittle than it is beautiful — and that she cannot be too much guarded in her behaviour towards the undeserving of the other sex."

Elizabeth lifted up her eyes in amazement, but was too depressed to make any reply. Mary, however, continued to console herself with such kind of moral platitudes.

In the afternoon the two elder Miss Bennets were able to be for half an hour by themselves; and Elizabeth instantly took the opportunity to make many enquiries, which Jane was equally eager to satisfy. After joining in general lamentations over the dreadful conclusion of this event, which Elizabeth considered as all but certain, and Miss Bennet could not assert to be wholly impossible, the former continued the subject by saying, "But tell me all and everything about it which I have not already heard. Give me farther particulars. What did Colonel Forster say? Had they no hint of anything before the elopement took place? They must have seen them together."

"Colonel Forster did admit that he had often suspected some preference, especially on Lydia's side, but nothing to give him any alarm. I am so grieved for him! His behaviour was attentive and kind to the utmost. He *was* coming to us, in order to assure us of his concern, before he had any idea of their not being gone to Scotland: when that seemed to no longer be the case, it hastened his journey."

"And was Denny convinced that Wickham would not marry? Did he know of their intention to go off? Had Colonel Forster seen Denny himself?"

"Yes; but when questioned by *him*, Denny denied knowing anything of their plan, and would not give his real opinion about it."

"And till Colonel Forster came himself, not one of you entertained a doubt, I suppose, of their being really married?"

"How was it possible that such an idea should enter our minds! I felt a little uneasy — a little fearful of my sister's happiness with him in marriage, because I knew that his conduct had not been always quite right. My father and mother knew nothing of that; they only felt how imprudent a match it must be, for financial reasons. Kitty then told us, with a very natural triumph on knowing more than the rest, that in Lydia's last letter she had prepared her for such a step. She had known, it seems, of their being in love with each other, for many weeks."

"But not before they went to Brighton?"

"No, I believe not."

"And did Colonel Forster appear to think poorly of Wickham himself? Does he know his real character?"

"I must confess that he did not speak so well of Wickham as he formerly did. He believed him to be imprudent and extravagant. And since this sad affair has taken place, it is said that he left Meryton greatly in debt; but I hope this may be false."

"Oh, Jane, had we been less secret, had we told what we knew of him, this would not have happened!"

"Perhaps it would have been better," replied her sister. "But to expose the former faults of any person without knowing their present character seemed unjustifiable. We acted with the best intentions."

"Could Colonel Forster repeat the particulars of Lydia's note to his wife?"

"He brought it with him for us to see."

Jane then took it from her pocketbook, and gave it to Elizabeth. These were the contents —

"MY DEAR HARRIET, —

You will laugh when you know where I am gone, and I cannot help laughing myself at your surprise tomorrow morning, as soon as I am missed. I am going to Gretna Green, and if you cannot guess with who, I shall think you a simpleton, for there is but one man in the world I love, and he is an angel. I could never be happy without him, so think it no harm to be off. You need not send them word at Longbourn of my going, if you do not want to, for it will make the surprise the greater, when I write to them, and sign my name "Lydia Wickham." What a good joke it will be! I can hardly write for laughing. I shall send for my clothes when I get to Longbourn; but I wish you would tell Sally to mend a great slit in my worked muslin gown before they are packed up. Goodbye. Give my love to Colonel Forster. I hope you will drink to our good journey. —

Your affectionate friend, LYDIA BENNET."

"Oh! Thoughtless, thoughtless Lydia!" cried Elizabeth, when she had finished it. "What a letter this is, written at such a moment! But at least it shows that *she* was serious about marriage. Whatever he might afterwards persuade her to do, it was not on her side a *scheme* of infamy. My poor father! How shocked he must have been!"

"I never saw anyone so affected. He could not speak a word for a full ten minutes. Mother took ill immediately, and the whole household was in such confusion!"

"Oh! Jane," cried Elizabeth, "was there a servant belonging to it who did not know the whole story before the end of the day?"

"I do not know. I hope there was. But to be secretive at such a time is very difficult. My mother was in hysterics, and though I endeavoured to give her every assistance in my power, I am afraid I did not do as much as I might have done! But the horror of what might possibly happen almost caused me to lose my faculties."

"Your care of her has been too much for you. You do not look well. Oh that I had been with you! You have had every care and anxiety upon yourself alone."

"Mary and Kitty have been very kind, and would have shared in every fatigue, I am sure, but I did not think it right for either of them. Kitty is slight and delicate; and Mary studies so much, that her hours of repose should not be disturbed. Our aunt Phillips came to Longbourn on Tuesday, after Father went away; and was so good as to stay till Thursday with me. She was of great use and comfort to us all. And Lady Lucas has been very kind; she walked here on Wednesday morning to console us, and offered her services, or any of her daughters', if they could be of use to us."

"It would have been better if she had stayed home," cried Elizabeth. "Perhaps she *meant* well, but, during such a misfortune as this, one cannot see too little of one's neighbours. Assistance is impossible; consolation insufferable. Let them triumph over us at a distance, and be satisfied."

She then proceeded to inquire into the measures which her father had intended to pursue, while in town, for the recovery of his daughter.

"He meant, I believe," replied Jane, "to go to Epsom, the place where they last changed horses, and talk with those on duty, and see if he could learn anything from them. His principal object must be to discover the number of the coach which took them from Clapham. It had come with a fare from London; and as he thought the circumstance of a gentleman and lady's removing from one carriage into another might be noticed, he meant to make enquiries at Clapham. If he could discover at what house the coachman had let them out, he determined to make enquiries there, and hoped it might not be impossible to discover the number of the coach. I do not know of any other designs that he had formed; but he was in such a hurry to be gone, and his spirits so greatly disturbed, that I had difficulty finding out even as much as this."

CHAPTER 48

The whole party was hoping for a letter from Mr. Bennet the next morning, but the mail came in without bringing a single line from him. His family knew him to be, on all common occasions, a most negligent correspondent; but at such a time they had hoped for greater effort. They were forced to conclude that he had no good news to send; but even of *that* they would have been glad to be certain. Mr. Gardiner had waited only for the letters before he set off.

When he was gone, they were certain at least of receiving constant information of what was going on, and their uncle promised, at parting, to convince Mr. Bennet to return to Longbourn as soon as he could, to the great consolation of his sister.

Mrs. Gardiner and the children were to remain in Hertfordshire a few days longer, as she thought her presence might be useful to her nieces. She shared in their care of Mrs. Bennet, and was a great comfort to them in their hours of freedom. Their other aunt also visited them frequently, and always, as she said, with the design of cheering and heartening them up. As she never came without reporting some fresh instance of Wickham's extravagance or dishonesty, however, she seldom went away without leaving them more dispirited than she found them.

All Meryton seemed striving to disparage the man who, but three months before, had been almost an angel of light. He was declared to be in debt to every tradesman in the place. Everybody felt that he was the wickedest young man in the world; and everybody began to say that they had always distrusted the appearance of his goodness. Elizabeth, though she did not believe half of what was said, believed enough to make her confidence of her sister's ruin still more certain. Even Jane, who believed still less of it, became almost hopeless, more especially as the time was now come when, if they had gone to Scotland, they must in all probability have heard some news of them.

Mr. Gardiner left Longbourn on Sunday, and on Tuesday his wife received a letter from him. It told them that, on his arrival, he had immediately found his brother and persuaded him to come to Gracechurch Street. Mr. Bennet had been to Epsom and Clapham, before his arrival, but without gaining any satisfactory information; and he was now determined to inquire at all the principal hotels in town, as Mr. Bennet thought it possible they might have gone to one of them, on their first coming to London, before they procured lodgings. Mr. Gardiner himself did not expect any success from this effort, but as his brother was eager, he meant to assist him. He added that Mr. Bennet seemed wholly disinclined at present to leave London, and promised to write again very soon. There was also a postscript to this effect —

"I have written to Colonel Forster to desire him to find out, if possible, from some of the young man's acquaintances in the regiment, whether Wickham has any relations or connections who would be likely to know in what part of the town he has now concealed himself. At present we have nothing to guide us. Colonel Forster will, I dare say, do everything in his power to satisfy us. But, on second thought, perhaps Lizzy could tell us what relations he has now living, better than any other person."

Unfortunately it was not in Elizabeth's power to give any information of the kind. She had never heard of his having had any relations, except a father and mother, both of whom had been dead many years. It was possible, however, that some of his companions in the regiment might be able to give more information; and, though she was not very hopeful, it did give her something to look forward to.

Every day at Longbourn was now a day of anxiety; but the most anxious part of each was when the mail was expected. The arrival of letters was the first grand object of every morning's impatience. Through letters, whatever of good or bad was to be told would be communicated, and every succeeding day was expected to bring some news of importance.

But before they heard again from Mr. Gardiner, a letter arrived for their father, from a different quarter, from Mr. Collins; which, as Jane had received directions to open all that came for him in his absence, she accordingly read. Elizabeth, who knew what curiosities his letters always were, looked over her shoulder and read it likewise. It was as follows –

"My dear Sir, — I feel myself called upon, by our relationship, and my situation in life, to console with you on the grievous affliction you are now suffering, of which we were yesterday informed by a letter from Hertfordshire. Be assured, my dear sir, that Mrs. Collins and myself sincerely sympathise with you and all your respectable family, in your present distress, which must be of the bitterest kind. It is my only desire to alleviate so severe a misfortune, and comfort you in a circumstance that must be of all others most afflicting to a parent's mind. The death of your daughter would have been a blessing compared to this. And it is the more to be lamented, because there is reason to suppose, as my dear Charlotte informs me, that this behaviour of your daughter has proceeded from a faulty degree of indulgence. At the same time, for the consolation of yourself and Mrs. Bennet, I am inclined to think that her own disposition must be naturally bad, or she could not be guilty of such an enormity at so early an age. Whatever the case, you are grievously to be pitied; in which opinion I am not only joined by Mrs. Collins, but likewise by Lady Catherine and her daughter, to whom I have related the affair. They agree with me in believing that this false step in one daughter will be injurious to the fortunes of all the others; for who, as Lady Catherine herself condescendingly says, will connect themselves with such a family? And this consideration leads me moreover to reflect, with augmented satisfaction, on a certain event of last November; for had Elizabeth accepted my proposal, I must have been involved in all your sorrow and disgrace. Let me advise you then, my dear sir, to console yourself as much as possible, to throw off your unworthy child from your affection forever, and leave her to reap the fruits of her own heinous offence. — I am, dear Sir," etc., etc.

Mr. Gardiner did not write again till he had received an answer from Colonel Forster; and then he had nothing of a pleasant nature to send. It was not known that Wickham had a single relation with whom he kept up any connection, and it was certain that he had no close living relatives. His former acquaintance had been numerous; but since he had been in the militia, it did not appear that he was on terms of particular friendship with any of them. There was no one, therefore, who could be pointed out as likely to give any news of him. And in the wretched state of his own finances, there was a very powerful motive for secrecy, in addition to his fear of discovery by Lydia's relations, for he had left very considerable gambling debts behind him. Colonel Forster believed that more than a thousand pounds would be necessary to clear his expences at Brighton. He owed a good deal in the town, but his gambling debts were still more formidable. Mr. Gardiner did not attempt to conceal these particulars from the Longbourn family. Jane heard them with horror. "A gambler!" she cried. "This is wholly unexpected. I had no idea of it."

Mr. Gardiner added in his letter that they might expect to see their father at home on the following day, which was Saturday. Rendered spiritless by the failure of all their endeavours, he had yielded to his brother-in-law's entreaty that he would return to his family, and leave the business of finding Wickham and Lydia to him. When Mrs. Bennet was told of this, she did not express so much satisfaction as her children expected, considering what her anxiety had been before.

"What, is he coming home, and without poor Lydia?" she cried. "Surely he will not leave London before he has found them. Who is to make Wickham marry her if he comes home now?"

As Mrs. Gardiner now desired to be at home, it was settled that she and her children should go to London at the same time that Mr. Bennet came from it. The coach, therefore, took them the first stage of their journey, and brought its master back to Longbourn.

When Mr. Bennet arrived, he had all the appearance of his usual philosophic composure. He said as little as he had ever been in the habit of saying; made no mention of the business that had taken him away, and it was some time before his daughters had courage to speak of it.

It was not till the afternoon, when he joined them at tea, that Elizabeth ventured to introduce the subject; and then, on her briefly expressing her sorrow for what he must have endured, he replied, "Say nothing of that. Who should suffer but me? It has been my own doing, and I ought to feel it."

"You must not be too hard on yourself," replied Elizabeth.

"You may well warn me against such an evil. Human nature is so prone to fall into it! No, Lizzy, let me once in my life feel how much I have been to blame. I am not afraid of being overpowered by the impression. It will pass away soon enough."

"Do you believe they are in London?"

"Yes; where else can they be so well concealed?"

"And Lydia used to want to go to London," added Kitty.

"She is happy, then," said her father drily, "and her residence there will probably be of some duration."

Then, after a short silence, he continued —

"Lizzy, I bear you no ill-will for being justified in your advice to me last May, which, considering the event, shows some greatness of mind."

They were interrupted by Miss Bennet, who came to fetch her mother's tea.

"This is a dramatic display," cried he, "which does one good; it gives such an elegance to misfortune! Another day I will do the same: I will sit in my library, in my nightcap and gown, and give everyone as much trouble as I can; — or, perhaps I may defer it till Kitty runs away."

"I am not going to run away, papa," said Kitty fretfully. "If *I* should ever go to Brighton, I would behave better than Lydia."

"*You* go to Brighton. I would not trust you anywhere near it for fifty pounds! No, Kitty, I have at last learned to be cautious, and you will feel the effects of it. No officer is ever to enter my house again, nor even to pass through the village. Balls will be absolutely prohibited, unless you are dancing with one of your sisters. And you are never to go out of doors till you can prove that you have spent ten minutes of every day in a rational manner."

Kitty, who took all these threats in a serious light, began to cry.

"Well, well," said he, "do not make yourself unhappy. If you are a good girl for the next ten years, I will take you to a military parade at the end of them."

CHAPTER 49

Two days after Mr. Bennet's return, as Jane and Elizabeth were walking together in the garden behind the house, they saw the housekeeper coming towards them, and, concluding that she came to call them to their mother, went forward to meet her. But, instead of the expected summons, when they approached her, she said to Miss Bennet, "I beg your pardon, madam, for interrupting you, but I was in hopes you might have got some good news from town, so I took the liberty of coming to ask."

"What do you mean, Hill? We have heard nothing from town."

"Dear madam," cried Mrs. Hill, in great astonishment, "don't you know there is an express come for the master from Mr. Gardiner?."

Away ran the girls, too eager to get in to have time for speech. They ran through the hallway into the breakfast-room; from thence to the library — their father was in neither; and they were on the point of seeking him upstairs with their mother, when they were met by the butler, who said —

"If you are looking for my master, ma'am, he is walking towards the little wood."

Upon receiving this information they instantly passed through the hall once more, and ran across the lawn after their father, who was deliberately pursuing his way towards a small wood on one side of the pasture.

Jane, who was not so much in the habit of running as Elizabeth, soon lagged behind, while her sister, panting for breath, came up with him, and eagerly cried out —

"Oh, papa, what news — what news? Have you heard from our uncle?"

"Yes, I have had a letter from him by express."

"Well, and what news does it bring — good or bad?"

"What is there of good to be expected?" said he, taking the letter from his pocket. "Perhaps you would like to read it."

Elizabeth impatiently caught it from his hand. Jane now came up.

"Read it aloud," said their father, "for I hardly know myself what it is about."

"Gracechurch Street, *Monday, August 12.*
MY DEAR BROTHER, — At last I am able to send you some tidings of my niece, and such as, upon the whole, I hope will give you satisfaction. Soon after you left me on Saturday, I was fortunate enough to learn in what part of London they were. The particulars I reserve till we meet: it is enough to know they are discovered. I have seen them both — "

"Then it is as I always hoped," cried Jane. "They are married!"
Elizabeth read on –

"I have seen them both. They are not married, nor can I find that there was any intention of getting married; but if you agree to the terms which I have ventured to make on your side, I hope it will not be long before they are. All that is required of you is to assure to your daughter her equal share of the five thousand pounds secured among your children after the decease of yourself and my sister; and, moreover, to enter into an engagement of allowing her, during your life, one hundred pounds per annum. These are conditions which, considering everything, I had no hesitation in complying with, as far as I thought myself privileged, on your behalf. I shall send this by express, so that no time may be lost in bringing me your answer. You will easily comprehend, from these particulars, that Mr. Wickham's circumstances are not as hopeless as they are generally believed to be. The world has been deceived in that respect; and I am happy to say there will be some little money, even when all his debts are discharged, to settle on my niece, in addition to her own fortune. If, as I conclude will be the case, you send me full powers to act in your name throughout the whole of this business, I will immediately give directions to Haggerston for preparing a proper settlement. There will not be the smallest occasion for your coming to town again; therefore stay quietly at Longbourn, and depend on my diligence and care. Send back your answer as soon as you can. We have judged it best that my niece should be married in our home, and I hope you will approve. She comes to us today. I shall write again as soon as anything more is determined. — Your's, etc.
EDW. GARDINER."

"Is it possible?" cried Elizabeth, when she had finished. "Can it be possible that he will marry her?"
"Wickham is not so undeserving, then, as we have thought him," said her sister. "My dear father, I congratulate you."
"And have you answered the letter?" said Elizabeth.
"No; but it must be done soon."
Most earnestly did she then entreat him to lose no more time before he wrote.
"Oh! My dear father," she cried. "Come back and write immediately. Consider how important every moment is in such a case."

"Let me write the letter for you," said Jane, "if you dislike the trouble yourself."

"I dislike it very much," he replied, "but it must be done."

And so saying, he turned back with them, and walked towards the house.

"And may I ask — " said Elizabeth, "but the terms, I suppose, must be complied with?"

"Complied with! I am only ashamed of his asking so little."

"And they *must* marry! Yet he is *such* a man!"

"Yes, yes, they must marry. There is nothing else to be done. But there are two things that I want very much to know: one is, how much money your uncle has laid down, to make it possible; and the other, how I am ever to pay him."

"Money! My uncle?" cried Jane. "What do you mean, sir?"

"I mean, that no man in his senses would marry Lydia on so slight a temptation as one hundred a year during my life, and fifty after I am gone."

"That is very true," said Elizabeth, "though it had not occurred to me before. His debts to be discharged, and something still to remain! Oh! It must be my uncle's doings! Generous, good man, I am afraid he has distressed himself. A small sum could not do all this."

"No," said her father. "Wickham's a fool if he takes her with a farthing less than ten thousand pounds. I should be sorry to think so ill of him, in the very beginning of our relationship."

"Ten thousand pounds! Heaven forbid! How is half such a sum to be repaid?"

Mr. Bennet made no answer, and each of them, deep in thought, continued silently till they reached the house. Their father then went to the library to write, and the girls walked into the breakfast room.

"And they are really to be married!" cried Elizabeth, as soon as they were by themselves. "How strange this is! And for *this* we are to be thankful. That they should marry, small as is their chance of happiness, and wretched as is his character, we are forced to rejoice. Oh, Lydia!"

"I comfort myself by thinking," replied Jane, "that he certainly would not marry Lydia if he had not a real regard for her. Though our kind uncle has done something towards clearing him, I cannot believe that ten thousand pounds, or anything like it, has been advanced. He has children of his own, and may have more. How could he spare even five thousand pounds?"

"If we are ever able to learn what Wickham's debts have been," said Elizabeth, "and how much is settled on his side on our sister, we shall exactly know what Mr. Gardiner has done for them, because Wickham has not sixpence of his own. The kindness of my uncle and aunt can never be repaid. Their taking her home, and affording her their personal protection, is such a sacrifice to her advantage as years of gratitude cannot enough acknowledge. By this time she is actually with them! If such goodness does not make her grateful now, she will never deserve to be happy! What a meeting for her, when she first sees my aunt!"

"We must endeavour to forget all that has passed on either side," said Jane. "I hope and trust they will be happy. His consenting to marry her is a proof, I believe, that he has come to a right way of thinking. Their mutual affection will steady them, and I flatter myself they will settle so quietly, and live in so rational a manner, as may in time make their past imprudence forgotten."

"Their conduct has been such," replied Elizabeth, "as neither you, nor I, nor anybody can ever forget. It is useless to talk of it."

It now occurred to the girls that their mother was in all likelihood perfectly ignorant of what had happened. They went to the library, therefore, and asked their father whether he would not wish them to make it known to her. He was writing, and, without raising his head, coolly replied —

"Do as you please."

"May we take the letter to read to her?"

"Take whatever you like."

Elizabeth took the letter from his writing table, and they went upstairs together. Mary and Kitty were both with Mrs. Bennet: one communication would, therefore, do for all. After a slight preparation for good news, the letter was read aloud. Mrs. Bennet could hardly contain herself. As soon as Jane had read Mr. Gardiner's hope of Lydia's being soon married, her joy burst forth, and every following sentence added to its exuberance. To know that her daughter would be married was enough. She was disturbed by no fear for her happiness, nor humbled by any memory of her misconduct.

"My dear, dear Lydia!" she cried. "This is delightful indeed! She will be married! I shall see her again! She will be married at sixteen! So wonderfully young! My good, kind brother. I knew how it would turn out. I knew he would manage everything! How I long to see her! And to see dear Wickham too. But the clothes, the wedding clothes! I will write to my sister about them immediately. Lizzy, my dear, run down to your father, and ask him how much he will give her. Stay, stay, I will go myself. Ring the bell, Kitty, for Hill. I will get dressed in a moment. My dear, dear Lydia! How merry we shall be together when we meet!"

Her eldest daughter endeavoured to minimize the intensity of these raptures, by leading her thoughts to the obligations which Mr. Gardiner's behaviour laid them all under.

"For we must attribute this happy conclusion," she added, "in a great measure to his kindness. We are persuaded that he has pledged himself to assist Mr. Wickham with money."

"Well," cried her mother, "it is all very well. Who should do it but her own uncle? If he had not had a family of his own, I and my children must have had all his money, you know; and it is the first time we have ever had anything from him, except a few presents. Well! I am so happy! In a short time I shall have a daughter married. Mrs. Wickham! — How wonderful it sounds! And she only turned sixteen last June. My dear Jane, I am in such a flutter, that I am sure I can't write; so I will dictate, and you write for me. We will settle with your father about the money afterwards; but the things should be ordered immediately."

She was then proceeding to all the particulars of fabric, and would shortly have dictated some very plentiful orders, had not Jane, though with some difficulty, persuaded her to wait till her father was at leisure to be consulted. One day's delay, she observed, would be of small importance; and her mother was too happy to be as obstinate as usual. Other schemes, too, came into her head.

"I will go to Meryton," said she, "as soon as I am dressed, and tell the good, good news to my sister Phillips. And as I come back, I can call on Lady Lucas and Mrs. Long. Kitty, run down and order the carriage. Some fresh air will do me a great deal of good, I am sure. Girls, can I do anything for you in Meryton? Oh! Here comes Hill! My dear Hill, have you heard the good news? Miss Lydia is going to be married; and you shall all have a bowl of punch to make merry at her wedding."

Mrs. Hill began instantly to express her joy. Elizabeth received her congratulations among the rest, and then, sick of this folly, took refuge in her own room, that she might think with freedom.

Poor Lydia's situation must, at best, be bad enough; but that it was no worse, she had need to be thankful. She felt it so; and though, in looking forward, neither happiness nor prosperity could be justly expected for her sister, in looking back to what they had feared only two hours ago, she felt all the advantages of what they had gained.

CHAPTER 50

Mr. Bennet had very often wished before this period of his life that, instead of spending his whole income, he had saved a portion of it for the better provision of his children, and of his wife, if she outlived him. He now wished it more than ever. Had he done his duty in that respect, Lydia need not have been indebted to her uncle for whatever of honour or credit could now be purchased for her. The satisfaction of prevailing on one of the most worthless young men in Great Britain to be her husband might then have rested in its proper place.

He was seriously concerned that a cause of so little advantage to anyone should be forwarded at the sole expense of his brother-in-law, and he was determined, if possible, to find out the extent of his assistance, and to pay him back as soon as he could.

When Mr. Bennet had first married, thrift was held to be perfectly useless; for, of course, they were to have a son. This son would ensure that the widow and younger children would be provided for. Five daughters successively entered the world, but still no son. Mrs. Bennet, for many years after Lydia's birth, had been certain that he would come. This event had at last been despaired of, but it was then too late to be saving. Mrs. Bennet had no interest in frugality, and her husband's desire to remain free of debt had alone prevented their exceeding their income.

Five thousand pounds was settled on Mrs. Bennet and the children. But in what proportions it should be divided amongst the latter depended on the will of the parents. This was one point, with regard to Lydia, at least, which was now to be settled, and Mr. Bennet could have no hesitation in accepting the proposal before him. In terms of grateful acknowledgment for the kindness of his brother-in-law, though expressed most concisely, he then delivered on paper his approval of all that was done, and his willingness to fulfil the agreements that had been made for him. He had never before supposed that, could Wickham be prevailed on to marry his daughter, it would be done with so little inconvenience to himself as by the present arrangement. It would scarcely cost him anything; for, what with her board and pocket money, and the continual presents which passed to her through her mother's hands, Lydia's expenses had been quite high indeed.

That it would be done with such trifling effort on his side, too, was another very welcome surprise; for his chief wish at present was to have as little trouble in the business as possible. When the initial anger which had produced his activity in seeking her were over, he naturally returned to all his former dullness. His letter was soon dispatched; for, though slow to undertake such business, he was quick in its execution. He begged to know farther particulars of what he was indebted to his brother, but was too angry with Lydia to send any message to her.

The good news quickly spread through the house, and with proportionate speed through the neighbourhood. It was borne in the latter with only mild disappointment. It would have been more for the advantage of conversation had Miss Lydia Bennet become fallen; or, as the happiest alternative, been secluded from the world, in some distant farmhouse. But there was much to be talked of in her marrying; and the good-natured wishes of all the spiteful old ladies in Meryton lost but little of their spirit in this change of circumstances, because with such a husband her misery was considered certain.

It had been two weeks since Mrs. Bennet had been downstairs, but on this happy day she again took her seat at the head of her table, and in high spirits. No sentiment of shame could dampen her triumph. The marriage of a daughter, which had been the first object of her wishes since Jane was sixteen, was now on the point of being accomplished, and her thoughts and her words were focused entirely on the business of setting up the new household. She was busily searching through the neighbourhood for a proper home for her daughter, and, without knowing or considering what their income might be, rejected many as deficient in size and importance.

"Haye Park might do," said she, "if the Gouldings would leave it — or the great house at Stoke, if the drawing room were larger; but Ashworth is too far off! I could not bear to have her ten miles from me; and as for Purvis Lodge, the attics are dreadful."

Her husband allowed her to talk on without interruption while the servants remained. But when they had withdrawn, he said to her, "Mrs. Bennet, before you take any or all of these houses for your son and daughter, let us come to a right understanding. Into *one* house in this neighbourhood they shall never have admittance. I will not encourage the impudence of either by receiving them at Longbourn."

A long dispute followed this declaration; but Mr. Bennet was firm. It soon led to another, and Mrs. Bennet found, with amazement and horror, that her husband would not advance a schilling to buy clothes for his daughter. He protested that she should receive from him no mark of affection whatever on the occasion. Mrs. Bennet could hardly comprehend it. That his anger could be carried to such a point of inconceivable resentment as to refuse his daughter a privilege without which her marriage would scarcely seem valid exceeded all that she could believe possible. She was more aware of the disgrace which the lack of new clothes must reflect on her daughter's marriage than to any sense of shame at her eloping and living with Wickham for two weeks before it took place.

Elizabeth was now most heartily sorry that she had, from the distress of the moment, been led to make Mr. Darcy acquainted with their fears for her sister. Since her marriage would so shortly give the proper termination to the elopement, they might hope to conceal its unfavourable beginning from all those who were not immediately on the spot.

She had no fear of its spreading farther through his means. There were few people upon whose discretion she would have more confidently depended. But, at the same time, there was no one whose knowledge of a sister's shameful behavior would have mortified her so much. Had Lydia's marriage been concluded on the most honourable terms, it was not to be supposed that Mr. Darcy would connect himself with a family where, to every other objection, would now be added an alliance and relationship of the nearest kind with the man whom he so justly scorned.

From such a connection she could not wonder that he would recoil. The wish of securing her regard, which she had assured herself of his feeling in Derbyshire, could not in rational expectation survive such a blow as this. She was humbled, she was grieved; she felt sorry for it, though she hardly knew why. She longed to be esteemed by him once more, though she could no longer hope to be benefited by it. She wanted to hear of him, when there seemed the least chance of gaining information. She was convinced that she could have been happy with him, when it was no longer likely they should meet.

What a triumph for him, as she often thought, could he know that the proposals which she had proudly rejected only four months ago, would now have been gladly and gratefully received! He was as generous, she doubted not, as the most generous of men; but still he was mortal, and must feel vindicated by such a reversal of sentiment.

She began now to comprehend that he was exactly the man who would most suit her. His understanding and temper, though unlike her own, would have answered all her wishes. It was a union that must have been to the advantage of both; by her ease and liveliness, his mind might have been softened, his manners improved; and from his position in life and knowledge of the world, she must have received benefit of greater importance.

But no such happy marriage could now teach the admiring multitude what marital felicity really was. A union of a different kind, and preventing the possibility of the other, was soon to be formed in their family.

How Wickham and Lydia were to support themselves financially, she could not imagine. But how little of permanent happiness could belong to a couple who were only brought together because their passions were stronger than their virtue, she could easily guess.

Mr. Gardiner soon wrote again to his brother. To Mr. Bennet's acknowledgments he briefly replied, with assurances of his eagerness to promote the welfare of any of his family; and concluded with a request that the subject never be mentioned to him again. The principal purpose of his letter was to inform them that Mr. Wickham had decided to resign from the Militia.

"It was greatly my wish that he should do so," he added, "as soon as his marriage was decided upon. And I think you will agree with me that a removal from that corps is highly advisable, both on his account and my niece's, as their behavior has been so infamous. It is Mr. Wickham's intention to go into the army; and among his former friends there are still some who are able and willing to assist him. He has the promise of an ensigncy in a regiment now quartered in the north. It is an advantage to have it so far from this part of the kingdom. He has potential; and I hope among different people, where they may each have a character to preserve, they will both be more prudent. I have written to Colonel Forster to inform him of our present arrangements, and to request that he will satisfy the various creditors of Mr. Wickham in and near Brighton, with assurances of speedy payment, for which I have pledged myself. And will you give yourself the trouble of carrying similar assurances to his creditors in Meryton, of whom I shall include a list according to his information? He has enumerated all his debts; I hope in that regard at least he has not deceived us. All his debts will be paid within a week. They will then join his regiment, unless they are first invited to Longbourn; and I understand from Mrs. Gardiner that my niece is very desirous of seeing you all before she leaves the south. She is well, and sends her best wishes to you and her mother. — Your's, etc., E. Gardiner."

Mr. Bennet and his daughters saw all the advantages of Wickham's resignation from the militia as clearly as Mr. Gardiner had. But Mrs. Bennet was not so well pleased with it. Lydia's being settled in the north, just when she had expected most pleasure and pride in her company, for she had by no means given up her plan of their residing in Hertfordshire, was a severe disappointment. Besides, it was such a pity that Lydia should be taken from a regiment where she was acquainted with everybody, and had so many favourites.

"She is so fond of Mrs. Forster," said she, "it will be quite shocking to send her away! And there are several of the young men, too, that she likes very much. The officers may not be so pleasant in the regular army."

His daughter's request, for such it might be considered, of visiting her family before she set off for the north, received at first an absolute negative. But Jane and Elizabeth, who agreed in wishing, for the sake of their sister's feelings, that she should be acknowledged at such a time by her parents, urged him so earnestly, yet so rationally and so mildly, to receive her and her husband at Longbourn, as soon as they were married, that he was prevailed upon to act as they wished. And their mother had the satisfaction of knowing that she would be able to show her married daughter in the neighbourhood before she was banished to the north. When Mr. Bennet wrote again to his brother, therefore, he sent his permission for them to come; and it was settled that, as soon as the ceremony was over, they should proceed to Longbourn. Elizabeth was surprised, however, that Wickham would consent to such a scheme; and had she consulted only her own feelings, any meeting with him would have been the last object of her wishes.

CHAPTER 51

Their sister's wedding day arrived, and Jane and Elizabeth felt sorry for her, probably much more sorry than she felt for herself. The carriage was sent to meet them, and they were to return in it by dinner time. Their arrival was dreaded by the elder Miss Bennets, and Jane more especially, who ascribed to Lydia the feelings which would have attended herself, had *she* been the culprit, and she was wretched in the thought of what her sister must endure.

They came. The family were assembled in the breakfast room to receive them. Smiles decked the face of Mrs. Bennet as the carriage drove up to the door. Her husband looked impenetrably grave, and her daughters were alarmed, anxious, uneasy.

Lydia's voice was heard in the hall; the door was thrown open, and she ran into the room. Her mother stepped forwards, embraced her, and welcomed her with rapture. She gave her hand with an affectionate smile to Wickham, who followed his lady, and wished them both joy.

Their reception from Mr. Bennet, to whom they then turned, was not quite so cordial. He scarcely opened his lips. The unconcerned demeanor of the young couple, indeed, was enough to provoke him. Elizabeth was disgusted, and even Miss Bennet was shocked. Lydia was Lydia still — untamed, unabashed, wild, noisy, and fearless. She turned from sister to sister, demanding their congratulations. When at length they all sat down, she looked eagerly round the room, took notice of some little alteration in it, and observed, with a laugh, that it was a great while since she had been there.

Wickham was no more distressed than herself; but his manners were always so pleasing that, had his character and his marriage been exactly what they ought, his smiles and his open demeanor would have delighted them all. Elizabeth had not before believed him quite equal to such confidence; but she sat down, resolving within herself to draw no limits in future to the shamelessness of a shameless man. *She* blushed, and Jane blushed; but the cheeks of the two who caused their discomposure suffered no variation of colour.

There was no lack of conversation. The bride and her mother could neither of them talk fast enough; and Wickham, who happened to sit near Elizabeth, began enquiring after his acquaintance in that neighbourhood with a good-humoured ease which she felt very unable to equal in return. They seemed each of them to have the happiest memories in the world. Nothing of the past was recollected with pain; and Lydia spoke voluntarily of subjects which her sisters would not have alluded to for the world.

"Only think of its being three months," she cried, "since I went away! It seems but two weeks, I declare; and yet there have been things enough happened in the time. Good gracious! When I went away, I am sure I had no more idea of being married till I came back again! Though I thought it would be very good fun if I was."

Her father lifted up his eyes. Jane was distressed. Elizabeth looked expressively at Lydia, but she happily continued — "Oh! Mama, do the people hereabouts know I am married today? I was afraid they might not be aware of it. We overtook William Goulding in his carriage, and I was so determined he should know it that I let down the side-glass next to him and took off my glove and let my hand just rest upon the window-frame, so that he might see the ring; and then I bowed and smiled like anything."

Elizabeth could bear it no longer. She got up and ran out of the room, and returned no more till she heard them passing through the hall to the dining parlour. She then joined them in time to see Lydia, with great excitement, walk up to her mother's right hand, and hear her say to her eldest sister, "Ah, Jane, I take your place now, and you must go lower, because I am a married woman!"

It was not to be supposed that time would give Lydia that sense of shame from which she had always been so wholly free. Her ease and good spirits increased. She longed to see Mrs. Phillips, the Lucases, and all their other neighbours, and to hear herself called "Mrs. Wickham" by each of them. In the meantime, she went after dinner to show her ring, and boast of being married, to Mrs. Hill and the two housemaids.

"Well, Mama," said she, when they were all returned to the breakfast room, " what do you think of my husband? Is not he a charming man? I am sure my sisters must all envy me. I only hope they may have half my good luck. They must all go to Brighton. That is the place to get husbands. What a pity it is, Mama, we did not all go."

"Very true; and if I had my way, we would have. But, my dear Lydia, I don't at all like your living so far away. Must it be so?"

"Oh, Lord! Yes, there is nothing to be done for it. I shall like it more than anything. You and papa, and my sisters, must come down and see us. We shall be at Newcastle all the winter, and I dare say there will be some balls, and I will take care to get good partners for them all."

"That sounds wonderful!" said her mother.

"And then, when you go away, you may leave one or two of my sisters behind you; and I dare say I shall get husbands for them before the winter is over."

"I thank you for my share of the favour," said Elizabeth, "but I do not particularly like your way of getting husbands."

Their visitors were not to remain more than ten days with them. Mr. Wickham had received his commission before he left London, and he was to join his regiment in two weeks.

No one but Mrs. Bennet regretted that their stay would be so short, and she made the most of the time by visiting with her daughter and having very frequent parties at home. Wickham's affection for Lydia was just what Elizabeth had expected to find it — not equal to Lydia's for him. She had scarcely needed a moment to be satisfied that their elopement had been brought on by the strength of her love rather than by his. She would have wondered why, without loving her, he chose to elope with her at all, had she not felt certain that his flight was rendered necessary by distress of circumstances. And, if that were the case, he was not the kind of young man who would resist an opportunity of having a companion.

Lydia was exceedingly fond of him. He was her dear Wickham on every occasion; no one could compare to him. He did everything best in the world; and she was sure he would kill more birds when hunting season began than anybody else in the country.

One morning, soon after their arrival, as she was sitting with her two elder sisters, she said to Elizabeth –

"Lizzy, I never gave *you* an account of my wedding, I believe. You were not present when I told Mama and the others all about it. Are you not curious to hear how it was managed?"

"Not, really," replied Elizabeth. "I think there cannot be too little said on the subject."

"La! You are so strange! But I must tell you how it went off. We were married, you know, at St. Clement's, and it was settled that we should all be there by eleven o'clock. My uncle and aunt and I were to go together; and the others were to meet us at the church. Well, Monday morning came, and I was in such a fuss! I was so afraid, you know, that something would happen to put it off, and then I would have been quite frantic. And there was my aunt, all the time I was dressing, preaching and talking away just as if she was reading a sermon. However, I did not hear more than one word in ten, for I was thinking, you may suppose, of my dear Wickham. I longed to know whether he would be wearing his blue coat.

"Well, and so we breakfasted at ten, as usual. I thought it would never be over; for, by the bye, you are to understand that my uncle and aunt were horridly unpleasant all the time I was with them. If you'll believe me, I did not once put my foot out of doors, though I was there for two weeks. Not one party, or scheme, or anything! Well, and so, just as the carriage came to the door, my uncle was called away upon business to that horrid man, Mr. Stone. And then, you know, when once they get together, there is no end of it. Well, I was so frightened, I did not know what to do; for my uncle was to give me away; and if he was late the marriage would have to be postponed to another day. But, luckily, he came back again in ten minutes' time, and then we all set out. However, I recollected afterwards, that if he _had_ been prevented going, the wedding need not be put off, for Mr. Darcy might have done as well."

"Mr. Darcy!" repeated Elizabeth, in utter amazement.

"Oh, yes! He was to come there with Wickham, you know. But, gracious me! I quite forgot! I ought not to have said a word about it. I promised them so faithfully! What will Wickham say? It was to be such a secret!"

"If it was to be secret," said Jane, "say not another word on the subject. You may depend upon my seeking no further."

"Oh! Certainly," said Elizabeth, though burning with curiosity. "We will ask you no questions."

"Thank you," said Lydia, "for if you did, I should certainly tell you all, and then Wickham would be angry."

On such encouragement to ask, Elizabeth was forced to put it out of her power by leaving the room.

But to live in ignorance on such a point was impossible; or, at least, it was impossible not to press for information. Mr. Darcy had been at her sister's wedding. Guesses as to the meaning of it, rapid and wild, hurried into her brain; but she was satisfied with none. Those that best pleased her, as placing his conduct in the noblest light, seemed most improbable. She could not bear such suspense; and hastily seizing a sheet of paper, wrote a short letter to her aunt, to request an explanation of what Lydia had said, if it were compatible with the secrecy which had been intended.

"You may readily comprehend," she added, "what my curiosity must be to know how a person so unconnected with any of us, and — comparatively speaking — a stranger to our family, should have been among you at such a time. Pray write instantly, and let me understand it; unless it is to remain in the secrecy which Lydia seems to think necessary; and then I must endeavour to be satisfied with ignorance."

"Not that I _shall_, though," she added to herself, and she finished the letter. "And, my dear aunt, if you do not tell me in an honourable manner, I shall certainly be reduced to tricks and stratagems to find it out."

CHAPTER 52

Elizabeth had the satisfaction of receiving a quick answer to her letter. She was no sooner in possession of it than, hurrying into the little wood, where she was least likely to be interrupted, she sat down on one of the benches, and prepared to be happy; for the length of the letter convinced her that it did not contain a denial.

"Gracechurch Street, *Sept. 6.*

My dear Niece, — I have just received your letter, and shall devote this whole morning to answering it, as I foresee that a *little* writing will not comprise what I have to tell you. I must confess myself surprised by your application; I did not expect it from *you*. Don't think me angry, however, for I only mean to let you know that I had not imagined such enquiries to be necessary on *your* side. If you do not choose to understand me, forgive my impertinence. Your uncle is as much surprised as I am, and nothing but the belief of your being a party concerned would have allowed him to act as he has done. But if you are really innocent and ignorant, I must be more explicit.

On the very day of my coming home from Longbourn, your uncle had a most unexpected visitor. Mr. Darcy called, and talked with him for several hours. It was all over before I arrived; so my curiosity was not so dreadfully piqued as *yours* seems to have been. He came to tell Mr. Gardiner that he had found your sister and Mr. Wickham, and that he had seen and talked with them both — Wickham repeatedly, Lydia once. From what I can gather, he left Derbyshire only one day after we did, and came to town with the resolution of hunting for them. The motive professed was his conviction of its being his fault that Wickham's worthlessness had not been so well known as to make it impossible for any young woman of character to love or confide in him. He generously attributed the whole to his mistaken pride, and confessed that he had before thought it beneath him to lay his private actions open to the world. His character was to speak for itself. He called it, therefore, his duty to step forward, and endeavour to remedy an evil which he had caused. If he *had* *another* motive, I am sure it would never disgrace him. He had been some days in town before he was able to discover them; but he had knowledge that we did not; and the consciousness of this was another reason for his resolving to follow us.

There is a lady, it seems, a Mrs. Younge, who was some time ago governess to Miss Darcy, and was dismissed from her charge, though he did not say why. This Mrs. Younge was, he knew, intimately acquainted with Wickham; and he went to her for information as soon as he got to town. But it was two or three days before he could get from her what he wanted. She would not betray her trust, I suppose, without bribery, for she really did know where her friend was to be found. Wickham, indeed, had gone to her on their first arrival in London, and had there been room in her house, they would have taken up their abode with her. At length, however, our kind friend procured the wished-for address. He saw Wickham, and afterwards insisted on seeing Lydia. His first object with her, he acknowledged, had been to persuade her to leave her present disgraceful situation, and return to her friends as soon as they could be prevailed on to receive her, offering his assistance as far as it would go. But he found Lydia absolutely resolved on remaining where she was. She cared for none of her friends; she wanted no help of his; she would not hear of leaving Wickham; she was sure they should be married some time or other, and it did not much matter when. Since such were her feelings, it only remained, he thought, to secure and expedite a marriage, which, in his very first conversation with Wickham, he easily learned had never been *his* design. He confessed himself obliged to leave the regiment on account of some gambling debts which were very pressing; and laid all the ill consequences of Lydia's flight on her own folly alone. He meant to resign his commission immediately; and as to his future situation, he could say very little about it. He must go somewhere, but he did not know where, and he knew he should have nothing to live on.

Mr. Darcy asked him why he had not married your sister at once. Though Mr. Bennet was not imagined to be very rich, he would have been able to do something for him, and his situation must have been benefited by marriage. But he found, in reply to this question, that Wickham still cherished the hope of more effectually making his fortune by marrying someone from a wealthy family.

They met several times, for there was much to be discussed. Wickham, of course, wanted more than he could get, but at length was persuaded to be reasonable.

Everything being settled between *them*, Mr. Darcy's next step was to make your uncle acquainted with it, and he first visited Gracechurch Street the evening before I came home. But Mr. Gardiner could not be seen, and Mr. Darcy found, on further inquiry, that your father was still with him, but would leave town the next morning. He did not judge your father to be a person whom he could so properly consult as your uncle, and therefore readily postponed seeing him till after the departure of the former. He did not leave his name, and till the next day it was only known that a gentleman had called on business.

On Saturday he came again. Your father was gone, your uncle at home, and, as I said before, they had a great deal of talk together.

They met again on Sunday, and then *I* saw him too. It was not all settled before Monday: as soon as it was, the express was sent off to Longbourn. But our visitor was very obstinate. I fancy, Lizzy, that obstinacy is the real defect of his character after all. He has been accused of many faults at different times, but *this* is the true one. Nothing was to be done that he did not do himself, though I am sure your uncle would most readily have settled the whole.

They discussed it for a long time, which was more than either the gentleman or lady concerned in it deserved. But at last your uncle was forced to yield, and instead of being allowed to be of use to his niece, was forced to put up with only having the probable credit of it, which went sorely against the grain. I really believe your letter this morning gave him great pleasure, because it required an explanation that would rob him of his borrowed feathers, and give the praise where it was due. But, Lizzy, this must go no farther than yourself, or Jane at most.

You know pretty well, I suppose, what has been done for the young people. His debts are to be paid, amounting, I believe, to considerably more than a thousand pounds, another thousand in addition to her own settled upon *her*, and his commission purchased. The reason why all this was to be done by him alone was such as I have given above. It was because of him, because of his reserve and want of proper consideration, that Wickham's character had been so misunderstood, and, consequently, that he had been received and noticed as he was. Perhaps there was some truth in *this*; though I doubt whether *his* reserve, or *anybody's* reserve, can be enough to explain his zealous attention in the matter. But in spite of all this fine talking, my dear Lizzy, you may rest perfectly assured that your uncle would never have yielded, if we had not believed Mr. Darcy partial to you.

When all this was resolved on, he returned again to his friends, who were still staying at Pemberley. But it was agreed that he should be in London once more when the wedding took place, and all money matters were then to be finalised.

I believe I have now told you everything. It is a relation which you tell me is to give you great surprise; I hope at least it will not afford you any displeasure. Lydia came to us; and Wickham had constant access to the house. *He* was exactly what he had been when I knew him in Hertfordshire; but I would not tell you how little I was satisfied with *her* behaviour while she stayed with us, if I had not perceived, by Jane's letter last Wednesday, that her conduct on coming home was exactly the same, and therefore what I now tell you can give you no fresh pain. I talked to her repeatedly in the most serious manner, representing to her all the wickedness of what she had done and all the unhappiness she had brought on her family. If she heard me, it was by chance, for I am sure she did not listen. I was sometimes quite provoked, but then I remembered my dear Elizabeth and Jane, and for their sakes had patience with her.

Mr. Darcy was punctual in his return, and, as Lydia informed you, attended the wedding. He dined with us the next day, and was to leave town again on Wednesday or Thursday. Will you be very angry with me, my Dear Lizzy, if I take this opportunity of saying (what I was never bold enough to say before) how much I like him? His behaviour to us has, in every respect, been as pleasing as when we were in Derbyshire. His understanding and opinions all please me. I thought him very sly; — he hardly ever mentioned your name. But slyness seems the fashion.

Pray forgive me if I have been very presuming; or at least do not punish me so far as to exclude me from Pemberley. I shall never be quite happy till I have been all round the park. A low carriage, with a nice little pair of ponies, would be the very thing.

But I must write no more. The children have been wanting me this half-hour.
Your's, very sincerely,
M. Gardiner."

The contents of this letter threw Elizabeth into a flutter of spirits, in which it was difficult to determine whether pleasure or pain bore the greatest share. The vague and unsettled suspicions which uncertainty had produced of what Mr. Darcy might have been doing to forward her sister's match were proved beyond their greatest extent to be true! He had followed them purposely to town, he had taken on himself all the trouble and mortification attendant on such a search, and he was reduced to meet — frequently meet, reason with, persuade, and finally bribe — the man whom he always most wished to avoid, and whose very name it was punishment to him to pronounce. He had done all this for a girl whom he could neither regard nor esteem. Her heart did whisper that he had done it for her. But it was a hope shortly checked by other considerations, for surely his affection for her, a woman who had already refused him, could not overcome a sentiment so natural as abhorrence against a relationship with Wickham. Brother-in-law of Wickham! Every kind of pride must revolt from the connection. He had, to be sure, done much — she was ashamed to think how much. But he had given a reason for his interference, which seemed to supply motive enough. It was reasonable that he should feel he had been wrong, and desire to correct it. Though she could not believe that she was his principal object, she could perhaps believe that his partiality for her might have played a part in his liberality. It was painful, exceedingly painful, to know that they owed an obligation to a person whom they would never repay. They owed the restoration of Lydia, her character, everything to him. Oh! How heartily did she grieve over every ungracious sensation she had ever encouraged, every saucy speech she had ever directed towards him. For herself, she was humbled; but she was proud of him. Proud that in a cause of compassion and honour he had been able to get the better of himself. She read over her aunt's commendation of him again and again. It was hardly enough; but it pleased her. She was even sensible of some pleasure, though mixed with regret, on finding how steadfastly both she and her uncle had been persuaded that affection still existed between Mr. Darcy and herself.

She was roused from her seat and her reflections by some one's approach, and before she could strike into another path she was overtaken by Wickham.

"I am afraid I interrupt your solitary ramble, my dear sister?" said he, as he joined her.

"You certainly do," she replied with a smile, "but it does not follow that the interruption must be unwelcome."

"I should be sorry indeed if it were. *We* were always good friends, and now we are better."

"True. Are the others coming out?"

"I do not know. Mrs. Bennet and Lydia are going in the carriage to Meryton. And so, my dear sister, I find from our uncle and aunt that you have actually seen Pemberley."

She replied in the affirmative.

"I almost envy you the pleasure, and yet I believe it would be too much for me, or else I could see it while on my way to Newcastle. And you saw the old housekeeper, I suppose? Poor Reynolds, she was always very fond of me. But of course she did not mention my name to you."

"Yes, she did."

"And what did she say?"

"That you were gone into the army, and, she was afraid, had not turned out well. At such a distance as *that*, you know, things are strangely misrepresented."

"Certainly," he replied, biting his lips.

Elizabeth hoped she had silenced him; but he soon afterwards said –

"I was surprised to see Darcy in town last month. We passed each other several times. I wonder what he can be doing there."

"Perhaps preparing for his marriage with Miss de Bourgh," said Elizabeth. "It must be something particular to take him there at this time of year."

"Undoubtedly. Did you see him while you were at Lambton? I thought I understood from the Gardiners that you had."

"Yes; he introduced us to his sister."

"And do you like her?"

"Very much."

"I have heard, indeed, that she is uncommonly improved within this year or two. When I last saw her she was not very promising. I am very glad you like her. I hope she will turn out well."

"I dare say she will; she has got past the most trying age."

"Did you go by the village of Kympton?"

"I do not recollect that we did."

"I mention it because it is the living which I ought to have had. A most delightful place! Excellent Parsonage House! It would have suited me in every respect."

"How should you have liked making sermons?"

"Exceedingly well. I should have considered it as part of my duty, and the exertion would soon have been nothing. One ought not to repine; but, to be sure, it would have been such a thing for me! The quiet, the retirement of such a life, would have answered all my ideas of happiness!

But it was not to be. Did you ever hear Darcy mention the circumstance when you were in Kent?"

"I *have* heard, from authority which I thought *as good*, that it was left you conditionally only, and at the will of the present patron."

"You have! Yes, there was something in *that*; I told you so from the first, you may remember."

"I *did* hear, too, that there was a time when sermon-making was not so palatable to you as it seems to be at present — that you actually declared your resolution of never taking orders, and that the business had been compromised accordingly."

"You did! And it was not wholly without foundation. You may remember what I told you on that point, when first we talked of it."

They were now almost at the door of the house, for she had walked fast to get rid of him, and, unwilling for her sister's sake to provoke him, she only said in reply, with a good-humoured smile —

"Come, Mr. Wickham, we are brother and sister, you know. Do not let us quarrel about the past. In the future, I hope we shall be always of one mind."

She held out her hand; he kissed it with affectionate gallantry, though he hardly knew what to think, and they entered the house.

CHAPTER 53

Mr. Wickham was so perfectly satisfied with this conversation that he never again provoked his dear sister Elizabeth by introducing the subject. And she was pleased to find that she had said enough to keep him quiet.

The day of his and Lydia's departure soon came, and Mrs. Bennet was forced to submit to a separation which, as her husband by no means approved her scheme of their all going to Newcastle, was likely to continue at least a year.

"Oh! My dear Lydia," she cried, "when shall we meet again?"

"Oh, Lord! I don't know. Not these two or three years, perhaps."

"Write to me very often, my dear."

"As often as I can. But you know married women have never much time for writing. My sisters may write to *me*. They will have nothing else to do."

Mr. Wickham's adieus were much more affectionate than his wife's. He smiled, looked handsome, and said many thoughtful things.

"He is as fine a fellow," said Mr. Bennet, as soon as they were out of the house, "as ever I saw. He simpers, and smirks, and endeavours to win our affection. I am prodigiously proud of him. I defy even Sir William Lucas himself to produce a more valuable son-in-law."

The loss of her daughter made Mrs. Bennet gloomy for several days.

"I often think," said she, "that there is nothing so bad as parting with one's friends. Life is so forlorn without them."

"This is the consequence of a daughter's marrying," said Elizabeth. "It must make you better satisfied that your other four are single."

"It does no such thing. Lydia does not leave me because she is married, but only because her husband's regiment happens to be so far away. If that had been nearer, she would not have gone so soon."

But the spiritless condition which this event threw her into was shortly relieved, and her mind opened again to the agitation of hope, by some news which then began to be circulated. The housekeeper at Netherfield had received orders to prepare for the arrival of her master, who was coming down in a day or two, to hunt there for several weeks. Mrs. Bennet was quite excited. She looked at Jane, and smiled, and shook her head by turns.

"Well, well, and so Mr. Bingley is coming down, sister" (for Mrs. Phillips first brought her the news). "Well, so much the better. Not that I care about it, though. He is nothing to us, you know, and I am sure *I* never want to see him again. But, however, he is very welcome to come to Netherfield, if he likes. And who knows what *may* happen? But that is nothing to us. You know, sister, we agreed long ago never to mention a word about it. And so, it is quite certain he is coming?"

"You may depend on it," replied the other, "for Mrs. Nicholls was in Meryton last night; I saw her passing by, and went out myself on purpose to know the truth of it; and she told me that it was certain. He comes down on Thursday at the latest, very likely on Wednesday. She was going to the butcher's, she told me, to order some meat on Wednesday, and she has several ducks just fit to be killed."

Miss Bennet had not been able to hear of his coming without changing colour. It was many months since she had mentioned his name to Elizabeth; but now, as soon as they were alone together, she said —

"I saw you look at me today, Lizzy, when my aunt told us the news. I know I appeared distressed, but don't assume to know the cause. I was only confused for the moment, because I felt that I *should* be looked at. I do assure you that the news does not affect me either with pleasure or pain. I am glad of one thing — that he comes alone; because we shall see the less of him. Not that I am worried about *myself*, but I dread other people's remarks."

Elizabeth did not know what to make of it. Had she not seen him in Derbyshire, she might have supposed him capable of coming there with no other view than what was acknowledged. But she still thought him partial to Jane, and she only wondered if he was coming there *with* his friend's permission, or if he was bold enough to come without it.

"Yet it is hard," she sometimes thought, "that this poor man cannot come to his own house without raising all this speculation! I will leave him to himself."

In spite of what her sister declared, and really believed to be her feelings, Elizabeth could easily perceive that her spirits were affected by it. They were more disturbed, more unstable, than she had often seen them.

The subject which had been so warmly discussed between their parents about a year ago was now brought forward again.

"As soon as ever Mr. Bingley comes, my dear," said Mrs. Bennet, "you will visit him, of course."

"No, no. You forced me into visiting him last year, and promised, if I went to see him, he should marry one of my daughters. But it ended in nothing, and I will not be sent on a fool's errand again."

His wife expressed to him how absolutely necessary such an attention would be from all the neighbouring gentlemen, on his returning to Netherfield.

"'Tis an etiquette I despise," said he. "If he wants our company, let him seek it. He knows where we live. I will not spend *my* hours running after my neighbours every time they go away and come back again."

"Well, all I know is that it will be abominably rude if you do not visit him. But, however, that shan't prevent my asking him to dine here, I am determined. We must have Mrs. Long and the Gouldings soon. That will make thirteen with ourselves, so there will be just room at the table for him."

Consoled by this resolution, she was the better able to bear her husband's incivility; though it was very mortifying to know that her neighbours might all see Mr. Bingley, in consequence of it, before *they* did. As the day of his arrival drew near —

"I begin to be sorry that he comes at all," said Jane to her sister. " I could see him with perfect indifference, but I can hardly bear to hear it thus perpetually talked of. My mother means well, but she does not know — no one can know — how much I suffer from what she says. Happy shall I be when his stay at Netherfield is over!"

"I wish I could say something to comfort you," replied Elizabeth, "but it is wholly out of my power. You must feel it, and the usual satisfaction of preaching patience to a sufferer is denied me, because you have always so much."

Mr. Bingley arrived. Mrs. Bennet, through the assistance of servants, contrived to have the earliest tidings of it, that the period of anxiety and fretfulness on her side might be as long as possible. She counted the days that must pass before their invitation could be sent — hopeless of seeing him before. But, on the third morning after his arrival in Hertfordshire, she saw him from her dressing room window enter the pasture and ride towards the house.

Her daughters were eagerly called to partake of her joy. Jane resolutely kept her place at the table, but Elizabeth, to satisfy her mother, went to the window. She looked — she saw Mr. Darcy with him, and sat down again by her sister.

"There is a gentleman with him, Mama," said Kitty. "Who can it be?"

"Some acquaintance or other, my dear, I suppose; I am sure I do not know."

"La!" replied Kitty, "It looks just like that man that used to be with him before — Mr. What's-his-name. That tall, proud man."

"Good gracious! Mr. Darcy! And so it does, I vow. Well, any friend of Mr. Bingley's will always be welcome here, to be sure; otherwise I must say that I hate the very sight of him."

Jane looked at Elizabeth with surprise and concern. She knew little of their meeting in Derbyshire, and therefore felt for the awkwardness which must attend her sister, in seeing him almost for the first time after receiving his explanatory letter. Both sisters were quite uncomfortable. Each felt for the other, and of course for themselves; and their mother talked on of her dislike of Mr. Darcy, and her resolution to be civil to him only as Mr. Bingley's friend, without being heard by either of them. But Elizabeth had sources of uneasiness which could not be suspected by Jane, to whom she had never yet had courage to show Mrs. Gardiner's letter, or to relate her own change of sentiment towards him. To Jane, he could be only a man whose proposals she had refused and whose merit she had undervalued. But to her own more extensive information, he was the person to whom the whole family were indebted, and whom she regarded herself with an interest, if not quite so tender, at least as reasonable and just as what Jane felt for Bingley. Her astonishment at his coming — at his coming to Netherfield, to Longbourn, and voluntarily seeking her again, was almost equal to what she had known on first witnessing his altered behaviour in Derbyshire.

The colour, which had been driven from her face, returned for half a minute with an additional glow, and a smile of delight, as she thought for that space of time that his affection and wishes must still be unchanged. But she knew now what to think.

"Let me first see how he behaves," said she, "it will then be early enough for expectation."

She sat intently at her needlework, striving to be composed, and without daring to lift her eyes, till anxious curiosity carried them to the face of her sister as the servant approached the door. Jane looked a little paler than usual, but more sedate than Elizabeth had expected. On the gentlemen's appearing, her colour increased; yet she received them with tolerable ease, and with a propriety of behaviour equally free from any symptom of resentment, or any unnecessary desire to please.

Elizabeth said as little to either as civility would allow, and sat down again to her work, with an eagerness which she did not often give it. She had ventured only one glance at Darcy. He looked serious, as usual, more like he had looked in Hertfordshire than when she had seen him at Pemberley. But, perhaps, he could not in her mother's presence be what he was before her uncle and aunt. It was a painful, but not an improbable, conclusion.

Bingley she had likewise seen for an instant, and in that short period saw him looking both pleased and embarrassed. He was received by Mrs. Bennet with a degree of civility which made her two daughters ashamed, especially when contrasted with the cold and ceremonious politeness of her curtsey and welcome to his friend.

Elizabeth particularly, who knew that her mother owed to the latter the preservation of her favourite daughter from infamy, was hurt and distressed to a most painful degree by a distinction so ill-applied.

Darcy, after enquiring of her how Mr. and Mrs. Gardiner were — a question which she could not answer without confusion — said scarcely anything. He was not seated by her; perhaps that was the reason of his silence; but it had not been so in Derbyshire. There he had talked to her family when he could not talk to her. But now several minutes elapsed without bringing the sound of his voice; and when occasionally, unable to resist the impulse of curiosity, she raised her eyes to his face, she as often found him looking at Jane as at herself, and frequently on no object but the ground. More thoughtfulness, and less anxiety to please than when they last met, were plainly expressed. She was disappointed, and angry with herself for being so.

"Could I expect it to be otherwise?" said she. "Yet why did he come?"

She was in no humour for conversation with anyone but him; and to him she had hardly courage to speak.

She inquired after his sister, but could do no more.

"It is a long time, Mr. Bingley, since you went away," said Mrs. Bennet.

He readily acknowledged it. "I began to be afraid you would never come back again. People *did* say you meant to leave the place entirely at the end of September; but, however, I hope it is not true. A great many changes have happened in the neighbourhood since you went away. Miss Lucas is married and settled. And one of my own daughters. I suppose you have heard of it; indeed, you must have seen it in the papers. It was in the *Times* and the *Courier*, I know; though it was not put in as it ought to be. It was only said, 'Lately, George Wickham Esq., to Miss Lydia Bennet,' without there being a syllable said of her father, or the place where she lived, or anything. It was my brother Gardiner's doing, and I wonder how he came to make such an awkward business of it. Did you see it?"

Bingley replied that he did, and made his congratulations. Elizabeth dared not lift up her eyes. How Mr. Darcy looked, therefore, she could not tell.

"It is a delightful thing, to be sure, to have a daughter well married," continued her mother. "But, at the same time, Mr. Bingley, it is very hard to have her taken away from me. They are gone down to Newcastle, a place quite northward, it seems, and there they are to stay I do not know how long. His regiment is there; for I suppose you have heard of his leaving the militia, and of his being gone into the regular army. Thank Heaven! He has *some* friends, though perhaps not as many as he deserves."

Elizabeth, who knew this to be levelled at Mr. Darcy, was in such misery of shame that she could hardly keep her seat. It drew from her, however, the exertion of speaking, which nothing else had so effectually done before; and she asked Bingley whether he meant to make any stay in the country at present. A few weeks, he believed.

"When you have killed all your own birds, Mr. Bingley," said her mother, "I beg you will come here, and shoot as many as you please on Mr. Bennet's manor. I am sure he will be vastly happy to oblige you, and will save all the best of the coveys for you."

Elizabeth's misery increased at such unnecessary attention! Were the same fair prospect to arise at present as had flattered them a year ago, everything, she was persuaded, would be hastening to the same vexatious conclusion. At that instant she felt that years of happiness could not make Jane or herself amends for moments of such painful confusion.

"The first wish of my heart," said she to herself, "is never more to be in company with either of them. Their society can afford no pleasure that will atone for such wretchedness as this! Let me never see either of them again!"

Yet the misery, for which years of happiness were to offer no compensation, received soon afterwards material relief from observing how much the beauty of her sister rekindled the admiration of her former lover. When first he came in, he had spoken to her but little, but every five minutes seemed to be giving her more of his attention. He found her as beautiful as she had been last year — and as good-natured, though not quite so chatty. Jane was anxious that no difference should be perceived in her at all, and was really persuaded that she talked as much as ever. But her mind was so busily engaged that she did not always realize when she was silent.

When the gentlemen rose to go away, Mrs. Bennet was mindful of her intended civility, and they were invited to dine at Longbourn in a few days time.

"You are quite a visit in my debt, Mr. Bingley," she added, "for when you went to town last winter you promised to take a family dinner with us as soon as you returned. I have not forgot, you see; and I assure you I was very much disappointed that you did not come back and keep your engagement."

Bingley looked a little embarrassed at this reflection, and said something of his having been prevented by business. Then they went away.

Mrs. Bennet had been strongly inclined to ask them to stay and dine there that day; but, though she always kept a very good table, she did not think anything less than two courses could be good enough for a man on whom she had such anxious designs, or satisfy the appetite and pride of one who had ten thousand a year.

CHAPTER 54

As soon as they were gone Elizabeth walked out to recover her spirits; or, in other words, to dwell without interruption on those subjects that must deaden them more. Mr. Darcy's behaviour astonished and vexed her.

"Why, if he came only to be silent, grave, and indifferent," said she, "did he come at all?"

She could settle it in no way that gave her pleasure.

"He could be still amiable, still pleasing to my uncle and aunt, when he was in town; and why not to me? If he fears me, why come hither? If he no longer cares for me, why be silent? Irritating, irritating, man! I will think no more about him."

Her resolution was for a short time involuntarily kept by the approach of her sister, who joined her with a cheerful look, which showed her better satisfied with their visitors than Elizabeth.

"Now," said she, "that this first meeting is over, I feel perfectly easy. I know my own strength, and I shall never be embarrassed again by his coming. I am glad he dines here on Tuesday: it will then be publicly seen that on both sides, we meet only as common and indifferent acquaintances."

"Yes, very indifferent indeed," said Elizabeth laughingly. "Oh, Jane! Be careful."

"My dear Lizzy, you cannot think me so weak as to be in danger now."

"I think you are in very great danger of making him as much in love with you as ever."

They did not see the gentlemen again till Tuesday; and Mrs. Bennet, in the meanwhile, was giving way to all the happy schemes which the good-humour and common politeness of Bingley, in half an hour's visit, had revived.

On Tuesday there was a large party assembled at Longbourn, and the two, who were most anxiously expected, were exactly on time. When they entered the dining room, Elizabeth eagerly watched to see whether Bingley would take the place which, in all their former parties, had belonged to him, by her sister. On entering the room he seemed to hesitate; but Jane happened to look round, and happened to smile: it was decided — he placed himself by her.

Elizabeth, with a triumphant sensation, looked towards his friend. He bore it with noble indifference, and she would have imagined that Bingley had received his sanction to be happy, had she not seen his eyes likewise turned towards Mr. Darcy, with an expression of half-laughing alarm.

His behaviour to her sister was such, during dinner time, as showed an admiration of her. Though more guarded than formerly, this persuaded Elizabeth that, if left wholly to himself, Jane's happiness, and his own, would be speedily secured. Though she dared not depend upon the event of their marriage, she still received pleasure from observing his behaviour. It gave her all the animation that her spirits could boast; for she was in no cheerful humour. Mr. Darcy was almost as far from her as the table could divide them. He was on one side of her mother. She knew how little such a situation would give pleasure to either. She was not near enough to hear any of their conversation; but she could see how seldom they spoke to each other, and how formal and cold was their manner whenever they did. Her mother's ungraciousness made the sense of what they owed him more painful to Elizabeth's mind; and she would, at times, have given anything to be privileged to tell him that his kindness was neither unknown nor unfelt by the whole of the family.

She was in hopes that the evening would afford some opportunity of bringing them together; that the whole of the visit would not pass away without enabling them to enter into something more of conversation than the mere ceremonious salutation accompanying his entrance. Anxious and uneasy was the period which passed in the drawing room before the gentlemen came. It was wearisome and dull to a degree that almost made her uncivil. She looked forward to their entrance as the moment on which all her chance of pleasure for the evening must depend.

"If he does not come to me *then*," said she, "I shall give him up forever."

The gentlemen came; and she thought he looked as if he would have answered her hopes; but, alas! The ladies had crowded round the table where Miss Bennet was making tea and Elizabeth pouring out the coffee, so that there was not a single vacancy near her. And on the gentlemen's approaching, one of the girls moved closer to her than ever, and said, in a whisper —

"The men shan't come and part us, I am determined. We want none of them, do we?"

Darcy had walked away to another part of the room. She followed him with her eyes, envied everyone to whom he spoke, had scarcely patience enough to help anybody to coffee, and then was enraged at herself for being so silly!

"A man who has once been refused! How could I ever be foolish enough to expect a renewal of his love? Is there one among the sex who would not protest against such a weakness as a second proposal to the same woman? There is no indignity so abhorrent to their feelings!"

She was a little revived, however, by his bringing back his coffee cup himself, and she seized the opportunity of saying, "Is your sister at Pemberley still?"

"Yes, she will remain there till Christmas."

"And quite alone? Have all her friends left her?"

"Mrs. Annesley is with her. The others have been at Scarborough these three weeks."

She could think of nothing more to say; but if he wished to converse with her, he might have better success. He stood by her, however, for some minutes in silence; and, at last, on the young lady's whispering to Elizabeth again, he walked away.

When the tea-things were removed, and the card tables placed, the ladies all rose, and Elizabeth was then hoping to be soon joined by him, when all her views were overthrown by seeing him fall a victim to her mother's avarice for whist-players, and in a few moments after seated with the rest of the party. She now lost every expectation of pleasure. They were confined for the evening at different tables, and she had nothing to hope, but that his eyes were so often turned towards her side of the room as to make him play as unsuccessfully as herself.

Mrs. Bennet had planned to keep the two Netherfield gentlemen until supper, but their carriage was unluckily ordered before any of the others, and she had no opportunity of detaining them.

"Well girls," said she, as soon as they were left to themselves, "what say you to the day? I think everything has passed off uncommonly well, I assure you. The dinner was as well prepared as any I ever saw. The venison was roasted perfectly — and everybody said they never saw so fat a haunch. The soup was fifty times better than what we had at the Lucas's last week. Even Mr. Darcy acknowledged that the partridges were remarkably well done, and I suppose he has two or three French cooks at least. And, my dear Jane, I never saw you look more beautiful. Mrs. Long said so too, for I asked her whether you did not. And what do you think she said besides? 'Ah! Mrs. Bennet, we shall have her at Netherfield at last.' She did indeed. I do think Mrs. Long is as good a creature as ever lived — and her nieces are very well-behaved girls, and not at all beautiful: I like them very much."

Mrs. Bennet, in short, was in very great spirits. She had seen enough of Bingley's behaviour to Jane to be convinced that she would get him at last. And her expectations of advantage to her family, when in a happy mood, were so far beyond reason that she was quite disappointed at not seeing him there again the next day to make his proposals.

"It has been a very agreeable day," said Miss Bennet to Elizabeth. "The party seemed so well selected, so suitable one with the other. I hope we may often meet again."

Elizabeth smiled.

"Lizzy, you must not do so. You must not suspect me. It mortifies me. I assure you that I have now learned to see him as an agreeable and sensible young man, without having a wish beyond it. I am perfectly satisfied, from what his manners now are, that he never had any design of engaging my affection. It is only that he is blessed with greater sweetness, and a stronger desire of generally pleasing, than any other man."

"You are very cruel," said her sister; "you will not let me smile, and are provoking me to it every moment."

"How hard it is in some cases to be believed!"

"And how impossible in others!"

"But why should you wish to persuade me that I feel more than I acknowledge?"

"That is a question which I hardly know how to answer. We all love to instruct, though we can teach only what is not worth knowing. Forgive me; and if you persist in indifference, do not make *me* your confidante."

CHAPTER 55

A few days after this visit Mr. Bingley visited again, and alone. His friend had left him that morning for London, but was to return in ten days' time. He sat with them for over an hour, and was in remarkably good spirits. Mrs. Bennet invited him to dine with them, but, with many expressions of regret, he confessed himself engaged elsewhere.

"Next time you call," said she, "I hope we shall be more lucky."

He should be particularly happy at any time, and if she would give him leave, would take an early opportunity of visiting them.

"Can you come tomorrow?"

Yes, he had no engagement at all for tomorrow; and her invitation was thus readily accepted.

He came, and his arrival was so early that the ladies had not yet dressed. In ran Mrs. Bennet to her daughters' room, in her dressing-gown, and with her hair half-finished, crying out, "My dear Jane, make haste and hurry down. He is come — Mr. Bingley is come — he is, indeed. Make haste, make haste. Here, Sarah, come to Miss Bennet this moment, and help her on with her gown. Never mind Miss Lizzy's hair."

"We will be down as soon as we can," said Jane, "but I dare say Kitty is closer to being dressed than either of us, for she went upstairs half an hour ago."

"Oh! Forget Kitty! What has she to do with it? Come, be quick, be quick! Where is your sash my dear?"

But when her mother was gone, for reasons of propriety, Jane could not be persuaded to go down without one of her sisters.

The same anxiety to get them alone was visible again in the evening. After tea Mr. Bennet retired to the library, as was his custom, and Mary went upstairs to play piano. Two obstacles of the five being thus removed, Mrs. Bennet sat looking and winking at Elizabeth and Kitty for a considerable time, without making any impression on them. Elizabeth ignored her; and when at last Kitty looked up, she very innocently said, "What is the matter, Mama? Why do you keep winking at me? What am I to do?"

"Nothing, child, nothing. I did not wink at you."

She then sat still five minutes longer; but, unable to waste such a precious occasion, she suddenly got up, and saying to Kitty, "Come here, my love, I want to speak to you," took her out of the room. Jane instantly gave a look to Elizabeth, which spoke of her distress at such scheming, and her entreaty that *she* would not give in to it.

In a few minutes, Mrs. Bennet half-opened the door and called out, "Lizzy, my dear, I want to speak with you."

Elizabeth was forced to go. "We may as well leave them by themselves, you know," said her mother, as soon as she was in the hall. "Kitty and I are going upstairs to sit in my dressing room."

Elizabeth made no attempt to reason with her mother, but remained quietly in the hall till she and Kitty were out of sight, then returned to the drawing room.

Mrs. Bennet's schemes for this day were ineffectual. Bingley was everything that was charming, except the professed lover of her daughter. His ease and cheerfulness rendered him a most agreeable addition to their evening party; and he bore with the ill-behaved mother, and heard all her silly remarks, with a forbearance and command of countenance particularly appreciated by her eldest daughter.

He scarcely needed an invitation to stay to supper; and before he went away, a plan was formed, chiefly through his own and Mrs. Bennet's means, of his coming the next morning to shoot with her husband.

After this day, Jane said no more of her indifference. Not a word passed between the sisters concerning Bingley; but Elizabeth went to bed in the happy belief that all must speedily be concluded, unless Mr. Darcy returned within the stated time. She felt tolerably persuaded that all this must have taken place with that gentleman's approval.

Bingley was punctual, and he and Mr. Bennet spent the morning together, as had been agreed upon. The latter was much more agreeable than his companion expected. There was nothing of presumption or folly in Bingley that could provoke his ridicule, or disgust him into silence; and he was more communicative and less eccentric than the other had ever seen him. Bingley of course returned with him to dinner, and in the evening Mrs. Bennet's invention was again at work to get everybody away from him and her daughter. Elizabeth, who had a letter to write, went into the breakfast room for that purpose soon after tea; for as the others were all going to sit down to cards, she could not be needed to counteract her mother's schemes.

But on returning to the drawing room when her letter was finished, she saw, to her infinite surprise, there was reason to fear that her mother had been too ingenious for her. On opening the door she perceived her sister and Bingley standing together over the hearth, as if engaged in earnest conversation. The faces of both, as they hastily turned round and moved away from each other, told all. *Their* situation was awkward enough; but *hers*, she thought, was still worse. Not a syllable was uttered by either; and Elizabeth was on the point of going away again when Bingley, who as well as Jane had sat down, suddenly rose, and whispering a few words to her sister, ran out of the room.

Jane could have no secrets from Elizabeth where confidence would give pleasure; and instantly embracing her, acknowledged with the liveliest emotion that she was the happiest creature in the world.

"'Tis too much!" she added. "Far too much. I do not deserve it. Oh! Why is not everybody as happy?"

Elizabeth's congratulations were given with a sincerity, a warmth, a delight, which words could but poorly express. Every sentence of kindness was a fresh source of happiness to Jane. But she would not allow herself to stay with her sister, or say half that remained to be said, for the present.

"I must go instantly to Mother," she cried. "I would not on any account allow her to hear it from anyone but myself. He is gone to ask Father already. Oh! Lizzy, to know that what I have to relate will give such pleasure to all my dear family! How shall I bear so much happiness?"

She then hastened away to her mother, who had purposely broken up the card party and was sitting upstairs with Kitty.

Elizabeth, who was left by herself, now smiled at the rapidity and ease with which everything was settled, though it had previously given them so many months of suspense and frustration.

"And this," said she, "is the result of all his friend's meddling! Of all his sister's falsehood and contrivance! The happiest, wisest, most reasonable end!"

In a few minutes she was joined by Bingley, whose discussion with her father had been short and to the purpose.

"Where is your sister?" said he hastily, as he opened the door.

"With my mother upstairs. She will be down in a moment, I dare say."

He then shut the door, and coming up to her, claimed the good wishes and affection of a sister. Elizabeth honestly and heartily expressed her delight in the prospect of their relationship. They shook hands with great cordiality; and then, till her sister came down, she had to listen to all he had to say about his own happiness, and about Jane's perfections. In spite of his being enraptured, Elizabeth really believed all his expectations of happiness to be rationally founded, because they had for basis the excellent disposition of Jane, and a general similarity of feeling and taste between her and himself.

It was an evening of delight to them all. The satisfaction of Miss Bennet's mind gave a glow of such sweet animation to her face that she looked more beautiful than ever. Kitty simpered and smiled, and hoped her turn was coming soon. Mrs. Bennet could not give her consent or speak her approbation in terms warm enough to satisfy her feelings, though she talked to Bingley of nothing else for half an hour. And when Mr. Bennet joined them at supper, his voice and manner plainly showed how really happy he was.

Not a word, however, passed his lips in allusion to it, till their visitor took his leave for the night; but as soon as he was gone, he turned to his daughter and said —

"Jane, I congratulate you. You will be a very happy woman."

Jane went to him instantly, kissed him, and thanked him for his goodness.

"You are a good girl," he replied, "and I have great pleasure in thinking you will be so happily settled. I have not a doubt of your doing very well together. You are each of you so complying that nothing will ever be resolved on; so easy that every servant will cheat you; and so generous that you will always exceed your income."

"I hope not so. Imprudence or thoughtlessness in money matters would be unpardonable in *me*."

"Exceed their income! My dear Mr. Bennet," cried his wife, "what are you talking of? Why, he has four or five thousand a year, and very likely more." Then, addressing her daughter, "Oh! My dear, dear Jane, I am so happy, I am sure I shan't get a wink of sleep all night. I knew this day would come. I always said it must be so at last. I was sure you could not be so beautiful for nothing! I remember when I met him, when he first came into Hertfordshire last year, I thought how likely it was that you should end up together. Oh! He is the handsomest young man that ever was seen!"

Wickham and Lydia were all forgotten. Jane was incontestably her favourite child. At that moment she cared for no other. Her youngest sisters soon began to make requests of her for objects of happiness which she might in the future be able to dispense.

Mary petitioned for the use of the library at Netherfield, and Kitty begged very hard for a few balls there every winter.

Bingley, from this time, was of course a daily visitor at Longbourn — coming frequently before breakfast, and always remaining till after supper — except when some barbarous neighbour, who could not be enough detested, had given him an invitation to dinner and he felt obliged to accept.

Elizabeth had now but little time for conversation with her sister; for while he was present, Jane had no attention to bestow on anyone else. But she found herself considerably useful to both of them, in those hours of separation that must sometimes occur. In the absence of Jane, he always attached himself to Elizabeth for the pleasure of talking of her; and when Bingley was gone, Jane constantly sought the same means of relief.

"He has made me so happy," said she one evening, "by telling me that he was totally ignorant of my being in town last spring! I had not believed it possible."

"I suspected as much," replied Elizabeth. "But how did he account for it?"

"It must have been his sister's doing. They certainly did not approve of his acquaintance with me, and I cannot wonder at, since he might have chosen so much more advantageously in many respects. But when they see, as I trust they will, that their brother is happy with me, they will learn to be contented, and we shall be on good terms again; though we can never be what we once were to each other."

"That is the most unforgiving speech," said Elizabeth, "that I ever heard you utter. Good girl! It would vex me, indeed, to see you again duped by Miss Bingley's pretended regard."

"Would you believe it, Lizzy, that when he went to town last November, he really loved me, and nothing but a persuasion of *my* being indifferent would have prevented his coming down again?"

"He made a little mistake, to be sure; but it is to the credit of his modesty."

Elizabeth was pleased to find that he had not betrayed the interference of his friend; for, though Jane had the most generous and forgiving heart in the world, she knew it was a circumstance which must prejudice her against him.

"I am certainly the most fortunate creature that ever existed!" cried Jane. "Oh! Lizzy, why am I thus singled from my family, and blessed above them all? If I could but see *you* as happy! If there *were* but such a man for you!"

"If you were to give me forty such men, I never could be as happy as you. Till I have your disposition, your goodness, I never can have your happiness. No, no, let me find my own path; and perhaps, if I have very good luck, I may meet with another Mr. Collins in time."

The situation of affairs in the Longbourn family could not be long a secret. Mrs. Bennet was privileged to whisper it to Mrs. Philips, and *she* ventured, without any permission, to do the same with all her neighbours in Meryton.

The Bennets were speedily pronounced to be the luckiest family in the world, though only a few weeks before, when Lydia had first run away, they had been generally proved to be marked for misfortune.

CHAPTER 56

One morning, about a week after Bingley's engagement with Jane had been formed, as he and the females of the family were sitting together in the dining room, their attention was suddenly drawn to the window by the sound of a carriage. They soon perceived a four-horse carriage driving up to the house. It was too early in the morning for visitors, and besides, the carriage did not belong to any of their neighbours. Neither the carriage nor the uniform of the servant who preceded it were familiar to them. As it was certain, however, that somebody was coming, Bingley instantly prevailed on Miss Bennet to avoid the confinement of such an intrusion and walk with him in the garden. They both set off, and the curiosity of the remaining three continued, though with little satisfaction, till the door was thrown open, and their visitor entered. It was Lady Catherine de Bourgh.

They had expected to be surprised; but their astonishment was beyond description, and on the part of Mrs. Bennet and Kitty, though she was perfectly unknown to them, even inferior to what Elizabeth felt.

She entered the room with an air more than usually ungracious, made no other reply to Elizabeth's salutation than a slight inclination of the head, and sat down without saying a word. Elizabeth had mentioned her name to her mother on her ladyship's entrance, though no request of introduction had been made.

Mrs. Bennet was flattered by having a guest of such high social status, and received her with the utmost politeness. After sitting for a moment in silence, she said, very stiffly, to Elizabeth —

"I hope you are well, Miss Bennet. That lady, I suppose, is your mother?"

Elizabeth replied that she was.

"And *that*, I suppose, is one of your sisters?"

"Yes, madam," said Mrs. Bennet, delighted to speak to Lady Catherine. "She is my second youngest. My youngest was recently married, and my eldest is somewhere about the grounds, walking with a young man, who, I believe, will soon become a part of the family."

"You have a very small yard here," returned Lady Catherine, after a short silence.

"It is nothing in comparison of Rosings, my lady, I dare say; but, I assure you, it is much larger than Sir William Lucas's."

"This must be a most inconvenient sitting room for the evening in summer: the windows are west-facing."

Mrs. Bennet assured her that they never sat there after dinner, and then added —

"May I take the liberty of asking your ladyship whether you left Mr. and Mrs. Collins well?"

"Yes, very well. I saw them the night before last."

Elizabeth now expected that she would produce a letter for her from Charlotte, as it seemed the only probable motive for her visit. But no letter appeared, and she was completely puzzled.

Mrs. Bennet, with great civility, begged her ladyship to take some refreshment; but Lady Catherine very resolutely, and not very politely, declined eating anything. Then she stood up and said to Elizabeth —

"Miss Bennet, there seemed to be a prettyish kind of a little wood on one side of your lawn. I should be glad to take a turn in it, if you will favour me with your company."

"Go, my dear," cried her mother, "and show her ladyship about the different walks. I think she will be pleased with the grounds."

Elizabeth obeyed, and, running into her own room for her parasol, attended her noble guest downstairs. As they passed through the hall, Lady Catherine opened the doors into the dining parlour and drawing room, and pronouncing them, after a short survey, to be decent looking rooms, walked on.

Her carriage remained at the door, and Elizabeth saw that her waiting woman was in it. They proceeded in silence along the gravel walk that led to the wood; Elizabeth was determined to make no effort for conversation with a woman who was now more than usually disagreeable.

"How could I ever think her like her nephew?" she thought.

As soon as they entered the wood, Lady Catherine began in the following manner: —

"You can be at no loss, Miss Bennet, to understand the reason for my journey here. Your own heart, your own conscience, must tell you why I come."

Elizabeth looked at her with genuine astonishment.

"Indeed, you are mistaken, madam. I have not been at all able to account for the honour of seeing you here."

"Miss Bennet," replied her ladyship, in an angry tone, "you ought to know that I am not to be trifled with. But, however insincere *you* may choose to be, you shall not find *me* so. My character has ever been celebrated for its sincerity and frankness, and in such moment as this I shall certainly not depart from it. A report of a most alarming nature reached me two days ago. I was told that not only your sister was on the point of being most advantageously married, but that *you*, that Miss Elizabeth Bennet, would in all likelihood be soon afterwards united to my nephew — my own nephew — Mr. Darcy. Though I *know* it must be a scandalous falsehood — though I would not insult him by supposing the truth of it possible, I instantly resolved on setting off for this place, that I might make my sentiments known to you."

"If you believed it impossible," said Elizabeth, colouring with astonishment and contempt, "I am surprised you took the trouble of coming so far. What could your ladyship mean by it?"

"I came to insist upon having such a report universally contradicted."

"Your coming to Longbourn, to see me and my family," said Elizabeth coolly, "will be rather a confirmation of it; if, indeed, such a report is in existence."

"If! Do you then pretend to be ignorant of it? Was not this rumour started by you and your family? Do you not know that such a report is spread abroad?"

"I never heard that it was."

"And can you likewise declare that there is no *foundation* for it?"

"I do not pretend to possess equal frankness with your ladyship. *You* may ask questions which *I* shall not choose to answer."

"This is not to be borne! Miss Bennet, I insist on being satisfied. Has he, has my nephew, made you an offer of marriage?"

"Your ladyship has declared it to be impossible."

"It ought to be so; it must be so, while he retains the use of his reason. But *your* cunning arts may, in a moment of infatuation, have made him forget what he owes to himself and to all his family. You may have drawn him in."

"If I have, I shall be the last person to confess it."

"Miss Bennet, do you know who I am? I have not been accustomed to such language as this. I am almost the nearest relation he has in the world, and am entitled to know all his dearest concerns."

"But you are not entitled to know *mine*; nor will such behaviour as this ever entice me to be more frank."

"Let me be rightly understood. This match, to which you aspire, can never take place. No, never. Mr. Darcy is engaged to *my daughter*. Now, what have you to say?"

"Only this: that if he is so, you can have no reason to suppose he will make an offer to me."

Lady Catherine hesitated for a moment, and then replied —

"The engagement between them is of a peculiar kind. From their infancy they have been intended for each other. It was the wish of *his* mother, as well as of hers. While in their cradles, we planned the union: and now, at the moment when the wishes of both sisters would be accomplished in their marriage, to be prevented by a young woman of inferior birth, of no consequence in the world, and wholly unallied to the family! Do you pay no regard to the wishes of his friends — to his tacit engagement with Miss De Bourgh? Are you lost to every feeling of propriety and delicacy? Have you not heard me say that from his earliest hours he was destined for his cousin?"

"Yes, and I had heard it before. But what is that to me? If there is no other objection to my marrying your nephew, I shall certainly not be kept from it by knowing that his mother and aunt wished him to marry Miss De Bourgh. You both did as much as you could, in planning the marriage; its completion depended on others. If Mr. Darcy is neither by honour nor inclination bound to his cousin, what is to stop him from making another choice? And if I am that choice, why may not I accept him?"

"Because honour, decorum, and prudence all forbid it. You cannot expect to be acknowledged by his family or friends if you wilfully act against the inclinations of all. You will be censured, slighted, and despised by everyone connected with him. Your marriage will be a disgrace; your name will never even be mentioned by any of us."

"These are heavy misfortunes," replied Elizabeth. "But the wife of Mr. Darcy must have such extraordinary sources of happiness that she could, upon the whole, have no cause for regret."

"Obstinate, headstrong girl! Is this your gratitude for my attentions to you last spring? Is nothing due to me on that score?

"Let us sit down. You are to understand, Miss Bennet, that I came here with the determined resolution of carrying my purpose, and I will not be dissuaded from it. I am not accustomed to submitting to any person's whims.."

"*That* will make your ladyship's situation at present more pitiable; but it will have no effect on *me*."

"I will not be interrupted! Hear me in silence. My daughter and my nephew are intended for each other. They are descended, on the maternal side, from the same noble line; and on the father's, from respectable, honourable, and ancient, though untitled families. Their fortune on both sides is splendid. They are destined for each other by the voice of every member of their respective houses; and what is to divide them? The upstart pretensions of a young woman without family, connections, or fortune. Is this to be endured? But it must not, shall not be. If you knew what was best for you, you would not wish to leave the sphere in which you have been brought up."

"In marrying your nephew I should not consider myself as leaving that sphere. He is a gentleman; I am a gentleman's daughter: in that regard we are equal."

"True. You *are* a gentleman's daughter. But who was your mother? Who are your uncles and aunts? Do not imagine me ignorant of their condition."

"Whatever my connections may be," said Elizabeth, "if your nephew does not object to them, they can be nothing to you."

"Tell me, once and for all, are you engaged to him?"

Though Elizabeth preferred not to answer this question, she was forced to say, after a moment's deliberation, "I am not."

Lady Catherine seemed pleased.

"And will you promise me never to enter into such an engagement?"

"I will make no promise of the kind."

"Miss Bennet, I am shocked and astonished. I expected to find a more reasonable young woman. But do not deceive yourself into a belief that I will ever give up. I shall not go away till you have given me the assurance I require."

"And I certainly *never* shall give it. I am not to be intimidated into anything so wholly unreasonable. Your ladyship wants Mr. Darcy to marry your daughter; but would my giving you the wished-for promise, make *their* marriage at all more probable? Supposing him to be attached to me, would *my* refusing to accept his hand make him wish to bestow it on his cousin? Allow me to say, Lady Catherine, that the arguments with which you have supported this extraordinary application have been as frivolous as the application was ill-judged. You have greatly mistaken my character if you think I can be convinced by such persuasions as these. How far your nephew might approve of your interference in *his* affairs, I cannot tell; but you have certainly no right to concern yourself in mine. I must beg, therefore, to be imposed upon no longer."

"Not so hasty, if you please. I have by no means finished. To all the objections I have already urged, I have still another to add. I am no stranger to the particulars of your youngest sister's infamous elopement. I know it all: that the young man's marrying her was a patched-up business, at the expense of your father and uncle. And is *such* a girl to be my nephew's sister-in-law? Is *her* husband, is the son of his late father's steward, to be his brother-in-law? Heaven and earth — of what are you thinking? Are the halls of Pemberley to be thus polluted?"

"You can *now* have nothing farther to say," she resentfully answered. "You have insulted me in every possible way. I must now return to the house."

And she rose as she spoke. Lady Catherine rose also, and they turned back. Her ladyship was highly incensed.

"You have no regard, then, for the honour and credit of my nephew! Unfeeling, selfish girl! Do you not consider that a connection with you must disgrace him in the eyes of everybody?"

"Lady Catherine, I have nothing farther to say. You know my sentiments."

"You are then resolved to have him?"

"I have said no such thing. I am only resolved to act in that manner which will, in my own opinion, result in my happiness, without deference to *you*, or to any person so wholly unconnected with me."

" You refuse, then, to oblige me. You refuse to obey the claims of duty, honour, and gratitude. You are determined to ruin him in the opinion of all his friends, and make him the contempt of the world."

"Neither duty, nor honour, nor gratitude," replied Elizabeth, "has any possible claim on me in the present instance. No principle of either would be violated by my marriage with Mr. Darcy. And with regard to the resentment of his family or the indignation of the world, if the former *were* kindled by his marrying me, it would not give me one moment's concern — and the world in general would have too much sense to join the scorn."

"And this is your opinion! This is your final resolve! Very well. I shall now know how to act. Do not imagine, Miss Bennet, that your ambition will ever be gratified. I came to convince you. I hoped to find you reasonable; but depend upon it, my wishes *shall* be accomplished."

In this manner Lady Catherine talked on till they were at the door of the carriage, when, turning hastily round, she added —

"In taking leave of you, Miss Bennet, I send no compliments to your mother. You deserve no such attention. I am most seriously displeased."

Elizabeth made no answer, and, without attempting to persuade her ladyship to return into the house, walked quietly into it herself. She heard the carriage drive away as she proceeded upstairs. Her mother impatiently met her at the door of the dressing room to ask why Lady Catherine would not come in again and rest herself.

"She did not want to," said her daughter.

"She is a very fine looking woman! And her calling here was quite civil! For she only came, I suppose, to tell us the Collinses were well. She was on a journey somewhere, I dare say, and so, passing through Meryton, thought she might as well visit you. I suppose she had nothing particular to say to you, Lizzy?"

Elizabeth was forced to indulge in a little falsehood here, for to acknowledge the substance of their conversation was impossible.

CHAPTER 57

The oppression of spirits which this extraordinary visit threw Elizabeth into could not be easily overcome, nor could she for many hours learn to think of it with anything but anger. Lady Catherine, it appeared, had actually taken the trouble of this journey from Rosings for the sole purpose of breaking off her supposed engagement with Mr. Darcy. From what the report of their engagement could originate, Elizabeth was at a loss to imagine; till she recollected that *his* being the intimate friend of Bingley, and *her* being the sister of Jane, was enough, perhaps, to plant the idea. She had not herself forgotten to feel that the marriage of her sister must bring them more frequently together. And her neighbours at Lucas Lodge, therefore (for through their communication with the Collinses the report, she concluded, had reached Lady Catherine), had determined the marriage between Mr. Darcy and Elizabeth to be almost certain and immediate.

While considering Lady Catherine's words, however, she could not help feeling some uneasiness as to the possible consequence of her persisting in this interference. From what she had said of her resolution to prevent their marriage, it occurred to Elizabeth that she must be planning to speak to her nephew. How *he* might take a similar representation of the evils attached to a connection with her, she could not guess. She knew not the exact degree of his affection for his aunt, or her influence over him, but it was natural to suppose that he thought much higher of her ladyship than *she* did. And it was certain that, in enumerating the miseries of a marriage with *one* whose immediate connections were so unequal to his own, his aunt would be appealing directly to his pride. With his notions of dignity, he would probably feel that the arguments which to Elizabeth had appeared weak and ridiculous contained much good sense and solid reasoning.

If he had been wavering before as to what he should do, which had often seemed likely, the advice and entreaty of so near a relation might settle every doubt. In that case, he would return no more. Lady Catherine might seek him while passing through London, and his plan to come again to Netherfield must be amended.

"If, therefore, an excuse for not keeping his promise should come to Mr. Bingley within a few days," she added, "I shall know how to understand it. I shall then give up every expectation, every wish of his constancy. If he is satisfied with only regretting me, when he might have obtained my affections and hand, I shall soon cease to regret him at all."

The surprise of the rest of the family, on hearing who their visitor had been, was very great; but they obligingly satisfied it with the same kind of assumption which had appeased Mrs. Bennet's curiosity, and Elizabeth was spared from much teasing on the subject.

The next morning, as she was going downstairs, she was met by her father, who came out of his library with a letter in his hand.

"Lizzy," said he, "I was going to look for you. Come into my room."

She followed him thither, and her curiosity to know what he had to tell her was heightened by the belief of its being in some manner connected with the letter he held. It suddenly struck her that it might be from Lady Catherine, and she anticipated with dismay all the consequent explanations.

She followed her father to the fireplace, and they both sat down. He then said —

"I have received a letter this morning that has astonished me exceedingly. As it principally concerns yourself, you ought to know its contents. I did not know before that I had *two* daughters on the brink of matrimony. Let me be the first to congratulate you."

The colour now rushed into Elizabeth's cheeks in the instantaneous conviction of its being a letter from the nephew instead of the aunt. She was unsure whether most to be pleased that he explained himself, or offended that his letter was not addressed to her, when her father continued—

"You look self-conscious. Young ladies have great insight in such matters as these, but I think I may defy even *your* ability to discover the name of your admirer. This letter is from Mr. Collins."

"From Mr. Collins! and What can *he* have to say?"

" He begins with congratulations on the approaching nuptials of my eldest daughter, of which, it seems, he has been told by some of the good-natured, gossiping Lucases. I shall not toy with your impatience by reading what he says on that point. What relates to you is as follows: 'Having thus offered you the sincere congratulations of Mrs. Collins and myself on this happy event, let me now add a short hint on the subject of another; of which we have been told by the same authority. Your daughter Elizabeth, it is presumed, will not long bear the name of Bennet after her elder sister has resigned it, and the chosen partner of her fate may be reasonably looked up to as one of the most illustrious personages in this land.'

"Can you possibly guess, Lizzy, who is meant by this? — 'This young gentleman is blessed, in a peculiar way, with everything the heart of mortal can most desire — splendid property, noble kindred, and extensive patronage. Yet, in spite of all these temptations, let me warn my cousin Elizabeth, and yourself, of what evils you may incur by accepting this gentleman's proposals, which, of course, you will be inclined to take immediate advantage of.'

"Have you any idea, Lizzy, who this gentleman is? But now it comes out —

"'My motive for cautioning you is as follows: we have reason to imagine that his aunt, Lady Catherine de Bourgh, does not look on the match with a friendly eye."

"*Mr. Darcy*, you see, is the man! Now, Lizzy, I think I *have* surprised you. Could he or the Lucases have named any man, within the circle of our acquaintance, who was *less* likely to command your affection? Mr. Darcy, who never looks at any woman but to see a blemish, and who probably never looked at *you* in his life! It is astonishing!"

Elizabeth tried to join in her father's pleasantry, but could only force one reluctant smile. Never had his wit been directed in a manner so little agreeable to her.

"Are you not amused?"

"Oh! Yes. Pray read on."

"'After mentioning the likelihood of this marriage to her ladyship last night, she immediately, with her usual condescension, expressed what she felt on the occasion. It then became apparent that, on account of some family objections on the part of my cousin, she would never give her consent to what she termed so disgraceful a match. I thought it my duty to give the speediest intelligence of this to my cousin, that she and her noble admirer may be aware of about the gravity of the situation, and not run hastily into a marriage which has not been properly sanctioned.' Mr. Collins, moreover, adds, 'I am truly rejoiced that my cousin Lydia's sad business has been so well hushed up, and am only concerned that their living together before the marriage took place should be so generally known. I must not, however, neglect the duties of a clergyman, or refrain from declaring my amazement, at hearing that you received the young couple into your house as soon as they were married. It was an encouragement of vice; and had I been the cleric of Longbourn, I should very strenuously have opposed it. You ought certainly to forgive them, as a Christian, but never admit them in your sight, or allow their names to be mentioned in your hearing." *That* is his notion of Christian forgiveness! The rest of his letter is only about his dear Charlotte's expectation of a child. But, Lizzy, you look as if you did not enjoy it. You are not going to pretend to be affronted at an idle report, I hope. For what is the purpose of living, but to make sport for our neighbours, and laugh at them in our turn?"

"Oh!" cried Elizabeth, "I am excessively amused. But it is so strange!"

"Yes, *that* is what makes it so amusing. Had they named any other man, it would have been nothing; but *his* perfect indifference, and *your* pointed dislike, make it so delightfully absurd! As much as I detest writing, I would not give up Mr. Collins's correspondence for anything. Nay, when I read a letter of his, I cannot help giving him the preference even over Wickham, as much as I value the shamelessness and hypocrisy of my son-in-law. And pray, Lizzy, what did Lady Catherine say about this report? Did she come to refuse her consent?"

To this question his daughter replied only with a laugh; and as it had been asked without the least suspicion, she was not distressed by his repeating it. Elizabeth had never been more at a loss to make her feelings appear what they were not. It was necessary to laugh, when she would rather have cried. Her father had most cruelly mortified her by what he said of Mr. Darcy's indifference. She could do nothing but wonder at such a lack of discernment, or fear that, perhaps, instead of his seeing too *little*, she might have imagined too *much*.

CHAPTER 58

Instead of receiving any such letter of excuse from his friend, as Elizabeth half expected, Mr. Bingley was able to bring Darcy with him to Longbourn before many days had passed after Lady Catherine's visit. The gentlemen arrived early; and, before Mrs. Bennet had time to tell him of their having seen his aunt, Bingley, who wanted to be alone with Jane, proposed their all walking out. It was agreed to. Mrs. Bennet was not in the habit of walking. Mary could never spare time, but the remaining five set off together. Bingley and Jane, however, soon allowed the others to outstrip them. They lagged behind while Elizabeth, Kitty, and Darcy were to entertain each other. Very little was said by either. Kitty was too afraid of him to talk, Elizabeth was secretly forming a desperate resolution, and thought that perhaps he might be doing the same.

They walked towards the Lucases, because Kitty wished to call upon Maria; and as Elizabeth saw no occasion for waiting, when Kitty left them she went boldly on with him alone. Now was the moment for her resolution to be executed, and while her courage was high, she immediately said —

"Mr. Darcy, I am a very selfish creature, and for the sake of giving relief to my own feelings I care not how much I may be wounding yours. I can no longer help thanking you for your unparalleled kindness to my poor sister. Ever since I have known it, I have been most anxious to acknowledge to you how gratefully I feel it. Were it known to the rest of my family, I should not have merely my own gratitude to express."

"I am exceedingly sorry," replied Darcy, in a tone of surprise, "that you have been informed of what may, in a mistaken light, make you feel a sense of obligation when none is owed. I did not think Mrs. Gardiner was so little to be trusted."

"You must not blame my aunt. Lydia's thoughtlessness first betrayed to me that you had been concerned in the matter; and, of course, I could not rest till I knew the particulars. Let me thank you again and again, in the name of all my family, for that generous compassion which caused you to take so much trouble, and bear so many mortifications, for the sake of finding them."

"If you *must* thank me," he replied, "let it be for yourself alone. That the wish of giving happiness to you might add force to the other enticements which motivated me, I shall not attempt to deny. But your *family* owe me nothing. Much as I respect them, I truly thought only of *you*."

Elizabeth was too much embarrassed to say a word. After a short pause, her companion added, "You are too generous to trifle with me. If your feelings are still what they were last April, tell me so at once. *My* affections and wishes are unchanged; but one word from you will silence me on this subject forever."

Elizabeth, feeling the awkwardness and anxiety of his situation, now forced herself to speak; and immediately, though not very fluently, gave him to understand that her sentiments had undergone a complete transformation, and she now received with gratitude and pleasure his present assurances. The happiness which this reply produced was such as he had probably never felt before, and he expressed himself on the occasion as sensibly and as warmly as a man in love can be expected to. Had Elizabeth been able to look at him, she might have seen how well the expression of heartfelt delight diffused over his face became him. But, though she could not look, she could listen, and he told her of feelings which, in proving of what importance she was to him, made his affection every moment more valuable.

They walked on, without knowing in what direction. There was too much to be thought, and felt, and said, for attention to anything else. She soon learned that they were indebted for their present good understanding to the efforts of his aunt, who *did* call on him in her return through London, and there relate her journey to Longbourn, its motive, and the substance of her conversation with Elizabeth. She dwelt emphatically on every expression of the latter which led her to seek the promise from her nephew which *she* had refused to give. But, unluckily for her ladyship, its effect had been exactly the opposite.

"It gave me a hope," said he, "as I had scarcely ever allowed myself to feel before. I knew enough of your disposition to be certain that had you been absolutely, irrevocably decided against me, you would have acknowledged it to Lady Catherine frankly and openly."

Elizabeth coloured and laughed as she replied, "Yes, you know enough of my *frankness* to believe me capable of *that*. After abusing you so abominably to your face, I could not hesitate to abuse you to all your relations."

"What did you say of me that I did not deserve? For, though your accusations were ill-founded, formed on mistaken premises, my behaviour to you at the time had merited the severest reproof. It was unpardonable. I cannot think of it without abhorrence."

"Let us not argue about who bears the greater share of blame for the events of that evening," said Elizabeth. "The conduct of neither, if strictly examined, was fully justified. But since then we have both, I hope, improved in civility."

"I cannot be so easily reconciled to myself. The recollection of what I then said — of my conduct, my manners, my expressions during the whole of it — is now, and has been many months, inexpressibly painful to me. Your rejection, so aptly applied, I shall never forget: 'Had you behaved in a more gentlemanlike manner.' Those were your words. You know not, you can scarcely conceive, how they have tortured me. It was some time, I confess, before I was reasonable enough to see the truth of them."

"I certainly did not expect them to make so strong an impression. I had not the smallest idea of their being ever felt in such a way."

"What you said made perfect sense. You thought me then devoid of every proper feeling; I am sure you did. I shall never forget the expression on your face as you said that I could not have proposed to you in any possible way that would convince you to accept me."

"Oh! Do not repeat what I then said. These recollections will not do at all. I assure you that I have long been most heartily ashamed of it."

Darcy mentioned his letter. "Did it," said he, "did it *soon* make you think better of me? Did you, on reading it, give any credit to its contents?"

She explained what its effect on her had been, and how all her former prejudices had been gradually removed.

"I knew," said he, "that what I wrote must give you pain; but it was necessary. I hope you have destroyed the letter. There was one part, especially the opening of it, which I should dread your having the power of reading again. I can remember some expressions which might justly make you hate me."

"The letter shall certainly be burned, if you believe it essential to the preservation of my regard; but my opinions are not, I hope, quite so easily changed as that implies."

"When I wrote that letter," replied Darcy, "I believed myself perfectly calm and cool; but I am now convinced that it was written in a dreadful bitterness of spirit."

"The letter, perhaps, began in bitterness; but it did not end so. The adieu is charity itself. But think no more of the letter. The feelings of the person who wrote and the person who received it are now so vastly different from what they were then, that every unpleasant circumstance surrounding it ought to be forgotten. You must learn to see as I do, and think only of the past as its remembrance gives you pleasure."

"I can give you credit for such a philosophy. But I have a very different one. Painful recollections will intrude, which cannot, which ought not, to be ignored. I have been a selfish being all my life, in practice, though not in principle. As a child I was taught what was *right*; but I was not taught to correct my disposition. I was given good principles, but left to follow them in pride and conceit. Unfortunately, an only son (for many years an only *child*), I was spoiled by my parents, who, though good themselves, allowed, encouraged, almost taught me to be selfish and overbearing. I cared for none beyond my own family circle, thought poorly of the rest of the world, and judged the sense and worth of others to be far less than my own. Such I was, from eight to eight-and-twenty; and such I might still be but for you, dearest, loveliest Elizabeth! What do I not owe you! You taught me a lesson, hard indeed at first, but most advantageous. By you I was properly humbled. I came to you without a doubt of my proposals being accepted. You showed me how insufficient were all my efforts to please a woman so worthy of being pleased."

"Had you then persuaded yourself that I would accept you?"

"Indeed I had. What will you think of my vanity? I believed you to be wishing for, expecting my proposals."

"My manners must have been at fault, but not intentionally, I assure you. I never meant to deceive you, but my spirits often lead me wrong. How you must have hated me after *that* evening!"

"Hate you! I was angry, perhaps, at first, but my anger soon began to take a proper direction."

"I am almost afraid of asking what you thought of me when we met at Pemberley. "

"Indeed, I felt nothing but surprise."

"Your surprise could not be greater than *mine* when you first arrived. My conscience told me that I deserved no extraordinary politeness, and I confess that I did not expect to receive *more* than what was due."

"My object *then*," replied Darcy, "was to show you, by every civility in my power, that I was not so bitter as to resent the past. I hoped to obtain your forgiveness, and lessen your ill opinion, by letting you see that your criticisms of my character had been attended to. How soon any other thoughts introduced themselves, I can hardly tell, but I believe in about half an hour after I had seen you."

He then told her of Georgiana's delight in making her acquaintance, and of her disappointment at its sudden interruption. This naturally led to the cause of that interruption, and she soon learned that his resolution of following her from Derbyshire in quest of her sister had been formed before he left the inn. His gravity and thoughtfulness there had arisen from no other struggles than how he was to go about the search for Wickham and Lydia.

She expressed her gratitude again, but it was too painful a subject to each to be dwelt on farther.

After walking several miles in a leisurely manner, and too distracted to pay any attention to their route, they found at last, on examining their watches, that it was time to be at home.

"What could have become of Mr. Bingley and Jane!" was a question which introduced the discussion of *their* affairs. Darcy was delighted with their engagement; his friend had given him the earliest information of it.

"I must ask whether you were surprised?" said Elizabeth.

"Not at all. When I went away, I felt that it would soon happen."

"That is to say, you had given your permission. I guessed as much."

And though he protested against the term, she found that it had been pretty much the case.

"On the evening before my going to London," said he, "I made a confession to him which I believe I ought to have made long ago. I told him of all that had occurred to make my former interference in his affairs absurd and intrusive. His surprise was great. He had never had the slightest suspicion. I told him, moreover, that I believed myself mistaken in supposing, as I had done, that your sister was indifferent to him. As I could easily perceive that his attachment to her continued, I felt no doubt of their happiness together." Elizabeth could not help smiling at his easy manner of directing his friend.

"Did you speak from your own observation," said she, "when you told him that my sister loved him, or merely from my information last spring?"

"From the former. I observed her closely during the two visits which I made, and I was convinced of her affection."

"And your assurance of it, I suppose, carried immediate conviction to him."

"It did. Bingley is most unaffectedly modest. His humility had prevented his depending on his own judgment in so important a decision, but his reliance on mine made everything easy. I was obliged to confess one thing which for a time, and not unjustly, offended him. I could not allow myself to conceal that your sister had been in town three months last winter — that I had known it, and purposely kept it from him. He was angry. But his anger, I am persuaded, lasted no longer than he remained in any doubt of your sister's sentiments. He has heartily forgiven me now."

Elizabeth longed to observe that Mr. Bingley had been a most delightful friend — so easily guided, that his worth was invaluable; but she checked herself. She remembered that he had yet to learn to be laughed at, and it was rather too early to begin. In anticipating the happiness of Bingley, which of course was to be inferior only to his own, he continued the conversation till they reached the house. In the hall they parted.

CHAPTER 59

"My dear Lizzy, where can you have been walking to?" was the first question Elizabeth received from Jane as soon as she entered the room, and from all the others when they sat down to eat. She had only to say in reply that they had wandered further than she had been used to. She coloured as she spoke; but neither that, nor anything else, awakened a suspicion of the truth.

The evening passed quietly, unmarked by anything extraordinary. The acknowledged lovers talked and laughed; the unacknowledged were silent. Darcy was not of a disposition in which happiness overflows into joviality. And Elizabeth, agitated and confused, rather *knew* that she was happy, than *felt* herself to be so; for, besides the immediate embarrassment, there were other difficulties yet to be faced. She anticipated what would be felt in the family when her engagement became known. She was aware that no one liked him but Jane, and even feared that with the others it was a *dislike* which not all his fortune and influence might do away.

At night she opened her heart to Jane. Though suspicion was very far from Miss Bennet's general habits, she was absolutely incredulous here.

"You are joking, Lizzy. This cannot be! Engaged to Mr. Darcy! No, no, you shall not deceive me. I know it to be impossible."

"This is a wretched beginning indeed! I am sure nobody else will believe me, if you do not. Yet, indeed, I am in sincere. I speak nothing but the truth. He still loves me, and we are engaged."

Jane looked at her doubtingly. "Oh, Lizzy! It cannot be. I know how much you dislike him."

"*That* is all to be forgot. Perhaps I did not always love him as much as I do now. But in such cases as these a good memory is unpardonable. This is the last time I shall ever remember it myself."

Miss Bennet looked at her in amazement. Elizabeth again, and more seriously, assured her of its truth.

"Good Heaven! Can it be really so? Yet now I must believe you," cried Jane. "My dear, dear Lizzy, I would — I do congratulate you; but are you certain — forgive the question — are you quite certain that you can be happy with him?"

"There can be no doubt of that. It is settled between us already that we are to be the happiest couple in the world. But are you pleased, Jane? Shall you like to have such a brother?"

"Very, very much. Nothing could give either Bingley or myself more delight. But we considered it, we talked of it as impossible. And do you really love him quite well enough? Oh, Lizzy! Do anything rather than marry without affection. Are you quite sure that you feel what you ought to do?"

"Oh, yes! You will only think I feel *more* than I ought to do, when I tell you all."

"What do you mean?"

"Why, I must confess that I love him more than Bingley. I am afraid you will be angry."

"My dearest sister, now *be* serious. I want to talk very seriously. Let me know everything that I am to know without delay. Will you tell me how long you have loved him?"

"It has been coming on so gradually that I hardly know when it began. But I believe I must date it from my first seeing his beautiful grounds at Pemberley."

Another entreaty that she would be serious, however, produced the desired effect, and she soon satisfied Jane by her solemn assurances of attachment. When convinced on that point, Miss Bennet had nothing farther to wish.

"Now I am quite happy," said she, "for you will be as happy as me. I always valued him. Were it for nothing but his love of you, I must always have esteemed him; but now, as Bingley's friend and your husband, there can be only Bingley and yourself more dear to me. But, Lizzy, you have been very secretive, very reserved with me. How little did you tell me of what passed at Pemberley and Lambton! I owe all that I know of it to another, not to you."

Elizabeth told her the motives of her silence. She had been unwilling to mention Bingley; and the unsettled state of her own feelings had made her equally avoid the name of his friend. But now she would no longer conceal from her his role in Lydia's marriage. All was acknowledged, and half the night spent in conversation.

"Good gracious!" cried Mrs. Bennet, as she stood at a window the next morning. "That disagreeable Mr. Darcy is coming here again with our dear

Bingley! What can he mean by being so tiresome as to be always coming here? I had no notion but he would go shooting, or something or other, and not disturb us with his company. What shall we do with him? Lizzy, you must walk out with him again, that he may not be in Bingley's way."

Elizabeth could hardly help laughing at so convenient a proposal, yet was really vexed that her mother should be always giving him such insults.

As soon as they entered, Bingley looked at her so expressively, and shook hands with such warmth, as left no doubt of his having been told the good news. He soon afterwards said aloud, "Mrs. Bennet, have you no more lanes hereabouts in which Lizzy may lose her way again today?"

"I advise Mr. Darcy, and Lizzy, and Kitty," said Mrs. Bennet, "to walk to Oakham Mount this morning. It is a nice long walk, and Mr. Darcy has never seen the view."

"It may do very well for the others," replied Mr. Bingley; "but I am sure it will be too much for Kitty. Won't it, Kitty?"

Kitty admitted that she had rather stay at home. Darcy professed a great curiosity to see the view from the Mount, and Elizabeth silently consented. As she went upstairs to get ready, Mrs. Bennet followed her, saying —

"I am quite sorry, Lizzy, that you should be forced to have that disagreeable man all to yourself. But I hope you will not mind it: it is all for Jane's sake, you know; and there is no need for you to talk to him, except just now and then. So do not inconvenience yourself."

During their walk, it was resolved that Mr. Bennet's consent should be requested in the course of the evening. Elizabeth reserved to herself the application for her mother's. She could not determine how her mother would take it; sometimes doubting whether all his wealth and grandeur could be enough to overcome her abhorrence of the man. But whether she were violently set against the match, or violently delighted with it, it was certain that her manner would be equally bad. She could no more bear that Mr. Darcy should hear the first raptures of her joy than the first vehemence of her disapproval.

In the evening, soon after Mr. Bennet withdrew to the library, she saw Mr. Darcy rise also and follow him, and her agitation on seeing it was extreme. She did not fear her father's opposition, but he was going to be made unhappy. That it should be through her means, that *she*, his favourite child, should be distressing him by her choice, should be filling him with fears and regrets in disposing of her, was a wretched reflection. She sat in misery till Mr. Darcy appeared again, when, looking at him, she was a little relieved by his smile. In a few minutes he approached the table where she was sitting with Kitty, and, while pretending to admire her work, said in a whisper, "Go to your father; he wants you in the library." She went immediately.

Her father was walking about the room, looking grave and anxious. "Lizzy," said he, "what are you doing? Are you out of your senses to be accepting this man? Have not you always hated him?"

How earnestly did she then wish that her former opinions had been more reasonable, her expressions more moderate! It would have spared her from explanations and professions which it was exceedingly awkward to give; but they were now necessary, and she assured him of her attachment to Mr. Darcy.

"So you are determined to have him? He is rich, to be sure, and you may have more fine clothes and fine carriages than Jane. But will they make you happy?"

"Have you any other objections," said Elizabeth, "than your belief of my indifference?"

"None at all. We all know him to be a proud, unpleasant sort of a man; but this would be nothing if you really liked him."

"I do, I do like him," she replied, with tears in her eyes. "I love him. Indeed he has no improper pride. He is perfectly amiable. You do not know what he really is. Please do not pain me by speaking of him in such terms."

"Lizzy," said her father, "I have given him my consent. He is the kind of man, indeed, to whom I would never dare refuse anything which he condescended to ask. I now give it to _you_, if you are resolved on having him. But let me advise you to think better of it. I know your disposition, Lizzy. I know that you could be neither happy nor respectable unless you truly esteemed your husband — unless you looked up to him as a superior. Your lively disposition would place you in the greatest danger in an unequal marriage. You could scarcely escape discredit and misery. My child, let me not have the grief of seeing _you_ unable to respect your partner in life. "

Elizabeth, still more affected, was earnest and solemn in her reply; and she explained at length, by repeated assurances that Mr. Darcy was really the object of her choice, the gradual change which her views of him had undergone. She related her absolute certainty that his affection was not the work of a day, but had stood the test of many months, and enumerated with energy all his good qualities. She was, in the end, able to overcome her father's disbelief, and reconcile him to the match.

"Well, my dear," said he, when she ceased speaking, "I have no more to say. If this be the case, he deserves you. I could not have parted with you, my Lizzy, to anyone less worthy." To complete the favourable impression, she then told him what Mr. Darcy had voluntarily done for Lydia. He heard her with astonishment.

"This is an evening of wonders indeed! And so, Darcy did everything — made up the match, gave the money, paid the fellow's debts, and got him his commission! So much the better. It will save me a world of trouble and thrift. Had it been your uncle's doing, I must and _would_ have paid him;

but these passionate young lovers do everything their own way. I shall offer to pay him tomorrow: he will rant and storm about his love for you, and there will be an end of the matter." He then recollected her embarrassment a few days before, on his reading Mr. Collins's letter; and after laughing some time, allowed her at last to go, saying, as she left the room, "If any young men come for Mary or Kitty, send them in, for I am in a generous mood."

Elizabeth's mind was now relieved from a very heavy weight, and, after half an hour's quiet reflection in her own room, she was able to join the others with tolerable composure. Everything was too recent for good humour, but the evening passed tranquilly away. There was no longer anything to be dreaded, and the comfort of ease and familiarity would come in time.

When her mother went up to her dressing room at night she followed her, and made the important communication. Its effect was most extraordinary; for, on first hearing it, Mrs. Bennet sat quite still, and uttered not a syllable. It was many, many minutes before she could comprehend what she heard, though in general she was supportive of anything that was for the advantage of her family, or that came in the shape of a lover to any of them. She began at length to recover, to fidget about in her chair, get up, sit down again, and wonder.

"Good gracious! Lord, bless me! Only think! Dear me! Mr. Darcy! Who would have thought it? And is it really true? Oh, my sweetest Lizzy! How rich and how important you will be! What spending money, what jewels, what carriages you will have! Jane's is nothing to it — nothing at all. I am so pleased — so happy. Such a charming man! So handsome! So tall! Oh, my dear Lizzy! Pray apologise for my having disliked him so much before. I hope he will overlook it. Dear, dear Lizzy! A house in London! Everything that is charming! Three daughters married! Ten thousand a year! Oh, Lord! What will become of me? I shall go quite mad."

This was enough to prove that her approval need not be doubted; and Elizabeth, rejoicing that such a reaction was heard only by herself, soon went away. But before she had been three minutes in her own room, her mother followed her. "My dearest child," she cried, "I can think of nothing else! Ten thousand a year, and very likely more! 'Tis as much as a Lord! But, my dearest love, tell me what dish Mr. Darcy is particularly fond of, that I may have it tomorrow."

This was a sad omen of what her mother's behaviour to the gentleman himself might be. Elizabeth found that, though in the certain possession of his warmest affection, and secure of her relations' consent, there was still something to be wished for. But the morrow went much better than she expected; for Mrs. Bennet luckily stood in such awe of her intended son-in-law that she ventured not to speak to him, unless it was in her power to offer him any attention, or mark her deference for his opinion.

Elizabeth had the satisfaction of seeing her father taking pains to get acquainted with him, and Mr. Bennet soon assured her that he was rising every hour in his esteem.

"I admire all my sons-in-law highly," said he. "Wickham, perhaps, is my favourite; but I think I shall like *your* husband quite as well as Jane's."

CHAPTER 60

Elizabeth's spirits soon rising to playfulness again, she asked Mr. Darcy to account for his having ever fallen in love with her. "How could you begin?" said she. "I can comprehend your going on charmingly, when you had once made a beginning; but what could set you off in the first place?"

"I cannot name the hour, or the spot, or the look, or the words, which laid the foundation. It is too long ago. I was in the middle before I knew that I *had* begun."

"My beauty you had early withstood, and as for my manners — my behaviour to *you* was at least always bordering on the uncivil, and I never spoke to you without rather wishing to give you pain than not. Now, be sincere; did you admire me for my audacity?"

"For the liveliness of your mind, I did."

"You may as well call it audacity at once. It was very little less. The fact is that you were sick of civility, of deference, of intrusive attention. You were disgusted with the women who were always speaking and looking and thinking for *your* approval alone. I interested you because I was so unlike *them*. Had you not been really amiable, you would have hated me for it; but, in spite of the pains you took to disguise yourself, your feelings were always noble and just. In your heart you thoroughly despised the persons who so zealously courted you. There — I have saved you the trouble of accounting for it; and really, all things considered, I begin to think it perfectly reasonable. To be sure, you knew no actual good of me — but nobody thinks of *that* when they fall in love."

"Was there no good in your affectionate behaviour to Jane, while she was ill at Netherfield?"

"Dearest Jane! Who could have done less for her? But make a virtue of it by all means. My good qualities are under your protection, and you are to exaggerate them as much as possible. In return, it belongs to me to find occasions for teasing and quarrelling with you as often as possible, and I shall begin immediately by asking you what made you so unwilling to come to the point at last? What made you so shy of me when you first called, and afterwards dined here? Why, especially when you called, did you look as if you did not care about me?"

"Because you were grave and silent, and gave me no encouragement."

"But I was embarrassed."

"And so was I."

"You might have talked to me more when you came to dinner."

"A man who had felt less might, but I admired you too much for such risks."

"How unlucky that you should have a reasonable answer to give, and that I should be so reasonable as to admit it! But I wonder how long you *would* have gone on if you had been left to yourself! I wonder when you *would* have spoken, if I had not asked you! "

" Lady Catherine's unjustifiable endeavours to separate us were the means of removing all my doubts. I My aunt's intelligence gave me hope, and I was determined at once to know everything."

"Lady Catherine has been of infinite use, which ought to make her happy, for she loves to be of use. But tell me, what did you come down to Netherfield for? Was it merely to ride to Longbourn, and be embarrassed? Or did you have other plans?"

"My real purpose was to see *you*, and to judge, if I could, whether I might ever hope to make you love me. My avowed one, or what I avowed to myself, was to see whether your sister was still partial to Bingley, and, if she was, to make the confession to him which I have since made."

"Shall you ever have courage to announce to Lady Catherine what is to befall her?"

"I am more likely to need time than courage, Elizabeth. But it ought to be done; and if you will give me a sheet of paper, it shall be done directly."

"And if I had not a letter to write myself, I might sit by you, and admire the evenness of your writing, as another young lady once did. But I have an aunt too who must not be longer neglected."

From an unwillingness to confess how much her intimacy with Mr. Darcy had been overestimated, Elizabeth had never yet answered Mrs. Gardiner's long letter. But now, having news to communicate which she knew would be most welcome, she was almost ashamed to find that her uncle and aunt had already lost three days of happiness, and immediately wrote as follows —

"I would have thanked you before, my dear aunt, as I ought to have done, for your long, kind, satisfactory detail of particulars; but, to tell the truth, I was too cross to write. You supposed more than really existed. But *now* suppose as much as you choose; give free reign to your fancy, indulge your imagination in every possible flight which the subject will afford, and unless you believe me actually married, you cannot greatly err. You must write again very soon, and praise him a great deal more than you did in your last. I thank you, again and again, for not going to the Lakes. How could I be so silly as to wish it! Your idea of the ponies is delightful. We will go round the Park every day. I am the happiest creature in the world. Perhaps other people have said so before, but not one with such justice. I am happier even than Jane: she only smiles, I laugh. Mr. Darcy sends you all the love in the world that he can spare from me. You are all to come to Pemberley at Christmas. — Yours, etc."

Mr. Darcy's letter to Lady Catherine was in a different style, and still different from either was what Mr. Bennet sent to Mr. Collins, in reply to his last.

"Dear Sir, — "I must trouble you once more for congratulations. Elizabeth will soon be the wife of Mr. Darcy. Console Lady Catherine as well as you can. But, if I were you, I would stand by the nephew, who has more to give. — Your's sincerely, etc."

Miss Bingley's congratulations to her brother on his approaching marriage were all that was affectionate and insincere. She wrote even to Jane on the occasion, to express her delight, and repeat all her former professions of regard. Jane was not deceived, but she was affected, and could not help writing her a much kinder answer than she knew was deserved.

The joy which Miss Darcy expressed on receiving similar information was as sincere as her brother's in sending it. Four sides of paper were insufficient to contain all her delight, and all her earnest desire of being loved by her sister-in-law.

Before any answer could arrive from Mr. Collins, or any congratulations to Elizabeth from his wife, the Longbourn family heard that the Collinses were coming themselves to Lucas Lodge. The reason of this sudden removal was soon evident. Lady Catherine had been rendered so exceedingly angry by the contents of her nephew's letter that Charlotte, really rejoicing in the match, was anxious to get away till the storm was blown over. At such a moment the arrival of her friend was a sincere pleasure to Elizabeth, though in the course of their meetings she must sometimes think the pleasure dearly bought, because Mr. Darcy was exposed to all the pomp and tiresome civility of her husband. He bore it, however, with admirable calmness. He could even listen to Sir William Lucas, when he complimented him on carrying away the brightest jewel of the county, and expressed his hopes of their all meeting frequently at St. James's, with very decent composure.

Mrs. Philips was another, and perhaps a greater, tax on his forbearance; and though Mrs. Philips, as well as her sister, stood in too much awe of him to speak with the familiarity which Bingley's good-humour encouraged, yet, whenever she *did* speak, she must be indelicate. Nor was her respect for him, though it made her more quiet, at all likely to make her more elegant. Elizabeth did all she could to shield him from the frequent notice of either, and was ever anxious to keep him to herself, and to those of her family with whom he might converse without mortification. Though the uncomfortable feelings arising from all this took from the season of courtship much of its pleasure, it added to the hope of the future. She looked forward with delight to the time when they should be removed from society so little pleasing to either, to all the comfort and elegance of their family circle at Pemberley.

CHAPTER 61

Happy for all her maternal feelings was the day on which Mrs. Bennet got rid of her two most deserving daughters. With what delighted pride she afterwards visited Mrs. Bingley, and talked of Mrs. Darcy, may be guessed. I wish I could say, for the sake of her family, that the accomplishment of her earnest desire in the marriage of so many of her children produced so happy an effect as to make her a sensible, amiable, well-informed woman for the rest of her life. It did not, though perhaps it was lucky for her husband, who could still be amused by a wife who was invariably silly.

Mr. Bennet missed his second daughter exceedingly; his affection for her drew him oftener from home than anything else could do. He delighted to visit Pemberley, especially when he was least expected.

Mr. Bingley and Jane remained at Netherfield only a year. So near a vicinity to her mother and Meryton relations was not desirable even to *his* easy temper, or *her* affectionate heart. The darling wish of his sisters was then gratified: he bought an estate in a neighbouring county to Derbyshire, and Jane and Elizabeth, in addition to every other source of happiness, were within thirty miles of each other.

Kitty, to her very material advantage, spent most of her time with her two elder sisters. In society so superior to what she had generally known, her improvement was great. She was not of so ungovernable a temper as Lydia: and, removed from the influence of Lydia's example, she became, by proper attention and management, less ignorant and more civil. From the farther disadvantage of Lydia's society she was of course carefully kept; and though Mrs. Wickham frequently invited her to come and stay with her, with the promise of balls and young men, her father would never consent to her going.

Mary was the only daughter who remained at home, and she was necessarily drawn from the pursuit of accomplishments by Mrs. Bennet's being quite unable to sit alone. Mary was obliged to mix more with the world, but she could still moralize over every morning visit. As she was no longer mortified by comparisons between her sisters' beauty and her own, it was suspected by her father that she submitted to the change without much reluctance.

As for Wickham and Lydia, their characters underwent no significant change from the marriage of her sisters. He was certain that Elizabeth must now become acquainted with whatever of his ingratitude and falsehood had before been unknown to her before. But, in spite of everything, he was not wholly without hope that Darcy might yet be prevailed on to make his fortune. The congratulatory letter which Elizabeth received from Lydia on her marriage explained to her that, by his wife at least, if not by himself, such a hope was cherished. The letter was to this effect —

"MY DEAR LIZZY, — "I wish you joy. If you love Mr. Darcy half as well as I do my dear Wickham, you must be very happy. It is a great comfort to have you so rich, and when you have nothing else to do, I hope you will think of us. I am sure Wickham would like a place at court very much, and I do not think we shall have quite money enough to live upon without some help. Any place would do, of about three or four hundred a year: but, however, do not speak to Mr. Darcy about it, if you had rather not. — Your's, etc."

As it happened that Elizabeth had *much* rather not, she endeavoured in her answer to put an end to every entreaty and expectation of the kind. Such relief, however, as it was in her power to afford, by the practice of thrift in her own private expenses, she frequently sent them. It had always been evident to her that such an income as theirs, under the direction of two persons so extravagant in their desires and heedless of the future, must be very insufficient. Whenever they changed their quarters, either Jane or herself were sure of being applied to for some little assistance towards discharging their bills. Their manner of living was unsettled in the extreme, even after the end of the war. They were always moving from place to place in quest of affordable living space, and always spending more than they ought. His affection for her soon sunk into indifference. Hers lasted a little longer, and in spite of her youth and her manners, she retained all the claims to reputation which her marriage had given her.

Though Darcy could never receive *him* at Pemberley, yet, for Elizabeth's sake, he assisted him farther in his profession. Lydia was occasionally a visitor there, when her husband was gone to enjoy himself in London or Bath; and with the Bingleys they both of them frequently stayed so long that even Bingley's good-humour was overcome, and he proceeded so far as to *talk* of giving them a hint to be gone.

Miss Bingley was very deeply mortified by Darcy's marriage, but as she thought it advisable to retain the right of visiting at Pemberley, she dropped all her resentment. She was fonder than ever of Georgiana, almost as attentive to Darcy as before, and was even tolerably civil to Elizabeth.

Pemberley was now Georgiana's home, and the attachment of the sisters was exactly what Darcy had hoped to see. They were able to love each other as well as they intended. Georgiana had the highest opinion in the world of Elizabeth, though at first she often listened with an astonishment bordering on alarm at her lively, teasing manner of talking to her brother. He, who had always inspired in herself a respect which almost overcame her affection, she now saw the object of open pleasantry. From Elizabeth's example she began to comprehend that a woman may take liberties with her husband which a brother will not always allow in a sister more than ten years younger than himself.

Lady Catherine was extremely indignant on the marriage of her nephew, and indulged in all the genuine frankness of her character in her reply to the letter which announced its arrangement. Her language was so very abusive, especially of Elizabeth, that for some time all correspondence was at an end. But at length, by Elizabeth's persuasion, he was prevailed on to overlook the offence, and seek a reconciliation. After a little farther resistance on the part of his aunt, her resentment gave way, either to her affection for him, or her curiosity to see how his wife conducted herself. She condescended to visit them at Pemberley, in spite of that pollution which its halls had received, not merely from the presence of such a mistress, but the visits of her uncle and aunt from the city.

With the Gardiners they were always on the best terms. Darcy, as well as Elizabeth, really loved them; and they were both ever sensible of the warmest gratitude towards the persons who, by bringing her into Derbyshire, had been the means of uniting them.

ABOUT THE AUTHOR

Gerry Baird lives in Utah with his wife and three children. He is an avid Jane Austen fan, and when he's not writing he spends his time playing piano and guitar. He is also the owner of Creative Resurgence, a productivity coaching company for creatives. Learn more at www.creativeresurgence.com

Made in the
USA
Columbia, SC